CHAOS ~ KISSED

Also by W. V. Fitz-Simon

THE WITCH OF CHEYNE HEATH

By Dawn, A Witch (Prequel Novelette)

Chaos & Cabernet (Prequel Novella)

Waking the Witch

Craftwork

Spells & Drugs And Rock 'n' Roll (Novelette)

Spellshock

Paint it Black

THE SHINING CONTINENT

Sins of the Poet (prequel novella)

The Third Secret

~ THE LIBRARY OF THE DAMNED ~
BOOK 1

CHAOS ~ KISSED

W. V. FITZ-SIMON

Dedo Press

New York

For Lee

who embodies the very best of friendship. Thank you for always being there.

LONDON

1993

1

CALLUM FOSTER KNOCKED ON the door and took out his timepiece, a brass pocket watch encased in a thin, transparent crystal box specially treated to shield its contents from the wild magic raging inside him. His tattoos kept the magic in check, but unshielded technology always suffered around him.

Noon. Four hours since the warning came through of another spontaneous flare-up. The longer he took to find it, the more likely someone would end up cursed like him.

He knocked on the door again: three sharp raps. "Geoffrey! Geoffrey Cooke!"

An hour for Jessica to come up with an image they could use. Half an hour to trace it to Bristol. Two and a half hours to drive from the Library of the Damned with Jessica and Rafe working frantically in the back seat to locate the source of her vision, who may or may not have anything to do with the flare-up. Everything involved with wild magic—Chaos, as the sorcerers insisted on calling it—was frustratingly uncertain. Right until the moment it cursed you.

No answer. He pressed one ear against the door. No sounds from inside. He slipped a hand into the pocket of his blue canvas workman's jacket to take out his knife, but someone swore on the steps behind him.

"Bloody plastic bag." A woman in her seventies struggled at the top of the steps with a split grocery bag in one hand and a large bottle of milk in the other. A box of cereal and a packet of digestive biscuits lay at her feet and four oranges rolled away from her across the landing.

Callum slipped his knife back into his pocket and stooped to retrieve an orange. Perhaps she could tell him something about Geoffrey Cooke. "Here, let me help you with that."

"I can do it myself!" She snapped at him as she bent over, wobbled slightly, and pressed her milk-burdened arm against the wall to steady herself.

"Are you sure?" He rounded up the remainder of the oranges as she scooped the cereal and digestive biscuits into the crook of her arm.

"My oranges, please." She turned toward him, the boxes wedged against her bosom to act as a scoop for the fruit. "You're one of his boys, I suppose." She eyed him with distaste and shuffled toward the other door on the landing.

Callum pushed down the urgent impatience that had him bouncing on his toes and smiled his best friendly and nonthreatening smile.

"Geoffrey? He's my cousin." He took a gamble that he and Geoffrey Cooke were feasibly related. Jessica's vision had led them here, but Callum only found out his name from the doorbell buzzers downstairs. Cooke was a sufficiently generic British name. Hopefully Callum's equally generic Celtic appearance would be a convincing family resemblance.

The woman softened, but only slightly, and balanced her bottle of milk precariously atop the oranges so she could fish her keys out of the pocket of her dress.

"Have you seen him?" Callum readied himself to leap into action should the bottle fall. "We had a family dinner last night and he never showed up."

"I'm sure I don't keep track of his comings and goings. It's disgusting the things he gets up to in there. Loud music at all hours of the morning. *Men* coming and going. He should be ashamed of himself."

Callum sighed. Nothing like a little bracing bigotry before lunch to awaken the appetite.

"Would you look at this for me?" He opened his jacket to display an ornate brooch, an acquisition of the Library from a refugee of the French Revolution. Its appearance softened the beholder's memory and made them forget the wearer. Though it was only a gentle manipulation, not an utter violation like the curse of forgetting that plagued Callum, using it still made him uncomfortable. All memory was precious.

Her key in the lock, she turned to look and blinked. A shadow of confusion drifted across her face. By the time she returned to opening her door, she was oblivious to his presence. Best the general public didn't know about magic, wild or tamed.

The landing clear, he took out his knife and slid it from its sheath. One of a pair, its gently curving blade of alchemical silver picked up emanations from the air around it. He held it up to the door, scanning for traces of wild magic, but the blade remained dull. He leaned in close and sniffed. The blade often picked up different things than his altered senses, but he didn't smell anything other than the varnish on the door.

Getting into the flat was easy. He always carried a few items from the Library's collection with him when he was on the job, artifacts twisted by wild magic to have unusual properties. Nothing that would cause harm, of course. He draped a linen handkerchief that once belonged to the painter, Francis Bacon, over the doorknob, and the lock clicked open.

He paused in the doorway and took in the flat, a pang of sadness and self-pity seeping in at the sight of the family photos on the shelves, the stack of dog-eared paperbacks on a side table, and the rumpled sweatshirt draped haphazardly over the arm of the couch, signs of a normal life untouched by magic of any kind.

He sniffed and swallowed, tasting the air. No telltale coppery bitterness at the back of his throat that marked the presence of wild magic, only a slight tingle across the tattoos on his back and limbs from the presence of the artifacts he was carrying. His altered senses didn't detect the familiar fragrances of lavender, frankincense, sandalwood, or any of the other scents that typically accompanied the many flavors of tamed magic wielded by sorcerous cabals. Only dust and cleaning fluid, and the stale mustiness of an old, long-inhabited building.

He went to the window to wave up Jessica and Rafe who waited anxiously on the street below for his signal. They made it upstairs quickly, Callum waiting by the door so as not to upset anything for Jessica and her clairvoyance.

"All clear?" Jessica, usually a diminutive bundle of head-shaved aggression, hovered nervously on the far side of the threshold peering through the sapphire-lensed spectacles that dampened her often-overwhelming visions. She'd lived with her curse for five years now. It was almost unheard of for someone to suffer the kiss of Chaos twice, but she still hadn't shaken the fear of it.

Callum couldn't blame her.

"It's all yours." He waved his hand and bowed deeply, welcoming her in.

She scowled and stepped across as if through a portal to another world which, in a sense, she was. Their lives at the Library couldn't be more different than that of a thirty-year-old professional living in Bristol.

She pushed forward, Rafe at her heels, but Callum grabbed his sleeve and held the librarian back. "What did I tell you, old man?"

Rafe looked sheepish, his tousled mop of salt-and-pepper hair framing his lined, apologetic face. He only rarely joined them in the field. His enthusiasm at being with them was both endearing and infuriating. His bumbling wasted time, and any delay put Callum on edge.

"Right, right. Let Jessica have first crack at it." Rafe held his cane tightly and tapped the sterling silver tip impatiently against the sole of his shoe, his free hand gripping his satchel, ready to spring into action as soon as Callum gave the word.

Jessica removed the sapphire-lensed spectacles, filters for the visual hallucinations that constantly assaulted her, making it almost impossible to see the real world around her. She stepped inside, and looked around the one-bedroom flat, modestly decorated with mid-range mass-produced furniture. Comfort and style on a budget.

"Getting anything?" asked Callum.

She ran her fingers across her shaved scalp as she looked around. A good sign.

"I think so. A lot of the usual jumble. Dropping his house keys and taking off his coat when he gets in from work … " She pointed at a small woven basket on a side table by the front door. "They're still here. Might want to look at that with one of your widgets, Rafe."

Rafe shifted to go further, but Callum held him back. "Not yet. Give her a second longer."

She walked through the living room and stuck her head into the kitchen and bedroom before returning. "It should be okay to come in. Just don't touch anything until I say so."

"You're up." Callum patted Rafe on the shoulder.

The librarian went to the coffee table, opened his satchel, and laid out his tools on a silk scarf. Some were actual tools: a claw hammer, a Phillips screwdriver, and a pair of dressmaker's shears. The rest were a mishmash of mundane objects: a palm-sized address book, a gnawed number two pencil, a bead prayer necklace, a porcelain teacup, and several other odd knickknacks you might find in a charity shop. Callum's tattoos shivered.

"That's a lot of gear." He stood over Rafe as the librarian kneeled at the coffee table, hands clad in a pair of white suede gloves embossed with sigils to protect him from the side-effects of Chaos as he adjusted the position of each artifact into a grid.

The gloves always seemed like overkill. Rafe was already cursed. A little more Chaos flowing through his body wouldn't make much difference.

The librarian glanced up at Callum, beaming with excitement. "I've been wanting to try these beauties. This one," he picked up the gnawed pencil, "has the unique ability—"

"Callum!" called Jessica from the bedroom, interrupting what could easily have been a ten-minute lecture on the powers and provenance of the artifact. "Take a look at this."

Rafe followed—pencil in one hand, cane in the other—as Callum went to join her.

"At least we know one thing about him for sure," said Callum at the sight of the posters on the wall. "He's gay."

"How do you know?" Rafe peered around him. "Is it something your tattoos are telling you?"

Callum and Jessica exchanged a knowing smile. He joined Jessica at the foot of the bed. "No, the posters."

A giant Marilyn Monroe stared down from the wall peering through a gauzy scarf, flanked by Liza Minelli reminding everyone in no uncertain terms how to spell her name, and Gloria Swanson glaring with displeasure at William Holden clutching a starlet to his chest.

Rafe's brow wrinkled in befuddlement as he took the posters in. "How does being an aficionado of movie stars of the Hollywood studio system mean he's homosexual?"

Jessica snorted, and Callum swatted her lightly on the shoulder.

"Be kind," he whispered. "I'll tell you later, old man. Jess, what did you want us to see?"

On the bedside table stood a picture of three young men in their twenties in bathing suits laughing and drinking extravagant cocktails at a bar on some exotic Mediterranean beach, and Callum wondered how many centuries it was since he had been that young. At least eight, though he couldn't remember anything before nineteen sixty-two.

"I'm seeing a dinner party." Jessica slipped on her spectacles and spun around in a little twirl, admiring herself in the full-length mirror propped against one wall of the bedroom. Her black tulle crinoline spun out, revealing more of the hot pink and black leopard print leggings beneath it. She always made the effort to dress like a rockstar. The best Callum could muster was the look of an Irish dockworker at the pub after Sunday mass.

"Any sign of Chaos?"

"Possibly? I can't be sure. There's a lot going on." She shook her head and peered at the books on a shelf by the bed.

Callum's tattoos shivered again. "Rafe, do me a favor and step outside? Your cane and the pencil are getting in the way."

Rafe's cane, the only thing that prevented him from disintegrating into a mound of dust, was an artifact of considerable power.

"Oh yes." He grimaced and backed out of the room. "Sorry, sorry."

"And cover the rest of your kit to be on the safe side."

"Callum?" called Rafe from the other room.

"If we can find something truly meaningful to him," said Jessica, "I can locate him."

"Callum!"

"I'll check the living room." Callum stepped out of the bedroom. Five gun-wielding men in black military fatigues surrounded Rafe. The librarian clutched his satchel and cane across his body as if they might protect him.

"Foster!" came a gruff voice from the doorway. "Get your people out, now!"

2

THE SMELL OF LAVENDER rolled over Callum, his altered senses picking up the magic emanating from the soldiers' enchanted weapons. His shock at the sudden arrival of troops from the Cottage boiled away. Yet another delay to finding Geoffrey Cooke before Chaos took him.

"What the hell is going on," he barked at anyone who'd listen. Three of the soldiers turned their weapons on him before tilting the barrels down. Rafe might be pale as a ghost, but guns didn't faze Callum. A bullet wound would be painful, but even a shot to the head would heal. Eventually. "This is an active investigation. You can't be here!"

The Cottage, the nation's front line against supernatural threats, were supposed to be their allies, working in tandem with the Library to keep the general public safe from things that go bump in the night, but their style of investigation was about as delicate as a brick through a shop window.

"I said, get your people out!" Biggs, the head of the unit assigned to the Library on the odd occasion when they needed extra muscle, waved the soldiers deeper into the flat. "Secure the site, fellas."

"You have no authority here," said Callum as the soldiers spread out, one of them escorting Rafe onto the landing. "The Royal Charter explicitly gives the Library of the Damned—"

Biggs turned on him, his teeth bared in a tense snarl. They were the same height, tall for your average twentieth-century male, but the solid mass of Biggs's torso made Callum seem an elfin waif in comparison. If they'd met at a bar, Callum might be tempted to flirt, but Biggs was stubborn, dismissive, and ornery. And very, very straight. Not Callum's type at all.

"Listen!" said the agent. "We've had four vampire nests in the last six days."

Callum blinked with surprise. That was more than in the past five years put together. Vampires were feral predators, all trace of their humanity leached from them by the kiss of Chaos. The vampire contagion manifested spontaneously like all afflictions of wild magic. Anyone bitten unlucky enough not to be killed would turn in a matter of minutes. The British Isles would be overrun by feral undead in days without the Cottage to stop it. A shocking revelation, but it had little to do with him.

"So what? It's lunchtime! Unless someone's come up with undead sunscreen, I think we're okay."

"Her Grace invoked clause seventeen. You're not doing anything without us until she gives the all-clear."

A black-uniformed soldier escorted a squirming Jessica out to the landing.

"They're making a mess of everything!" Jessica dug the heels of her hobnailed boots into the carpet, but she was so petite, her escort dragged her out with ease.

"Come on," said Biggs. "They'll make sure the place is safe, and then you can putter around to your heart's content." He touched a small disk in his ear as Callum went out. The smell of lavender spiked. "We've got the bookworms."

Callum growled under his breath and clenched his fists with frustration, but there was nothing he could do. He followed Biggs out onto the landing. The agent joined his two underlings from Frayn Unit. Clarke seemed, as usual, like she would happily munch on a handful glass, while Hudson wore his familiar bland expression. With their studiously nondescript clothing, the three of them looked more like inspectors from the local Council than members of the British Security Service.

Biggs leaned against the wall and inserted a brass and rubber earpiece into his ear. The smell of lavender crested again. Though the agents weren't sorcerers themselves, their sorcerous bosses at the Cottage gave them all kinds of odd devices, modern technology merged with alchemy, arcane artifice, and who knew what else to use in the field. He scowled.

"Bugger," hissed Clarke and brushed her shoulder-length brown hair aside to touch her own earpiece.

"Everything okay?" asked Callum.

Biggs turned his back on him and leaned heavily against the wall.

"We lost Auden Unit," said Hudson. Usually the only cheerful one of the three, his face was pale.

"The whole unit?" Callum was shocked. Cottage strike teams were the best of the best, recruited from the Special Air Services.

Hudson, looking ready to lose his breakfast, nodded. "All but three died sterilizing the outbreak. The survivors were all infected. The support teams had to execute them."

"Fuck. I'm sorry, mate."

"Site secured," said one of the soldiers as they filed out and down the stairs. Keeping the neighbors from being curious about an armed paramilitary squad traipsing through a Bristol neighborhood was far more than Callum's brooch could handle, but it was Biggs's problem. The Cottage had more reliable resources for this kind of thing.

Jessica fumed silently at his side, clearly ready to give the soldiers a good kicking for messing up her investigation.

"Easy, luv," whispered Callum. "You're peeling the paint off the walls."

"They know my bloody curse isn't science," she muttered under her breath. "If everything's not exactly right … "

She was far too hard on herself. He'd seen how effective her visions could be. Thirty-two people were living happy, uncursed lives thanks to her work over the past five years.

"Get on with it," barked Biggs without bothering to turn around. "I've got better things to do than be your babysitter."

Callum closed his eyes, took a deep breath to calm himself, and left the agents to their comms. "Come on. Let's see what we can salvage from this mess."

Rafe took a step toward the door, but Callum held him back so Jessica could go through first.

"Right, right," said the librarian. "Of course." He backed away and bowed as she passed.

She stepped across the threshold and groaned as she walked through the flat. "They've ruined it!"

"Can you find anything?" said Callum.

"Maybe?" She sighed and headed back to the bedroom. "Look for meaningful objects. Rafe, bring your thingamajigs. Maybe you can pick up a trace."

Callum stood in the living room and looked around. Which of the flat's many possessions would be most important to a thirty-year-old gay man? If only he could remember his own youth, though being gay in the twelfth century probably didn't have much in common with being gay today. Thankfully, the law in nineteen ninety-three wasn't so big on executions.

On a fifties cabinet filled with vinyl sat an expensive record player with a pair of four-foot speakers on either side. He squatted and flicked through the record collection: Broadway and West End musical soundtrack albums, long players by David Bowie, Donna Summer,

Bronski Beat. He stopped when he found a copy of a nineteen-fifties Maria Callas recording protected by a plastic sheath.

"Bingo."

He slipped it under his arm and headed for the kitchen. It was small—enough room for a stove, a decent-sized fridge, a sink, and some counter space—but everything was neat and clean. Suspended from the ceiling hung a rack of high-quality pots and pans. The missing man liked to cook. A quick rummage through the drawers turned up a small wooden box containing a Japanese chef's knife. He opened the box and took out the blade.

"What a beauty," he whispered to himself. He knew a thing or two about knives.

He spun the implement around in his grip, feeling its balance, and tossed it in the air, sending it spinning butt over tip. The handle fell into his grip cleanly as if magnetized by his palm. This would do.

Back in the bedroom, he dropped his prizes on the duvet. "Try these."

Jessica kneeled by the bed and slid her spectacles onto her scalp. She nodded. "Yes. I'm picking up something."

Callum looked around the bedroom. On one of the bookshelves stood a trio of framed photos. Each was a picture of the same two people, a man and a woman, clearly siblings, the man one of the swimsuited trio from the picture by the bed. He and his sister shared the same jawline, the same nose, the same straight brown hair. In all the pictures, the man was smiling, but the woman's face was fixed in a serious scowl.

"Geoffrey Cooke, I presume." Callum reached for one of the photos. As he took it from the shelf, the bitter taste of copper exploded in the back of his throat, and his heart began to pound. He waved the picture at Jessica and Rafe.

"I've got something."

3

CALLUM PEERED THROUGH THE windshield up at the full moon shining down on the abandoned thirteenth-century monastery and shivered. Never a great way to start the evening. "Are you sure this is the place?"

Jessica, sapphire-lensed spectacles black in the dashboard light against the glow of her pale skin, inspected the photo, the Maria Callas album on her lap, and looked up at the ruins.

"Yes." She wound down the window.

A familiar smell of springtime country evenings wafted into the car triggering the yearning of a memory just beyond the range of Callum's conscious awareness. He pushed the sensation away knowing the memory would never crest. Worrying at it would only be distracting, and he needed his wits about him.

"I'm certain." Jessica took off her spectacles to stare into the night. "Everything's pointing to that building."

He turned off the engine and pocketed the keys.

"You have to tell me how you do that sometime."

She slipped her spectacles back into place and shrugged. "It wouldn't make any sense to you. I see a lot of chaotic images, like the kind of dreams you get after a big curry dinner. Mad to anyone else, but obvious to me."

Chaotic. Something all three of them in the car knew a lot about.

"Rafe," he swiveled around to look at his friend in the back seat. "What do you have for me?"

Age was treating Rafe well. His hair fell across his handsome, lined face as he tried to simultaneously read a road map in one hand and a slim volume in the other by the glow of a flashlight wedged between his jaw and shoulder.

"Trentham Abbey." The librarian abandoned the map so he could comb his hair out of the way with one hand and aimed the flashlight at the book. "Founded in eleven thirty-six. A Cistercian monastery."

"The white monks," said Callum, without knowing how he knew it, a feeling he was well used to.

"Yes." Rafe nodded. "That's exactly right. Founded with the blessing of the Plantagenets. The Abbey is original, but the attached house dates back to the late seventeen hundreds. Built by the family that claimed the property after the monasteries were broken in the Reformation."

He put the book down and picked up another from the tumbling piles on the seat beside him, a glossy traveler's guide to the area. "It's been closed up since the sixties. Another lesser stately British pile."

"Why would a successful young professional from Bristol," said Callum, "have left home on a Thursday evening without telling anyone where he was going and show up in an abandoned eleventh-century monastery?"

Jessica and Rafe exchanged quizzical shrugs.

"You're the ancient immortal," said Jessica. "You tell us."

Headlights pulled up behind them, their minders from the Cottage. Callum sighed and opened the car door. "We'd better figure it out quickly before our babysitters decide to storm the walls and startle the current inhabitants. I doubt Somerset's population of foxes and crows will take kindly to the disturbance."

He slipped out of the Range Rover and felt it immediately. A wave of shivers caressed the tattoos across his arms, legs, and back, and the familiar acrid, coppery taste of wild magic spread across the back of his throat. He pulled his scruffy tweed coat tighter around him, armor against the chill.

"Yep," he said to the dark. "This is the place." Jessica emerged from the other side of the Rover, too short to see at first until the moonlight caught her pale, shaved scalp. "Should you stay in the car?"

She took off her spectacles and slipped them into the pocket of her vintage leather biker jacket.

"In this light, I can see as well as you. Better. With my visions, I'll know what's coming before you do."

"Do you see it?" He rounded the car to stand next to her and look up the hill.

She nodded, her bald head bobbing in the moonlight. "The Chaos? I do. It's light. Strong enough to be a concern, but not enough to be a worry."

They had as many words for shades of wild magic as the Inuit had words for snow.

"Rafe," he said as the librarian got out of the car. "Don't forget your cane. I don't want to be running around in the moonlight with a dustpan and brush trying to put you back together."

"Quite right, my boy. Quite right." Rafe ducked back inside to retrieve the artifact.

He and Rafe had known each other for thirty years. Rafe was sixty-two and Callum was … Well, at least eight hundred years old according to the journals kept in trust by the Library of the Damned, not that he could remember anything further back than thirty years. Even so, they still played the game that they were both the age they appeared to be.

Though Callum, Jessica, and Rafe were all Chaos-kissed, Callum was the only one who couldn't seem to die. Get buggered up to the point of death, yes, an unpleasant experience he would go a long way not to repeat, but no curse, or boon, or spell would stick to him thanks to the intensity of the Chaos within him.

"What's up with the spooks?" said Jessica.

The three members of Frayn Unit sat in their car, a nondescript black Vauxhall Cavalier, with all the interior lights on. Biggs sat staring into space in the front passenger seat, one elbow resting on the car door, playing absently with his curly black hair and scowling at nothing, while his two underlings held a conversation each with their head down as they fiddled with something in their laps. No doubt more of their arcane devices.

"Maybe they're reporting in?" Callum raised his arms to stretch the past three hours of driving through country lanes from his body. He might look young, but he certainly didn't feel it. "As long as they stay in the car, they can do what they like."

"Flashlights, anyone?" Rafe reemerged with cane in one hand and a trio of small flashlights sticking out at awkward angles in the other.

He held out the lights for the others to take. Callum reached behind Jessica for one, but she made no move.

"Oh!" Rafe's eyes widened, realizing the faux pas of offering her a flashlight to someone with her curse. "Oh, I'm so sorry."

Jessica smiled and held out a hand. "Don't worry about it. I'll take one. I can use it as a club to cosh anyone over the head who comes at me in the dark."

She hefted the aluminum flashlight twice, flipped it deftly the wrong way round with one hand, and slid it into a pocket of her skirt. The girl might be petite and cursed, Callum thought, but he wouldn't want to run into her in a back alley after midnight. He'd seen what she could do with her hobnailed boots.

"They're up to something." Jessica looked over at the Cavalier. "Their hoodoo is lighting up the car like a beacon."

Biggs knocked on the windshield and beckoned Callum over.

"The master summons me," said Callum with his back to the spook. There was no way the man could lip read from within the car with the lights on like that, but Callum was never sure what other skills operatives of the Cottage had. They were masters of arcane surveillance, after all.

Biggs rolled down his window as Callum approached.

"The oracles are telling us there are spikes on the board all around here. Keep your arse clean. I don't want to have to wade in there to pull you out of a mess."

Callum leaned against the car roof, stuck his head into the window, and leered. A whiff of lavender wafted out of the car at him. He wondered what this bunch of hardened spies would think if they knew they walked around smelling like a field of summer flowers.

"This is not my first haunted house, love." He waggled his eyebrows suggestively. "And I know my way around a mess better than you ever will." He winked, and the spook scowled at him.

"This isn't a game, Mr. Foster. Chaotic Influence is nothing to play with." The cabals all had weird highfalutin jargon for anything supernatural, as if the idea of calling it all magic like anyone else was beneath them.

Callum sighed, rolled his eyes, pushed off the car, and walked away.

"Read my fucking file, arsehole," he muttered, sick of the attitude, "and then say that to me."

"Everything okay?" Rafe pointed his lit flashlight down, and the glow illuminated his face from below.

"They're giving him the usual hard time," said Jessica.

"Oh, pay them no mind, dear boy. They're intimidated by you. They hate a mystery they can't solve." He shook himself like a wet dog. "There's a nip in the air. Shall we?"

Callum would normally have found a walk in the woods in the moonlight with friends a delightful way to spend an evening. The deepening taste of copper in the back of his throat rather ruined it.

They clambered over the stone wall that surrounded the abbey grounds, Jessica vaulting over it and Callum helping Rafe across. Rafe wasn't feeble by any stretch of the imagination, just a little clumsy.

They trudged up through the trees and grass to the top of the hill, where the ruined shell of the abbey stood to their left, and the later house to their right. They stopped at the tree line and Callum turned to Jessica. "Where to first?"

She looked around through her sapphire spectacles and again without them. "The Chaos is thick like a fog. It's masking everything. All I can see is purple mist."

"I doubt our missing upwardly mobile professionals would be hanging out in that," Callum turned his flashlight on the gray, lichen-covered stone of the Abbey. Its roof was missing, and the back wall had partially crumbled.

"Ahead we go, then." Rafe, unperturbed by the deep creepiness of the night, made off toward the front door of the house.

"Rafe!" Callum snagged his sleeve and pulled him back. "What have I told you about the direct approach?"

He didn't join them on field trips often, but they needed his research skills. Rafe nodded vigorously.

"Yes, of course. How foolish of me. It rarely gets you the results you want. We try the back door?"

"We'll do a quiet circuit around the house, then assess how we're going in."

"Excellent plan!" said Rafe, and immediately tried to take off in the other direction, but Callum held him back.

"Let me go first, old man."

"Yes, yes. Capital idea. So sorry. It's so much fun to be out and about with you."

'Out and about' was what Rafe called the alternating waves of tedium and terror the assignments he sent Callum and Jessica out on. His last time out with them, to the Channel Islands to track down a linen handkerchief that had the unfortunate property of turning anyone who touched it to ice, had ended with Callum's hands blackened by frostbite. What would have killed a normal person, for Callum, meant a month and a half of humiliating help in every part of his life— *every* part—while his bandage-wrapped hands healed. 'Out and about' was rarely fun.

It didn't take long to walk around the mansion and find an innocuous back door.

"They were definitely here." She stepped back from the door to look up at the house, "But I'm getting a lot of confusion."

"Confusion?" said Callum. Being unable to give a decisive answer was unusual for her.

"I can't tell if it's because of the Chaos, or something else." She strode back a few paces the way they came and looked into the trees. "I see a lot of walking around, through the house and the woods, but aimless drifting without interacting with each other much. I see other presences, maybe five or six more."

She drifted a few paces toward the abbey ruins.

"They congregated here. I can see them standing around, listening to someone talk. But after that, they all vanish. I see nothing. It's like the mists part for a moment, and then close in again, obscuring everything."

Callum switched off his flashlight to see the house and abbey better in the moonlight. He felt a ripple across his tattoos and the hairs on the back of his neck stood at attention. Something was very off.

"Have you seen that kind of thing before?" asked Rafe.

"I suppose so," said Jessica. "If someone knows what they're doing, it doesn't take much to mask themselves from me." She turned in a slow circle, raising and lowering her spectacles every so often. "Do you smell any sorcerers?"

"Fee fie foe fum." Callum sniffed the air.

No lavender, no frankincense, no old, varnished wood or bright and citrusy lemon, nor any other fragrances provoked by the strange sensory confusion the kiss of Chaos had bestowed on him, none of the scents an acolyte of the twenty-odd sorcerous cabals might give off.

"I smell the blood of no one. Just Chaos. I'm going to need a stiff whiskey after all this to get the taste out of my mouth. Are you sure of the sequence of events? They started in the house, then went to the abbey?"

She nodded.

"And do you know how long ago?"

"I can't tell. Recently. After the dark of the moon."

Magic, wild and tamed, ebbed and flowed with the tides. "So, any time in the last three days. Off to church we go," said Callum.

Rafe struck out toward the abbey, and Callum lurched forward to grab him by the belt.

"Rafe! Come on. Don't make my life harder than it needs to be."

"Sorry, sorry." Rafe speared the damp earth beneath them with the tip of his cane as if to anchor himself to the spot. "Two steps behind at all times."

"Just don't go running off."

Jessica slipped her arm around Rafe's. "Us support staff will stick together and let fussy Celtic daddy have all the fun."

Callum snorted. "As if you could. Flashlights off."

Rafe turned his off and plunged them into night.

The wide gothic arch greeted them like a dark maw. Callum had a general policy against entering the expected way, so he steered them around to the ruined side wall. The interior of the abbey wasn't much different to the exterior. Open to the air, moonlight shone down over the grassy earth at an angle, leaving one side shrouded in darkness. He stopped shy of the interior.

"Can you see who they were talking to?" whispered Callum.

Jessica paused before answering, slipping her glasses off for a moment.

"No, but there's twelve of them."

"Twelve?! Where did the others come from?"

"No idea," said Jessica, "but now that I've seen them, I can trace them back to their point of origin if needs be."

A sudden pungent whiff filled Callum's nostrils, a mixture of burning matches and sulfurous rotten eggs.

"You smelled something," said Jessica. "It was like a cloud passed over you."

The smell lasted only a second, the bitter copperiness of Chaos reasserting itself.

"It's gone."

"What was it?"

Callum paused before answering, hoping his vast ocean of lost memories might give him a clue.

Nothing.

He grimaced and shook his head.

"Look over there." Rafe peered into the darkness on the other side of the abbey. "What's that?"

Callum could make out some kind of mound in the gloom. He sniffed the air but smelled nothing new. The mound didn't seem to move, and his miswired senses gave him no other warnings of what it might be, so he stepped across the wall to approach.

"They gathered over there." She led Rafe to the center of the abbey. "They were here for a good while. Agitated at first, then they all calmed down. Then nothing."

The moonlight was bright enough that Callum had trouble making out details of the mound in the shadows, so he turned on his flashlight.

A pile of animal carcasses. Dogs, mongrels, all about the same size, about thirty pounds, stacked haphazardly atop each other as if tossed aside. He squatted to examine the nearest, touching its rump. The body was still warm under his fingers, but only just. He ran the flashlight up the length of the poor animal but could see no cause of death.

He turned it over. Its tongue lolled out of its mouth, its eyes frozen in the blank stare of death. A twinge of sorrow rose up in him, but if it was from simple compassion for another creature or driven by something deeper, a dog-owner's affinity, he couldn't tell. He hadn't owned a dog in the thirty years since he last lost his memory. But before that?

He stumbled back at the sight of what he saw on the dog's body. Its throat had been ripped open, a jagged tear slicing through fur and skin, leaving flesh and sinew and bone exposed to the night. There was no sign of blood.

"Bugger," he swore as he pushed himself up and scanned the darkness.

Vampires.

4

NO TELLTALE IRIDESCENT EYES in the shadows reflecting the moonlight, but vampires tended to nest near the place they were turned. They were sure to all still be on the grounds. How many had Jessica seen? A dozen.

He jumped up and ran to the others.

"Once we get clear of the Chaos," Jessica turned to Rafe, "I'll need a little time to lock in on them, but the personal effects I have will help—"

"We have to leave," said Callum. "Now."

"Dear boy," said Rafe, oblivious to Callum's urgency, "This is fascinating. I'm so glad you let me tag along this time. I'm learning so—"

Callum grabbed them both by the sleeve and pulled them with him toward the ruined wall.

"Vampires, Rafe," he hissed, trying not to raise his voice. Vampires were olfaction-dominant, but their hearing was pretty sharp.

Rafe and Jessica tensed and scanned the darkness for threat when they should have been moving. He dragged them behind him. If only he had thought to bring his knives. The security of knowing Frayn Unit were with them made him careless.

"Move as fast as you can without making noise."

It might buy them time, but the second they began to sweat, there would be no hiding.

They picked up the pace, so he let go of them, letting them follow behind. He led them from the abbey back to the house and the main drive. It was wide and open, the trees a few yards from the gravel trail. It would offer them no cover, but at least they'd be able to see the vampires coming.

"Jess, can you see anything?"

She took off her glasses. "Too much Chaos," she whispered back.

Their feet crunched on the gravel. He could imagine the predators gathering in the dark beyond the trees. The road was two hundred yards down the hill. They'd never make it.

"My god, look," said Rafe when they were no more than fifty feet away from the house.

Pinpoints of blue firefly light glittered in the trees, winking on and off.

"Keep moving," said Callum.

The vampires were keeping their distance, following them from within the tree line. That wasn't right. They should have been all over them at first sight. Vampires were feral predators, all trace of their humanity leached from them by the kiss of Chaos.

A blur in the darkness before them materialized into the shape of a woman, short and pale, short dark hair framing her face. Dressed in jeans and an oversized sweater, she looked more like an art history college tutor than a ravening undead monster.

She smiled, her fangs protruding from between her lips.

Instinct buried in his lost memories screamed at him that something was wrong, something even more wrong than being hunted by undead monsters, but he didn't have time to process. He snatched

Rafe's cane from him and swung it at the vampire's head like a cricket bat. The handle and tip were sterling silver, not the alchemical blend his knives were forged from, but good enough to slow a vampire down.

Vampires were faster than humans, even the rare, long-lived ones like Callum. The embodiment of primal urges, vampires rarely thought, never spoke, and moved with terrifying swiftness, but this one had only begun to react as the cane came down upon her. Prepared to feint an expected preternaturally fast-moving parry, Callum wasn't using his full strength, and the cane's handle only clipped her on the temple, but silver was silver, even if only sterling, and the skin around her temple seared and darkened.

She cried out and clutched the side of her head. "You little shit!" Her vowels had the plummy roundness of the privately educated.

Adrenaline charging up his limbs, Callum flipped the cane in his grip without thinking and stabbed it at her, aiming for her heart. She brushed the cane to one side and the tip lanced at her chest, tearing fabric and crunching into her upper ribs and collarbone. She cried out with pain as he drew the cane back and struck her again in the head with the handle with his full strength, knocking her to the ground. He might look lightweight but, thanks to constant training, he was strong.

"Run!" he cried.

The vampires in the trees remained in the darkness, reflective eyes winking out and back. Rafe and Jessica might have a chance.

"But my cane." Rafe reached for his anchor to human form.

"If I can't get it back to you in time, turning into a mound of dust will be the best thing for you. Run! And don't stop till you reach the spooks."

Jessica grabbed Rafe's hand, and they took off down the hill as the vampire cried out with rage and pushed herself up to her feet. The silver burns were already beginning to heal.

"Unexpected." She leered dangerously and cracked her knuckles, "but not unwelcome. This will be fun."

He didn't understand what he was seeing. He had helped burn out several vampire nests in his surviving memory, and his instincts, screaming at him to run from the eyes in the dark beyond, couldn't reconcile the woman. There was no question she was undead. Silver didn't burn mortals like that—

He took too long wrestling with what was going on. She leapt at him, covering the short distance between them quickly—quicker than a human by far, yet still slower than a vampire—her fingernails extended into talons that matched her fangs, giving Callum only a fraction of a second to turn, crouch, and throw her over his shoulder. She fell on her back, hard. Her pale skin glowed in the moonlight.

"Damn you!" she shouted, but before she could spin up, he stabbed her in the neck with the tip of the cane, he had been aiming at her heart, pulled it back and struck her in the head again, this time holding the handle against her, pressing the silver handle into her skin until it began to sizzle.

She screamed, a high-pitched screech that rapidly scaled up to the ultrasonic and became a sharp pressure against his eardrums. The glowing eyes in the darkness broke cover.

That did it, he thought and ran.

The vampires should have swarmed him within seconds, but his pounding legs outdistanced them, and he reached the road to run into Biggs and his two subordinates, Hudson and Clarke, waving their firearms in his face. He ran past them to where Jessica and Rafe stood on the far side of the country lane by the cars. Gulping down great lungfuls of air, he tossed the cane at Rafe who snatched at it and held it against his chest like a cherished infant.

"Get … in … the … car," Callum gasped, pulling Jessica and Rafe with him as he staggered over, his thighs beginning to seize after the sudden effort.

"Where are they?" Biggs called out. "Where the fuck are they?"

Callum had fully expected them to be overrun by now, but Biggs and the other two stood fanned out across the entrance to the drive, covering the empty darkness with their firearms.

"Get as far away from here as possible." Callum handed the car keys to Rafe as he reached into the driver's side door to retrieve his knives in their scabbards. "Go straight to the Cottage and warn them. They need to send a sterilization team."

"We can't leave you," said Rafe.

Jessica, two-thirds his height, clamped her hands around him and pushed him to the car door. "Come on. We have to do as he says."

He looked stricken, but climbed into the driver's seat as Jessica ran around to the passenger side, one hand on the hood of the car to guide her.

The knives, according to Callum's journals, were five hundred years old, forged by a Venetian alchemist and procured for him by the custodian of the Library of the Damned of the time, a man for whom Callum had felt great affection. According to his journals. He had no memory of the man.

He clipped the scabbards to his belt as the Range Rover drove away behind him.

One less thing to worry about. He'd be much more effective without having to keep them safe.

The knives felt good in his hands, a deep familiarity that connected him to all his lost memories. Thick hunting knives with a Saracen curve to the tip, the alloy of the blades caught the moonlight and held it in a glow that trailed off into the night as he spun and swung them to warm up his shoulders. The metal, enchanted to be fatal to the deathless and the undead, gave off a bright, astringent smell that energized him and sharpened his focus.

Better than a shot of Arabic coffee.

He joined Biggs and the other two at the entrance to the still-empty drive.

"Why are you still here?" said Biggs, his entire being focused on a single point in the darkness up the hill. Sweat poured down his brow. "You should have left with the others."

"There's a dozen undead up there. You need the help."

"Fuck off." Biggs sneered. "This is no place for civilians."

Callum waved the blade of one of his knives in Biggs's field of vision. The moonglow trailed behind it like phosphorescence in seawater.

"I've got alchemical silver. What do you have?"

Biggs scowled and grunted.

Plain bullets, then.

They might break bones, but a shot to the head or heart would only slow the vampires down. Only alchemical silver would finish them off.

"And what will you do if you get nicked?"

An open wound of any size would leave Biggs and his team vulnerable to the vampiric contagion. Ten minutes after infection, if they were still alive, they'd no longer be human.

"Turn my gun on myself," said Biggs. "Standard protocol."

"You know I'm immune, right? I'm already cursed. Can't get another one."

Biggs paused, his only concession. "Fuck. Where are they?"

He was right. The vampires should have followed Callum down the hill at the very least.

"They're young. They fed recently, and I whacked one of them with silver. Young vampires can be skittish about their boundaries until they get hungry. Maybe they went to ground."

He thought of the pile of drained dogs, all large enough to sate a vampire's thirst. Convenient that they somehow had enough to feed twelve.

"I don't like it," said Biggs. "You sent the old man to warn the Cottage?"

Callum nodded. It was an hour's drive away.

"We can't wait that long," said Biggs. The risk of the vampiric contagion spreading was too great. "Hudson, get on the line to HQ. Get me authorization to go in."

"Sir, regulations—"

"Fuck regulations! What have I told you about getting that rod out of your arse? Get on the line, now!"

Biggs might be an arrogant prick, Callum thought with grudging respect, but he wasn't a coward. The odds weren't great, but he'd seen the spook's team in action.

Hudson lowered his weapon and darted back to the car. He slid into the back seat and bowed his head, fiddling with some arcane communications device in his lap, obscured from view.

Above them a shadow passed across the moon, plunging them momentarily into complete darkness. The fetid stench of matches and rotten eggs filled Callum's nostrils in an explosive burst, only to fade and be replaced by the soft lavender emanating from Biggs and Clarke.

"What the fuck was that." Biggs scanned the skies frantically, but no terror descended on them from above. Unlike in books and movies, vampires couldn't fly.

"A low-flying plane?" said Callum, though that didn't explain the smell of sulfur. Whatever it was, it was heading away from them, so not an imminent threat.

Callum took a deep breath. He didn't deliberately put himself into dangerous situations, but sometimes he was the only one who could do anything. "I'm going in."

"No." Biggs glanced briefly at him, quickly returning his attention to the drive. "You don't have authorization."

Callum grinned.

"*You* don't have authorization. I'm not in your chain of command. Come back me up when Her Majesty gives you clearance."

5

CALLUM SLIPPED INTO THE trees that ran along the drive. Walking up the middle of the road in the bright full moon was more folly than even he dared attempt. The moonglow emanating from the blades quickly dissipated, though there was enough ambient light to leave behind a faint phosphorescence. He knew people with the skills to go unnoticed on Regent's Street at midday. He wasn't that adept, but he had learned a thing or two in the last thirty years of his life he could remember. Body odor he could do little about other than stay downwind.

With Biggs and Clarke behind him and out of sight beyond the trees, he stopped and cocked his head to one side to listen. The undead made natural wildlife nervous, making the birds, voles, and insects all clam up, but they tended to recover quickly. The unnerving silence of the woods holding its collective breath against imminent danger was disturbed by the hoot of an owl. So, the vampires had retreated, probably to their nest.

A nocturnal walk in the woods with friends was always pleasant, but hunting brought Callum to life, all his senses sharpened to a fine point, his body loose and poised, ready to spring into action.

A vampire nest had to be lightproof so they wouldn't all combust at sunrise. The vampire contagion was a vicious curse that threatened all of humanity. Luckily, Chaos was capricious, inconsistent, and often contradictory in the ways it warped reality. If there was some controlling intelligence behind the contagion, it would surely have created a less vulnerable predator. A vampire's strengths centered mainly around its instinctive viciousness and single-minded intent to feed plus an unfortunate ability to weaken the minds of its intended victims with eldritch suggestion. It had a surprising number of weaknesses. If you knew what you were doing and could get to the vampire before it got to you, you had a fifty-fifty chance of survival. Worse odds and the British Isles would have been inundated with the undead millennia ago. He shuddered to think how screwed they'd all be if a sorcerer with dominion over Chaos put some thought into it. Luckily, wild magic was the only kind that didn't have sorcerers to guide its power.

The moon moved lower on the horizon as he made his way up the hill, silent footstep by silent footstep, deepening the shadows that cloaked him from sight. With any luck, dawn would be near, and he could let nature do the heavy lifting. Or maybe he could barricade the doors and set the house on fire. The difference between courage and foolishness would only be determined in the light of day.

A healthy dose of primeval fear pounded in his chest as he dashed across the drive into the shadow of the house, and he made his way around to the back door. Vampires not being all that worried about security, the door wasn't locked. He slipped inside and closed the door quietly behind him, the sounds of night fading into the random creaks and clicks of an old house. Closing his eyes to focus his other senses, he sniffed the air, hoping to get a whiff of what might be in there with him. Vampires—ironically, given that it had no effect on them—

smelled of garlic to him, but the acrid taste of Chaos was too overpowering.

The windows of the house were all shuttered, but the residual glow of starlight still in his knives gave him enough dim illumination to make his way around without bumping into the walls. With his attention on the ceiling as much as the floor, he edged deeper into the house in search of the door to the cellar.

Twin pinpoints of reflected starlight glittered in the room to his left and the hairs on the back of his neck stood to attention. He braced himself for the vampire's rushed attack, but the glittering eyes didn't move. Not one to question an advantage, he launched himself at the creature, starlight trailing from his blades like a knight's banner, and sliced. It stepped back with expected vampiric swiftness, avoiding a cut to its torso, the blade instead grazing its arm. Its flesh sparked with the brief flare of a lit match and smoldered, but the spark quickly died. It would take a wound to the creature's torso for the alchemical silver to do much damage, and a pierced heart to deliver it the natural death the kiss of Chaos had robbed it of.

The creature hissed loudly, its white teeth catching the starlight, and came at him, talons drawn. A vampire attacked with single-minded ferocity, but this one seemed off: slower and with no precision. He ducked and turned into it as it swung at him, its talons missing him by a hair's breadth, and stabbed upward with both blades, slicing into its arm. The wound was deep enough that the flesh ignited. The vampire screeched and flapped its arms, a one-winged demon in the darkness casting distorted shadows on the walls.

Callum spun and embedded both blades into the creature's chest. One pierced its heart. It disintegrated in a torrent of flames that burned itself out in a second.

He staggered back, panting, not believing his luck. That was too easy.

Holding himself as still as he could, he listened for movement, any sign that the remainder of the nest might have heard the scuffle and decided to investigate, but five, seven, breaths passed, and he heard nothing.

Until he heard a whimper, a muffled sound coming from somewhere in the room with him.

He held one knife up so that the captured starlight emanating from the blade might show him what it was. In the corner of the room was a huddled lump about the size and shape of a man trying to make himself as small as possible.

He made a move toward the figure, and it shrunk away from him, trying to press itself into the corner.

Not the actions of a vampire.

"It's okay," he whispered as he sheathed one of the knives, crouched, and reached out his free hand to touch the figure, but the man whimpered and flinched.

He held the blade to his face to illuminate it. "See? I'm not one of them. No shining eyes."

A pale face peeked out from behind the lapels of an overcoat.

"I'm Callum. What's your name?"

"Geoffrey," came a man's voice from the doorway. "How you hanging in there?"

Callum spun around. The eyes of the figure standing in the doorway glittered and glowed in the starlight from the knife. A vampire.

But vampires didn't talk.

At the sight of Callum and his blade, the strange undead creature hissed and lunged forward, but Callum, nerves wound taut to breaking, tossed the knife into his left hand and used his right to grab the vampire's outstretched arm and throw him over his shoulder across the room. The undead creature's body crashed into the wall beside the cowering man who pushed himself up to his feet and staggered away. Callum leapt on the vampire, buried his blade into its heart, and jumped back as the flames took it.

The vampire had known the other man, Geoffrey. How it had been able to speak, Callum couldn't fathom, so he put it out of his head. Able to hold a conversation, but slower and weaker was a tradeoff Callum was willing to live with and puzzle out later.

"Are you injured?"

Geoffrey shook his head.

"Any scratches? Did they draw blood? Did they spit on you?"

Any of these things would mean a quick loss of mortality and a painful transformation under the contagion.

"N-no."

Callum pushed him against the wall and held him there as he held up the blade to see the man better.

"Please don't kill me," Geoffrey croaked.

Young, early twenties, dark hair and a scruff of beard. Scrawny and unathletic build.

Callum held the blade to the man's eyes, but the irises and pupils only glistened with tears. He pulled the collar of the man's shirt down to inspect his neck. No marks of any kind. He checked his wrists. All clear.

"I'm not going to hurt you. How long have you been here?"

"I … I dunno. Since the evening?"

Several hours. He would have turned long ago if he'd been infected. But why did they leave him unbled and unturned?

"I'm going to get you out of here, but you have to stay close to me, and you have to do *exactly* as I say. Understand?"

Geoffrey swallowed and nodded vigorously.

The easiest path out would be to retrace his steps to the back door. Any number of vampires might be out in the woods, but at least he'd be able to see them coming.

"We're going out this door, turning left, and heading down the passage to the back door. Got it?"

"Got it."

"Stay in front of me."

Callum spun Geoffrey around with his free hand and, gripping the fabric of his coat like a child's harness, pushed him forward.

"Wait," he said, and peered out of the doorway.

No sign of glittering eyes or creeping shadows.

"Go."

He pushed him into the passage, blade held above them to light the way, only to walk into the barrel of a gun.

6

"Get that thing out of my face," said Biggs at the other end of the pistol, waving Callum's blade down.

Around the barrel was wrapped a piece of parchment inscribed with text, held in place by a length of twine. A strong smell of lavender wafted toward Callum. Behind him, Hudson and Clarke brandished pistols with the same attachment, a work of High Influence, presumably to make their weapons effective against the vampires.

Biggs shifted his aim over Callum's shoulder to the house beyond, and Hudson and Clark fanned out on either side of them.

"Who's this?" Biggs didn't bother to look at the newcomer. "You checked him?"

"He's clear," said Callum. "Found him huddled in a corner."

"They left him here untouched? Something's very wrong. We took out three on the way up, but they were mooning around like undergrads on mushrooms."

"I took out two in here. Same thing. One of them even spoke."

"Fuck! Hudson, get this guy down to the car, and keep an eye on him. HQ will want to question him."

Hudson nodded once with military precision and beckoned Geoffrey to follow.

"Come on," he whispered. "Let's get you to safety."

Geoffrey looked ready to burst into tears as the agent led him away.

"Here's the plan," whispered Biggs. "Clarke cooked up an incendiary bomb from our gear." Clarke wore a backpack, the straps pulling her cotton shirt tight across her chest. "We set the bomb, detonate from outside, and pick off any stragglers. Where's the stairs?"

"Haven't got that far," said Callum. "This way, I think."

He gestured deeper into the house with his knife, and Biggs and Clarke stepped around him to take the lead.

The house was large, the ground floor a series of rooms opening out onto a central hallway, the main staircase sweeping down toward the front.

A pair of glowing eyes glittered from the ceiling above them, out of the agents' field of vision.

"Three o'clock," Callum had no idea if this was part of the agent's vernacular, but it always worked in the movies.

A dark figure jumped down on them, but the two agents reacted quickly, sidestepping and firing up at it, their bullets bright like tiny suns trailing starstuff behind them. One hit the vampire in the leg, which instantly began to burn. The other grazed its shoulder. The wound glowed with the red of dying embers. The vampire hissed in pain, but kept moving, bearing down on Biggs, but Clarke shot it in the back and must have hit its heart. It exploded in flames, the body falling on Biggs. Callum kicked it off him, and Biggs rolled onto his front to smother the patches of flame that had ignited on his clothing.

"Boss, you okay?" Clarke trained her gun on the ceiling.

"I'm fine." Biggs pushed himself up and retrieved his gun. "This is so fucked. Why aren't they swarming?"

As if on cue, three more glittering-eyed figures leapt out at them, jumping down from the upstairs landing. Biggs and Clarke opened fire, sunfire bullets streaking through the gloom. Biggs got one squarely in the heart and it burst into flames that lit up the hallway and burned themselves out by the time the body hit the floor. His second shot struck the leg of another, which began to smolder, but the vampire ignored it, landing in a crouch and leaping at Biggs.

Clarke shot the third in the head. Flames gushed out of its eyes and mouth before it collapsed, dead, the head shot enough to end it, but not to cause its entire body to burn.

Biggs backed himself into a wall to get away from the remaining vampire and emptied his clip into it, missing its heart, so it kept coming, but it ignored Callum, who darted behind it, grabbed it by the shoulder to brace himself, and plunged his alchemical silver blade into the creature's back. It burned fast.

The three of them pulled together, standing back-to-back in case any more came.

Two more did, the first materializing out of the dark to grab Clarke from the side. She screamed as it buried its talons into her and tried to aim at it, but it was too close. It sank its fangs deep into her mouth and ripped out her throat. Blood spewed everywhere. There would be no need to check that she might have caught the contagion and been turned.

It all happened too quickly for Callum to save her. With her limp body still in the vampire's arms as it tried to consume as much of her remaining blood as it could, he spun his knife back-handed, grabbed it by the back of its neck and severed its spine, the burning wound finishing the job of decapitating it. The head tumbled away, and Callum let it disappear into the darkness. The head wouldn't survive, but the body might.

He rolled the body on its back and stabbed it in the heart, an idiotic move, he realized, as the flames ignited Clarke's clothing and the backpack containing the incendiary device. He'd been wounded to the point of death six times that he could remember, but none of them had been from dismemberment. He didn't want to find out if that was something his curse would let him recover from.

Gunshots rang out behind him as Biggs took out another vampire, the body dropping to its knees and collapsing face first onto the ground.

"Bomb!" shouted Callum, and grabbed Biggs by the collar, half dragging him to the back door and out into the night. They cleared the house as the bomb exploded, the shock wave knocking them into the grass. Callum rolled over onto his back as the flames engulfed the whole building.

"Fuckfuckfuckfuck," said Biggs by his side as he untangled a new clip from his pocket and fed it into his gun. "It got me! I think it got me!"

In the light cast by the raging blaze that consumed the house, Biggs was covered in black fluid. If it was his own blood, he would certainly be infected, but if it was only the ichor that the contagion turned the vampire's blood into, he might be okay.

Biggs turned the gun on himself, pressing the barrel into his neck under his chin and aiming it up at his brain. His fingers scrabbled at the hilt and trigger, trying to get proper purchase.

"No!" shouted Callum, and leapt at the gun, wrenching it from Biggs's hands and tossing it aside.

Biggs rolled onto his hands and knees and scrambled toward it, but Callum tackled him, wrapping his arms around Biggs's neck and tangling their legs together as he rolled onto his back.

"What are you doing!" shouted Biggs. "It got me! I'm going to turn! I need the gun."

"You don't know that." Callum gritted his teeth as he struggled to restrain the resisting agent. "All we can do is wait."

"Fuck you! I don't want to turn. I don't want to end up like that. You have to kill me."

"If you turn, I will," grunted Callum. A dozen people had succumbed irrevocably to the contagion before he could do anything. He wasn't going to lose someone else. "I promise. Just wait. Just wait."

They struggled like that, rolling around in the grass as Biggs, slowly losing strength, tried to get free.

The sky began to lighten above the blaze with the first glimmer of dawn. If Biggs was turning, Callum wouldn't even have to stab him in the heart. Sunlight would do the job as quickly and definitively.

A ray of sunlight peeked over the treetops and hit them squarely in the eyes, but nothing happened. No smoldering flesh, no burning limbs. Biggs would be okay. Callum released his grip.

The agent rolled off him onto his hands and knees. He buried his face in the grass and wept.

7

BIGGS SOBBED HIMSELF DRY while Callum pretended to keep an eye out for any vampires that might have been forced into the open morning by the inferno, waiting for the strike team to arrive. Callum wished he could have done more to comfort the agent, but their relationship had never been friendly. Biggs was exactly like all the other operatives of the Cottage: too shell-shocked by the insanity they dealt with on a daily basis to be in touch with their emotions. When Hudson drove the car up the drive to see what he'd missed, Biggs pulled himself up, ramrod stiff, showing none of the feelings he had wept into the grass moments ago.

The strike team helicopter descended on them half an hour later, avenging angels that had taken too long to put on their sandals and togas and had missed the heavenly war. Soldiers in black fatigues poured out of the copter and spread out across the property, machine guns raised and presumably loaded with some form of alchemical ammunition concocted to take out the undead. Vampires were notorious for finding bolt holes to wait out the sun.

Three of the strike team tried to make Callum, Biggs, and Hudson submit to a humiliating examination to make absolutely, definitely sure they hadn't been infected by the contagion, but Callum told them to bugger off. The fact that they were standing in sunlight without burning up like roman candles should be enough. The strike team knew he was from the Library, and Cottage operatives were all instructed to defer to anyone on its staff, the Library's Royal Charter granting them consideration if not superiority. Biggs looked on, uncharacteristically withdrawn and permitting Callum to speak on his behalf.

The strike team bundled the three of them and Geoffrey, the survivor, into the helicopter to be taken to the Cottage for debriefing. Callum pressed himself into his seat as the abbey grounds fell away beneath them. Terrified of heights for fear of what a fall might do to him, he stuffed his hands under his thighs and gripped the edge of the seat as they flew into the bright morning, unable to feel the relief of not being held captive and bled dry for an eternity. The vampires had behaved so unexpectedly. He was no expert on the undead, like Rafe, but he had never heard of vampires deviating from the norm.

Biggs and the survivor sat across from him, sharing the same haunted look in their eyes, a look Callum knew well. He'd seen it time and time again in all the years he could remember working for the Library in every survivor of the ravages of Chaos and its byproducts.

The Cottage itself was the idea of a small country home an incredibly wealthy and out of touch person might have. The actual Cottage sat in a wealthy suburban town at the limits of Greater London. The seat of power of Euphemia Graham, Sorceress to the Crown, it was the hub of a compound housing alchemist's workshops, archives, and other ateliers of the sorcery of High Influence, including a three-story eyesore of a nineteen-seventies office block the local council had failed valiantly to prevent being built that housed the less magical operations of the supernatural division of the British Security Service. After Euphemia Graham had established the Cottage in the nineteen-fifties, the comings and goings of operatives at all the hours of day and night through a prim and proper suburban town had undermined the covert nature of her affairs, so the Cottage's heliport was relocated to a field some miles out of town.

The helicopter touched down at around midday to be met by a vintage black Rolls Royce and two unmarked black Vauxhall Cavaliers. Callum and Geoffrey were each bundled into one of the nondescript cars, while Biggs was escorted to the Roller. A tall, long-haired blond woman in her mid-thirties dressed in smart clothes modeled after a traditional riding outfit, complete with jodhpurs and knee-high leather boots, ushered him in, and the three cars drove off to the Cottage in a convoy with the Roller at the lead.

"My boy!" Relief radiated from Rafe as he opened his arms to embrace Callum. "They refused to tell us what was going on. We feared the worst."

Rafe's natural woody, astringent fragrance of witch hazel crested above the intense smell of lavender that had assaulted Callum the moment he slipped into the car and had followed him into the Cottage's office building where Rafe and Jessica were being held in a waiting room with as much charm as a National Health dentist's office.

"It was a close call." Callum plonked himself down between Rafe and Jessica. Jessica squeezed his hand and took off her sapphire-lensed glasses to look at him with her eerie, gold-tinged eyes. "We lost Clarke, but I found a survivor."

"A survivor," said Rafe. "How can that be?"

"There was something off about the whole thing. The vampires weren't acting like they usually do. One even said something."

Rafe scowled. "Said something? That's impossible. According to both Labrax and Theophilus, the vampire contagion changes the shape of the human brain, annihilating the capacity for speech and recognition of language entirely."

"It clearly spoke the survivor's name. And their reaction times were slower. Still dangerous, but off."

Rafe's eyes glazed over as he retreated into that place he went whenever he was in research and analysis mode. Jessica stared at Callum with her eyes that saw little that was real, but everything that was true.

"What?" said Callum. "What do you see?"

She paused before answering, opened her mouth to speak, shook her head, and replaced her glasses.

"It was too vague. A shadow behind you. A man. Maybe? Sorry."

He squeezed her hand. He had to figure out a way to get her to be less hard on herself.

One of the four doors that lined the waiting room opened and Biggs emerged. Callum rose to greet him, but the agent refused to meet his gaze and made for the entrance.

"Biggs!" Callum strode across the waiting room to catch up with him.

The agent stopped at the swinging doors with his back to Callum, hesitated as if deciding, and turned to face him, expressionless.

"How are you feeling?" Callum refused to be put off by the agent's gruffness.

The faintest of scowls flickered across Biggs's face.

"Good," he said, but Callum wasn't convinced. "I'm good."

"If you need someone to talk to—"

"I said I'm good." Biggs turned to go, stopped, and turned back. "I appreciate it, but I'm fine."

He shouldered his way through the swinging doors and left.

"He is anything but good," said Jessica from behind Callum, Rafe at her side.

"I recognize that look," said the librarian. "Keep an eye on him. Don't let him fall through the cracks."

Operatives of the Cottage tended not to last more than a few years. The things they had to deal with took a toll. Retirement often involved a hearse or a straitjacket. It was part of the Library's charter to make sure that didn't happen, but Euphemia Graham's underlings weren't a talkative bunch, even among themselves.

The door Biggs had emerged from opened and out stepped the blond woman in riding gear. Her eyes were a hard, crystalline blue, her face lean, her features angled. "Ah, there you are." She spoke with immaculate vowels and precise consonants as sharp as her cheekbones. "Esme Cavendish, Frayn Unit's supervisor. You must be Rafe Torvalds."

She reached out to shake Rafe's hand. He obliged with his usual charming smile that over the years had etched its marks on his face. His eyes were also blue, but the blue of a summer sky that makes everyone beneath it shed a few pounds of their burden. Esme Cavendish, however, was not affected. Her smile never quite reached her eyes.

"Callum Foster and," she flipped open the leather folio in her hands and checked her notes, "Jessica Harris. Glad you could come in. Would you join me inside?"

She opened the door wide so that they could enter, and ushered them into a gray, cramped, and depressing conference room, the spartan table surrounded by six uncomfortable-looking chairs.

"Do have a seat." She took the head of the table, laid her folio out before her, opened it to reveal a stack of papers and a lined notepad covered in miniscule and rigidly margined handwriting, and took out a Montblanc pen. "Commander Biggs walked me through the details of the encounter, but I'd like to hear them again from your perspective."

"Certainly." Rafe smiled affably. "Happy to be of help."

He shot Callum a worried glance. The Library and the Cottage were technically on the same team, but each side prized their secrecy. The Cottage pried constantly. Callum was convinced they were angling for a way to fold the Library into their organization. He dreaded what Euphemia Graham might do with the knowledge secured in the Hidden Galleries. He didn't trust her an inch.

Rafe led her through the preamble: the vague warning the previous morning from the Cottage's department of oracles, the frantic drive to Bristol, the objects they had found that led them to Trentham Abbey.

Cavendish asked exhaustive questions and took copious notes, even more so when Callum described what happened at Trentham. She asked all the questions about the vampire nest Callum would have expected, and he answered them with frank and open honesty until what happened after he and Biggs had escaped the inferno came up. Callum took an easy guess that Biggs hadn't brought up their scuffle. Operatives of the Cottage had it drilled into them that anyone under the slightest suspicion of infection with the vampire contagion should be immediately terminated. For the security of the nation. That Biggs had allowed Callum to overpower him and prevent him from taking his own life, even though he had been fine, would be a major black mark against his career. He would have been walked out of the conference room in irons.

The smell of lavender intensified. Cavendish, unlike Biggs and the rest of Frayn Unit, must be a fully initiated acolyte of Euphemia Graham. Their magic had a unique sensitivity to the telling of lies and the keeping of secrets. She must suspect something and be trying to cast a spell on him, but Callum stared her directly in the eye, his expression devoid of tells, confident in the knowledge that the wild magic that raged inside him kept in check by his tattoos would stymie any attempt she might make to catch him out.

"Excellent," she said with no enthusiasm as she returned her pen to her jacket and closed the folio. "Thank you for your cooperation. An agent will take you to your car. You're free to go."

Rafe stood before she did. "I wish to be present at the questioning of the survivor."

She paused before speaking, her face an emotionless and intimidating blank canvas. "I'm afraid that—"

"It is my right under the royal charter to be present at the debriefing of any subject of the realm that has been directly impacted by Chaotic Influence to advocate for their wellbeing and to offer them counsel."

Rafe excelled at meeting the Cottage head on with all their ridiculous jargon. Sorcerers thought themselves too refined to call magic what it was, calling it Influence instead. If it quacked like a duck and drank human blood because it had been corrupted by wild magic, then it was a magic duck, not an aquatic avian suffering from the adverse transmutational effects of Chaotic Influence, or however else they might refer to it in their paperwork. The only jargon that worked for Callum was calling wild magic Chaos.

Chaos felt right.

Cavendish blinked rapidly, the slightest crinkles folding around her eyes as she processed his request. "Very well. Follow me."

She led them down the corridor deeper into the building and paused at another unmarked door with one hand on the doorknob. "Only you, Mr. Torvalds."

"Mr. Foster and Ms. Harris are my advisors," said Rafe with a warm and nonconfrontational smile. Callum marveled at how he made it work for him. "I require them to be present with me."

Cavendish exhaled a tiny, sharp breath, her only concession to frustration. The Library's royal charter was meticulously explicit. If Chaos was involved and subjects of the realm had been affected, the Library of the Damned—terrible name, but it dated back to its foundation in the fifteenth century—was required to be involved.

"You may observe only," she said, "while the interrogation is in progress. Find yourselves seats out of the way. I don't want to hear a peep out of you."

"Of course," said Rafe. "We wouldn't dream of interrupting you."

8

CAVENDISH PUSHED THROUGH THE door into a darkened room. A red "exit" sign above cast a seedy glow. A line of pin lights led the way up a central aisle between five rows of seats with the feel of several art house cinemas in the West End Callum had enjoyed over the years. She turned her back on them and stalked through the darkness to a seat on the aisle in the front row, letting them find their own way. Rafe led them to the row behind her and all the way to the end.

As the door clicked shut, the entire front wall disappeared, revealing a cold, white room beyond. At the desk, facing them, Geoffrey slumped in his seat sitting on his hands looking diminished and dejected, staring blankly, unaware of their presence.

Cavendish removed from the pocket of her jacket a slim, black Bakelite box with a rotary telephone dial embedded on its surface and five unmarked buttons beneath it. Crossing her legs and resting her folio on her thigh, she pressed one of the buttons and dialed three numbers.

"You may begin," she said.

A door in the white room beyond opened and a round-faced man in his twenties dressed in a dark suit and tie entered. He brought with him a dull red plastic cafeteria tray bearing a large carafe of water and a single glass.

"Mr. Cooke." The man smiled pleasantly and placed the tray down on the table out of Geoffrey's reach. "I do apologize for making you wait. If you'll answer a few questions for me, we can have you on your way home by dinner."

Geoffrey's blank stare zeroed in on the carafe of water. His knee began to bounce up and down.

"I hope the medical staff took good care of you," said the interrogator.

Tucked under one arm was a pad which he placed on the table in front of him. He took out a pen and leaned back against his seat in a casual slump. He slid out from the pad an official-looking form, which he skimmed.

"Yeah," said Geoffrey, not taking his eyes off the carafe. "Yeah, they were great."

"Oh, good. I see they gave you a clean bill of health. That is a relief. You must be exhausted after such a harrowing experience."

The door to the viewing room opened and in slipped a tall, slender figure. The woman was in her sixties, dressed in a black Chanel suit with white trim, pale stockings, and black high-heeled shoes, her short salt and pepper hair styled in waves and curls that emphasized her sharp cheekbones. Callum knew exactly who she was from the way the smell of lavender blossomed to the point of cloying.

He leaned in to Jessica and Rafe, who hadn't noticed the new arrival.

"Euphemia Graham," he whispered. The sorcerer in charge and advisor to the Crown on all matters of supernatural security.

Unfazed, Rafe only glanced at her quickly, but Jessica removed her glasses and stared. Her golden eyes glowed faintly in the gloom.

"Strewth." Her mouth fell agape.

"Sweetie, you're drooling." Callum shoved her gently with his shoulder. She had a weakness for powerful women that got her in all sorts of trouble.

"Like I'd ever have a shot at that." She replaced her spectacles.

"Don't sell yourself short. I've every confidence you'll meet the dark sorceress of your dreams, and you can tie each other up to your heart's content."

She snorted and slumped deeper in her seat. Rafe scowled at them for misbehaving.

"Would you like a glass of water?" said the interrogator.

Geoffrey grunted and nodded. The interrogator filled the glass and handed it to him. He snatched it and chugged the entire glass down without stopping to breathe. He wiped his mouth and placed the glass on the table in front of him, his fingers wrapped around it like talons.

"Dehydration," whispered Callum. "They should have given him an IV drip. What are they playing at?"

"We're trying to understand what exactly happened, and I hope you can help us fill in some blanks," said the interrogator.

"Yeah, yeah," said Geoffrey, his eyes fixed on the carafe. "I don't remember much. It's all a blur."

The interrogator scrunched up his face in a reasonable facsimile of sympathy, though Geoffrey was more interested in the water. The interrogator didn't offer him another glass.

"Of course. The entire experience must be confusing for you. How did you come to find yourself in Trentham? You live in Bristol, I believe." He glanced down at the medical form. "Clifton."

"Yeah, I dunno. I don't remember."

"What's the last thing you do remember, Mr. Cooke?"

Geoffrey blinked and focused on the interrogator for the first time.

"I got off work on Thursday, went down the pub with my mates for a drink. I remember not staying late 'cause I wanted to go for a run the next morning. I caught a cab home … "

He trailed off and stared into the distance, his eyes darting around as he tried to remember what he did next, but his expression became more and more distressed. Jessica sat up and leaned forward.

"Do you see something," whispered Rafe.

"He was beguiled. I see the figure of a woman standing over him."

"Can you describe her?"

She shook her head. "It's too vague. Something's messing up the impression."

"And what did you do next, Mr. Cooke," said the interrogator. "After you returned home."

Geoffrey squinted as if it might bring his memories into focus. "I called my sister."

He didn't sound confident.

"Your sister, Lucinda?" The interrogator pulled out another sheet of paper from his pad and scanned it with the tip of his pen. "We have your phone records here. The only call you made that day was at oh-seven-hundred hours that morning to London. Are you sure you went home?"

"Yeah," said Geoffrey, more definite this time. "Yeah, I remember some dickhead got the cab I wanted, and I had to wait for another. I remember getting into the cab."

"But you didn't call your sister when you got home."

"No, I did." Geoffrey scowled. "I spoke to her. She told me … "

He trailed off again.

"What did she tell you?" said the interrogator.

"It's a strong beguilement," whispered Jessica. "He's trying to break through the fog, but it's fighting back."

"She told me … "

The interrogator began to move his pen from side to side, the golden tip of the cap gleaming in the overhead light, in an apparently casual, absentminded gesture, but neither Callum nor Rafe were fooled.

"No." Rafe rose from his chair. "I insist you stop this immediately!"

Jessica and Callum shifted in their seats so Rafe could make his way down the row to confront Esme Cavendish.

"Mesmerism may not be used on subjects of the Crown without consent!"

"Sit down, Mr. Torvalds." Cavendish didn't bother to look up.

"I will not sit down!" He shuffled around to put himself directly between her and the transparent wall. "This is outrageous behavior. He is clearly distressed. You have no right to treat him this way."

She stood and glared down at him.

"I have every right to question him however I see fit." A scornful sneer spread across her face. "He is the rare survivor of a vampire infestation. And he is still under the effect of its beguilement. I need to know how he became ensnared and how he survived. The safety of the nation depends on it."

"Mr. Foster and your agents sterilized the contagion, did they not?" Rafe snapped back. Under normal circumstances a calm and unassuming man, when an innocent had been violated by wild magic, he became a pit bull. "There is no imminent threat. The young man has been through a horrendous ordeal. He must be allowed to rest and recover so the beguilement can fade. There are other, less invasive ways to get the information you seek."

"This is the Cottage, Mr. Torvalds, not a wellness retreat. I don't have the time or the resources to hold his hand and feed him tea and cakes while he returns to his senses."

"Yes, but I do. This is precisely why the Library was chartered. I will call the Palace if I have to."

By "palace," he meant St. James, the seat of the Shadow Council that supervised the Cottage, and not Buckingham. Callum doubted the Royal Family knew the first thing about sorcery and wild magic.

Cavendish pressed a button on her box. "Remove and detain Mr. Torvalds and his associates immediately."

The door opened and three operatives in expensive suits entered. Callum and Jessica rose as two of them approached. The third stalked down the aisle toward Cavendish and Rafe. Callum still had his knives on him, but he couldn't use them, no matter how much he wanted to.

"You won't be able to call anyone from a holding cell." Cavendish sneered at him.

Rafe stepped away from the operative to face Euphemia Graham across the seats. "There are other ways to contact someone than the telephone. The Master of the Dagger will be most unhappy to hear how you're treating Her Majesty's law-abiding subjects!"

It was a clever bluff. Callum knew they had no other way to get word out if they were detained, but Euphemia Graham didn't. The Library was in Cheyne Heath, a borough of London the local witches had carved out as a refuge from sorcery. Magic didn't work there the way it did everywhere else in the British Isles. Graham couldn't spy on them in there by supernatural means, and any operatives who dared to enter were summarily expelled by the witches. She had no idea what Rafe could or couldn't do.

"Stand down." Graham spoke as softly as if telling someone at her table it was their turn to play their hand at cards.

The operatives fell back immediately and left the room. Graham rose to follow them.

She stopped at the door and turned back. "You have five days to find out what happened. After that, I'm coming for him."

"The witches won't let you into the neighborhood," said Rafe.

Graham smiled. It wasn't pleasant.

"There are other ways to retrieve someone than my officers or High Influence, Mr. Torvalds."

She knew he had been bluffing. The threat of confinement had been merely a feint, a test of his resolve.

The door opened for her, and she walked out.

9

IT WAS LATE AFTERNOON before they were able to bundle Geoffrey into the Rover and get him away from the Cottage. Callum drove them into the nearby town and stopped at a local chip shop to get them drinks and dinner. All four of them wolfed their fish and chips down, and Geoffrey chugged back a large bottle of water. They sat in silence with greasy fingers and full bellies once they were all finished, the tension of the past day softened enough to make them all feel human again.

"We can take you home," said Rafe in the back seat with Geoffrey as Callum and Jessica tidied up the remains of the meal, "but we're almost to London. We wouldn't get you back to Bristol till late. Why don't you stay the night with us at the Library? We can drive you back home in the morning after you've had a proper night's rest."

Rafe had no intention of letting Geoffrey go home, Callum knew, until they were certain he would be okay. It would take some time to help the poor chap process what had happened, and, if he couldn't, they had ways of blurring his memories to make living with his brush with the undead tolerable.

"That would be great," said Geoffrey, barely able to lift his head. "Thank you."

He slumped down into his seat, closed his eyes, and fell asleep.

"Well, then." Rafe settled in himself. "Let's get home. I'll be happy to see the back of the past twenty-four hours."

"Your wish is my command," said Callum.

The drive into London was uneventful, most of the traffic heading the other way as commuters wended their way from their jobs in the big city back to their safe and normal homes. What must that be like, Callum wondered.

The tattoos across the back of his body tingled as they crossed from Fulham into Cheyne Heath, and the ordered flow of Influence that gave sorcerers their power broke down. When the witches of Cheyne Heath claimed the entire borough for themselves a few years ago and somehow managed to undo millennia of sorcerous control, Callum thought he would have to leave, but wild magic left to its own devices didn't have to mean the catastrophic turbulence of full-on Chaos. The man-made order of High Influence pressed against his supernaturally jumbled senses, a constant buzz at the upper range of his hearing, the perpetual screech of braking cars at the edge of his perception. Cheyne Heath's primordial wildness came as a relief, the comfort of returning home to the familiar. And Chaos manifested only slightly more often here than it did in the outer world. It was a small price to pay for the occasional moment of peace and quiet.

Three streets into the neighborhood, a pair of women waved them down from a corner. Witches checking up on them. Callum slid to a halt and wound down the window.

"Mr. Foster." The shorter of the two witches, a bright-smiled pepper pot of a woman dressed in floral prints and a straw hat with a bunch of berries attached to the brim, stuck her head in. Her companion, a Chinese witch in a denim skirt and a bright Mickey Mouse shirt faced the way they had come, her expression an irate scowl.

Though thoroughly magical, neither woman gave off an odor to Callum's scrambled senses, the absence of fragrance differentiating their power from that of sorcerers. "How delightful to see you all!"

Rafe, in the passenger seat, leaned in to speak to her. "Mrs. Dearing, what a lovely surprise. I do hope you're not out at this hour on our account?"

The witches of Cheyne Heath kept close track of the few sorcerers they allowed into their sanctuary, but the Library of the Damned they usually let come and go in peace.

"Oh, not at all." The witch took a deep breath and held her face up to the moonlight as if it were the sun. "We're out for a lovely evening stroll."

She saw Geoffrey in the back seat and raised an eyebrow.

"Do be careful, though." She glanced uneasily toward Fulham. "The wolves are at the door. Mrs. Graham has turned her vigilant eye upon us."

"I fear that might be our fault," said Rafe.

The witch looked again at Geoffrey and slipped a hand into her pocket. Callum felt a shiver run across his tattoos. She was casting some kind of spell.

"Oh, you poor dear," she said to Geoffrey. "You have had a hard time, haven't you! Well, you're in good hands. Dear Mr. Torvalds will see you right. And we'll make sure she doesn't get in your way, Mr. Torvalds. Enjoy your evening. Don't be strangers!"

She stepped away from the car and joined her friend. The two witches exchanged words, smiled, and waved as Callum drove away.

The Library of the Damned was housed in a red-brick Victorian mansion directly across the border from Fulham. Callum found them a parking spot across the road while Rafe woke Geoffrey up as gently as possible.

"You live here?" Geoffrey stared up at the imposing building as Rafe fumbled with his keys to open the front door.

"Yep," said Callum. "Most of the building is library, but there are a few residential rooms on the upper floors."

"That's crazy. My flat's the size of a postage stamp."

Geoffrey's voice dropped to a hushed whisper as he stepped foot inside. The vestibule was small for such a large building. Red brick walls surrounded a black and white stone tiled floor, the room dominated by the carved wooden doors that led into the Library. On either side stood brass Moorish braziers that radiated dim light and an earthy fragrance from a mechanism within that Rafe tended to on a weekly basis to tame any magic, wild or otherwise, within the building.

"This way, dear boy." Rafe led Geoffrey up a staircase to the right. "It's a bit of a walk, I fear. Five flights. Think you can manage it?"

"Yeah, yeah," said the young man, awed enough by the building to forget the madness he had lived through, if only for the night.

"I'm still wired." Jessica collapsed into one of the dark carved wood chairs pushed up against the walls as Geoffrey and Rafe disappeared upstairs. "Let's go out for a drink!"

All Callum wanted to do was go up to his room, shut the door, and immerse himself in his books.

"Oh, come on! You never want to go out." Jessica pouted. Maybe her visions gave her a window to his thoughts. Probably she could see the lack of enthusiasm written on his face. "You'd think someone a thousand years old would have learned how to have a good time."

"I can't. I need to get everything that's happened down on paper before I forget it. You know that." He had twenty more years before he was guaranteed to lose all his memories again, but that only made him more desperate to record as much as possible while he could.

She growled with frustration. "Useless, the pair of you! It's like living in a monastery!"

"You could go out on your own."

"Oh, sure." She kicked the chair leg with the heel of her boot. "Go down the pub and spend an hour chatting someone up only to discover they're a figment of someone else's imagination? Or worse, get killed crossing the road from walking into a car I couldn't see because I was too busy trying not to get trampled by horses from a hundred years ago. Not likely."

She pushed herself up and headed wearily for the stairs, her black tulle crinoline drooping around her shins. Outside the Library, where magic flowed freely, even with her sapphire spectacles walking around was a challenge. In here, she made her way with full confidence, even in the dark. She'd lived with them for five years, since the accident that had changed her, and she knew her way around every nook and cranny Rafe would allow her access to.

"Somewhere out there." She trudged away, her feet leaden on the stairs, "is a jug of gin and tonic with my name on it, lost and alone."

Callum sank into the seat she left behind and took in the darkness and the silence, the red brick walls of the Library a shield against the potential madness and danger of the world outside.

Callum's digs were in the attic, all the way at the top of the building, shielded by a network of wards and sigils that disconnected him magically from the library so that the arcane energies of its contents wouldn't eat away at his tattoos and, should his tattoos fail, the wild magic that raged within him wouldn't wreak havoc in the stacks and the galleries beneath them. He kept the large room as it had been when the librarian of thirty years ago, a prickly man Callum had not connected with the way he had with Rafe, found him after he had lost his memory. Beneath the large skylight, he had a bed, a dresser, an armchair, and a side table. In the nineteen-fifties, right before the last time Callum had lost his memories, he had apparently secured the funds for a renovation and now he also had electricity and a small bathroom with a shower to use within the protective boundary. He even had a hotplate, a kettle, and a small fridge so he didn't have to walk down two floors to the kitchen for milk for his tea.

His attic might have little in the way of comforts, but it was far from empty. Laden bookshelves covered one entire wall from floor to ceiling housing a thousand volumes of Callum's journals from his four hundred years at the Library, plus a cache of two or three hundred scrolls Rafe had unearthed in a crypt beneath a parish church in Wales in seventeen thirty-seven, the earliest of which dated back to the eleventh century. On the side table by his armchair lay his current journal next to a volume from the eighteenth century he was halfway through. In the back of each volume, he kept a record of how many times he had reread the volumes. This one he had reread six times.

He dropped into the armchair and picked up his current journal, a hardback notebook from a case Rafe had bought for him, clothbound and embossed with Callum's name in gold. Some days he was better at taking notes of the events of the day. Some entries documented every feeling, every thought, every small moment of joy he had experienced. Others were little more than a short string of terse sentences. Today the words flowed from his pen.

"Friday, September 10th, 1993—Vampire nest. A new breed? One survivor (!) Rafe saved him from the clutches of the Cottage … "

Lost in his writing, he barely registered the knock on the door.

"Callum, dear boy," came Rafe's voice from the other side. "May I enter?"

He finished the sentence he was writing and rose to open the door. "Come in, come in!" He glanced at the bookshelves as he passed and sighed. "Have a seat, old man."

He waved Rafe to the armchair.

The librarian perched on its arm and laid his cane across his lap. "I think you should take Jessica out for a drink."

A volume of his journals from the fifteenth century perched on the windowsill caught Callum's eye. Wasn't there something about vampires in there? "I have to get everything down before I forget it."

Rafe peered at the writing in the open journal beside him. "It looks like you have already."

Callum snatched up the volume on the windowsill and remembered another that had mentioned something about the possible origins of the vampire contagion. He ran his fingers across a shelf to find it. Seventeenth century, definitely. "Maybe tomorrow, Rafe—"

"Callum." Rafe came up behind him and placed a hand on his shoulder. "It's important. For both of you. I'm going to have to insist. You just survived a vampire infestation. At the very least, do it for Jessica. She won't go out otherwise, and I'm worried about her."

Callum sighed out frustration and exhaustion in equal measures. She had been increasingly moody and irritable over the past few months, spending more and more time locked in her room blaring music.

"All right." He returned the journals to the shelf, pulling them out halfway to see where they were. "I'll take her to the Bull and Pig."

Rafe's expression brightened. "A capital idea! You love that place."

Only partially refreshed and revitalized by a shower and a change of clothes, Callum stuck his head into the common area of the Library's residence, an open plan kitchen and living room that filled the entire floor two stories down from the attic, to find Rafe at the dinner table with his ubiquitous stack of research materials. The sun had gone down, so he had pulled a standing lamp over to help him read.

"You look nice." Rafe pulled off his reading glasses to let them dangle from the cord around his neck and beamed. "I told Jessica. She's getting ready."

Callum had slipped out of his usual uniform of well-worn jeans, a plain white t-shirt, and a canvas jacket into black slacks and a burgundy collared shirt, the cuffs buttoned so it covered his tattoos. Dressing up a bit always did wonders for how he felt. "Want to come?"

Rafe smiled and shook his head. "I must stay here and keep an eye on our guest."

"You could bring him along. It might be a good distraction."

"Perhaps in a day or two if he feels stronger. The experience took a lot out of him."

"I know how he feels. You ready," he asked Jessica as she walked in. She had changed into a men's blue pinstripe suit with only a black bustier underneath. "You know, we're only going to the Bull and Pig."

"You're not the only one who likes to dress up." She dismissed him with a wave and went over to Rafe to kiss him on the top of his head. "I checked in on Geoffrey. He's sound asleep, but there's nightmares on the way."

Rafe grimaced, closed his books, and stood. "I'd better burn some incense. A witch I met in Morel Market last week gave me a blend of sage that might be quite helpful."

Rafe was like catnip to witches: a Chaos-kissed straight man who knew about their Craft and valued them enough to let them get on with it without judgment. He'd had long-term relationships with three witches since Callum had known him. They never lasted, though. His curse was too much of a hurdle.

"I'll check up on him when we get back." Callum followed Jessica downstairs.

Coats on and ready to hit the town, Callum opened the front door to find a familiar figure on the front step.

"Biggs?" Callum hardly recognized him. Instead of the stuffy Cottage-approved security service drag he always wore at work, Biggs was dressed in a pair of black, pleated trousers with a black t-shirt under a black leather jacket, his only concession to color the gold chain he wore around his neck. He cleaned up well. "Do you need something?"

The agent bobbed uncomfortably on the step, brow furrowed.

"My boss said I should come and talk to you. About what happened."

"You told her!" It came out sharper than Callum intended. He winced internally, worried about what the Cottage might do to Biggs.

"About the ... ?" He trailed off and brushed his neck. "Fuck, no. Of course not. I'm not an idiot."

Biggs softened, probably realizing his usually belligerent manner was not the best tack to take to get whatever it was he was after. "Sorry. She wanted you lot to clear me for service."

"Oh," said Callum, wary. According to the charter, any agent of the Cottage directly exposed to Chaos was supposed to be counseled by the Library, but no one ever did it. What could have caused Esme Cavendish to enforce the rules this time?

"I wanted to come and talk to you," said the agent, distress in his expression, tension in his body and the hunch of his shoulders. "Take you up on your offer."

"What's up, boys," said Jessica from behind Callum. She had found her coat, a charcoal gray cashmere overcoat, and had wrapped a black feather boa around her neck to protect her against the cool evening breeze.

"Biggs is joining us for a drink."

"What?" said the agent.

"Come on, mate." Callum clapped him on the shoulder and led him down the steps. "We're going to the Bull and Pig for a pint. It's a ten-minute walk from here."

"Don't you want to, you know, talk?" Biggs frowned, confused.

"Like therapy?" Callum laughed. "I'm no psychiatrist."

"Don't sell yourself short." Jessica slid her arm around his so he could lead her. "He's an excellent shoulder to cry on if you ever need it."

Callum led the two of them down the street, Biggs following a pace behind.

"Tonight, we'll be colleagues having a drink after work, nothing else." Callum breathed in the night air. "If more needs to be done, we can do it tomorrow."

10

"HOW DID YOU GET past the witches?" asked Jessica as they made their way through the shabby streets of Cheyne Heath, her arm through Callum's. "They take special glee in ejecting you lot the second you step foot in the neighborhood. Did they not challenge you?"

"I dunno." The agent shrugged. "A couple of women stopped me as I was getting out of the car and asked me the time. Were they witches?"

"What did they look like?"

"A cranky Eastern European woman and an Indian granny in a pink sari."

"Where did you park?" said Callum.

"Two doors down from you."

Callum chuckled. "They probably smelled the Chaos on you and assumed you were with us."

Biggs stopped at the sight of the Bull and Pig. "It's a fucking poof's paradise."

The traditional Victorian public house building that was the premises for the pub had been tarted up by the owners with a pink and yellow neon sign depicting a bull doing something unspeakable to a pig that was still technically against the law in the United Kingdom of Great Britain and Northern Island.

Callum put a hand on Biggs's chest to block his path.

"None of that, understand?" He stared the agent in the eye. "If you're going to be a prick you can fuck right off."

"Yeah, yeah." Contrite, Biggs bobbed his head in agreement. "Sorry."

"All right." Callum clapped him on the back. "First round's on me."

Inside, the pub had been decorated as if it existed in a parallel universe where all the right angles were a little off, and the colors were all shifted three shades toward pink. It was its usual half-full for a Friday. More a neighborhood hangout for the local queer community and artists than a destination party place, it only filled up after pride marches or on Saturday nights when they had bands in. Jessica and Biggs found them a booth while Callum hit the bar.

The bartender was new to Callum, though he hadn't been in for a month or two. Late twenties, broad-shouldered, and a couple of inches taller, the bartender wore a tight-fitting white tank top that showed off ropes of muscle, and chest hair that tufted out of the neckline. A large, elaborately carved wooden bead strung on a thin black leather necklace rested suggestively at the base of his throat, and a close-cropped beard sprawled up his face toward his wide-set blue eyes.

"What can I get you?" He had a strong Scottish accent, his white teeth catching the pink neon light that surrounded the mirror behind the bar.

Callum realized he needed to get laid. "Pint of bitter, a lager, and a gin and tonic, please."

"Coming right up."

Callum's thoughts drifted to the vampire nest. A new breed. Had that ever happened before? He shouldn't be surprised, they were creatures of Chaos, after all. The contagion had first been recorded in the fourteenth century, but there were no detailed records or studies of it. People were too concerned with stamping it out before the whole country was overrun. His journals were useless in these situations. Too many pages of chronological entries. He might get lucky, flick through a volume at random, and come across a passage with more information about whatever challenge he was up against, but that was rare. It would be so much easier if he could remember. What good was being so long-lived if you could only recall as much as anyone else? He should make some kind of index, or a reading order for the next time he found himself wandering around the city having forgotten everything about himself.

The bartender returned with the drinks. "He's fit."

"Excuse me?"

The Scot smiled, his eyes glittering in the overhead light.

"The feller at the end of the bar you've been staring at for the past five minutes. I think he's alone. You should go for it."

He winked, and Callum felt his heart flutter. He *really* needed to get laid.

"Not tonight." He over-tipped like he always did. "I'm with friends. Cheers."

At the booth, Callum found Biggs huddled forward with a stricken expression as he listened to Jessica.

"A conversion camp?" said the agent. "Like brainwashing?"

Jessica slumped back in her chair and played with the thick pewter ring around her thumb. "Yes, like brainwashing. My parents thought they could torture the gay out of me."

She glanced up at Callum as he placed the drinks on the table, squinted hard, and reached for her gin and tonic, only missing it by a hair. He slid it the rest of the way into her hand. She sat back and took a sip.

"My girlfriend came to get me, but we were already driving away when she arrived. She stepped out in front of the car to stop us, but my Dad didn't see her till the last moment. He swerved, but still hit her. I got out to help her, but she was already dead. I remember screaming myself raw. I was so angry and so scared all at the same time. And then the world shifted."

"Shifted?" Biggs gripped his pint mug so hard his knuckles turned pale.

"I don't know how else to describe it. I felt powerful all of a sudden, like I could do anything. I was surrounded by a light so bright it burned my eyes. Then I passed out and woke up in a hospital bed, only I didn't know it right then because all I could see was clouds. Big, purple clouds of smoke."

"And that's what you can see now?"

She shook her head. "Now it's like there's a transparent movie screen in front of my face. I can sort of see through it, but the movie on the screen gets in the way."

"Fuck."

"Yeah." She grimaced and took another sip of her drink.

Biggs frowned at the foamy head of his beer as if it contained the answers to all his problems. "Something like that happened to my mate, Clive. He got recruited to the Cottage at the same time I did. A week after we got out of training, they found him screaming his head off running through the cars in Oxford Circus. Never saw him again."

Callum had. He remembered the incident. He and Rafe were called in to help, but there was nothing they could do.

Biggs turned to Callum. "Is that what happened to you?"

Callum shrugged as he took a swig of his lager. "Can't remember."

Biggs frowned, irritated. "Come on!"

"No, really. I can remember a few years back, and then nothing."

Biggs took a deep draft of his beer and wiped the foam from his mouth with the back of his hand. "Is that going to happen to me?"

Callum and Jessica exchanged a look.

"Not necessarily." Callum sounded unconvincing even to himself.

They sat in silence for a while, watching the patrons come and go, the quiet chatter of normal people having a normal Thursday night unburdened by the knowledge of magic and the terrors that lurked out of sight in the nooks and crannies of reality.

Biggs broke the silence. "How's Cooke doing?"

"As well as can be expected," said Jessica. "So, not great."

"How are you guys going to help him?"

"Be there for him," said Callum, suspecting they weren't only talking about Geoffrey. "Let him realize he's not crazy, he's not alone. That we're here for him."

"Sounds like a good plan." The agent swallowed another mouthful of lager and took his time savoring it. "And what about the nest? The boss said the governor gave you five days to figure out—"

"No case talk," said Jessica.

"Yeah." Biggs relaxed, sinking back into the bench. "Probably just as well. They put me on medical leave for two weeks. Two weeks! What the hell am I going to do? Sit around on my arse twiddling my thumbs all day?"

He launched into a litany of frustrations with working for an organization only tangentially associated with the government and the arcane rules of sorcerers that made no sense to anyone who'd ever worked in the real world, even a spook.

Between the alcohol and the conversation, Callum felt the edge he had been riding ever since they got home begin to soften. He let his attention wander to the other drinkers and made brief eye contact with the man sitting at the bar the hot bartender had tried to get him to pick up. He wasn't bad-looking: slender, medium height, fair hair and skin, a charming smile and an easy manner as he chatted with an older lesbian couple who hung on his every word.

"Another round?" He gulped back the last of his pint.

"My turn." Biggs made to stand, but Callum waved him down.

"You get the next one. Same again?"

"Get us some snacks as well," said Jessica. "No pork scratchings. They're disgusting."

Movement in the corner of his eye caught Callum's attention as he waited at the bar, a roadie type setting up gear for a performance on the tiny stage in the corner.

"Dutch courage." The bartender slid a shot of whiskey toward him across the counter.

"Hm?" said Callum, confused.

"You and he," the Scot nodded to the man at the end of the bar, "have been eyeing each other up for the past hour. One of you has to make a move."

Callum smiled. It was a tempting thought. "I'm not really up for it tonight."

"Shame. I'd like to see you go home with someone, even if it's not me." The bartender flicked his eyebrows up and down in a quick, but obvious come-on, made all the more alluring by his broad and warm smile.

Callum laughed and knocked back the whiskey. To his surprise, it was quite good. Not top shelf, but certainly not from the well.

"Let's see how the evening develops. Two lagers, a gin and tonic, and a packet of crisps, please."

"Coming right up." The bartender picked up an empty pint glass the wrong way round, tossed it in the air, and caught it in an impressive display of manual dexterity.

Music began to play from the speakers by the sides of the stage, an extended loop of the distinctive opening bars of "Diamonds Are Forever."

"Ladies and gentlemen." A deep and resonant voice echoed around the room. "Thilady Missgrace!"

As the lights dimmed and a mist sprung up throughout the pub, Callum was hit by a potent fragrance of sandalwood. There weren't many sorcerers who could successfully wield their powers in the wild magic of Cheyne Heath, but one of the spheres, the many houses of sorcery, had achieved unparalleled control: a cabal of illusionists who owned a nightclub within the borders of the borough, all of them drag performers *par excellence*. This should be good.

Blue firefly lights winked on and off throughout the pub as a long and slender arm emerged from the side of the stage clad in a sleeve of squares of glass that caught the beam of an invisible spotlight and reflected it in a thousand shards that caught the mist. The performer stepped out onto the stage, her entire outfit covered like a lithe and sinewy mirror ball, and the entire pub exploded with light. As she stalked the stage and gyrated, lip synching to the plaintive, gut-wrenching wail of Shirley Bassey proclaiming the uselessness of men, the room was transformed by magic. It was a subtle effect, the walls shifting and receding, a bright and giant moon shining down upon them that might have been a cardboard cutout, or a moon that shone over the landscape of a dream. The altered room was only set dressing, suggestive details to enhance the performer. No one was looking around them to wonder what had happened to the Bull and Pig. All eyes were on the sorceress, Thilady Missgrace. When the song ended, the crowd erupted into rapturous applause.

A hand squeezed Callum's shoulder, and a voice spoke in his ear. "Callum."

He turned to find the man at the end of the bar standing there, smiling at him. Callum hadn't realized how handsome he was. He had the most striking violet eyes flecked with gold that made Callum want to lose himself in them.

"It's good to see you," said the stranger.

"I'm sorry," said Callum, confused. Exhaustion, the beer, the shot of whiskey, the performance all made it hard for him to think. "Do I know you?"

11

WOOD DIGGING AWKWARDLY INTO his thigh. His face flushed with heat. The room shifting around him like a spinning top with its momentum almost spent. His back pressing into a hard, uncomfortable surface. His head pounding like he'd been hit with a brick.

"Closing time, mate."

"What?" Callum looked up at the bartender standing over him and panicked, his heart pounding a vigorous staccato rhythm in his chest. "What time is it?"

"Almost twelve. We're closing up. I'm going to have to kick you out in a moment."

Callum took a deep breath, and another, and another, trying to steady himself. He had lost time again. It happened occasionally, a few hours inexplicably vanishing from his memory every year or so, the gaps between incidents getting shorter and more frequent as the days advanced toward his inevitable loss of everything he knew.

I'm Callum Foster. Callum Foster. Rafe Torvalds and Jessica Harris are my friends. I live at the Library on Consul Street.

He repeated his name again and again like a mantra. He was okay. He still knew who he was.

"Must have been some powerful drugs you were on," said the bartender. "What was it, ketamine?"

Callum turned his head to look up at him, but his brain objected. A lance of bright pain sparked between his temples.

"Are you all right?" The bartender slid into the booth next to him.

Callum swallowed, trying to get some moisture back into his throat so he could answer.

"Yeah," he croaked. "Yeah, I'm fine. Sorry, I need a second."

The bartender began to look worried.

"You don't look fine. Hang on." He darted back to the bar, leaned across it, fished out a bottle of water, and unscrewed the cap.

"Here." He offered it to Callum. "Drink this."

Callum chugged the cold water down in one long drag. His head didn't appreciate being tipped back, but the water was an elixir that returned him to life. "Thank you."

"What did you take?"

"I didn't. I didn't take anything."

The bartender scowled. "That fucker. He must have slipped you something. Are you sure you're okay? He didn't do anything to you?"

Callum rubbed his temples. The headache was subsiding, but he was still disoriented, confused.

"What are you talking about?"

"I thought you got lucky. I saw you and him slip into the bathroom together."

"Who?"

"The guy at the bar who was chatting you up. He came over to you after the first number."

"The number … "

Memory glimmered at Callum through the fog in his brain. Shirley Bassey. Diamonds are Forever. Performed by a sorcerer. The song finished and …

That was where his memories ended. So, only two or three hours lost. That wasn't too bad.

He remembered he hadn't come to the bar alone. "Bugger! Jessica! I left her all alone with Biggs."

She was going to kill him.

"Do you need me to take you somewhere?" The bartender placed a hand on his back. "St. Decuman's is around the corner."

Callum closed his eyes for a second. The bartender's hand felt so good, a calming weight steadying his nerves. He wanted to lean in and be held in his arms. Was he that starved of physical affection?

"I'm fine, thank you." He placed a hand on the bartender's shoulder, not to push him away, but to ask for some space. The big man got the message and eased back but kept close, one arm behind Callum ready to catch him should he take a turn. "You're very kind, thank you. I'm okay. I will be okay. It happens to me every so often. It's like a seizure. I lose a little bit of time. I'll be fine if I can get home and rest."

"Do you live nearby?"

"Yeah. Yeah, I do. Ten minutes away."

"All right. Hang on here a moment." The bartender rose, picked up a denim jacket on the counter, and called out to someone in the back. "Bill, I'm all done. You okay locking up?"

"Yeah, no problem," came the response.

The Scot held out a hand to help Callum up. "I'll walk you home."

"Really, there's no need. I'll be—"

Callum stumbled as he got to his feet, but the bartender slipped in to catch him.

"I'll walk you home. Come on."

The cool night air felt good against Callum's skin, the damp chill filling his lungs and clearing the fog as it seeped into his brain.

"My name's Rory, by the way," said the bartender.

"Red-haired king."

"Excuse me?"

"That's what Rory means in Gaelic." Another one of those things Callum knew without knowing how. "Red-haired king."

Rory laughed and tousled his mop of thick black hair.

"Not a good name for me, then."

"Oh, I don't know. You carry yourself like a king."

Oh god, thought Callum, inwardly cringing. *Next, you'll be asking him if he comes here often.*

Rory's cheeks darkened the slightest shade. Was he blushing?

"Are you cold?" Rory held up his jacket. "Do you want this?"

Callum smiled. He was usually the knight in shining armor sweeping in to save the day. Well, not shining armor. Jeans and a t-shirt at best.

"I'm fine thank you, Rory. My name's Callum."

"Oh, you're Scottish, too? I thought I detected an accent."

Rory's face lit up at the possible connection to his homeland, but Callum had no idea where he was from or how he got the name. According to one of his earliest journals, he had attempted to find out. He'd been able to retrace his travels as far north as Dumfries, but the trail had ended there.

"Originally. I have family up that way," he lied. Or maybe it was the truth. He had no way of knowing. "But I traveled around a lot. I haven't seen you at the pub before."

"I got to London at the beginning of the summer last year. Been working at the Bull and Pig for about a month."

They reached a zebra crossing. Rory grazed Callum's arm to stop him from stepping out and looked both ways, even though the nearest car was two streets off. On the other side, he caught Callum looking at him. His face flushed, his cheeks darkening in the streetlights.

God, he's cute.

"What brought you down to London?" Callum stuffed his hands into the pockets of his jeans and hugged his arms close. His jacket wasn't particularly warm. Perhaps he should have taken Rory up on the gallant offer.

"Ah, you know. I grew up in a small town near Inverness. Not so great for the gays."

Callum nodded. He was surrounded by people for whom him being gay wasn't an issue. Many people weren't so lucky.

They walked in silence for a while, a good silence, both enjoying the night and each other's company.

"This is me," said Callum when they reached the Library.

Rory's eyes widened as he looked up at the building.

"You live here?"

"I work here. I'm a caretaker. I have a room in the attic."

"Nice job."

"I like it."

Rory looked up at the full moon as it emerged from behind the clouds and frowned, one hand worrying at the carved bead that nestled in the cleft between his collarbones. "So, you sure you're okay?"

"Yes, I'm fine. I'll be back to normal by tomorrow morning."

The silence between them grew awkward. Callum didn't want to put him off, but he was also in no condition to ask Rory in. And Rory seemed to be working through a calculus of his own.

"Well, don't be a stranger, yeah?" Rory glanced up at the moon. "Stop by tomorrow or something and let me know you're okay."

"I can do that."

Rory backed away a few paces before heading off. "You promise?"

Callum laughed. "I promise. Get home safe."

He watched the big man walk off in the direction of the pub. Halfway down the street, Rory turned back, caught Callum looking after him and beamed from ear to ear.

I think I might be in trouble, thought Callum as he took out his keys.

12

"WHAT THE HELL HAPPENED to you," came a voice from the darkness that made Callum jump and his heart pound in his chest.

He turned on the lights in the common area to reveal Jessica sitting in an armchair in the corner in her purple silk pajamas scowling at him, arms and legs crossed, her slippered foot bouncing with fury.

"Crap, Jess, you scared me half to death." He pulled out a chair at the dining table and collapsed into it, his whole body vibrating, the shock a serious setback to recovering from the lost time. "Why are you hiding in the dark?"

"It's never dark for me, genius." She jumped up from the chair and stormed over. "I can't believe you would disappear and leave me alone with Biggs like that! What were you doing?"

She was such a tiny person, barely taller standing than he was sitting, but she still intimidated him.

"I'm so sorry. I didn't mean to. I lost time again."

About to lash into him further, she stood there with her mouth open, frowning as she tried to process what he had said.

"You lost time?"

"I was watching the performance at the bar, and the next thing I know, they're kicking me out because the place is closed."

She pulled out the chair next to him, sat, and touched the back of her hand to his brow as if taking his temperature. "Are you okay?"

Though she only touched him lightly, it was still too strong for his throbbing head. He brushed her hand away. "I remember who I am. I remember who you are. I've got another twenty years before I have to start worrying."

She took off her glasses, held his hands, and looked at him with her golden eyes.

"Yes, but the last time it happened was four months ago. That's too soon, isn't it?"

He tried to pull his hands away so he could get himself a glass of water, but she held him fast.

"Don't move. I'm looking you over." Her eyes darted around, sometimes looking at him directly, sometimes focusing on the air around him. A wave of shivers spread across his tattoos as the wild magic trapped within him responded to her probing. After a long minute, she released him and sat back in the chair.

"Dammit!" She put her glasses back on. "I've never been with you so soon after it's happened. I thought I might be able to see more than usual."

"Any luck?"

The achy throbbing of his head cooled for a moment as a spark of hope kindled within him. None of them understood the extent of the abilities her curse had afflicted her with. Perhaps he might finally learn something.

She removed her glasses again.

"I'm seeing jumbled vignettes. I can usually tell if what I'm seeing is a vision of something real, or dream impressions. These, I can't. And they're beginning to fade."

The spark of hope extinguished, and he suddenly felt so tired, desperate for bed.

"Unless … " She spread her fingers wide and pressed them into the table, something she always did when she was weighing up her options. "Come."

She snatched his hand and pulled him out of the common room to the stairs. For such a petite human being, she was fast, and Callum had to hustle to keep up without tripping. With one hand on the wooden banister to steady her, she scuttled down the stairs in her velvet slippers, threatening to pull him tumbling down behind her.

"Slow down!"

If he fell and broke his neck, he could be paralyzed for weeks before his body found a way to heal itself.

"There's no time. We have to get there before the images fade completely."

"Where are we going?"

"Keep up!"

She led him all the way down to the ground floor and the double doors that led to the library, the braziers lit on either side giving off a deep red glow. When he realized where she was taking him, he pulled her up short.

"We can't go in there," he whispered as if Rafe, all the way up at the top of the building in his room, could hear. "Rafe would have a conniption."

And rightly so. The Library was filled with things that went bump in the night to spectacular and devastating effect. No one was allowed access to the collection's artifacts without express permission from the librarian by order of the Crown, and Rafe only gave it on the rarest of occasions.

"Do you want to know what happened?" She placed a hand on the door and scowled at him as he hesitated. "Do you want to wait until it happens again?"

He'd searched in vain for answers for thirty years that he could remember, and according to his journals for hundreds before that.

"Let's go." He followed her through the doors.

The main floor of the library itself was a vast room four stories high filled from carpeted floor to cavernous ceiling with bookshelves, a network of galleries snaking around the upper levels of the stacks to give access to the books. In daytime, it was lit by sunlight from high, two-story windows and strategically placed lights, but now, in the middle of the night, the only light was the unsettling glow from the braziers that cast unnerving shadows.

Jessica led him all the way down the central aisle to the very end. The books up here were mostly innocuous, all the dangerous stuff secured in the Hidden Galleries below them, but still, he kept close to her. Rafe, Jessica, and he were all skittish around so much wild magic. Even though the worst had already been done to them and Chaos rarely struck twice. Rarely, but not never.

She stopped at the gated elevator at the end of the aisle.

"No," he said when she took out a ring of keys and used one to unlock the gate. "We're not going down there. How did you even get a key?"

"I know where all Rafe's secrets are hidden." She grinned, her cherubic face turned demonic by the light of the braziers, opened the gate, and stepped into the elevator.

"And a few of yours, too. Is this why you've lived so long?" Her lips curled up into a taunting sneer. "You're too afraid to take risks?"

A small part of him nagged that this was reckless. A very small part. He ignored it and stepped in next to her. She slid the gate closed and pressed the button for the eighth sub-basement. The elevator lurched into action and Callum flinched, certain that Rafe would somehow feel it through the building.

The eighth sub-basement housed one of the many Hidden Galleries that contained the more dangerous artifacts of Chaos that the librarians and their helpers had retrieved through the centuries. Organized by an arcane system that only Rafe properly understood, the gallery floors were each a wide, low-ceilinged expanse filled with glass-fronted cases containing the artifacts.

"What I'm looking for is back here." Jessica led him on a labyrinthine path through the cases, past decks of playing cards, buckets and mops, precious jewels, children's storybooks, salt and pepper shakers, hand-drawn maps and more, objects both mundane and unusual that had all been transformed by wild magic into items of power.

"Here we are." She finally stopped before a case tucked away against one wall. "The works of Madame Morozova."

The case had the name Morozova engraved on a plaque above it. Jessica reached up and opened a compartment.

"What are you doing?" said Callum.

She reached into the cabinet and took out a globe of crystal about the size of a bowling ball and its stand.

"Don't worry. It's perfectly safe." She held it up in her hands and turned it about as if inspecting it through her sapphire spectacles as anyone with normal vision might. He wondered what she saw.

"Bring the cloth, would you?" She turned with confidence and strode away, only to bump into another case. "Blast. The lower galleries tend to shift around slightly after hours. You'll have to guide me." She looked behind her to find him staring at her, mouth agape in shock at the casual ease with which she handled something so potentially dangerous. "Don't just stand there. Hurry!"

He snatched the red velvet cloth that remained in the compartment and took her arm.

"Take us to one of the work desks."

Spaced evenly throughout the gallery were large, dark oak tables a visitor might use to examine an artifact. He led them to the nearest.

"Madame Morozova was uniquely gifted in bending Chaos to her will to create artifacts with specific abilities. They're all remarkably stable. Spread the cloth on the table." She placed the globe in its stand on the cloth on the tabletop. "Take a seat."

"She made this intentionally? Was she a sorcerer?"

Artifacts were Chaos-Kissed the same way he and Jessica were. Wild magic was called down by intense emotion, derangement, acts of massive folly, or merely the whim of fate. Rarely was it possible to summon it intentionally, and rarer still was it possible for a person to make it do its bidding.

"Remarkably, she was not," said Jessica, taking a seat across the table from him, "in the traditional sense. She gave no oath of fealty to any of the Spheres of Influence, nor was she acknowledged by the Convocation of Saints, and yet she was an effective mage in her own way. Obsessed with psychic phenomena and contacting the other side, and, by all accounts, a convincing clairvoyant. I've been dying to give this thing a try."

She reached out for his hands around the orb.

He leaned forward. "Do I need to do anything?"

"Look into the crystal ball and tell me if something appears."

She removed her glasses, the soft golden radiance of her eyes matched by the warm glow cast by a nearby brazier, and took his hands in hers.

"Good," she said. "There's still a trace."

They sat in silence in the gloom for a long moment.

"How do you get it to work?" he asked.

"No ide—Oh!"

She squeezed his hands as a dim purple light began to flicker within the orb, somewhere between a tendril of smoke and a flame.

"It's glowing," he said.

"I know. Hush."

Her eyes darted around, her head turning as she tracked Callum knew not what with her sight.

"So much wild Chaos within you. Your tattoos can hardly contain it all. I see fragments, images of you flashing by. I can hardly make them out. It's you in a jumble of times. Your clothing keeps changing. Sometimes it's medieval, sometimes modern, sometimes filthy and threadbare, sometimes expensive and refined. I'm starting to get the hang of this."

The smoky flame within the orb began to grow and seep out as a glowing mist that spread across the velvet cloth, making his skin crawl with nerves. He had to keep reminding himself that it couldn't hurt him, probably, or he would pull away from her and banish her visions.

"God," she said. "I never realized how old you really are … Wait." She cocked her head to one side as if trying to hear better. "There's always someone with you. It's always a man."

"Who is he?"

"It's a different person every time, but they all have the same eyes. Odd. Violet irises with flecks of gold."

The last vestiges of his throbbing head dissipated.

"Damn." She released him and cupped the orb in her hands.

"What's happening?"

The mist and flame vanished, leaving them in gloom.

"I'm sorry." She rubbed her eyes and slipped on her glasses. "It's faded."

He slumped back in the chair and realized he had been clenching every muscle in his body. He took a deep breath to try and release all that tension.

"Have you ever seen someone with eyes like that?" She reached for his hand again, this time not a seer, but a friend.

"Violet and flecked with gold?" He racked his brain, but it wasn't familiar. "No, never."

"It might not be literal. The color might symbolize something. I'm sorry."

He leaned in and kissed her fingers. "No, it's good. Thank you for trying. I don't think there's anything in the journals like that, but now I have something to look for."

"She's coming," came a voice from the darkness next to them.

Above them stood a figure, its face distorted by shadows into something alien and monstrous.

"When she arrives," said the figure, "the work can begin."

13

CALLUM WAS UP AND out of his seat in one pounding heartbeat, his chair knocked back onto the carpet. Even Jessica was startled, jumping up and moving around the table to put it between her and the looming figure.

"Geoffrey?" As Callum's shock abated, the apparition's shadow-deformed features resolved into those of their troubled guest. "What are you doing here?"

"She's coming." His voice dreamy, his expression distant, Geoffrey looked around the dark gallery. "She will love this place. Here lay her forge for centuries, waiting for its moment to fulfill its purpose. And so many tools to help her carry out her master's will."

"I think he's sleepwalking." Jessica cocked her head to one side. "It looks like he's drifting through a shifting landscape of dream images."

Callum edged closer to him.

"Hey there, Geoffrey. How did you get down here?"

How did he? The elevator rattled like a pebble in a tin can kicked down a hill. There was no way it could have gone back up to the ground floor and down again without them hearing.

"For those who follow her," Geoffrey leaned in to examine the orb, "all places are open once the invitation's been made."

"Who is he talking about?"

"I see the woman standing behind him again," said Jessica, "shrouded in mist and shadow. He must still be beguiled."

"But how? The sterilization team would have wiped out any stragglers from the nest by now." Callum placed a hand on Geoffrey's arm to lead him upstairs. "Come on, Geoffrey. Let's get you back to bed."

The young man twisted free of his touch and danced out of reach.

"Oh, no," he chuckled. "I will not be caged. We will not be held. The night is ours, and we will ride it to the gates of hell to receive our reward."

"Jess, block the elevator. Make sure he doesn't slip away."

It was a straight shot from where they stood to the ancient lift with nothing in the way. She'd be able to reach it without hitting anything. She paced a wide arc around them to get past Geoffrey.

"Wait, wait, pretty lady," said Geoffrey. "Don't leave us. She will welcome you as warmly as she did me. You will relish in the power her kiss will bestow."

"I don't think so, buster." Jessica darted away into the gloom. "I've already had one life-changing kiss."

"But where is the night?" Geoffrey looked up as if in search of something on the ceiling. "She won't find me if I cannot taste the night."

"Let's get you back up to your room and tucked into bed, mate. Does that sound good?"

He grabbed Geoffrey's arm firmly, but the scrawny man twisted and thrashed like a fish struggling to get back to the water. He broke free and ran into the stacks.

"Bugger." Callum darted after him.

Geoffrey led him on a wild hunt through the display cabinets, always disappearing around another corner, tittering like a demented child, until Callum careened around a cabinet and barreled straight into him. They fell to the floor in a tangle of arms and legs.

"Look, look." Geoffrey pointed at a case against one wall. A deep blue glow emanated from one of the cabinets. "See how beautiful it is. That's what the master of my mistress wants, more than anything. Who knew I would find it here?"

He was up on his feet and away before Callum could restrain him and had the cabinet halfway open as Callum caught up. He threaded one arm under Geoffrey's and up around his neck in a half nelson and slammed the cabinet shut with his free elbow.

Geoffrey turned nasty, baring his teeth and grunting like an animal. With his free arm he grabbed and struck at Callum, but none of his blows landed. Callum hooked a leg around his, unbalanced him, and they fell to the floor once again.

"Jessica!" he shouted as he leaned all his weight into the struggling Geoffrey to keep him down. "I've got him! Get Rafe!"

Geoffrey went limp. Callum rolled off him, cautious in case it was a feint, but the young man was fast asleep and snoring.

"You did what!?!"

Rafe, in his blue and white striped pajamas and silk robe, froze with the coffee pot in one hand and an unfilled mug in the other as Callum and Jessica hovered by the doorway like two miscreant children ready to run from their punishment. Morning sunlight reflecting off the handle of Rafe's cane nestled in the crook of his elbow glinted in Callum's eyes.

"He's fine," said Callum, hoping to roll past their wrongdoing to the matter of Geoffrey's somnambulism. "He's in the guest room sleeping like a log."

Rafe placed the mug and pot on the kitchen counter, took a deep breath, and thrust his fingers into the unkempt mop of his hair. The tip of his cane knocked against the kettle.

"You snuck into the library—into the Hidden Galleries, no less—and *handled* an *artifact!* It took ten years of training before my predecessor allowed me into the sub-basements on my own. Do you realize the damage you could have done?"

"We were perfectly safe," said Jessica. "I wanted to use one of the Morozova articles. They're fully contained."

"I'm not worried about what might have happened to you." Rafe paced around the kitchen table in furious circles, stopping every other word to turn and berate them waving the handle of his cane above his head. "Even Morozova's creations bleed Chaos. You could have triggered a cascade and brought the whole of London down! What on earth could you have wanted with one of her instruments?"

"I lost time, Rafe," said Callum.

"And how did you get down there?" Rafe ranted on, not hearing him at first. "My keys … You lost time? But it's only been thirty years."

The knowledge settled on him, his agitation bleeding out of him in a sudden drop. He hugged Callum. His cane pressed into Callum's side.

"Oh, my boy. I'm so sorry. How do you feel?"

"I'm fine," said Callum as they separated.

Rafe sat at the kitchen table while Jessica poured him his coffee and placed it on a coaster in front of him.

"I understand now." He took a sip of the hot coffee and winced. "You went for the crystal orb. Did you discover anything significant?"

Jessica and Callum sat with him at the table.

"A succession of images." She removed her spectacles and rubbed her eyes. "From Callum's past, I think. He had a companion with him in each of them. The men all had the same unusual eyes, but that was it."

Rafe squeezed Callum's hand. "Does that mean anything to you?"

"Not a thing. I don't recall anything from the journals, but I can skim through them again."

"If you'll permit me, I want to run some tests."

The first sub-basement was filled with workrooms containing all manner of devices the library had accumulated over the centuries to measure and categorize wild magic.

"Of course, but we need to talk about Geoffrey."

Rafe groaned.

"What possessed you to take him down there?"

"We didn't," said Callum. "He just appeared. We don't know how he got in."

"He was beguiled," said Jessica.

"By what?" Rafe cupped his mug gingerly, testing its warmth.

"I saw the woman standing behind him again, like at the Cottage."

"And he kept talking about a woman who was coming for him," said Callum.

"I read the file on him the Cottage gave me." Rafe tried the coffee, found it cool enough, and took a swig. "Most of it is redacted, though I don't know why. He's a low-level accounts manager at an advertising agency. He has a sister, Lucinda, who he is apparently close to. Perhaps you should find her."

"Good idea," said Callum. "Do you know where?"

"It was redacted." Rafe sighed deeply. "Sometimes I'm convinced they want us to fail."

"There's something else."

"Ugh, don't tell me." Rafe bowed his head and shielded his eyes with one hand as if that might lessen the blow of the bad news he knew was about to come.

"He was drawn to a particular cabinet of artifacts. The cabinet was glowing."

Rafe took a deep breath, straightened up, and shook his head.

"No amount of coffee is going to prepare me for this, is it?"

"What's the lot number?" Rafe pored over a giant, leather-bound ledger he had perched on a lectern nearby.

"A-g-seven-five-six-two-four." Callum read off the engraved plaque above the cabinet.

Rafe paused as he flicked through the pages to find the entry and looked around.

"JESSICA! Get back here! You're on thin ice, my dear. Consider your browsing privileges suspended until further notice."

She appeared around a corner and stamped petulantly toward them. "Madame Morozova's objects are works of art! There's not a single recorded incident of mishap from using them."

"And, after a decade of training, you'll be able to get your hands on them. Ah, here we are."

"I've no intention of binding myself to this wretched place for the rest of my life." She squeezed Callum's arm. "Sorry, love. I know it's been a life saver for you."

Callum chuckled. Rafe had been trying to get her to become his trainee since the moment she came to live with them.

"Five items," read Rafe from the ledger, "found across a span of six hundred years in the environs of Bromsgrove, each with the ability to perform minor transmutations. An iron nail, a stainless-steel needle, a linen handkerchief, a medieval arrowhead, and a clockmaker's brass hand nut tool."

Callum peered into the cabinet and counted.

"They're all there."

Rafe joined Callum at the cabinet to look.

"Why would these five items, of all things, have been active? There's no record in the ledger of any incidents since they were placed there. Jessica, take a look, please."

"Oh, now am I allowed to touch the artifacts?"

"I said 'look'." Rafe ran his finger down the side of the page. "Keep your grubby fingers off the merchandise."

She scowled, went up on the tiptoes of her hobnailed boots, and removed her spectacles to peer into the cabinet.

"I only see four items in there. Describe them?"

"A nail," Rafe returned to the ledger to read off the list, "a needle, a handkerchief, an arrowhead, and a tool of some sort."

"The tool's missing."

"What?" Rafe pulled off his glasses and scowled, the reaction of an Oxford don to a failing student suddenly getting an 'A.' "That can't be right."

"There's something in there, but it's inert."

"Excuse me." Rafe stepped up to the cabinet. He hooked his cane in the crook of his elbow and put on the white suede gloves he used to handle artifacts of Chaos to unlock the cabinet. "Don't think for a second, Ms. Harris, that I've forgotten about you breaking into the gallery. We will have words later about how you achieved it."

He slid out the wooden platform upon which the artifacts were laid out, each in their own velvet-lined tray, and took it to the nearest worktable.

"They're all there," he said. Callum saw all five as well. "What do you mean, one's missing?"

Jessica reached across him and picked up the clockmaker's tool.

"No!" Rafe snatched at her hand to get her to drop it, but she yanked it out of reach and rolled the tool around in her fingertips, feeling the weight and texture of it.

"It's nothing," she said. "It's a piece of trim, a tassel. Like what you'd find hanging off a curtain in a stuffy old hotel. What does it look like to you?"

"An odd cross-like thing with a small socket wrench on one end and a tiny screwdriver on the other."

"I see the same thing," said Callum.

"Well, you're both wrong. Here." She tossed it at Rafe, who caught it in his gloves and felt it with his fingertips the way she had.

"Well, dress me up and call me Sally," said the librarian. "You're right."

14

"I MUST LEAVE THE matter of Geoffrey in your capable hands." Rafe stepped off the elevator on the first sub-basement, the four genuine artifacts and the impostor safely packaged up in a wooden box engraved in gold with arcane mathematical symbols designed to keep the world safe from the Chaos of whatever might be stored within it. "I have to understand what this means."

"It's you and me, kid," Callum said to Jessica as the elevator rattled up to the main floor.

"We need to find out who the woman is who's beguiling him." The elevator lurched to a halt, and she hauled the gate open. "I didn't like the sound of what he was saying about her."

"You saw all the vampires in the nest standing around looking at something in the abbey ruins. Could it have been Geoffrey's phantom mistress?"

Morning light flooded through the high windows above the stacks. In daylight the Library was quite lovely, not the eerie depository of madness it became after sundown.

Jessica shrugged.

"It could have been the Pope, for all I know."

"We need more information." He looked up at the large clock mounted above the Library entrance. He had never found a watch that could handle the wild magic raging within him. "It's seven-thirty now. We could be in Bristol by ten. It might help to find his sister, retrace his steps before he was beguiled, that kind of thing."

"Someone's going to have to keep an eye on Geoffrey." She jerked a thumb behind her at the elevator. "And his nibs."

Callum sighed. He loved that it was only the three of them, but more help would make so much of his life easier.

Jessica handed him a matchbook from the Bull and Pig with a phone number scribbled on it in ball-point pen.

"Call your new best friend, Commander Biggs. He's got nothing else to do. I'm not sure if he was giving me that to be friendly or to hit on me."

Callum grinned and raised a saucy eyebrow. "Maybe you should be the one to call him. I'm sure your mother would be overjoyed if you brought a military man home for Christmas."

She punched him in the arm. Hard.

Callum picked Biggs up in the Rover outside a nondescript row house in Chalk Farm.

"Where are we off to?" The agent slid into the car, immediately sank down in his seat and put his black-tasseled loafers up on the dashboard.

Callum did his best to stifle his irritation as he pulled into the street. Four hours of restless sleep and dreams of a man with violet and gold eyes looming over him were going to make it hard to act compassionately toward the agent. He reminded himself that Biggs had no obligation to help with the search for more information about Geoffrey Cook.

"Bristol. I thought we'd start at Cooke's flat."

Biggs leaned forward and rapped a brisk tattoo on the dashboard. "Westward ho, driver." He leaned back and grinned in satisfaction at his quip.

Callum wasn't sure if he preferred Biggs more on or off duty. On the job, the agent was surly and brusque, but at least he didn't say much. Two hours in the car with a relaxed and chatty Biggs might be more than he could handle. At least Callum had his knives with him, tucked away in a leather pouch under the driver's seat. Worst come to worst, he could always stab the man in the heart, though there was no guarantee that would be enough to shut him up.

"So how is the blighter?"

"Not good." Callum sighed inwardly as he negotiated the morning traffic. He was looking at a realistic three hours trapped in the car before they got to Bristol. "Jessica thinks he's beguiled, we need to find out by who, or what."

"Beguiled? Shouldn't the sterilization have taken care of that? I spoke to a mate in Shelley Unit this morning. He said they burned and bulldozed the entire property, just to be safe."

Shelley Unit, one of the Cottage's rapid response teams. All their units were named after British poets or playwrights. Callum had seen enough spy movies to know that was unusual for military intelligence.

"How many times have you come across a vampire nest?"

Biggs scowled. "Twice before."

"Didn't you notice a change in how they behaved this time?"

The agent snorted with derision. "Not really. I was too focused on not getting eaten or turned."

"Something was off. They were slower, and I heard one of them say something."

"So, you want to talk to them? What difference does it make if they're running slow? Isn't that a good thing? Makes 'em easier to kill."

"The vampire contagion was first discovered nine hundred years ago. There's a whole section on it in the Library. According to the record, it's never changed its effects in all that time. No one's been able to discover how it started."

Biggs rubbed his temples like he was massaging out a migraine.

"Nine hundred years. Fuck. I can't handle all this supernatural shit. Two years ago, I was happily surveilling neo-fascist skinheads in Wolverhampton. Now it's all sorcery and High Influence and more ways to die than I ever thought possible. Can we talk about something else? What happened to you last night? You get your wick wet?"

Rafe had a connection that kept tabs on the Cottage's file on Callum. They knew he was undying, but that was about it. They had no knowledge of what happened to him every half-century. Callum was inclined to keep it that way. It would do him no good to arouse the curiosity of Euphemia Graham. Her methods of getting answers to her questions were invasive and destructive. He would be overjoyed if she could find out more about his history, but the risk of her messing with his tattoos to see what happened when the wild magic inside him got loose was too great. The proof was there in his journals. His past selves had documented in red ink the rare times his tattoos had failed. None of them were pretty. People died.

And yet, he needed to make a connection with Biggs to make sure he was all right. The last head of Frayn Unit had been taken away in a strait jacket to an asylum run by the Cottage in Cornwall raving about tentacles lurking in his bathtub drain waiting to pull him down to hell. Callum had checked his flat to make sure his paranoid delusions weren't, in fact, the truth. You couldn't be too careful. He didn't want that happening to Biggs.

"I lose time." He kept his eyes on the road and white-knuckled the steering wheel. He never had a problem telling people he was gay but talking about his curse felt like ripping open his belly and showing off his intestines. "I look up and hours have passed, and I don't know what happened."

"Fuck. Is that part of … You know. Your thing?"

Callum smiled at Biggs's gift with words.

"I think so."

"Fuck. I saw you chatting up the barman and thought you were getting lucky. I thought blow jobs were like handshakes for poofs."

"Hey." Callum jerked the steering wheel sharply to the right a few degrees, making the car lurch momentarily to the side to underscore his point. The jolt made Biggs's feet slide on the dashboard, and he slipped further down in his seat. "Don't be a prick."

"It was only a joke."

"Jokes are funny. That was you being an arsehole."

Biggs pushed himself up in his seat and tucked his feet into the footwell.

"My last bird couldn't take a joke, either … "

He launched into a long-winded tale of his last relationship filled with sordid details that he didn't seem to realize showed him in a poor light. At least he was talking about himself. Callum had to take that as progress.

Traffic on the M4 was chock-a-block, leaving Callum plenty of time to stew as Biggs chattered away. From Slough to Reading, he kneaded the steering wheel until his knuckles ached, half holding his breath as his thoughts bounced between what might be happening to Geoffrey and what his unexpected time loss might mean. Finally, around Swindon, he took a deep breath and rolled out his neck.

"I'm going to pull in here for a bit," he said as he took the exit for a rest stop.

"Good idea. I need to shake hands with an old friend."

"What?" Biggs's meaning took time to sink in.

The agent bared his teeth in a grimace and waggled his eyes like an old vaudevillian, and Callum wished Jessica was with them. Off-duty Biggs was becoming increasingly surreal.

While Biggs went to find the gents, Callum paced the car park trying to put the time loss out of his mind and focus on Geoffrey, but his thoughts kept coming back to the men Jessica had seen in the orb, all with the same strange eyes. Were they metaphor or real? At first, he had been excited by the idea that they were all the same person and there might be someone else like him in the world, someone for whom age and death never came. Even if they weren't, perhaps the eyes were a metaphor for something that attracted these men to him, an idea that filled him with hope in an entirely different way. Rafe and Jessica were like family to him, but at night, when the moon rose or in the peaceful dark when whatever imminent threat that constantly filled his time had been averted, his attic room closed in around him, a solitary cell. In all the journals, he had made no mention of anyone significant in his life.

"You okay?" Biggs approached with a half-smoked cigarette.

"Yeah, just thinking."

The agent took a final drag and tossed the cigarette into the grassy verge beyond the tarmac. "Can you explain this beguiling thing? It's such a stupid name. I feel like I'm in a Christmas panto half the time, only one where the big bad wolf is real and ready to rip your throat out when you step off stage."

A young couple with a toddler in tow approached to get into the car next to them, so they both clammed up until they were back in the Rover.

"It's a way vampires attract prey." Callum pulled out of the car park and headed back to the motorway. "They're usually bound to a building or a plot of land, so it draws people to them. It usually only works on kith and kin, anyone close to who the vampire was before they turned."

"Yeah, I know that, but we killed them all."

"Yeah, but there's other things that can beguile, even artifacts. There's a theory the contagion came from an object that drew people to it."

"So, something or someone else lured Geoffrey Cooke to a nest of vampires, which then didn't touch him."

"Yeah, I don't get it either. But when does Chaos ever make sense?"

Biggs shook his head and grunted with disgust. "I don't know how you manage it."

"With a lot of help."

Geoffrey's flat was on a side street above a fish and chip shop, a solid old building that had fallen on shabbier times. Biggs looked up and down the street to see if anyone was watching and lifted his leg to kick the door in.

"What are you doing!" Callum stepped between him and the door before he committed property damage. "I have his keys!"

"Oh." Biggs almost seemed disappointed. "All right. If that's how you want to play it."

On the cramped landing, a small stack of junk mail sat next to Geoffrey's door. Callum glanced over at the neighbor's, but the old woman's door remained closed.

"Let me go in first," said Callum, cautious in case anything unexpected might be inside waiting to cause them mischief.

He stepped across the threshold a few paces in and stood in the corridor between the living room and the kitchen. No telltale aromas assaulted his senses, and the tattoos on the back of his body remained calm.

"All clear."

Biggs pushed past him into the living room and set to a careful search, leaving none of Geoffrey's possessions uninspected, but putting it all back so that it appeared undisturbed. Callum let him get on with it and went into the bedroom to soak up the atmosphere, but aside from the smell of deep frying seeping up from the chip shop downstairs, nothing untoward came to him.

"Nothing interesting," said Biggs as he came in behind Callum. "Any funny stuff in here?"

Callum shook his head as Biggs picked up another of the framed pictures Jessica had used to track Geoffrey to Trentham Abbey: Geoffrey and his sister sitting in a Greek restaurant, the sister looking annoyed at the camera's intrusion.

"His sister's a corker." He grinned at Callum. "We should question her next."

"Keep it in your pants, Casanova. But yes. That was my next stop. We need to find an address."

He slipped the photo out of the frame and into his pocket, in case it would help them in their search.

"You don't have it? I thought Cavendish gave you the file. Wait, don't tell me. It was heavily redacted."

"Yep."

"Bloody Cottage. They don't even trust their own people."

Biggs picked up the phone on the bedside table, checked his watch, and dialed.

"I can get it for us. Chezza," he said into the phone. "It's Biggs … Fuck off. You lost that money fair and square. You can try and win it back next week. Can you help me with an address?"

15

CALLUM FELT SOMETHING WRONG the moment he stepped out of the car. His tattoos chilled and contracted, drawing his skin tight. The effect only lasted for a second, the way your skin contracts and shivers in sudden cold, but the message was clear: wild magic.

"Get back in the car," he said as Biggs opened the door and started to get out.

"What?"

It might not be dangerous, but the hit was strong enough, and Biggs was his responsibility now. "I sense Chaos. Get back in and close the door. Do it!"

Confused and ruffled by the sharp command, Biggs sat back down and pulled the door shut.

Callum approached Lucinda Cooke's home, a large stone house in a swanky, tree-lined neighborhood. He peered into the living room window as he walked up to the front door and rang the bell. No lights, and no movement inside. He rang again and knocked, rapping the brass knocker hard. No answer.

He sniffed the air and smelled a dank odor, the mildewy funk of autumn leaves left in a damp heap too long. The smell of wild magic gone stale. Something strange had happened here, and, though the danger had passed, something in the house was preventing the Chaos from fully receding back into the ambient flow. It was probably safe for Biggs to leave the warded protection of the car. Putrescent remnants of wild magic rarely did more than cause bad dreams. He walked back to the Rover and rapped on the roof.

"Funny business?" said the agent as he emerged.

"Yeah. Had to be sure it was safe."

"Mm. Appreciate it."

Callum looked up at the higher floor of the house. The windows there were all dark. "I don't think anyone's home. We need to get in there. Something big happened, and there's still Chaos lingering around. At the very least, we need to dispel it."

"You got what you need to do that?"

"In the trunk."

"All right. Get your gear. I'll get us in."

Biggs made it halfway to the front door and stopped. "It's safe though, right?"

The agent was never usually this cautious when they were in the field. The possibility of being turned by the vampires must have shaken him.

Callum looked up at the house and opened his eyes wide, shifting his head to see it out of the corner of his eye. His garbled senses often came to life in moments of danger, sometimes as sounds, sometimes as flashes in the periphery of his vision, but there was nothing.

"Should be okay, but keep an eye out. And don't go in without me."

"Yeah, not a problem." Biggs disappeared around the side of the house.

The trunk held two suitcases of equipment for occasions such as these. Callum opened the nearest's combination lock and took out a cylindrical object wrapped in white suede embossed with gold symbols and tied up with a leather cord: the Scepter of Labrax, a sixteenth-century artifact created with the intent to dispel wild magic. Generally reliable, it had proven effective against stale Chaos before. And against anything feistier, it might be the edge that would get them out of the house unharmed. He untied the parcel and held the scepter in one hand. A globe about the size of an orange with a brass handle, its surface engraved with arcane symbols, it could double quite nicely as a mace if needed, but Callum retrieved his knives from the front seat and clipped the scabbards to his belt. If he used the scepter as a weapon, Rafe would have his head.

Biggs stuck his head out from behind the house and beckoned him over. The small garden was secluded from the neighbors by several well-placed trees. Breaking in this way wouldn't be seen. Biggs led him to a kitchen window.

"There's no alarm system. I checked." The agent saw the scepter and smiled brightly, as if Callum were carrying a bouquet of flowers. "That'll do. May I?"

Callum passed it to him, and he hefted it in his hand before stuffing it in the back pocket of his jeans while he removed his light blue sweatshirt. The shirt he held up against the kitchen window as he whacked it hard with the scepter. The grass broke with a muffled tinkle. Rafe would have a conniption at a precious artifact being used so rudely, but Callum had found the kiss of Chaos made the things it didn't destroy much more durable.

Biggs returned the scepter to Callum and draped his sweatshirt over the window frame to cover any remaining shards of glass.

"Hang on." Callum put a hand out to stop Biggs from going in. He stuck his head through and sniffed, reaching in and waving his arm around in case his tattoos picked up something. The tattoos remained calm, but the mildewy smell of decay filled his nostrils.

"I think we're good, but be careful."

"Yeah, yeah." For such a burly bruiser of a man, Biggs slid elegantly through the window and disappeared inside, only to open the kitchen door from within a moment later.

"Nice place." He stepped aside so Callum could enter.

The furniture was expensive and modern, but not particularly comfortable, a perfect location for stiff and formal dinner parties with uptight guests more interested in being seen than the meal.

"Hold off on the search." Callum held up the scepter.

Three brass rings banded the bottom of the handle, controls that altered the intensity of the scepter's effects. Too much and the stale Chaos might be rejuvenated. Not enough and the scepter would end up feeding it rather than dispelling it. For anyone else, the calibration process would be fraught with potential failure, but Callum had an advantage. He held the scepter close to his face and sniffed, adjusted the dials, and sniffed again, repeating the process until the odor wafting off the scepter matched that of the decaying funk. Satisfied, he placed the scepter on the floor, balancing it carefully upright, pressed the switch on the side, and stepped back.

"Don't look at it."

He turned his back on it. Biggs followed as the sound of an unwinding clockwork mechanism ticked quietly, ending with a loud click. Blue light flashed, and the smell of decay lessened, but didn't vanish.

"Is that it?" said Biggs.

"No, there's more. Probably upstairs."

The doorways on the ground floor were all open, so there was no need to use the scepter again down here, but he would have to go from room to room if any doors upstairs were closed.

Biggs moved to a bookshelf filled with titles pulled from the Times bestseller list, the dust jackets all immaculate as if the books were unread.

"Don't bother with a detailed search." Callum retrieved the scepter, taking care not to disturb the dials. "It'll be obvious."

"What are we looking for?" Biggs returned a copy of Salman Rushdie's *The Satanic Verses* to its place between a Nigella Lawson cookbook and a rock star's autobiography.

"The usual."

"Mm." Biggs nodded. "Something out of place that gives me the willies. Got it."

They spread out, checking the kitchen, the living room, and the dining room on their way to the stairs.

"I'll go first." Callum peered up, one hand on the banister.

Biggs chuckled. "Be my guest."

The upper level had four rooms, two on each side of the landing. Three of the doors, to bedrooms, were opened. The fourth was locked, the smell of decay wafting strongly off it.

"It's in here." He stepped aside to let Biggs at it.

The agent rattled the doorknob and gave the door a tentative push. "Give me some room."

He stepped away from the door, leaned back, and gave it three swift hard kicks with the sole of his boot. The third splintered the doorframe, and the door swung open.

The stench of decay billowed out at them.

"Ugh!" Biggs covered his nose and mouth.

"You can smell that?"

"Yeah, it's awful."

The curtains were drawn, and the room was dark, so the agent reached a hand in, found a light switch, and turned on the harsh overhead.

"I'm guessing that's what we're looking for," said Biggs at the sight of what lay inside.

16

THE CONTENTS OF THE room had all been pushed aside. A desk and its chair were shoved up against the wall under the windows, and a large Turkish rug had been rolled up to expose the hardwood floors. On the floor someone had drawn in chalk two concentric circles with intricate symbols carefully drawn between them. Within the circle had been drawn a five-pointed star, a half-burned-down black candle placed at each point. At the center of the circle was what looked like the charred remains of a bird.

"You're kidding me!" Biggs hovered in the doorway, letting Callum enter. "Is this what it looks like? Is this devil-worship crap?"

Callum crouched to inspect the writing in the circle. He recognized the arcane symbols: *mathematica infernalis,* developed by the Library in the sixteenth century to describe the effects of Chaos. Rafe used it all the time in his research and had tried to teach it to Callum, but he could never get the hang of it. Interspersed were other symbols, some he recognized as the kind sorcerers used, and some he was unfamiliar with.

"Not necessarily." From his crouch, he was able to peer under the desk and thought he could see something. "Could be angel-worship crap. Desperate people will seek any help they can."

"Angels? You're having me on."

"A person can worship whatever they like, but it doesn't mean anyone's listening." Callum thought he could hear something faint, right at the edge of his perception. "Hush a second."

He closed his eyes to listen better. There it was, the sound of whispered singing, a complex dirge of discordant tones he could only just distinguish from the sound of the occasional car passing by on the road outside. And was that the smell of sulfur? Mixed with the heavy, cloying scent of a burning herb.

He turned his head from side to side on the off chance that his arcane sensory impression had a direction to it.

There, behind the desk.

"Help with this, will you?" He went over to the window. "Be careful not to disturb the chalk."

"No chance of that." Biggs skirted the edge of the room to get around the circle. It took up much of the floor, leaving them only a little room to shift the desk.

"There's something down there I want to get at."

They moved the table enough that Callum could reach an arm down. He fished around with his fingertips until he touched what felt like a book. His tattoos contracted at the contact, pulling on his skin, and chilled by several degrees. Squeezing his shoulder between the edge of the desk and the wall, he could reach farther and grab the book.

"What you got?" said Biggs.

Callum held it up so they both could see: an old book bound in black leather burnished to a glossy sheen, a few inches thick. The pages inside, yellowed with age, were covered in columns of dense handwriting, some of it Latin, some of it Greek, some of it the symbols of *mathematica infernalis*. As he flicked through the pages, the coppery taste of Chaos spread down the back of his throat. "This is what I felt when I got out of the car."

"Then let's bugger off home." Biggs glanced anxiously at the chalk circle. "What do we do about that?"

Callum took out the scepter from his coat pocket. "Once I use this, we can clean it up safely."

"Uh-uh. Not touching it."

Callum sighed and put the book on the desk. He couldn't blame Biggs for not wanting to get his hands dirty with the circle. The agent's brow glistened with sweat and his whole body tensed, a whippet ready to run at the first loud noise.

Matching the stench coming off the book would be a challenge, which was why the scepter was less effective against active Chaos, but he already had it calibrated from using it when they entered the house. He placed the artifact on the table, slid the switch into position, and turned away. Biggs did the same.

The clockwork mechanism began to tick, but a high-pitched whine filled Callum's ears as the discordant whispering choir grew louder. The scepter began to vibrate. Something was wrong.

"Bugger!"

He spun around to grab the scepter and disarm it, but it was too late. The globe sparked, and the knot of electrical brightness exploded, knocking him and Biggs into the wall. The lights went out and the door slammed shut, plunging them into darkness. Sulfur and incense filled his nostrils. The taste of copper rose up in his gullet strong enough to make him gag.

"Biggs, you okay," he sputtered.

The agent groaned beside him. "What did you do?"

Not knowing how much room he had between the wall and the chalk circle, Callum gathered his legs underneath him to push himself to his feet and help Biggs up.

The crackle of electricity filled the air and every hair on Callum's body stood on end, the room suddenly lit by the eerie glow of tiny sparks arcing off every conductive surface.

"Time to go."

Callum pushed Biggs toward the door and grabbed for the book and scepter, but the book was hot enough to scorch him, and he dropped both.

"Door won't budge." Biggs reared back and kicked at it, but it held fast.

The deep orange-red glow of flames flickered through the tiny gap between the drapes. Callum pulled one open.

The pleasant tree-lined West Country street was gone, replaced by a barren landscape lanced through by jagged spires of rock that towered in the distance, the sky above them a backdrop of burning flames.

As Biggs hammered frantically at the unyielding door with his entire body, the chalk markings on the floor began to glow and the spent candles burst into flames. Callum took out one of his knives, thinking he might be able to cut through the door. The blade glowed a fierce red that matched the dark radiance of the burning sky.

The floor at the center of the circle splintered and exploded upward, and from the hole crawled a creature with broad shoulders and long arms that levered it up into the room. Its black, oily skin glistened around bone spikes that thrust out along its spine and down its arms and legs. Its head was little more than an enormous mouth with rows of crooked white teeth. It opened its jaws and screeched. It lunged at them, but the circle flashed bright, and the creature flinched back.

Next to Callum, Biggs had stopped attacking the door. He gawped at the creature, his mouth open, his face slack.

"Keep trying!" Callum drew his other knife, its blade glowing like its twin's, and stepped between the agent and the creature, ready to fight, but the creature was unable to cross the circle. Every time it tried, the circle flashed and forced it back. Frustrated, it threw its head up and roared, swinging its arms. The circle flashed repeatedly as the creature spun around, its long arms flailed with rage until it reached one segment that didn't respond when it swung. Realizing it had found a break in the circle, it turned, its bone-clawed hands straining in the air as if trying to part a heavy pair of doors.

"Oh, shit." Callum edged around the circle to face it, his knives up. "Get us out of here!"

The circle glowed brighter and brighter as the creature strained at the invisible barrier holding it prisoner, until the chalk burned away, setting it free. Callum crouched, ready to spring, but the creature swept out its massive arm and knocked him off his feet to crash into the wall. Winded, Callum slid to the floor as the creature went for Biggs.

It slammed its hands into the walls on either side of the agent, who pressed himself into the door to get away, and thrust its head at him. It opened its jaws.

Biggs screwed his eyes shut. The creature sniffed at the agent. Its long black tongue snaked out to taste him.

Callum took advantage of the creature's pause, raised his knives, and leapt at it. He plunged the knives into its back, the radiance of the blades glowing through its flesh, highlighting the pulse of its arteries and veins. It screeched and spun to fling Callum off it, but he pulled his knives out in time, gouging great furrows in its back as he was thrown into a wall.

It reared up, threw its head up, and cried out in a great wail of pain, leaving its throat open. Unsure whether a knife to the head or the heart would be a killing blow, Callum erred on the side of caution, crossed his wrists, leapt at the creature's throat, and stabbed it in both sides of its neck. With a roar of effort, he dragged the blades across the creature's throat, severing sinew and arteries, nearly decapitating the creature.

No blood spewed from its neck. Instead, it fell to the floor clutching at its throat as the wound knitted itself back together. The blades were useless against it. Callum needed another weapon.

As the creature recovered, hissing angrily, Callum dropped the knives and dove for the scepter. It thrummed in against his palm as he clasped the handle. With no time to calibrate the thing, he turned all the dials to their maximum setting. The brass globe sparked with power, great arcs of white lancing off it to pool on every surface. The creature rolled onto all fours and leapt at him, but he swung the scepter at its head with all his might. The globe connected, and all the tendrils of power converged on the creature, coursing around its torso and limbs. It screeched with pain, its wail growing louder as the tendrils brightened like the sun.

With a concussive snap, the brightness dimmed. The harsh overhead came on again, and soft West Country sunlight shone through the window. The creature and the hole in the floor vanished. Callum dropped to his knees, panting with exertion.

"Can you open the door?" he said to Biggs, who cowered in the corner, his eyes wide, his face pale with shock.

"OPEN THE FUCKING DOOR!" he shouted, hoping the profanity would snap some sense back into the agent.

Biggs gibbered something, scrambled to his feet, and did as he was asked. Before he could say anything, Callum rushed him and pushed him out onto the landing.

"Get me the two suitcases from the car boot. Quickly!"

There was no point explaining to him what he wanted from them. Biggs was in no shape to process complex instructions. Callum tossed him the car keys and slammed the door.

His nerves were so jangled by the creature, he couldn't tell if there was still Chaos churning in the room, but he edged around the chalk circle to the scepter and the book, eying the spot where the creature had broken through. A tiny smudge, barely large enough to notice, broke the line. The book was still on the desk. He hefted the scepter. It felt off in his grip, its balance all wrong. The three dials spun freely as he turned them without catching the mechanism within.

Rafe was going to kill him.

17

"Callum!" called Biggs from the cellar as Callum descended, arms laden with equipment. "You need to see this."

The agent had returned promptly with the two suitcases, the color returning to his face, and Callum, with many assurances that there would be nothing as bad that would happen to the agent, had sent him to search the house. With the proper equipment, securing the book was an easy matter. A pair of white suede gloves with gold-embossed sigils let him pick it up safely and slip it into a platinum and gold mesh bag that would render it inert until Callum could get it back to the Library and one of the heavy-duty storage cases in the Hidden Galleries. Hopefully any anger and disappointment Rafe might feel at Callum ruining one of his special treasures would be balanced out by his excitement at the retrieval of the book and the hours of research that would be required to trace its provenance.

He put the suitcases down in the hallway and descended the rest of the way to the cellar, a cold and damp unfinished basement lined with shelves packed with storage boxes. He found Biggs standing under a single lightbulb, stooped over a tarp draped over something in the middle of the concrete floor. Biggs stood and moved to one side so Callum could see. Under the tarp was the body of a woman, one corner turned back to expose her upper torso. In her twenties with short dark brown hair, the young woman's vacant eyes stared up into the lightbulb. Callum compared the face to the photo he had taken from Geoffrey's flat. The body was not Lucinda Cooke.

"Damn," Callum whispered.

"Look here."

Biggs pointed out her neck. A small incision had been cut into it.

"There's no blood," said Callum.

"Yeah, I checked all the drains. Whoever did this cleaned up well. Any idea why?"

Callum shook his head and shrugged. "A sacrifice for the ritual upstairs? Your guess is as good as mine."

Biggs snorted. "I doubt that. What do you want to do?"

Nothing came to Callum as he stared at the poor woman. Strange anomalies he could take in his stride, even the ones that tried to kill him. Though he was himself a strange anomaly, there was something unreal about them. A dead person, on the other hand, nothing was more real than that. He imagined all the people she must have known, all the moments of joy, all the possibilities that were now snuffed out.

"All right." Biggs took a white cotton handkerchief from the pocket of his jeans and used it to pull the tarp back over the dead woman. "My turn to be the boss. Get your stuff out of here and wait for me in the car."

Callum waited in the driver's seat as instructed. His hands began to shake as the charge of the encounter left his body, so he gripped the steering wheel hard and breathed deeply, trying to return himself to some kind of equilibrium. Half an hour later, Biggs emerged from the back of the house and slipped into the car.

"Drive," he said.

"Did you—"

"Just drive. Get us to the motorway, and I'll fill you in."

There was something calming about being on the endless river cars on the tarmac that stretched across the south, drawing them steadily onward, away from the horror in that house. Callum felt the ropes of tension in his neck and shoulders ease and his breath come more freely.

"I wiped our fingerprints," Biggs said eventually, "and called the Cottage. They'll clean the rest up."

"That's good. Without the book, the circle will be useless. It won't be any danger to them. And they'll investigate the murder?"

"They'll give it to Pinter Unit. They're the best at that kind of thing."

Callum sank back in his seat and eased up his grip on the steering wheel. As much as Rafe liked to keep the Library's affairs a secret, they weren't equipped to handle a murder investigation.

"Did you tell them about the book and the … "

He didn't know what to call the thing that crawled out of the floor and nearly ate them.

"Of course I fucking didn't!" Biggs scowled at him. "I'm already up to my neck in it. They'd throw me in the loony bin."

They both knew that wasn't only an expression.

The penny dropped for Callum as to what calling the Cottage when he was supposed to be on leave would mean. "What kind of trouble are you in?"

Biggs sighed. "Suspension? A shit desk job? After the last few days, I wouldn't object."

"I'm sorry for dropping you in it."

"Yeah." Biggs chuckled. "Next time you invite me along, I'll probably say no."

Callum barked a laugh in return. "Fair enough."

The agent slid up in his seat, shedding the semi-hypnotized state of a passenger driving down an endless road and returning to reality. "What was that thing? Was it real?"

Callum took a moment to ponder. It wasn't an easy question to answer. "Was it a creature from the abyss trying to eat us? Probably not? The witches say there's no afterlife, so there's probably no hell, either. Or heaven."

"*Probably* not!?"

"Things usually aren't what they seem where Chaos is concerned. Whatever it was, I've no doubt it could have killed us."

"Yeah, not both of us, though, right? You'd be fine."

"I haven't died yet, but that doesn't mean it can't happen." The image of the creature's head dangling from its neck held on only by a rope of sinew flashed across Callum's inner movie screen. "I haven't been decapitated, as far as I know."

A thought creeped its way into his conscious mind, a nagging question germinating into daylight. "It didn't attack you. It had you up against a wall and it didn't do anything."

Biggs stared out the window for a long minute before responding. "It only attacked you once you stabbed it in the back. Maybe it wasn't going to kill us."

The thought hung there between them, neither of them believing it.

Biggs sighed. "Can you drop me off at the Cottage? Cavendish will want to rip me a new one."

18

NO SOONER HAD CALLUM stepped foot in the foyer, than Rafe burst through from the Library, his ever-present notebook in one hand, his cane in the other.

"Thank god you're back!" Rafe waved the book and cane in the air like he was trying to scare off a flock of pigeons. "We've been robbed!"

"What are you talking about?" Callum was still wrestling with the creature and the grimoire. He didn't have room in his brain for yet another crisis.

"You must come with me." Rafe tucked his notebook under one arm and tried to pull Callum with him into the Library.

"Give me a moment." Callum stashed the suitcases in the coat closet. The front door was kept locked so people couldn't wander in off the street, but, still, it didn't feel safe to leave all that equipment and the grimoire out in the open. Rafe hovered at the library doors like a child waiting for permission to go to the loo. "What do you mean, we've been robbed?"

Rafe dragged him through into the library and the elevator to the Hidden Galleries. "I checked the records. The Bromsgrove artifacts were intact when they were assembled into a single lot in seventeen ninety-six. The librarian made a detailed description of each item, including several readings from the analytical tools they had at the time. Surprisingly accurate, in fact. The tools I use today have changed very little since then."

Amazing how quickly Rafe's train of thought could become derailed and careen off into a tangentially related rabbit hole. Best to cut him off quickly.

"The robbery, Rafe. Stay focused."

The librarian blinked rapidly, trying his best to redirect himself. Callum pressed the elevator button for the first sub-basement. The lurch of the elevator mechanism snapped Rafe back on track.

"Yes, a detailed analysis, which means the artifacts would have been handled extensively. There's no question the missing artifact was present. It was documented again in the great inventory of nineteen hundred, when the last artifact stolen by the Theosophists was finally retrieved. Since then, the collection has remained untouched."

The elevator clanged to a halt and Callum opened the gate for Rafe to scuttle through.

"Did you check the research request logs?" said Callum.

Members of the public—mostly sorcerers and the various underlings that served them, along with a small number of independent researchers and artifact hunters who had proven themselves loyal to the principles of the Library—were permitted to use the collection and view its artifacts after an extensive application process.

"Of course, dear boy." Rafe led him to a workroom far down the corridor on the right, one of the empty ones he rarely used. "I'm not an amateur. No one has requested access to that section, or even that floor, in a hundred years."

The workroom was a low, broad room with plaster walls yellowed by age and dark wood wainscoting. One wall was covered with a tryptic of blackboards, each blackboard with two more behind it, all hinged on one side so layers upon layers of calculations could be quickly displayed. The boards were empty. Callum had spent a refreshingly dull week fifteen years ago cleaning up the rooms Rafe didn't use, wiping away a century's worth of chalkings from librarians he was probably as close to as he was with Rafe but had no memory of. The blackboards in here were still pristine save for a square of calculations Rafe had chalked in the center one.

Dominating the room was a large and sturdy wooden table in the middle and an overhead light designed to illuminate the entire surface. Rafe had stacked a neat pile of books and ledgers at one end. Jessica sat slumped at the table at the other, her chin resting on the surface putting her at eye level with the forged artifact perched on a small, velvet-lined pedestal. She rolled her golden-glowing eyes around as if trying to look at everything in the room but the object.

"Aren't you keeping an eye on Geoffrey," asked Callum.

"He's been sleeping all day." She waved dismissively at him with her spectacles. "I left him a note telling him to buzz us on the intercom if he needs anything."

She stood, rubbed her eyes, and stretched. "I've tried everything I can, but it's a tricky bastard. It's not a spell. I can tell you that much. Witches' and sorcerers' spells each give me clear, specific impressions. Whatever's doing this seems like a natural phenomenon."

"An effect of Chaos?" Rafe placed his cane on the table and leaned over to get a closer look at the artifact.

"Uh-uh." She shook her head. "Natural like trees and flowers. I keep seeing glimpses of grassy fields and forests out of the corner of my eye."

Rafe pulled out a chair next to Jessica and sat so he could open his notebook and scribble down his thoughts.

"A natural charm, or a glamor, but not a witch's spell. Fascinating. I've never heard of such a thing. I must check the archive." He stared into space, his eyes darting about as he processed. "Perhaps I can visit the Ladies. They're bound to know something."

Rafe had a gaggle of witches who he adored that were endlessly coming to him with under the table requests for information.

"Let's keep that as a last resort, shall we?" said Callum. "If the Cottage or the Palace find out how wrapped around their fingers you are, there'll be hell to pay."

Rafe frowned, indignant. "We can't bring this to anyone official. It's exactly the kind of thing the parliament of sorcerers can use to seize the collection from us. Who else are we going to go to for information about a naturally occurring illusion but witches? And besides, the Ladies would never betray my confidence."

An illusion. That gave Callum an idea. The performer last night at the Bull and Pig was an illusionist. The likelihood of a sorcerer who used magic as performance art at gay bars being in the pocket of the Convocation of Saints was unlikely in the extreme. Perhaps they could provide some expert advice off the record. He could see if Rory knew how to get in touch with them.

The thought of the hot bartender brought a flutter to his chest that he decided to ignore. How could he explain all this supernatural drama to a civilian? Biggs could barely handle it, and it was his job. "Hold off on the witches for the time being. I have someone I can ask for advice."

"What's wrong?" Jessica took her glasses off and looked Callum up and down.

"Ah, yes. Glad you mentioned it. We have a new complication in the case of our friend upstairs."

The grimoire lay on the table in another of the empty workrooms. With the doors closed, each one was isolated from the others in case something nasty and Chaotic got out. Rafe had set up an elaborate armature of copper and brass mesh and rods on the table for further protection, and the grimoire was now mounted on a rack within it so Rafe could examine it with his white suede gloves in safety.

"The use of *mathematica infernalis* is quite complex." Rafe peered at the pages through an elaborate pair of goggles with multiple lenses he could swing in and out to change magnification. "See there and there?"

He pointed at sections of dense hand-written text that Callum could neither read nor understand from where he stood.

"These are based on theorems developed by Labrax in the seventeenth century, so the grimoire must be late seventeenth century at the earliest."

"Speaking of Labrax," said Callum, thinking of the ruined scepter.

"Hm?" Rafe looked up at him, but barely registered Callum's presence; he was so wrapped up in his analysis of the tome.

"Never mind." This was the kind of roll Rafe was best not derailed from. "Carry on."

"I recognize much of the sorcerer's script, but these other symbols are new to me. You say it reacted badly to the scepter?"

"'Badly' is an understatement." Callum pulled out a chair and collapsed into it. He desperately needed a nap. "We were transported to a hellscape, and a monster crawled out to greet us."

"A monster?" Jessica came up behind him and began to knead his shoulders, digging her strong fingers into knots of muscle the size of walnuts.

"Blessed be, you kind and generous angel," he said at the delicious pain. The knots put up a fight, but Jessica refused to back down, and his neck began to ease up. "It was dark, spikey, six-foot-four with terrifying teeth. Reminded me of a few ex-lovers."

He joked, but the memory of it made him shudder and the hair on the back of his neck ripple.

"There were symbols on the ground, yes? Like this?" Rafe turned the armature so Callum could see the grimoire's pages. Drawn on one side was the circle, the pentagram, and the writing.

"That's it."

Rafe turned the grimoire back to face him. "Hmm. A summoning circle."

He stood over the book in its armature, took out a small brass pendulum attached to a chain, and dangled it over. The pendulum immediately began to swing in an erratic sweep, jerking and skipping as if it were following the path of a labyrinth.

"I'll have to take this down to the laboratory. Perhaps the big machines can make sense of it. And I have a couple of trusted consultants I can bring in."

Jessica released Callum and removed her spectacles so she could peer at the pages.

"What do you see, my dear?" said Rafe.

'It's been through many hands in its lifetime. A lot of people feeling deeply, none of the emotions good. It's too much of a jumble. Sorry."

"I wish you would let me train you. Without your help, I fear we'll never get to the bottom of all—"

"Will you stop!" She slammed a fist down on the table. "I'm cursed! What use would I be to you? Leave me alone!"

She fled for the door, fumbled at the doorknob, and walked out.

Callum was out of his chair and after her like a shot, catching up with her in the corridor.

"Sweetie, are you okay?"

She spun around and stamped a hobnail boot like a frustrated child, tears streaming down her face. Callum wrapped his arms around her in a bear hug.

"He won't stop!" She sobbed into his chest. "Why won't he leave me alone? I can't go outside by myself. I can't read a book. I can't watch Coronation Street on the telly. I can barely even find the bloody milk in the fridge! I'm useless to anyone. All I can see is dreams and omens."

He stroked the back of her stubbled scalp.

"Okay," he said softly. "First of all, that's nonsense. Rafe and I would be lost without you. Think of all the ways your dreams and omens have helped us since you've come to live with us. You're far too hard on yourself. Yes, you're at a disadvantage compared to before, but there's no reason you can't be out and about and raising hell."

She pushed away from him and found the wall with her fingertips.

"Not you, too." She stalked off toward the elevator, a black-clad cloud of self-pity. "Leave me alone, the pair of you."

He sighed and went back to the workroom. There was no reasoning with her when she was in a funk like this.

"I worry we made a mistake, taking her in," said Rafe as Callum sat beside him by the armature and the book. "We've made it too comfortable here. We're too set in our ways, you and me. We can't challenge her the way she needs to flourish."

"Where else would she have gone?" Callum leaned on the table and rested his chin in his hands to stare at the book. "When we found her, she thought she was going mad."

He slumped in his chair and placed a hand on Rafe's back.

"I'm afraid you and I are the best chance she's got, old chap. We're going to have to do better by her."

19

WHEN CALLUM AWOKE, THE room was dark. Rubbing the sleep from his eyes, he rolled over to turn on the bedside light and check the clock. Nine-thirty. Not so bad. He still had plenty of time to get to the Bull and Pig before it closed.

He rolled out of bed and almost put on the worn jeans he had tossed on the floor on his way to crashing face first onto the mattress the night before, but the Bull and Pig wasn't the kind of place you showed up at looking like a donkey's arse. He didn't have a lot of clothing, aside from the stack of white t-shirts, two pairs of boots, and three dark-hued V-necked sweaters he cycled through on a daily basis. He dug out of the back of his closet a pair of black canvas trousers, a caramel leather jacket he hadn't seen since the early seventies, and a floral print shirt Jessica had forced him to buy the last time they took a walk down Morel Market.

He checked himself out in the mirror to make sure his tattoos weren't visible and looked at the clock. Ten. He had wasted half an hour preening.

"Idiot," he said to his reflection as he adjusted his collar and ruffled his hair in an attempt to make it spike up and not lie flat and lifeless like its usual impression of a bale of hay.

He passed by Jessica's room thinking he might drag her along, but the Indigo Girls song blaring through her closed door put him off. At least it wasn't the outlandish avant-garde wailing and speaking in tongues of Diamanda Galás she loved to shake the walls with when she was feeling particularly depressed. Indigo Girls meant she was on her way back.

His stomach gurgled to remind him he hadn't eaten since breakfast, and he ducked into the common room to find Geoffrey at the kitchen table devouring an enormous bowl of breakfast cereal.

"I'm sorry," Geoffrey mumbled around a mouthful of bran flakes. "I woke up starving."

"Please, help yourself." Callum stuck his head in the fridge. "We have tons of leftovers, you know. You should eat something healthy."

Callum took out several plastic containers and takeaway trays and laid them out on the kitchen counter. "That curry's excellent."

Geoffrey took another mouthful of cereal and rose to inspect the options Callum had laid out for him. He took the curry back to the table and proceeded to tuck in, alternating between stuffed mouthfuls of his two dishes. Callum opted for leftover kebab and taramasalata from the Greek restaurant down the road.

He sat munching on his food in silence watching while Geoffrey plowed through his meal, stopping occasionally to chug down milk from the glass he kept topped up in front of him. Callum could see being hungry like that after missing an entire day's meals, but the ravening speed with which Geoffrey wolfed down his food was alarming.

"How are you feeling," said Callum, partly to slow him down in case he ruptured something.

"Better." Geoffrey mumbled around his mouthfuls. "Stronger. Clearer. I felt wiped out after … "

He stopped, spoon in hand and food half chewed, and stared off into the distance, distress spreading across his face.

"Talking about it might help." Callum felt like a heel for wanting information about how Geoffrey found himself at Trentham more than wanting to help him. "Do you remember anything more about how you ended up there?"

"I got off work on Wednesday," Geoffrey spoke softly, his voice small, like a child being asked to recount a traumatic experience, "went down the pub with my mates for a drink. I remember not staying late, 'cause I wanted to go for a run the next morning. I caught a cab home."

Callum perked up. They were the exact same words Geoffrey had used when the Cottage had tried to interrogate him.

"I called Lucinda when I got home to arrange to get together because we hadn't seen each other in a few weeks. She wanted us to go up to London for a long weekend. I called in sick the next morning and rented a car to drive up. I must have got lost, and the next thing I knew I was at the place you found me. I remember I parked the car down the road and wandered up to the house to get directions."

He blinked, looked at Callum, and launched back into his meal.

Callum knew he hadn't called his sister, and there had been no cars parked on the road around the abbey. What was going on? Could his presence at Trentham be a coincidence? He might simply have got too close to the nest and been lured in, but his description of what happened came out rote, like he'd rehearsed it. Or did his sister set him up to go there? Maybe it had something to do with the summoning circle in Lucinda's study. A sacrificial offering?

"Have you called your sister? She must be wondering why you didn't show up."

Geoffrey paused, his glass of milk held suspended before his mouth as he drifted off again. It only lasted a moment, and he was back to his meal.

"Yeah, yeah, I called her. I called her last night. She's coming to get me."

Callum supposed that might be true. They hadn't been keeping close tabs on him while he was with them. If she did show up, it would save Callum the effort of tracking her down.

"When's she coming?"

Geoffrey grimaced at Callum. "I'm so sorry for imposing on you. You guys have been very kind to let me stay here."

Callum smiled and waved the apology away. "You can stay as long as you want."

"She said she has some things to take care of, but she wants to meet you. To thank you for looking after me. Our parents died when I was young. She's very protective of me."

"She sounds like a wonderful person."

A wonderful person who sacrifices young women to summon demons as a hobby, he thought, though there were so many unanswered questions about what happened in that house. He hoped Rafe could get some answers from the book. The Cottage was never going to share the results of their investigation with them.

"Let me know when she's coming, will you? I don't want to miss her." He looked at the clock. Ten-fifteen. He'd better get a move on. "I'm going out for a drink, want to come?"

Geoffrey shook his head around a mouthful of curry. "Thanks. I'm going back to bed."

Callum cleared up his plate and put it in the sink.

"Don't stay up too late."

He arrived at the Bull and Pig as drag bingo was wrapping up and the host was counting her tips, the happy buzz of the dispersing crowd a balm for his jangled nerves after the events of the day. Rory spotted him as he entered and his face lit up. He winked and went back to serving. When a stool opened up at the end of the bar, Callum sat and waited for the bartender to work his way down the bar toward him, customer by customer.

He tried not to stare at the handsome Scot at work. He was the kind of guy perfectly suited to being a bartender: charming, good-looking, and unflappable. If what Jessica saw with the crystal orb were true in some way, perhaps Rory could be the violet-eyed man at his side. For a while, at least, until the fact that Callum didn't age became too hard to conceal. His journals spelled out over and over again what he had done in the past. After ten years or so, he would find himself something to do that would take him away from the Library, perhaps hunting down an artifact or following the trail of misery left behind by someone Chaos-kissed. Apparently, there was always something he could do to keep himself out of London for a decade or so. He'd even been to Europe during the Second World War, but the magic of the Continent was a different beast to that of the British Isles, with its own rules and squabbles, and Callum had found himself yearning for the familiar wildness of home. He hadn't been close to anyone in the decades since he last lost his memory. Lovers he'd had, yes, but no one he felt close to.

"Hey." Rory snapped him out of his reverie. "Why so glum? You okay?"

Callum forced himself to brighten up, not a hard thing to do with that smile and those eyes fixed on him. "Yeah, yeah. Nothing a good night's sleep couldn't cure. Sorry, I was thinking about work."

"For the Library of the Damned?"

Callum's heart skipped a beat, and his smile froze. He was sure he hadn't mentioned the Library by name the night before.

Rory chuckled. "Don't worry, I wasn't stalking you. I passed by that way yesterday on my way to the market to pick up Bloody Mary supplies. We go through the mix like water. Can I get you a drink?"

Callum did his best to relax. He was far too on edge. The name of the Library was engraved on a plaque by the front door. Anyone could know about it. "A lager, please."

Rory scooted off down the bar to get him his beer and was back in an instant.

"Funny name, no?" He took Callum's money. "What kind of a library is it?"

Callum swigged back a good, solid mouthful of beer and let the taste of hops knock some sense into him.

"It's such a stupid name." He wiped his mouth with the back of his hand and tried not to stare at Rory's broad shoulders bursting through the straps of his tank top. Or the carved bead on his leather necklace resting in the dip between his collarbones. Or his lips. "It's a collection of esoteric books. Philosophy and magic, that kind of thing."

"Magic?" The smiling crinkles around Rory's blue-gray eyes stiffened for a moment, and his gaze flickered to the person sitting nearest to Callum at the bar three stools away. The night was beginning to wind down.

"Bunch of nonsense, really." Callum felt exposed, like he was suddenly losing ground in an interrogation. "Ancient alchemical treatises on turning lead into gold, that kind of thing. We've got a few valuable items that scholars always want to look at. It's very boring. Is it okay if I'm chatting with you," he said, desperate to change the subject before his weird job brought a rapid end to their conversation and any chance he might have of a tumble. "I don't want to keep you from your work."

The smile returned in full force.

"Of course! I'm happy for the company." He leaned in to whisper so no one else could hear. "Sunday nights are deadly dull. By now I'm usually counting the seconds till closing time."

He held his head there, close enough to kiss, for a moment longer than was merely friendly.

"Just a sec." Someone signaled for him at the other end of the bar, and he scampered off, giving Callum a chance to inspect the curve of his well-formed rump straining against the cotton of his trousers.

"I'm all yours," said the Scot as he came back and leaned on the bar, one hand resting only the width of a little finger away from Callum's.

Callum took another swig of beer. This guy was an accomplished flirt. He'd better get to business before fatigue and the beer went to his head. "You know the performer who was here last night?"

"Thilady Missgrace? She was good, no? Yeah, she's a regular. Very popular."

"Do you know how to get in touch with her? The Library's putting on a fundraiser and I thought she'd be great for the entertainment."

Rory raised an eyebrow. "I don't know her well, and Matt, who does the bookings, isn't here tonight. He'd have her number."

"Can I get in touch with him?"

Rory leaned back and thought for a moment, his face lighting up again as an idea formed in his beautiful head.

"I can do one better than that. She's performing at Bar de Bauche tonight. Be right back."

He disappeared through the garish plastic beaded curtain that separated the bar from the back of the house.

Bar de Bauche was the hallow—the stronghold and seat of power—of the cabal of illusionists this performer, Thilady Missgrace, belonged to. It was one of only two hallows that were able to remain in the borough of Cheyne Heath once the witches claimed it as their sanctuary. They were strict about their guest list. It was impossible to get in.

Rory came back five minutes later, pleased as punch.

"It's your lucky night, laddie. I got us on the list."

20

"HOW ON EARTH DID you manage that?" said Callum.

Rory waggled his eyebrows, his grin spreading from ear to ear.

"I'm a man with high connections in low places. I used to work there as a bouncer. My old boss is on the door tonight. He owes me."

"Wow. I'm impressed."

Callum was suddenly glad he'd bothered to dress up, though he was still going to stick out like a sore thumb. Bar de Bauche was more of a gown and tuxedo kind of place, and Callum owned neither.

"Ah, don't be. They're a loyal bunch there. Once you're in with them, you're always welcome. She goes on at midnight. We should get there in time."

"Thank you. That's extremely kind of you."

"Oh, nonsense. You deserve a good night out after the last one you had."

Waiting on the corner for the lights to change, Rory picked up Callum's hand in a soft, warm grip and ran his thumb over the back of it. Callum shivered.

"Nice tattoo." Rory traced the curlicue of dark ink that had peeked out from Callum's sleeve. Callum resisted the instinct to pull away and cover it up. "How far up does it go?"

Callum chuckled. This guy was so forward. He locked eyes with him.

"All the way up and all the way down," he said, holding the Scot's gaze without blinking.

I'm in so much trouble.

The flirting escalated to the point that Callum had to go to the gents to cool himself down. He couldn't risk messing up an invitation into the sorcerer's hallow. When he emerged, Rory was waiting for him, his denim jacket struggling to cover those broad shoulders.

"Come on." He took Callum's hand, interlocking their fingers, and dragged him out of the pub. "I'm going to have to close up for Bill for a week, but it'll be worth it."

They walked in silence for a while, the same comfortable quiet as the night before, though Callum ruined the mood for himself by worrying. If Rory had been a bouncer for the hallow, perhaps he knew about magic. Dare Callum tell him about his curse? In all the years since his last loss of memory, he had never once considered telling his occasional lovers the truth. How had Rory got so deep under his skin? He found himself going through the same litany of worries he had only read in his journals. When he came across the first passage where a past self had agonized over telling an infatuation the truth, he didn't recognize himself. He couldn't believe what a chump he was. But apparently, this was a cycle he went through. Every time. Always, there would be someone who would turn his head who he would eventually give in to, someone who he might or might not reveal everything, but who would consume him for years until his undying youth became a problem, or the losses of time increased, signaling the onset of the theft of his identity. And then there would be even more inner turmoil until he either fled or lost himself.

"Are you sure you're okay?" Rory broke the spell of his funk.

"Oh, yeah. Sorry. I had to drive all the way to Bristol and back today. It was a long time in the car."

"What were you doing there? Sorry, I don't mean to pry."

Callum caressed the back of Rory's hand with his thumb. "No worries. I was tracking down a book for the Library."

"Something fun?"

Rory's eyes caught the moonlight, shining for a brief instant before a cloud rolled over the clear, white disk hanging over them in the sky. Shining blue. Not violet. And no gold flecks. Callum realized how much anticipation he was bringing into this unexpected date. Keep going like this, and it would only turn out a disappointment.

"Fun? No. But important for the Library. How long did you work at Bar de Bauche?"

"About a year."

"Oh, wow. Was it your first job in town? How did you fall into that?"

If Rory had some background with the cabals up in Scotland, it might explain how he got the job so easily. Callum didn't know if he was hoping for it, or against it.

"Near enough. A woman helped me out with something when I first arrived, and her husband gave me a job. I owe a lot to those two."

Rory reached up with his free hand and fiddled with the bead on his necklace. A vague answer, but who knew what help a gay man from a small town up north might need when he first arrived in London, even one as strapping as Rory. Callum remembered how helpless and forlorn he was when he first awoke with no identity. If the librarian in those days hadn't been searching for him, he would have been an easy mark for anyone, assuming they survived the storm of Chaos that came when his tattoos burned away.

The conversation flowed easily as they wandered through the neighborhood, each of them asking questions that bordered on prying, though Callum had to stay on his toes not to reveal too much without seeming evasive or resorting to outright lies, made that much harder by having thirty years of adult experiences when he only looked twenty-seven.

They reached Bar de Bauche a few minutes before midnight. A small group of well-dressed patrons—men in suits and tuxedos, women in stylish evening gowns—lined up at the velvet ropes around the entrance, a pair of glass doors in the side of a brutalist concrete mountain Callum remember being built in the late sixties. Three bouncers stood behind the ropes vetting people as they came in, two of them broad-shouldered bruisers in black suits and ties with crisp white shirts, the third dressed all in black standing between them examining the guest list on a leopard print clipboard. Rory led them to the back of the queue.

"Quite a turnout for a Sunday night," said Callum.

Rory grinned. "Every night's a big deal here."

Callum imagined it would be, all of these people craving the reflective glow of sorcerous power, even if they didn't realize it.

"Alfie," said the Scot when they reached the rope, three other couples lined up behind them.

The doorman with the clipboard looked up at the sound of his name and broke into a smile.

"Brother, good to see you!"

The doorman wasn't as broad as the other bouncers, but he filled out his suit well. For a moment, jealousy welled up in Callum at the thought that this well-coiffed, dimple-cheeked looker might be competition for Rory's attention, but Alfie leaned across the rope, clasped Rory's hand, and wrapped an arm around him in the fraternal hug of bouncers everywhere.

"This is my friend, Callum," said Rory as Alfie unclipped the velvet rope so they could pass.

"Good to meet you, Callum. Packed house tonight, unfortunately. Can't offer you a table, but you're welcome to watch from the balcony or hang out at the bar."

The doorman nodded in greeting and reattached the rope to its stanchion as they passed. Callum felt the special thrill of being admitted somewhere others were not.

"Have a good time, boys." Alfie pulled one of the glass doors open for them. As they crossed the threshold, the phantom odor of sandalwood hit Callum's nostrils. A wide staircase carpeted in rich navy blue with an ornate, crowned "B" woven into it swept down, luring them on.

As they reached the low-ceilinged mezzanine landing, the strains of a high-pitched synthesized drone rang out through the club, and the house lights dimmed. The other patrons milling around them rushed down the remaining stairs to the club floor. Rory wrapped an arm around Callum's shoulders and hustled him along the balcony.

"This way." He spoke into Callum's ear to be heard above the music, and Callum felt the radiant heat of his lips against his skin. "It's my favorite spot."

He led them almost to the end of the balcony, next to a large palm tree in a giant, gilded pot that thrust up to the ceiling. Down below, the floor was covered with tables, each packed with excited spectators transfixed by the shimmering royal blue curtain across the stage lit by a single spotlight. The spotlight swung across the floor and narrowed in to settle at the center of a long table elevated on a low platform that lined the wall opposite them. A statuesque woman stood in the beam wearing an elaborate black dress modeled on the garb of a flamenco dancer, with a headdress that towered above her head. The crowd burst into rapturous applause.

Rory leaned into Callum to be heard. "That's La Davina."

Callum grinned and raised his eyebrows, nodding in recognition. He knew who La Davina was: by night an award-winning female impersonator who had played Royal Command Performances, by day the ruling sorcerer of the Sphere of Strength.

La Davina raised her arm in recognition of the adulation and gestured toward the stage. The spotlight snapped back to the curtain, which fell to the floor in a cascade of glittering fabric, to be whisked off into the wings by unseen hands. Light exploded from the stage and began to pulse in time with the electronic beat of the opening bars of "I Feel Love" by Donna Summer. The audience cheered as the beat repeated over and over in a loop without shifting into the rest of the song.

Callum realized Rory wasn't paying attention to the show and was looking at him. Pulsing shadows flickered across his face.

He whispered in Callum's ear. "Do you know how this works?"

"Do I know how a stage show works? Of course."

"No. Do you know how this," Rory waved a hand to encompass the entire club, "works? Do you know what's really going on here?"

Down below, a giant blue flower appeared on the stage, an enormous peony almost as tall as the proscenium arch, its petticoat petals thick and full, pulsing open slowly in time with the music. At its center hovered the performer in a long, velvet dress in matching blue, her long and slender, brown-skinned body encased in an armature of golden thorns. She floated down to the stage and the crowd went wild, jumping to their feet with applause.

"The flower, the lights, the performance," said Rory in his ear. "Do you know?"

And there was Callum's answer to the question that had been plaguing him since leaving the pub. The doubt was gone. Rory knew about what sorcerers insisted on calling Influence and Chaos, but which was magic, pure and simple, and Callum realized he was glad.

"Yes," he said into Rory's ear. "I know. This is all sorcery. Magic is real."

He held the back of Rory's head, threading his fingers through his thick brush of hair, and kissed him. The smell of highland fields, of heather, grass, and loam, washed over him as their lips parted and their tongues met.

21

THE PERFORMANCE BELOW MIGHT have lasted fifteen minutes or an hour, but Callum was oblivious to anything but Rory's body pressing against his, his long and powerful arms wrapped around him as they kissed. Only when the show finished, the crowd burst into applause, and the house lights went up, did Callum come back to himself. He pulled away from Rory enough to leave his lips free to speak.

"Should we go backstage?"

"We have a few minutes. It'll take her a little time to get to her dressing room. I'm sorry I made you miss the show."

Callum could have stayed there in the corner at the end of the balcony, in the dark behind the enormous palm tree, in Rory's arms forever. He pulled him close to kiss him again.

"You cannot continue to associate with the unwashed masses," came a voice from the other side of the dressing room door, the resonance of theatrical training cutting through the wood. "It's bad enough that you insist on cohabiting with a minion of another Sphere, but to consort with witches as well! And to serve them! This is not why I accepted your oath."

Callum and Rory stood in the dark in the cramped service corridor outside the dressing room.

"It's La Davina," whispered Rory.

"Should we leave?"

Rory shook his head and wrapped an arm around Callum's waist, sliding his hand into the back pocket of Callum's jeans.

"I don't serve them," said another voice, a younger man's. "They're my friends, and sometimes they need my help. And Joel isn't an acolyte. He only works for Fate and Fortune."

"Silence! You should know better than to talk back to me! I'm trying to help you. Our path is not an easy one. We are not like the other Spheres. Every iota of power we have we must struggle for. You will never advance, never fulfill your potential if you continue to squander your talents. You could be one of the greatest of your generation, if you would but apply yourself."

"I'm sorry, La Davina. I'll work harder, I promise."

"I will not require you to walk away from your partner. I sense the challenges of your relationship are good for your development, but I forbid you from using your talents to help those that are not your assigned charges."

"But Davina—"

"My word is final!"

The door opened and the statuesque flamenco dancer came out, stopping to turn back and point a dramatic finger at Thilady Missgrace, still in her blue gown and golden thorns.

"No. More. Witches!"

La Davina turned and stormed past Callum and Rory in a flurry of black lace, satin skirts and petticoats. In the dressing room, Thilady

Missgrace sank into a chair and slumped forward onto the dressing table with a dramatic sigh.

Rory knocked on the open door.

"Thilady?" he said quietly, hovering in the doorway, a six-foot-two and two-hundred-and-ten-pound man doing his best to be unassuming. "Is this a bad time?"

Thilady looked up from her slump.

"Rory! Alfie said you had something you wanted to talk to me about. Come in, come in. And shut the door behind you."

The dressing room was small and cramped with packed racks of garment bags lining the walls. Thilady stood, her body long and slender, and leaned elegantly against the table. "And who is this handsome gentleman you bring to my boudoir?"

She raised a hand for Callum to take and flashed a broad and radiant smile. He obliged and brushed his lips against the back of her hand.

"Callum Foster at your service, Ma'am."

"Why, Rory, my dear. You always have such excellent taste in men."

"He's a friend of Glinda," said Rory.

"Oh, thank heavens." Thilady sighed with relief, and slumped again, her regal bearing softening. "I thought I was going to have to pretend to take this all off the hard way. Please forgive me, Callum Foster, for shattering the illusion."

She traced her fingers in the air in an elaborate gesture, and her appearance changed. Her blue wig and the golden thorns vanished along with all her jewelry, leaving only her gown and makeup. She sat at the dressing table and pulled herself close so she could lean in and inspect her face in the mirror, her makeup glowing in the bright light of the bulbs that ringed it.

"Talk to me, boys, while I take off this warpaint."

She traced one eye with the tip of her index finger, and the elaborately sculpted eyebrow disappeared to reveal an ordinary one beneath.

"Thilady—" said Rory.

"Please, call me Johnny." Sections of her makeup disappeared with every stroke of her finger. "I've had enough pretentious artifice for one night."

"Johnny, Callum had something he wanted to ask you."

"I work for an organization called the Library of the Damned." Callum positioned himself so he and Johnny could see each other in the mirror.

"Intriguing!" Layer by layer, the face of the glamorous drag queen transformed into that of a young man about Rory's age. "How do I sign up for a library card?"

"It's a repository of books and artifacts associated with wild magic."

"Magic!" Finished with his unmasking, Johnny leaned back to inspect his work. "How refreshing to hear someone use that word. I'm so sick of all the incessant talk around here of High Influence, codexes, and ancient rites. It's like I joined the bloody Freemasons."

Satisfied, he stood and presented his back to Rory.

"Be a dear and unzip me, would you?"

The bartender carefully pulled down the zipper, and Johnny let the gown fall dramatically from his shoulders, leaving him bare-chested and wearing a pair of black leggings and combat boots.

"Pass me the t-shirt behind you?"

Callum retrieved a black Siouxsie and the Banshees concert shirt draped over one of the racks, and Johnny slipped it on over his wiry frame. He looked at himself in the mirror.

"Needs a little something extra."

He snapped his fingers, and the leggings became a pair of crisp black jeans that hugged his long legs. The picture on his shirt became covered in glitter that glimmered in the dressing table lights, casting multicolored sparkles on the walls.

"Much better. Now, how can I help the dramatically named Library of the Damned?"

"We've discovered we've had a robbery," said Callum. "One of the artifacts in our collection was stolen and replaced by an illusion we can't identify. I was hoping to get in an expert such as yourself to tell us more about it."

Johnny sighed and perched on the desk. "It sounds fascinating, but I'm sure you heard the old battleaxe. My days of being a sorcerer for hire are over."

Disappointed, Callum nodded. "I understand."

"Are you sure there's nothing you can do?" said Rory.

"I would love to help, but you know how our dear Saint Divine can be. I'm on the naughty step until she deems me worthy."

Johnny took a final look at himself in the mirror and, liking what he saw, grabbed a formless leather sack of a handbag.

"Tell you what." He slipped the bag over one shoulder. "Let me think about it. Perhaps I can refer you to someone else. Do you know anything about the illusion at all?"

Callum shook his head. "Only that it's not High Influence or witchcraft. It's some kind of natural magic."

"Natural?" Johnny raised an eyebrow and pursed his lips. "How intriguing. I've never heard of such a thing." He scowled. "No. No, no, no. You're extremely tempting, but I really can't. Rory, darling," he cupped the bartender's bearded cheek. "Lovely to see you."

He turned to Callum and eyed him up and down.

"And you, Mr. Foster, don't be a stranger."

He turned to leave but stopped in the doorway and draped himself across the doorframe in a seductive pose, winked, and vanished in a cloud of sparkling glitter that exploded, covered the two of them, and faded away. Callum laughed with delight.

"I'm sorry I wasn't helpful," said Rory.

Callum pulled him closer, reached up, and wrapped his arms around his neck.

"No worries. I'll find someone else." He kissed him. "Want to see the Library?"

Rory grinned, his bright, white-toothed smile spreading from ear to ear.

22

Waking up was never an easy thing for Callum. In those few seconds before memory and identity slunk back from their nighttime banishment, there was always a flutter of fear that it had happened, that, once again, everything important to him had been ripped away.

Not this morning. From the moment the flame of awareness kindled within him, he felt the weight of Rory's arm resting against his back and knew who he was. He turned to face him, trying not to disturb him, but the movement was enough to wake the broad hunk of a man.

"Morning." Callum spoke softly for fear of startling him and scaring him from the bed.

Half his face pressed into the pillow, Rory smiled. Callum slid across the sheets to kiss him.

"Oh, god." The Scot recoiled and covered his mouth. "My breath could wither a dragon. I'll be right back."

He slipped out from under the covers. Callum watched as he walked to the bathroom, taking in his naked body in the daylight shining through the blinds. He sighed, content in a way he couldn't remember feeling in years, and rolled onto his front, happy to doze until Rory's return.

"Your tattoos are incredible," said Rory standing above him. Callum would never get tired of his highland brogue. It felt like comfort. Like home. "May I look at them?"

"Knock yourself out."

Rory touched the back of Callum's neck with his fingertips, and Callum shivered with pleasure, a rare feeling, different from the reaction of his tattoos whenever he was in the presence of Chaos.

"That feels nice," he mumbled into his pillow.

The Scot traced the lines of ink down the back of his neck, across his shoulders, and down his arms. He pulled the sheets off him to follow the swirls and curlicues all the way down to Callum's heels. "They must have taken forever. Was it painful?"

"Yep, very. Twelve hours lying naked face down on a couch in a basement on Carnaby Street being poked with needles. Wouldn't do it again. If I didn't have to."

Rory slid his palm up Callum's leg, cupping his buttock on the way up to his back. Callum rolled over and pulled the Scot down onto him, trying not to think about those first few hours thirty years ago after awakening to obliviousness. The librarian at the time had found him quickly, but not before the raging, unfettered wild magic within him had caused bedlam, machinery failing, and illnesses that, up till that moment, had been only a probability suddenly hitting full force, heretofore sane people suddenly turning violently mad.

Kisses and caresses were always a pleasant way to redirect the flow of a conversation.

After a long while, they pulled apart to come up for air and Callum rested his head on Rory's chest.

"How did you find out?" said Rory eventually, and Callum knew he didn't mean about being gay.

He hated to lie, but he wanted this moment to last forever. Perhaps a half-truth would do. "I was cursed."

Rory held him tighter and kissed the top of Callum's head. "The memory loss?"

"Yeah."

"Do you know how it happened?"

Callum shook his head and left it at that. "How about you?"

"I always knew. It's a family thing. Up where I'm from, all sorts of strange things happen."

He, too, let it lie there without elaborating. So, they both had things to hide. Good to know. It made Rory less of the answer to Callum's dreams and perhaps someone real in all the turmoil of his daily life.

The grandfather clock downstairs struck eight, the deep, resonant chime rising through the stairwell, and the weight of everything pressed in on him, breaking the spell of contentment.

He pushed himself up, feeling the absence of Rory's embrace.

"I have to get to work."

"Oh." Rory's whole demeanor deflated with disappointment. "Of course. Yeah. Let me get out of your—"

Callum grabbed him as he slid to the edge of the bed in search of his underwear and pulled him down onto the sheets to kiss him.

"I'm not kicking you out," he said after disentangling his tongue from Rory's. "But I do have to get a move on. Want to have breakfast?"

Jessica was in the kitchen nursing her usual morning meal of a mug of black coffee, slumped in her chair so low, she was almost under the kitchen table, but she perked up when Rory came in behind him. Her jet-black eyebrows shot up above her spectacles, her early morning scowl changing to surprise.

She grinned. "Well, hello, boys."

"Jessica." Callum gestured toward Rory in a mock formal bow. "This is Rory. Rory, this is Jessica. She lives with us here at the Library and is an indispensable member of our team."

"Pleased to meet you, Rory." She leaned back in her chair, propped her feet up on the table, and rested her arm across the chair back, a gunslinger in bright pink fuzzy slippers greeting the new sheriff in town. "Where in Scotland are you from?"

"How did you … ?" said Rory.

"Don't show off." Callum slid her slippers off the table. "Jessica has the gift of divining all sorts of annoying things about a person. It's quite intrusive."

They exchanged fake smiles.

"From a village not far from Inverness," said Rory.

"Have a seat." Callum pulled out a chair and patted the back of it. "I'll see what I can rustle up for us."

"Rory from Inverness." Jessica leaned in across the table. "And where did you two meet?"

"Leave him alone." Callum threw a tea towel at her.

"I'm only asking a friendly question." She folded the towel neatly and placed it in front of her. "Callum so rarely has guests."

"Oh, really," said Rory, "not much of an entertainer?"

"Far from it. Our dear Callum lives a quiet and ascetic life."

"Hm." Rory raised a tart eyebrow. "I'm surprised to hear that after last night."

"Hey!" Callum returned with cereal, milk, and a pair of bowls, feigning outrage, though it warmed him to see Jessica feeling better and getting along with Rory. "No ganging up. This is supposed to be a safe space."

Rafe shuffled in in his pajamas, dressing gown, and slippers, his head already buried in a book, one of the many ledgers that documented the inventory of the Hidden Galleries. "Dear boy, Edgar Newman is coming in this morning to help me analyze the data. Did you have any luck—"

Rafe looked up to see Rory and stopped dead in his tracks.

"Oh!" He closed his book, tucked it under his arm, and stood there paralyzed by awkwardness.

Callum sighed. They all desperately needed company over, real company, not only lost souls like Geoffrey. "And this is Rafe, the librarian here."

Rory stood to shake Rafe's hand. "Pleasure to meet you, sir."

Rafe took it and stood there, mouth open, speechless.

"It's okay, old man." Callum poured milk into his and Rory's bowl. "He's in the family. He used to work at Bar de Bauche."

Rafe blinked rapidly and relaxed. "Oh! Well, that's all right then." He shuffled over to the coffee machine.

"What did you call me at the club last night?" said Callum around a mouthful of corn flakes.

Rory poured himself a bowl of cereal. "A friend of Glinda. Pass the sugar?"

"A friend of Glinda." Callum chuckled and shoved Rory gently with his shoulder. "I love it."

Callum had been half dreading bringing Rory down for breakfast, but Jess and Rafe acquitted themselves admirably. Rory seemed as into him standing on the front steps after as he had been the night before.

"I had a great time." Callum wrapped his arms around the bartender's neck and pulled him close for another kiss.

"Me, too." Rory dropped to the step below so they could be eye to eye. "Much better. Will I see you again?"

Callum hugged him tight.

"Of course you will, silly. Are you working tonight?"

"Yeah, the rest of the week. Have to pay off my debt to Bill."

"All right. I don't want to make a promise I can't keep. This nonsense," he gestured up at the Library, "can mean unexpected late nights, but if I can't make it in tonight, I'll call you. Is that good?"

"Yeah. Works for me."

Callum stood on the steps watching him go, only going back inside once Rory turned the corner and was gone.

23

CALLUM AND RAFE CAME down from the residence to find Jessica hovering by the front door.

"I'm going out," she said.

Dressed in a green explorer's jacket with a fake fur collar thrown over a silk-screened Sinead O'Connor t-shirt, tight black jeans and bovver boots, she had her long white cane in hand.

"You are?" said Callum, incredulous. She hadn't been out on her own in months, and she hated her cane with a passion.

"I can't be stuck in this mausoleum all day with you two anoraks."

Rafe looked at Callum, confused. "Anoraks?"

"She's calling us nerds," said Callum.

"Nerds? Isn't that an American sugar confection?"

"Geeks?"

"She's saying we bite the heads off chickens in a circus?"

Callum rolled his eyes. "I'm several hundred years older than you, and somehow, you're the one who's out of touch. She's calling us swots."

Rafe frowned and cocked his head to one side as he tried to make sense of what Callum had said.

"She's deriding us for valuing dedication and study?"

"Yes, old man. That's exactly what she's doing."

"But anorak? Isn't that what she's wea—"

"Sh-sh-sh. Best not aggravate her."

Throughout their entire exchange, Jessica had stood five feet from the front door, unmoving, a fierce look in her eyes.

"Have fun?" said Callum, curious if she would go through with it.

The doorbell rang, breaking her concentration, and she walked the remaining paces to the front door using the cane to tell her when she had reached it, though Callum knew she didn't need it inside the building, especially not with her spectacles on.

"Ms. Harris," said the man standing outside. "How are you this beautiful morning?"

"Perfectly fine thank you, Edgar. Do come in."

She shifted so Edgar Newman—a tall, lean, tweedy gentleman in his seventies with kind eyes and short, pure white hair and beard—could pass, walked out onto the front step, turned back, and stuck out her tongue at Callum as the door swung shut.

"Edgar, my good man," said Rafe. "Thank you so much for agreeing to join us."

"How could I refuse such an intriguing invitation." The older gentleman grinned, his smile broad and warm. "A summons to the Library of the Damned, no less. Mr. Foster." He reached out a hand for Callum to shake. "Always a pleasure."

"Likewise, Edgar. Likewise."

The smell of summer grass and damp earth filled Callum's nostrils, as it always did when Edgar was around, but the man was a scholar, not a sorcerer, and Callum had never been able to figure out what it meant.

"This way, dear fellow," said Rafe. "I've quite a treat for you. I need your input on something down in the Hidden Galleries."

Edgar's eyes lit up. "The Hidden Galleries? This is my lucky day."

Callum followed behind, the two men chattering away as Rafe led them to the elevator and the sub-basements. The easy bliss of his night with Rory was steadily fading, replaced by the jittery feeling of too much else going on. He didn't want to sit and wait for Thilady Missgrace to come through. For Johnny, he corrected himself. Sometimes he had trouble separating a performer's alter-ego from their offstage persona. He should pound the pavement and see if he could rustle up someone else. And the dead woman in Lucinda Cooke's basement. Handing the case over to the Cottage put him out in the cold. Still, he'd love to understand what Lucinda had been up to. Summoning a demon from hell—Callum had never known that was even possible— seemed outlandish and unlikely.

Edgar's eyes glittered with excitement at being given access to the Hidden Galleries, a rarity for someone not an initiated sorcerer, though he was only being taken to the workroom floor.

"And here it is." Rafe gestured to the grimoire in its protective armature.

Edgar leaned forward reverently to inspect the closed book.

"Fascinating." The low light over the table caught his white hair and made it glow. "What can you tell me about it?"

"Let's see what you think first, then we can compare notes. Here." Rafe gave him a pair of white suede work gloves. "Be sure to only touch it wearing these, and don't remove it from the armature."

Callum sat back in his chair to wait while Edgar proceeded to "hmm" and "hum" for the next fifteen minutes inspecting the grimoire, going through the pages with care. Callum tried to stay focused, but his mind drifted to Rory, to the feeling of his lips and his body pressing against him, to their limbs tangling together with the soft cotton of his bedsheets, and the smell of the high countryside that filled Callum's senses whenever he was near. He daydreamed of the two of them walking hand in hand across a Scottish hillside, of riding with him, their horses pelting through the night under the stars, a pack of hounds running with them, howling up at the moon.

"I think I have it," said Edgar, shattering Callum's reverie.

Had he fallen asleep?

"Seventeenth Century, most definitely. I can tell from the mixture of *mathematica infernalis* with the other writing systems. Such combinations were common at that time. Many sorcerers, especially of the more mystical traditions, were faddish on discovering what lay beyond the veil."

"The veil to the afterlife?" asked Rafe.

If what Callum had seen through the windows in Lucinda Cooke's office was any kind of afterlife, he would gladly stick with the witches' belief there was nothing after death. Though he had the luxury of feeling that way. Sometimes he thought it a blessing he lost his memory every fifty years. How many friends and lovers had he buried in his time? He was happy he would never know.

"And other realms," said Edgar. "There's a volume by Labrax that suggests there are many realms beyond our ken. Heavens and hells, lands of dream and nightmare. He divides the many planes of existence into the Within, that would be us, and the Without."

The mention of Labrax made Callum cringe inwardly. He had yet to break the news he had ruined one of Rafe's precious artifacts.

"Most of the treatises of that time," said Edgar, "are more interested in the heavenly hosts. Cherubim and Seraphim and all that. This fascinating tome," he turned the pages to a particular spread and swiveled the armature so they could see, "purports to contact Hell itself. It even has a ritual of summoning."

The pages showed the summoning circle and pentagram.

"Though I don't know how effective it would be, if Labrax's theories are correct. The realms of the Without are essentially unreal.

How could a creature from out there possibly exist here? What would sustain it?"

Callum and Rafe exchanged meaningful looks. The demonic apparition that attacked him might not be real in any material sense, but they both had experience with the damage the unreal could cause an unfortunate mortal who found themselves in the wrong place at the wrong time.

Edgar turned the book back to face him and flicked through the pages. "The author was onto something, however. This ritual might not penetrate the veil, but performed properly, it could very well bend the fabric of the Within and draw someone or something already here into this circle. Is this an acquisition from Mendelssohn? He loves specimens of the macabre such as this."

Callum perked up. A lead. Erich Mendelssohn, a dealer in artifacts and books of magic, had his fingers in many pies, most of them illegal.

"No, not Mendelssohn," said Callum. "It didn't come from any of the usual channels."

Edgar glanced between Callum and Rafe, expecting an elaboration, but neither of them took the bait.

"This Labrax volume," said Rafe. "Do you have it?"

"No, you do. It's in your restricted collection. I came across it last year when I was doing that research project for the Lord Chief Justice. How did I do? Was I right about the book?"

"Oh," said the librarian. "Oh yes. Perfectly. You know, there's something else I wonder if you would look at."

He meant the illusion. Callum, out of Edgar's line of sight, shook his head almost imperceptibly, but Rafe, for once, got the message. It wouldn't do to air the Library's dirty laundry especially to a visiting scholar like Edgar.

"The Labrax volume." Rafe's face lit up with inappropriately excessive enthusiasm. He would be useless under interrogation. "I haven't inspected it in some time. And you're much more fluent in the technical language of the era than I."

"I would be happy to do so. And I would love to have a closer look at this little gem."

"I'll leave you two to your fun and games," said Callum. "A pleasure to see you again, Edgar."

"Likewise, Callum." Edgar's eyes glimmered. "Likewise."

24

CALLUM RANG BIGGS'S BELL three times and was about to leave when the front door opened.

"What?" Dressed in a tattered t-shirt and a pair of sweatpants, Biggs squinted at him through sleep-heavy eyes, his hair flattened on one side of his head and sticking up at haphazard angles on the other. "Oh, it's you."

He waved Callum in as he shuffled to the door to his flat and stuck one hand down the crotch of his sweats to scratch himself. Glad though Callum was that he and the agent were feeling more comfortable around each other, he wasn't sure he wanted their relationship becoming that familiar.

Biggs's flat was a small one-bedroom with a galley kitchen down one side of the living room. With walls painted magnolia white and soft, comfortable furniture, the decor's feminine touch was ruined by a stationary bike covered with clothes in one corner and a stack of free weights next to it, a former partner's attempts at making a home slowly being erased by the detritus of Biggs's bachelor tendencies.

"Cuppa tea?" Biggs slouched to the electric kettle on the counter, flicked it on, and went through the cupboards to get what he needed.

"Thanks, mate. How did it go at the Cottage?"

Biggs gestured for him to sit at the table that divided the kitchen from the living room and plonked himself down across from him.

"Cavendish was not happy to see me." He rubbed his eyes in an attempt to banish sleep. "Even less when I told her about the body."

"Any consequences to you?" Callum would feel like crap if he got Biggs into trouble.

"My leave's over." Biggs grinned. "But she's got me on desk duty for the duration, night shifts. Which is worse than being forced to stay home. All that stuff's going on and you're sat there analyzing data. Not what I got into the Service for."

"I'm so sorry, mate."

"S'okay." The kettle pinged, and Biggs got up to make the tea. "What brings you my way?"

"Just wanted to see if you're okay and find out about the body. Any news?"

"Not yet. Pinter should report today. I'll let you know. How about the book?"

He handed a mug of tea to Callum and stood there, staring into space, his own mug held in front him, his expression blank.

"I'm starving," he said, life returning. "You hungry?"

He put the mug down roughly, splashing tea on the table, and went to the fridge. Callum grabbed a tea towel to clean up the spill before it soaked into the wood.

"I'm fine, thanks. Rafe had an expert in to look at it, and he gave us a lead, a dealer in Brent, up past Becklow Towers. I'm going to head over there in a second."

"I'll come with you," mumbled Biggs around a mouthful of pork chop. "Give me a moment to clean up."

He stuffed his mouth with more pork until his cheeks bulged out like a squirrel's and headed for the bedroom.

"You don't have to come," Callum called after him. "If you're working night shifts, you should get some rest."

"It's shuffling papers around and a lot of filing," Biggs called back from the bedroom, his voice muffled by the food in his mouth. "It'll be good to feel like I'm doing something useful."

Biggs took a fraction of the time it would have taken Callum to make himself look respectable. Walking to the Rover, in the reflections of car windows, they looked like gay and straight versions of the same person, both dressed in a nondescript uniform of jeans, t-shirt, and sweater, the perfect outfits to go unnoticed with the added benefit of being able to move around easily if trouble called for it. They drove to the dealer in silence, Biggs working his way through another pork chop, three bananas, and a bag full of trail mix.

Eric Mendelssohn's shop was a small storefront tucked away between a cobbler and a charity shop on a side street in the southern part of the borough, a few streets away from the border to Cheyne. A black storefront with two windows divided up into a checkerboard of smaller panes and a gold-leaf sign above the front door proclaiming, 'books to the trade,' it was uniquely uninviting for a retail establishment. Gold-leaf letters on the door read 'by appointment only,' but there was a light on in the back of the shop, so Callum rang the doorbell. When no one answered, he leaned on the doorbell, the aggressive trill cutting through the afternoon quiet.

A head stuck out from behind a bookcase, a scowl on the older man's face. Callum waved and showed his ID. It was little more than a standard library card, but the calligraphic "L-o-D" across it was recognizable to anyone who dealt with artifacts of Chaos.

The figure stamped to the front door and opened it, keeping it on the chain.

"What do you want!"

A tall, slender man, with lank dark hair and oily skin, his face was lined with deep grooves that shaped it into a mask of aggression.

"Mr. Mendelssohn." Callum did his best to be polite. "I'm from the Library of the Damned—"

"I can see that. By appointment only. It says so right there on the door." Mendelssohn jabbed a finger at the lettering.

"I'm sorry to disturb you, but I have a few questions to ask you about a book we believe you sold to someone recently."

"My client list is confidential."

"I realize that, Mr. Mendelssohn, but there's been a death connected to the book."

Callum shifted to one side to give Mendelssohn a better view of Biggs hovering over his shoulder. He felt the agent press in so the two of them became a wall of intimidation.

"My colleague here is from the Cottage." Biggs held up his own, much more official-looking, ID card. "Any help you might provide us would be gratefully appreciated."

A dealer like Mendelssohn wouldn't give a damn about being in the good graces of the Library, but the Cottage was another matter. The wrong kind of interest from them could mean Mendelssohn's entire business network drying up, the right kind, a possible source of income as a consultant. Callum was glad Biggs had offered to come with him.

Mendelssohn scowled at them, unmoving.

"A death?" he said, finally. "How?"

"The book was a grimoire. We need to determine if the death was incidental to the rituals described in it, or if it was a sacrifice."

Human sacrifice was heavily frowned upon by the Cottage, but only because of the threat it posed to national security. Any ritual requiring that much juice to get it going could jeopardize any number of irons the many sorcerous cabals had in the proverbial fire. There was nothing they hated more than the inconvenience of unregulated use of High Influence.

Mendelssohn blinked three times and closed the door to unhook the chain.

"Do you have the book?" He led them into the back of the shop, past floor-to-ceiling locked cabinets filled with volumes Rafe would have done anything to get his hands on. The air in the shop was stale and muggy, but that was all Callum sensed. No telltale coppery taste. Either there were no artifacts of Chaos on the premises, or the cabinets were well-shielded.

"It's being analyzed at the Library," said Callum.

Mendelssohn grumbled. With the exception of the extensively plotted heist by the Theosophists in the late eighteen-hundreds, objects that went into the Library never came out, which Callum was certain cut into the business of dealers like Mendelssohn who profited from the endless sale and resale of books that passed between practitioners of High Influence, sorcerous and otherwise.

"A grimoire, you say?" The dealer led them to a desk tucked away in the back. He sat and stared up at them, his face illuminated from below by the glow of his desk lamp. Expecting the shopkeeper might get out some kind of sales ledger, Callum prepared to wait patiently, but all Mendelssohn did was stare at him.

"On the subject of summoning the devil," said Callum.

Mendelssohn smirked. "The world isn't a religious fairy story. There's no devil hiding in the cupboard waiting to tempt and torment you. Just an endless host of demons stabbing each other in the back."

Callum and Biggs exchanged glances.

"Summoning demons, then."

The shopkeeper opened a drawer in his desk and took out a file folder containing an order book with most of the pages ripped out to leave only the pink carbon copies.

How many demonic grimoires must he sell in a week?

Mendelssohn stopped at a particular page and turned the pad face down on the table while he opened another drawer and took out a ledger and thumbed through the pages. He stopped at an entry. "Seventeenth century?"

"Yes."

"Leather bound?"

"Yes."

"Two hundred pages?"

"I suppose so."

"Hand-written?"

Callum did his best to suppress a sigh of frustration. "Yes, hand-written. Purchased, we believe, by a Lucinda Cooke."

Mendelssohn raised an eyebrow and grunted. "That was my sale, yes. Is she the one who died?"

"I'm not at liberty to say. Did you read the book?"

"I did."

Callum was ready to grab the man and throw him up against the wall. Biggs must have been feeling the same. The agent walked around the desk and perched on it uncomfortably close to Mendelssohn. He smiled, the wide, toothy, mirthless grin of a predator. Mendelssohn's shell of crankiness slipped. He swallowed.

"What was in it?" Biggs toyed with a bundle of pens stuffed into a coffee mug on the desk. He removed one and began to click the spring, holding up the pen as if he might stab the shopkeeper.

Unnerved, Mendelssohn gulped. "A t—taxonomy of the hosts of Hell," he stammered and clutched his ledger to his chest as if it might protect him, "a schema of the realms beyond the veil, and detailed instructions for three different rituals to summon denizens from the infernal realms."

He attempted a smile, a tremor in his cheeks.

"And was a human sacrifice required for any of these rituals, Mr. Mendelssohn?" Biggs placed the pen on the desk, tip down, holding it upright with an index finger on the spring mechanism. Mendelssohn eyed it nervously. Callum had always thought of Biggs as a blundering thug. He'd never suspected him capable of wielding his menace as finely as this. Callum was impressed.

"Ah, no. No human sacrifice, that is. Lesser animals. Doves, lambs, rabbits, that kind of thing. Nothing that would produce restricted intensities of Influence upon death."

Though most sorcerers preferred to think human beings were the only source of magic, it was an emanation of all life that thought and felt emotions. The more thinking and feeling the creature, the more Influence flowed from it into the vast reservoir that surged around the British Isles.

Thinking, feeling creatures. Like primates, horses, or dogs.

Dogs.

Why is that important? Some part of Callum stirred at the thought.

"A taxonomy of the hosts of hell," said Biggs. "Does that mean lists of demons?"

Mendelssohn nodded, the bobbing of his head so vigorous it made his chair squeak.

"Yes, with descriptions, their names and titles, their areas of expertise."

"Like a satanist's telephone directory."

Mendelssohn laughed, a surprised bark at what he thought was a joke, but Biggs's expression was serious, and the bookseller snapped his mouth shut, his teeth clacking.

"Yes. Yes, exactly like that."

"And what are these demons? Are they like Christopher Lee, all suave and debonair? Or are they monsters? Tall buggers covered in spikes with giant mouths and rows of fangs?"

Mendelssohn looked confused. It wasn't the kind of question he expected from a spook.

"Both, I suppose. But it's all fantasy. No one has ever pierced the veil. No one knows what's on the other side, if there even is one."

Fantasy didn't always mean harmless. That thing in Lucinda Cooke's study could have ripped Callum's head off if he hadn't used the scepter on it, something he wasn't certain he could recover from.

"Where did the book come from," said Callum. "Do you have others like it?"

Mendelssohn released his grip on the ledger, his white fingers regaining some blood flow as he looked at the entry for the grimoire.

"No, it's highly unusual. Found in an estate sale in Birmingham. From a collector. I was still establishing its provenance when I found a buyer for it."

"Lucinda Cooke? Did she ask for it specifically?"

"Not at all. I remember the transaction vividly. She wasn't one of my regular customers. The colleague who referred her to me said she was interested in spell craft, mesmerism, that kind of thing. Said she had seemingly limitless funds."

"A golden goose?"

"Yes. Yes, exactly."

"Did she seem like she knew what she was talking about? Or was she a dilettante?"

"Something between the two. A lay practitioner. She knew *mathematica infernalis* but wasn't an initiated sorcerer as far as I could tell."

The sorcerous cabals did their best to rule over magic with an iron fist, but there was always a demimonde of people who insisted on dabbling in things that could get them killed, or worse. If the high muckety-mucks of sorcery were to behave more like authoritarian fascists, Callum would be out of a job. Not necessarily a bad thing. He could use a few more cozy nights in.

"Write down the details of the sale for me," said Callum. Biggs took a pad from the desk and handed it and the pen to Mendelssohn, who scribbled it all down.

With the details in his pocket—Callum didn't have much hope they would lead to anything, but it was important to be thorough—he bade farewell to the dealer, but on the way out the door, Mendelssohn hovering behind them, he thought about the stolen artifact and the illusion that had covered up the theft.

"What do you know about natural magic?"

Mendelssohn, one hand on the door, looked confused. "Natural? All Influence is natural."

"I mean like plants and rocks. From the land?"

Mendelssohn spoke cautiously, as if being tested. "There's no such thing. Influence emerges from thought and feeling, from the complex psyche of man. What feelings does a rock have?"

In thirty years of memory and thousands of journal pages, Callum's only experience with magic was of the wild variety. He had no way of knowing if what Mendelssohn had claimed was true.

"Thank you for your help."

"Do you have a card or something?" The dealer hovered in the doorway. "In case I uncover more information?"

"I think he's talking to you," Callum said to Biggs. A contact at the Cottage would be a prize. A contact at the Library would be a pain in the arse. Rafe would confiscate half his inventory.

Biggs turned back to the dealer. "I don't have a fucking business card. If you come up with anything, we'll know."

Callum smirked as they walked to the car.

"We like to cultivate an air of aggressive omniscience," said the agent. "What was all that about? Natural magic?"

Callum considered brushing off the question, pretending it was nothing, but he was trying his best to be honest with Biggs.

"There's an issue with the collection. I can't really talk about it."

"To do with the book?"

"No, something else."

"You know, I'm already up to my neck in it with you lot. If the Cottage finds out about the book, they'll kick me out." He let the thought sink in and sighed. "Might not be a bad thing."

They turned the corner and walked into the glare of afternoon sunlight. Biggs winced and covered his face with his arm. "Bloody hell."

In the car, the agent resumed munching on his bag of trail mix. "I'm on duty in a couple of hours," he mumbled around a mouthful of nuts. "Come with me and I can get you briefed about the dead woman."

"Sounds good." Callum pulled out into the street.

"I'm parched. We can stop off for a quick pint on the way."

25

VISITING THE COTTAGE WHEN they hadn't recently pulled your arse out of the fire was a much less welcoming and streamlined experience. No helicopters and unmarked cars, no being whisked through to debriefing rooms. Even though Callum had been to the Cottage in an official capacity on a hundred occasions in the past thirty years, and who knew how many before that, they always gave him a hard time. After an hour of questioning, filling out forms, and waiting patiently while they vainly cast a torrent of spells on him, his head was spinning from the overpowering scent of lavender when a nameless attendant handed him a pass and Biggs came to rescue him from the gray, windowless tomb of an interrogation room.

"You know you're the only one they do that to, don't you?" The agent walked them through a maze of corridors to the incident rooms. "With everyone else, it takes about five minutes. The oracles pick up who's coming in the day before and all vetting is done overnight."

Interesting. Callum did not know that. "They're probably frustrated their spell work doesn't stick on me."

Biggs raised an eyebrow. "The curse?"

"Yeah. It takes a lot of wattage to get through."

Callum immediately regretted saying it. He hoped it wasn't a mistake. He didn't exactly have secrets, other than the ones the curse kept from him, but he didn't fancy being at someone's mercy.

Another windowless space, the incident room was low and dark. A dozen desks organized in neat rows covered the floor, two agents to a desk either talking on telephones, reading tarot cards, or using some other form of oracle. The long wall opposite the entrance was entirely covered with a whiteboard. Three different clusters of work—pictures, scrawled notes, and other evidence—were spread across it. Callum recognized a photo of the now-destroyed Trentham Abbey in the center of the board. Down one side of the room stood a bank of computers, a surprise to Callum as the only tech the Cottage usually used was a weird amalgam of High Influence, alchemy, and cobbled together elements from centuries past.

In one corner, perched on a high stool at a standing desk, Esme Cavendish reviewed a document an underling old enough to be her father had presented her. She saw Callum and Biggs enter and thrust the paper at her underling.

"Ah, Mr. Foster." She stalked over to meet them. "I hope you can enlighten me on a few points."

"What exactly did you tell her?" Callum muttered to Biggs out of the corner of his mouth.

"Only the big picture. She wouldn't want to hear the rest from me. Good luck."

He tapped Callum lightly on the arm and shuffled off down an aisle to claim a desk. He picked up a phone but kept one surreptitious eye on Callum.

"What's the story with this book?" Cavendish stared Callum down. In her riding boots, she towered over him by a good inch or more. "Do I have to open another file?"

"Did you find out the identity of the dead woman?"

"Listen, if there's a potential situation looming over us, it's imperative we get in there before it starts and cut it off at the knees."

"Quite so." Callum turned his face into as amiable a mask as he could. He could play this game of information chicken all night. He caught Biggs smirking out of the corner of his eye. "I imagine there's no indication if Lucinda Cooke was one of the vampires you sterilized in the nest?"

With her stature and beauty, Esme Cavendish must not be used to someone who didn't quail and buckle under the fierce gaze of her ice-blue eyes. If they had met socially, he would have found her attitude and strength fascinating. Perhaps it was because he was gay. The straight men he knew never seemed to appreciate a woman's strength. He smiled at her.

She grunted, the slightest hint of a guttural growl to show her frustration.

"Come."

She strode past him and out the door.

"The woman's name was Maggie Pelham." She led Callum deeper through the labyrinth of corridors. "She was thirty-two, two years older than Lucinda Cooke. They were lovers, partners, whatever you people like to call yourselves."

You people? Was Ms. Cavendish a bigot or trying to get under his skin?

"Lucinda Cooke purchased and moved into the house five years ago. Maggie Pelham joined her two years later."

"Cause of death?"

"See for yourself."

She pushed through a door and led him into a chilly room lit only by overhead fluorescents. At the center of the room stood a wheeled stretcher with a body under a sheet. In one corner, a woman in a white doctor's coat sat at a desk making notes on a medical chart.

"Out," barked Cavendish, and the woman scurried away, chart in hand.

Cavendish carefully turned down the sheet to reveal the body of Maggie Pelham, her skin gray and pallid under the light. "The cause of death was exsanguination. An incision was made here."

She pointed to the slit in Pelham's neck. It was small, no larger than a couple of inches, and placed exactly over the woman's jugular.

He knelt by the stretcher to inspect the clean slice through her flesh. "I saw it when we found the body. What is it? A knife wound?"

"The forensics girls tell me a surgical scalpel."

"There was no blood on the body, nor anywhere we could see in the rest of the house. Was she murdered somewhere else and hidden in the basement?"

"Not a clue."

He stood to see Maggie Pelham's face. She was a pretty woman with delicate features. He imagined her laughing, running her fingers through her hair, reading a book on the top deck of a bus. He leaned over and sniffed her forehead.

"What on earth are you doing," said Cavendish, outraged.

He ignored her. He smelled nothing unusual, but as he straightened up, was that a hint of sulfur? "Do you have a time of death? She's in remarkably good shape."

"Something is interfering with the body's decomposition. The cells are suffused with small traces of Influence."

"Someone cast a spell on her. Can you tell who?"

"We cannot. The Influence has a quality our alchemists are unable to identify."

"Sulfur." The word slipped out without him realizing. This was the third time he had smelled it.

"Excuse me?" Cavendish raised an eyebrow.

There'd be no benefit to telling her what he meant. The fragrances he smelled were entirely subjective. To tell her would do her no good, and the explanation would give away more about him than he trusted the Cottage to know.

"Sorry. Talking to myself. Were there other marks on her? Any indication of a struggle? Any indication of the body being cleaned up?

If she died from blood loss, there must have been some on her at some point."

Cavendish shook her head. "Nothing. Save for the incision, her body is as unblemished as a waxwork at Madame Tussauds. For all we know, she undressed, lay down on the cellar floor, and waited for someone to slit her neck."

It wasn't an outlandish suggestion. A spell could easily make a person act against their instinct for self-preservation.

"How did they get the blood out of her?" He stooped to look at the incision again. A vampire would have ripped her throat out and left blood all over the place.

"No idea, which is alarming. Neither the oracles nor the sensitives came up with anything. Whatever did this to her did not want to be found."

Callum raised an eyebrow. Cavendish's boss, Euphemia Graham, was greedy for secrets. Not knowing must be driving her insane. "How vexing for you."

"All right." Cavendish stalked over to the body and covered it with the sheet, taking her ball and going home. "Enough of this. Lucinda Cooke went missing three days before her brother's disappearance and six days before you discovered he was gone. In your statement, you said Ms. Harris sensed some form of assembly had happened in the abbey ruins. Has she been able to determine more about the meeting? Were they some form of vampire cult? It wouldn't be the first time civilians have dabbled in things that could kill them."

He had been so caught up with Geoffrey, Biggs, and Rory, he hadn't thought to follow up with Jessica. His time loss had derailed everything.

"Jessica said there was too much Chaos on the site. She wasn't able to glean more information than what she gave you."

"In the interrogation room, she said Geoffrey Cooke was beguiled. Have you any indication as to who or what was doing that to him?"

Callum suddenly felt like a schoolboy caught out for not doing his homework, a strange and specific sensation for someone who had no memory of his childhood.

"He keeps talking about his sister. He made the claim he called her, remember? Perhaps she's doing it."

"Perhaps?" She was thoroughly unimpressed by his suggestion. "And how would she have the ability to do that? Is it connected to the book you found?"

"Possibly. The book is a treatise on demonology. Summoning rituals and the like."

She rolled her eyes and shook her head.

"Demonology? So, it's nothing more than a fiction, a curiosity?"

"I wouldn't say that. The summoning circle attracted something nasty."

She snorted. "A demon from hell? We've had more vampire nests on British soil in the last five years than the entire century before and an unaccountable source of High Influence, and you bring me fairy tales? You're wasting my time, Mr. Fost—"

An almighty and deafening clanging blared from a speaker in one corner of the room.

"Bugger." Cavendish darted to the door.

"What is that?" Callum had to shout to make himself heard above the din.

"The incident alarm." She didn't bother to turn back to answer. "Make your own way out, Mr. Foster. And stay out of the way."

26

CALLUM RETURNED TO THE Library to find Thilady Missgrace, Johnny, holding court in the lobby, Jessica and Rafe laughing at something he had just said.

"Boys or girls?" Johnny placed an affectionate hand on Jessica's arm. He wore a tightly fitted suit made of iridescent purple Chinese silk with a matching fedora. In his well-manicured hand he carried a Frankenstein's monster of a handbag cobbled together from fragments of smaller bags.

"Excuse me?" Jessica, who usually looked so stylish even in her slouching-around-the-house clothes, was a Dickensian street urchin in comparison.

"What's your fancy? When the house lights go up and the old itch needs to be scratched, who do you turn to?"

"Girls." She grinned. "Most definitely girls."

"And are you single or taken?"

"Single. Do you know someone?"

"Darling," Johnny winked. "I know *everyone*. Even you, Mr. Torvalds. You have quite the reputation among the ladies of Cheyne Heath."

Rafe actually blushed. Callum couldn't believe it.

"And here we have the adorable Mr. Foster," proclaimed Johnny at the sight of Callum standing in the doorway. "Hearts have broken along the entire Morel Road at the news of his latest entanglement. Have you heard," he asked Jessica and Rafe with a conspiratorial air.

"Oh, yes." Rafe's eyes twinkled. "We've met the young gentleman."

"Rory's very nice," said Callum, uneasy that his crush was being talked about by others, "but we've only been out once."

"Hm," said Johnny. "So reserved. You can't fool me, darling. I've seen the way you look at each other."

Now it was Callum's turn to blush. "I thought you weren't allowed to help us?"

At this, Johnny sobered up.

"La Davina has the best intentions for me, but I can't turn my back on a mystery. Now, show me this illusion."

The door to the library opened, and Edgar emerged in his coat, his satchel over one shoulder. Surprised to see them there, he stopped and hovered awkwardly.

"Edgar," said Rafe. "All set?"

"Ah, yes," said the scholar, uncharacteristically timid. "I would like to come back once I've done some research."

"Of course, my good man. Any light you can shine on the problem will be much appreciated. Oh, I'm so sorry. May I introduce you to Johnny Suharto. Johnny, Edgar is a frequent user of the collection. He's quite a fixture around here."

Edgar bobbed his head in greeting. "A pleasure." He patted the pocket of his coat and looked in his satchel. "How foolish of me. I left my notebook downstairs. Is it all right if I go back and get it?"

"Of course," said Rafe. "You know the way."

Edgar ducked through the doors.

Rafe turned to Johnny. "You've never been to the Library, have you?"

"I'm sad to say I had never heard of it before darling Callum came a-calling," said Johnny, "knock-knock-knocking at my dressing room door."

"You must let me show you the highlights!"

Rafe led Johnny into the library in full tour guide mode.

Callum slipped his hand into Jessica's, and they followed close behind. "How are you feeling?"

"Better," she said after a beat. "I need to get out more."

"Yes, of course."

"On my own."

"You got it."

"And I need to make connections outside the Library."

"Makes sense. If you need anything from me, just ask. I want you to be happy."

She squeezed his hand. "That might take a bit of work."

"And I'll help you any way I can."

Edgar emerged from the workroom containing the grimoire as they stepped out of the rickety elevator.

"See you tomorrow?" said Rafe.

"Yes, yes." Edgar sidled past them clutching his satchel close to his body. "Tomorrow it is."

"What's the matter with him?" Jessica removed her spectacles to watch as the old scholar shuffled down the corridor.

"No idea." Rafe. "See anything?"

She replaced her spectacles and shrugged. "He's always been a bit odd. Like he's stepped through a portal from a different time."

"Oh my," said Johnny at the sight of the glamored artifact resting on its velvet pedestal on the large worktable. "I see what you mean. It's quite convincing. May I?"

"Please." Rafe pulled out a chair. "Make yourself at home."

Johnny beamed a mischievous smile. "How kind."

His Chinese silk suit transformed into a white lab coat cut in the style of a Victorian undertaker's jacket, the pants of the suit becoming black drainpipe trousers. He placed his chimeric handbag on the table and began to unload a series of objects which he arranged neatly in front of him. Callum and Jessica took seats across the table while Rafe sidled up to Johnny to observe over his shoulder.

"Fascinating. Are these your tools?" said the librarian.

Johnny laid out a pair of hand mirrors, a compact, three makeup brushes of different sizes, a pot of foundation, a string of pearls, three rings with absurdly large jewels set into them, a comb, a candle, and a packet of cigarettes. The fragrance of sandalwood drifted across the table toward Callum, mixed in with a peculiar headnote of pungent tea. Satisfied with what he had laid out, Johnny closed his bag and placed it on the floor under the table.

"Just a few bits and bobs."

"Remarkable." Rafe edged forward to get a closer look. "And so unusual. The implements of High Influence are usually much more arcane. Is this a mark of your sphere?"

"Decidedly not." Johnny waved his hand in a gesture that was part horror and part dismissal. "My sphere has little in the way of *accoutrements*. The High Influence of Strength involves a lot of fasting, chanting, and hand-sewing ballerina tutus and ball gowns. It's quite tedious. You must never repeat that. La Davina doesn't like her soiled unmentionables laid out for all the world to see."

"So, what's all this?"

"I've learned a few things in my time. The old ways are not always the best ways. My dearest friend is a witch. They have a more grounded perspective on the magical arts. La Davina does not approve of my methods."

He winked at Callum, sat back, closed his eyes, and took a deep breath.

"I am ready." He opened his eyes.

"Anything you can tell us about the illusion," said Rafe, "would be an immense help. The original artifact was last accounted for in nineteen-oh-two. Beyond that, it's all a mystery."

Johnny slid the velvet pedestal toward him and squinted at the odd, cross-like clockmaker's tool. "It's an extremely sophisticated glamor."

He opened the compact and used the larger of the brushes to collect a thick dusting of face powder on the bristles, which he proceeded to blow at the artifact. The dust collected in a cloud around it without dispersing. He held the two hand mirrors up on either side of the artifact and peered into the one in his right hand, which he held still as he adjusted the position of the one in his left. "Good heavens! Look at this."

Rafe peered into the mirrors.

"Look at the reflections. Follow them in about a dozen steps."

"Oh," Rafe cried. "Oh, my!"

"Come look, you two."

"You go." Jessica waved Callum forward.

"How thoughtless of me," Johnny said to her as Callum peered into the mirror. "Please forgive me."

"It's fine."

The recursive reflections in the hand mirrors stretched back into infinity, but, sure enough, about a dozen repetitions deep in a single reflection, instead of the clockmaker's tool, on the pedestal sat a tassel of the sort you might find on a curtain sash in a grand old hotel, exactly as Jessica had said.

Johnny put the mirrors down. "That's not something I've seen before." He looked up at Callum. "You told me something about it being 'natural' magic. What did you mean by that?"

Callum turned to Jessica. "You're up."

She leaned forward and removed her spectacles as she peered at the artifact.

"When I look at it, I see images of nature: a grassy field by a forest, wildflowers, a river flowing in the distance."

"Is it a specific place?" said Johnny. "Somewhere you recognize?"

She shook her head. "The elements are always the same, but the image itself changes."

"Curious. Have you tried to break the illusion?"

"I wouldn't know how," said Rafe.

"Probably just as well." Johnny put on the string of pearls and the three rings, two on his left hand, one on his right. "This sort of thing is best done by an expert."

He held his hands over the artifact and hummed something quietly under his breath. Callum recognized the tune: "La Vie En Rose."

"To be on the safe side," said Johnny, "Perhaps you should all step back."

Callum and the others took a step away from the table.

"All the way back."

They retreated to the walls. When he was satisfied, the sorcerer began to sing with a surprisingly beautiful voice. A glow appeared within the gemstones on the rings. The brighter the glow, the more forcefully Johnny sang. The smell of grass in summer, of humidity and wildflowers, filled Callum's nostrils.

A loud crack rang out from nowhere, and the temperature of the room dropped by ten degrees.

"Tricky little thing!" said Johnny.

"What happened?" Callum approached the table to peer at the artifact. The glamor still held.

"The kind of illusions my lot cast require focus and constant maintenance. Without me to sustain it, my outfit would dissipate."

His lab coat disappeared to reveal a brown suede jacket over a hot pink t-shirt with Tina Turner on it. The lab coat returned as quickly as it had vanished.

"This thing is self-sustaining. I don't know how it's possible. The amount of discipline required to weave something like this is staggering."

He sat back and ran his fingers through the tight crop of his black hair, pulling the skin of his face into a mask of sharp lines and steep angles.

"I don't have the right tools with me," he said after a long minute. "If I could take this with me, I could get a proper look under the hood."

Rafe frowned and shook his head. "Oh, I don't know. I don't think I can let it out of the building."

"It's not an artifact, old man," said Callum. "It's a tassel. It's perfectly safe. It is perfectly safe, isn't it?"

"Oh yes." Johnny picked it up and inspected it in the low work light. "Perfectly."

"In that case, yes," said Rafe. "We would appreciate any help we can get."

"And if you need another example to experiment with, I can track down one of the others."

"Others?" Rafe looked shocked. "There are more?"

"What was the purpose of the artifact this replaced?"

"Minor transmutations. Water into wine, cotton into silk, that kind of thing."

"Would someone who can walk in here unnoticed, steal something, and leave a copy without you ever knowing limit themselves to an artifact that turns water into wine? I imagine you have all sorts of treasures down here."

Johnny's laboratory outfit transformed into a Christmas panto version of a cat-burglar's garb: a tight-fitting black body suit with knee-high boots and a black sequined mask across his eyes that slanted up into a pair of cat ears.

Callum and Rafe stared at each other, appalled. They'd never even considered there could be more missing.

"Shall we see what else your crafty thief has stolen?" Johnny's outfit returned to the white lab coat.

He took one of the cigarettes from the packet and lit it with a chunky chrome lighter he took from his pocket.

"Oh, there's no smoking in the Library," said Rafe.

Johnny took a deep drag and blew the smoke at the smoldering tip of the cigarette, where it collected in a bubble.

"Don't worry, it's not tobacco. And the smoke will never touch your lovely books or your fascinating *objets*. This," he stood, and his outfit transformed into a three-piece tweed suit with a Victorian capelet across his shoulders and a deerstalker hat on his head, "is a particularly inquisitive blend of tea, and extremely non-regulation. Please never mention it to anyone outside this room. La Davina would have a conniption if she found out about it."

He picked up the glamored clockmaker's tool and waved it three times around the bubble of smoke.

"Are we all ready?" Johnny grinned at them, his eyes alight with excitement. "We might need to stay on our toes. It's a bit frisky. All set?"

"Ready," said Rafe.

"All right, my dear." Johnny addressed the cigarette. "Off you go."

A tendril of smoke snaked out of the bubble.

"Open the door for it, would you, ducky?" he asked Callum, who darted ahead and did as he was asked.

The tendril snaked out of the door and turned left.

"The game's afoot!" An enormous magnifying glass the size of a record appeared in Johnny's hand. He held it up to the cigarette and followed the trail of smoke out of the room.

27

THE TRAIL OF SMOKE led them all over the Hidden Galleries and even to the library above. By the time they were finished, after three hours of mounting horror, they returned to the workroom with illusionary replacements for a dozen books and thirty-odd artifacts. Rafe organized them on the table in silence as the others looked on. Even Jessica, who always did her best to hold herself above the erratic turbulence of Library affairs, was shaken, her cheeks leeched of color. This place that was a sanctuary for them all had been violated.

"I've organized everything according to their effects." Rafe stepped back and took in the three groups he had moved all the stolen objects into. He pointed to each group in turn. "Transmogrification and transformation, clairvoyance and inquiry into the esoteric cosmos, cryptozoology and anthropology."

This last was a stack of three large tomes.

"What's most curious to me is that everything here is ephemera." He opened one of his thick ledgers and turned the pages. "Even the artifacts are minimally potent. We have much more powerful examples that were left untouched."

Callum picked up one of the books, a volume on ancient creatures of mythology and terror. He opened it to a random page filled with printed text he found impossible to read. His eyes couldn't focus on the words. "Jess, can you see what I'm actually holding?"

She snapped out of her daze and removed her spectacles to look. "It's a cookbook. Mince pies and Christmas stuff."

"Bugger me!"

He sank into a chair. He'd always thought of himself as the Library's unofficial guardian. Even in his earliest journals he wrote about his commitment to its mission and protecting those who sought its refuge. It was the one thing that gave him purpose, and he'd botched the job up royally. "Who would do this? Who *could* do this? Every door and window is warded. Every item in the collection is tagged."

A jolt of purpose shook him out of his daze. Tagged. Every item had attached to it a hidden slip of paper bearing a string of symbols in *mathematica infernalis* that acted as a locator, drawing its power either from the Chaos the object gave off or from the magic in the air around it.

"The catalog." Rafe was already halfway out the door.

He led them up to the first sub-basement and the collection catalog, a small room lined with drawered cabinets containing an organized record of all the items in the Library. At its center stood a desk with Rafe's latest attempt at dragging the Library into the twentieth century: a large computer monitor and its accompanying tower stood next to it. Draped over both were strips of white suede embossed with symbols supposed to insulate the technology from the damaging effects of the Library's concentration of wild magic. Stacked in one of the closets in the lobby sat the fried electronic carcasses of his eight previous attempts.

On the far wall hung a large map of the British Isles studded with colored push pins to mark the locations where the artifacts of Chaos in the Library collection had been found. In front of it stood a table with a pyramid-like rig suspending a pendulum over the tabletop. From the cabinet beneath it, Rafe took out a map of the British Isles and slid it under the pendulum.

"This is so exciting," said Johnny.

Rafe went to the card catalog against one wall. "Let's see." He surveyed the labels on the grid of tiny drawers. "The Bromsgrove quintet."

He zeroed in on a drawer, flicked through the contents, and pulled out a card which he took to the pendulum. Referring to the information on the card, he calibrated the pendulum device with a series of dials, wheels within wheels. Satisfied, he pulled the pendulum bob off-center and let it swing.

An acidic metallic odor wafted toward Callum as the pendulum moved, signaling the rising of the magic powering the device.

"What's supposed to be happening?" Johnny whispered to Callum.

"The pendulum will tell us the location of the artifact, but it should have locked on by now."

"I don't understand." Rafe pulled his fingers through his tousled hair. "It has to be somewhere."

"Could the thief have removed the tag?" said Johnny.

Rafe blinked repeatedly, trying to wrap his mind around the suggestion.

"I suppose it's possible, but it would be hard. The tags were devised by John Dee himself. They've been in place since the foundation of the Library. I must check the others."

He darted out of the room.

"Is he all right?" asked Johnny.

"We're all a bit shaken," said Callum.

28

"THERE IS ONE MORE thing I can do for you," said Johnny on the front steps. The last glow of sunlight was dying in the sky. They had been down in the Hidden Galleries for hours. "I should be able to create an alarm, something that will tell you if your larcenous illusionist strikes again, though it may take me a couple of days."

"I truly appreciate your help," said Callum. "We all do."

Johnny hugged him, and the scent of sandalwood, the mark of the sorcerer's magic, enveloped him. When they parted, Johnny, the Sherlock Holmes drag replaced by a somber black suit, handed him a business card.

"My number. Call me day or night if you need my help. If I'm not there, tell my partner, Joel. He'll know how to find me. You must come for dinner one night. You'll love Joel. He's sturdy, like you." Johnny grinned and patted Callum's shoulder.

As Callum closed the door, the thin copper ward-wire around it caught his eye. He might not be much use to Rafe down in the galleries, but he could check all the building's wards and see if any were broken. It was a tedious and time-consuming job. Exactly what he needed to feel useful. There weren't many doors in and out of the building, but there were many, many windows, some of them large and high up, requiring ladders and much awkward climbing.

It was past nine when he finally made it up to the residence, with no sign of Jessica and Rafe. He was inspecting the windows in the common room, when he heard a moan coming down the hall from Geoffrey's room.

The small, spartan bedroom was a mess, the clothes someone from the Cottage had brought Geoffrey from Bristol strewn across the floor. He lay huddled in bed, blankets wrapped around him.

"Are you okay?" Callum perched on the edge of the bed.

Geoffrey clearly was not. His face was pale, and his body shivered.

"I'm so cold," he croaked. "So thirsty."

Callum put a hand on the young man's forehead. His skin was like ice and parchment-dry. A strange odor, decay mixed with something pungent over the unmistakable metallic bitterness of Chaos, wafted off him. He needed more help than Callum could give him.

"Hang in there. I'm going to get help."

He ran to the intercom on the wall in the common room and hit the buzzer, but all he got was a garbled crackle. They really needed to install a better intercom. He tore down the stairs two at a time, one hand on the wall to keep himself from tumbling arse over tit to a broken neck and months of recovery. The elevator to the Hidden Galleries had never been so slow.

He burst into the catalog room, out of breath.

"Something's wrong with Geoffrey," he blurted out as soon as he could find the words. "He's as cold as a block of ice and reeks of Chaos."

Rafe and Jessica, up to their elbows in ledgers and artifacts as they stooped over the map and pendulum, dropped what they were doing and followed Callum back to the elevator.

"My kit is in my office," said Rafe. "I have a few things in there that will stabilize him."

"Is it the beguiling?" Callum raised his voice to a shout to be heard above the rattling.

They shot out of the elevator and headed for the stairs but as they passed through the lobby, the doorbell rang, followed by a loud, insistent knocking.

Time seemed to slow for Callum as adrenaline surged through his bloodstream, some fundamental instinct for self-preservation aroused by the sound. Rafe, who was closest to the door, stopped in the middle of the room, his face suddenly blank, and turned to answer it. Callum watched in disbelief as his friend opened the door. "What are you doing?"

On the front step, lit from behind by the streetlamp, stood a tall woman with long, straight blonde hair that fell across the shoulders of her black cashmere overcoat. Her skin was pale, white as marble.

"Hello," she said, her voice low and melodious.

Jessica, one foot on the stairs, stopped and went to Rafe's side.

Callum recognized her immediately from the photos in Geoffrey's flat. Lucinda Cooke. An overwhelming odor of rotten eggs and garlic swept in through the front door, and the coppery bitterness of Chaos rose up in his throat so powerfully, he gagged.

"I believe my brother is staying here with you." Her lips parted to reveal white teeth, a pair of slender fangs protruding where her incisors should have been. Her eyes shone an iridescent blue in the light from the foyer. "I must see him. It's extremely urgent. Won't you invite me in?"

"No!" Callum lunged at Rafe and Jessica to pull them back, but he was too far away to get to them in time.

"Of course," said Rafe, as polite and accommodating as ever. All the hair on Callum's body stood at attention. "Do come in, won't you?"

One moment she was standing on the front step, the next she was in the middle of the lobby.

"What a curious place." She looked around the room, an explorer in a freshly unearthed tomb. "Close the door."

Rafe did as he was told, and he and Jessica stood passively in front of it, their expressions calmly blank.

"And you." She turned to Callum. "You're the dangerous one. The one I'm supposed to be wary of."

The tattoos on his back contracted and grew cold, and the stench of sulfurous garlic increased. She must be trying to beguile him the way she had Geoffrey. That she assumed she had succeeded might be his only advantage, so he stood stock still, as frozen to the spot as Rafe and Jessica, and tried not to flinch as she caressed his cheek.

"You're the same age as Geoffrey," she said.

Something caught her attention, and she looked up at the ceiling.

"The poor boy. He's in so much pain. I would have come sooner, but in one short night, you three ruined months of work. The master insisted I replace all the thralls you killed before he would let me come."

She turned to Jessica and Rafe. "Which of you shall I choose for Geoffrey's sacrifice?"

She moved so quickly, faster than a person should be able to. Her body blurred in the dim light of the lobby. She traced a finger down Rafe's neck.

"Too old. You might die before you've bled out. And there's a tiny flutter in your heart. You should get that seen to."

Lucinda laughed heartily, as if she'd made a joke.

"You, I think." She stepped back to take in Jessica. "You're smaller. I don't have much time, and you'll die quicker. And you're Geoffrey's type. Come with me, dear."

She took Jessica's hand and led her to the stairs.

The instant Lucinda turned her back on Callum, he lunged for Rafe and grabbed his cane. Lucinda heard the movement and spun around, blurring as she rushed at him, but it was too late. He raised the cane and swung it at her with all his might. The silver handle bashed into her temple and knocked her to the ground. The side of her face smoldered.

He struck her again, and a third and a fourth time, before she could recover. The blows were enough to break her hold on Rafe and Jessica. They both looked around, confused, as if awaking from a deep sleep.

"RUN!" Callum's cry snapped them back to reality. He struck the vampire one more time—the entire side of her head was now a blackened mass of seared flesh—and tossed the cane to Rafe. "Seal me in and get help."

Rafe had ways of locking the building down by supernatural means. Callum didn't know what this strange vampire could do, but it should be enough to slow her down until help arrived if he failed to stop her.

"But—" Rafe fumbled, almost dropping the cane.

Lucinda groaned.

"DO IT!"

Jessica didn't need to be told twice. She ran for Rafe and grabbed his arm, dragging him with her out the door. Callum didn't wait to see them go. Lucinda was already struggling to get up.

"Wanker!" She touched the side of her head and flinched as Callum tore past her and bounded up the stairs. His knives were in the attic, about as far away from him as they could possibly be. "I don't care what the master says. I'll make sure Geoffrey bleeds you slowly while I break every bone in your body!"

Callum only made it as far as the bottom floor of the residence before she caught up with him. Flowing up the stairs behind him, she struck him like a battering ram. The impact threw him into the wall, winding him. Looming over him, she backhanded him hard, knocking him sideways, his ears ringing and lights flashing in his eyes. She grabbed him by the back of his shirt and dragged all fourteen stone of him effortlessly up the stairs to the landing.

"Geoffrey!" she shouted. "Where are you?"

She cocked her head to one side, listening as Callum struggled to get his legs underneath him.

"There you are."

With nothing more than a casual toss, she hurled Callum down the corridor. He tumbled to a halt outside Geoffrey's door, and she dragged him in, throwing him to one side like a sack of potatoes.

"You poor thing." She sat on the bed next to Geoffrey and caressed his cheek. "It's okay. I'm here now. I made a terrible mess of it. Can you forgive me?"

She pulled Geoffrey's shivering body into her embrace and kissed the top of his head.

"You should have been the first person I brought into the fold, but I had to be certain it would be safe. The transition nearly killed me, and I had to be sure."

"Help me," he whimpered. "I'm so cold."

"I know, dear. You'll feel better very soon, I promise you. So much better, but we have to do this properly or you'll become another one of those feral beasts."

The room finally stopped spinning around Callum, and he had enough breath back in his body to get to his feet. He grabbed the wooden desk chair next to him and swung it at Lucinda, hoping to distract her so he could make it up to the attic and his knives, but she raised an arm to shield herself, and the chair shattered into splinters.

"Will you stop!" In a blurred flow of unnerving speed, she grabbed him and pulled him down onto the bed, her arms a steel cage around him, unyielding no matter how much he struggled. She pulled his head to one side exposing his neck.

"In a minute, you'll drink his blood," she said. "All of it. Every last drop."

The shivers wracking Geoffrey's body subsided. Wide-eyed, he pushed himself up on his hands so he could stare down at Callum, his entire body focused on Callum's neck.

"And you must do it slowly, savoring it. You mustn't gulp it down. You must drink him until his heart stops and the light in his eyes fades away. Do you understand?"

Geoffrey nodded, bobbing his head eagerly, a child about to open a present.

Callum knew—hoped—he wouldn't die, counting on his curse to hold and allow him to somehow foil Lucinda's plan and save Geoffrey from being turned, but he'd never been bled to the point of death before. How long would it take him to recover? Assuming this wasn't the one thing that could break his curse.

She sliced his neck open with a fingernail. He barely felt it.

"A tiny cut will be enough." She pressed a finger against his neck to stop the blood from flowing until she was ready.

"Please," said Geoffrey. "I'm so thirsty."

"Every drop, do you understand?"

Her brother bobbed his head. Were it not so gruesome, it might have been sweet.

She placed a hand on the back of his head and guided his mouth to Callum's neck, removing her finger so the blood could flow. Geoffrey latched on and began to suck.

"No, no," said Lucinda. "You mustn't be greedy. Let it flow into you. His life into yours."

Geoffrey stopped sucking, and Callum felt his tongue lapping against his neck. Between the battering and the blood loss, Callum's head began to swim. Geoffrey gagged and pulled away coughing, letting Callum's blood spill onto the rumpled bed sheets. Lucinda pressed a finger against the wound. Callum felt the itch that came whenever his body began to heal itself.

"What's the matter?" She stooped over her brother.

Geoffrey retched, spewing up Callum's blood, and clutched his throat.

"It burns," he croaked. "It's burning me."

A light began to glow deep within Geoffrey's body, growing brighter until it shone through his skin, illuminating arteries, veins, bones, and organs.

"Geoffrey!" She released Callum and tossed him aside. He pressed a hand against the cut in his neck to stanch the flow of blood as he sprawled across the floor.

"Help me!" Geoffrey reached out for his sister.

The stench of burning flesh filled the room as Callum staggered out the door, and a flash of heat seared his back. A bright explosion cast stark shadows on the corridor wall.

"GEOFFREY!" shrieked Lucinda, but Callum kept running, one hand pressing on the wound in his neck to keep the blood from seeping out.

He made it one floor up before Lucinda bore down on him, his knives still a lifetime away. She pushed him from behind, knocking him to his hands and knees. He lost more blood before he could reapply pressure to his wound.

"What did you do to him!" she shrieked.

He rolled onto his back and scrambled away from her across the floor as she stalked toward him and levered himself up the wall to his feet.

"Wild magic," he croaked. "Whoever told you I was dangerous was right."

He did his best to stand his ground, but it was all show. He had no idea how his blood had done that. A side effect of the Chaos within him reacting badly with the vampire contagion?

Without his knives, or even Rafe's cane, he had nothing to fight her with.

Nothing except his blood.

He hadn't lost much, less than a pint. How much could he waste before losing consciousness, he wondered as he removed the pressure from the wound.

"Stop that!" shrieked Lucinda.

The stench of sulfurous garlic rose around him as she tried to beguile him and failed. He smeared the blood on his neck, down his front, and on his hands. When he felt the first hint of wooziness creep up on him, he pressed the wound with his left hand so he could hold his other up like a weapon, fingers curled into claws.

He ran for her, staggering drunkenly across the few feet that separated them, but she slipped away in a shimmering blur. A second later he heard her hammering on the front door trying to get out.

"Let me out!" she shouted. "Let me out of this madhouse!"

While she tried to break through whatever Rafe had done to seal the building, Callum staggered up the last flight of stairs to the attic and his knives. His first stop was the bathroom for something to help put pressure on the wound. A bloody ghoul stared back at him from the mirror, the blood congealing into a sticky mess on his body and clothes.

No sooner had he retrieved one of his knives, still lying in its scabbard on a bookshelf, than Lucinda appeared in the attic doorway. He pressed the scabbard into the table with his knee to hold it fast as he pulled the blade free, and held the knife in front of him, a wadded-up facecloth pressed to his neck with his free hand.

"I don't know what you are," said the vampire, "but you can't hold me here."

He didn't bother to argue. He lunged and sliced at her with the knife, a foolish and desperate move. At his best, she would have dodged him easily. Half dead as he was, she blurred, and a ten-ton truck plowed into him and threw him against the wall. The knife and the facecloth fell from his hands.

As he scrabbled for the cloth to stanch the flow of blood, a fierce, concussive bang exploded in the room. Black-uniformed soldiers with heads obscured by face shields poured in through the door, semi-automatic weapons held at the ready. At the first sight of Callum lying bloody on the floor, the soldier in the lead turned on the dazed vampire and fired three short bursts into her. She screamed as her body ignited.

She burned like a Roman candle, reduced to nothing but ash in seconds.

A figure loomed out of the smoke and kneeled over Callum. Biggs snatched up the facecloth and pressed it against Callum's neck.

"MEDIC!" he shouted at the uniformed soldiers. "MAN DOWN!"

He scowled with worry as he crouched over Callum.

"Crikey, mate! Can't leave you alone for two seconds, can I?"

29

N O LESS THAN THREE different units from the Cottage traipsed through his attic while he sat patiently in his armchair waiting for the blood transfusion administered by the medic who had stitched up and bandaged the wound in his neck to finish. Jessica sat next to him, holding his hand, and Biggs hovered nearby, his jacket pulled tight around him as if shielding himself from a cold wind.

"How did this crew get past the witches," whispered Callum.

"Rafe brokered a truce. There's witches everywhere. I've never seen the Library this busy."

Even Esme Cavendish, who Callum had never even met before Trentham Abbey, had decided to pay them a visit, no doubt to make the most of the opportunity to gather as much information as possible about the Library and the witches' sanctuary. Callum imagined Rafe standing sentry in front of the doors to the collection, invoking the Royal Charter at anyone who attempted to pass.

"Geoffrey exploded?" asked Jessica, her spectacles perched on her head as she watched over him.

"Like I'd stabbed him in the heart with my knife."

Callum had been through the events of the night already with Cavendish as an assistant took copious notes, the interrogation ending abruptly when he recounted how Lucinda Cooke had said she had replaced the thralls of her master. Cavendish had disappeared downstairs to track this potential new vampire nest. The one good thing he could say about the Cottage was they gave a serious threat the consideration it deserved.

A member of the uniformed strike team picked up a journal from a shelf and began to flick through it.

"Hey," said Callum. "That's private!"

"Danny," said Biggs. "Do us a favor."

He went over and talked quietly to the agent who put the book down and cleared out, leaving Callum alone with him and Jessica.

"Cheers, mate." Biggs closed the door behind the agent and leaned against it. "You can chill out. They won't bother you anymore."

Jessica pulled Callum's blood-stained t-shirt closer to inspect it.

"See anything," he asked.

"A thick purple miasma. It's rich with Chaos."

"Bugger." They were going to have to go over his attic and the residence with a fine-toothed comb to be sure it was safe. "How come you never noticed this before?"

"You've never bled in front of me before." She dropped the shirt and wiped her fingers on his jeans. "Did you know that would happen?"

He shook his head. "I've never bled on a vampire before."

"Biggs." She slid her spectacles down and took Callum's hand. "Make yourself useful and get him some clean clothes."

"In the cupboard," said Callum as Biggs pushed away from the door. "Cheers, mate."

"When this is done," she touched the IV line hanging from the standing lamp by a plastic tie that dripped blood into his arm, "you should jump in the shower. This," she waved a hand to encompass him from head to toe, "is every shade of gruesome."

"Thanks, love. You're always so supportive."

She swatted his arm.

"Looks like you're done there," said Biggs as he brought over a pair of jeans and a t-shirt and put them on the table. "Let me."

With surprising gentleness, Biggs slid out the drip, tied it up and dropped it in the biohazard bag the medic had left behind, big enough for Callum's clothes as well. Callum stripped off his shirt and trousers, dropped them in, and put on the fresh clothes Biggs had brought him.

Moving tentatively, he got to his feet. Aside from the bruises from being knocked around by Lucinda Cooke, he felt okay. A soak in a tub of scalding hot water and a week of sleep would help, but he'd live. He always lived. He could already feel cool waves of healing spreading through his body.

"What time is it?"

He reached for Biggs's wrist to see his watch—it was eleven. Rory would be getting off work soon.

The agent's arm was cold, and his skin was dry.

"Are you feeling okay? You're ice cold."

Irritated, Biggs pulled his arm away. "Feeling a bit run-down, that's all."

Pieces of a puzzle Callum didn't know he had been assembling fell into place. He snaked a hand around Biggs' neck and pulled him close so he could smell him better.

"What the hell?!" Biggs pushed him away, but he'd caught a whiff: a faint odor of sulfur and garlic.

"I think you're infected. I think you caught the contagion at Trentham Abbey. In the fight in the house."

"What? No. The sun came up and shined on me and everything!"

"This is different. The contagion's changed. You've been exhibiting all the same symptoms as Geoffrey. Your grogginess, your hunger and thirst, and now the chill."

Callum's words began to sink in, and a look of horror spread across Biggs's face.

"Not all the symptoms." Jessica pushed her spectacles up on her head. "He's not beguiled."

"Maybe Lucinda and her master didn't know about him."

"Her master?" said Biggs.

"There was someone she answered to. Someone told her about me."

There was a knock on the door and one of the uniformed agents stuck her head in.

"We've got a lead on the nest. Cavendish wants all hands on deck."

"I'll be right there," said Biggs.

"She wants everyone downstairs now."

"I'll be right there!" Biggs snapped at her.

She scowled and closed the door. He dashed over to it and locked it.

"If they find out I might be infected," he whispered, "They'll shoot me on the spot. Or worse."

"What could be worse than that?" Jessica slipped her spectacles back on her head.

"They take people into one of the buildings and never let them out again, one of the alchemy labs. No one in the units knows what they get up to in there."

"Do we know for sure he's turning?" said Jessica.

Biggs began to swear, a whispered tirade of obscenities spewing from his lips.

"I suppose I could be wrong." Callum ran his fingers through his hair and found clumps of it stuck together with dried blood. "The smell of sulfur and garlic might be left over from the vampire."

"Sulfur and garlic!?!" Biggs sank into a crouch against the wall and buried his head in his hands. Jessica knew about Callum's scrambled senses, but it was news to the agent.

"Rafe could tell for sure," said Jessica. "He has the right equipment downstairs."

"You have to help me." Biggs, the big confident man, looked up at them like a small, frightened child. "Please. You have to help me."

"Even if you are turning, Lucinda Cooke was specific about what had to happen to finish the process," said Callum. "Don't drink anybody's blood slowly until they die, and you'll be fine."

Biggs whimpered and buried his head in his hands.

"Don't say anything," said Callum on the stairs. "Let me do the talking."

They reached the lobby to find a gaggle of agents surrounding Esme Cavendish all talking on enormous army field telephones. Four witches flanked them, scowling and crossed-arm pillars of discontent. Callum only recognized one of the women: Mrs. Dearing, the cheerful witch who had greeted them as they crossed the border into Cheyne Heath. He never would have imagined such a small woman could be so fearsome.

"Here he is, Ms. Cavendish," she said. "Up and about again, the poor dear. I think it's time you wrapped up here. Assemble your troops, and we'll escort you to the border."

Rafe took one look at the bloodied and disheveled Callum and rushed over to embrace him.

"Oh, my boy! I'm so glad to see you."

"Agent Biggs," said Cavendish. "The oracles were able to back-trace the vampire's movements since Trentham. We have three possible nest locations. I'm giving you Dickens Unit."

His own unit would be a huge deal for Biggs under normal circumstances, even if it were a field promotion.

"We have to keep Biggs here," Callum whispered in Rafe's ear. "He might have the contagion."

Rafe's eyes widened to the size of saucers, but he didn't let his dismay get in the way of what needed to be done.

"Mrs. Dearing, Ms. Cavendish," he called out as Cavendish and a worried-looking Biggs were halfway out the door. "A word please. It's important."

Mrs. Dearing grunted, the faintest wash of impatience shimmering across her expression. "What is it, Mr. Torvalds? It's time for your guests to be off."

"It's imperative that we have protection," said the librarian. "Lucinda Cooke came to us in search of her brother, and now both are dead. What if her mysterious master comes seeking revenge?"

Mrs. Dearing softened at the question. "Not a problem, at all. I'm sure I can find a witch or two to keep an eye on you."

"Ah, no, no." Rafe shot Callum a nervous glance. "Thank you so much for your kind and generous offer, but I feel someone from the Cottage would be preferable. In this instance."

Mrs. Dearing and Esme Cavendish both looked surprised. You could see the calculations running through Cavendish's mind. A presence in the Library would be a massive coup.

"Very well. If it's acceptable to all parties," she said, "I'll send a unit over."

"A unit?" Mrs. Dearing shook her head vigorously. "I'm afraid—"

"A unit won't be necessary," said Rafe. "Agent Biggs will suffice. He's worked closely with our team for some time now. His presence would not be a disruption, and he would be a perfect liaison."

The witch craned her neck to look up at Biggs standing next to her. Her hand slipped into a pocket in her dress.

"Very well," she said after a moment's consideration. "Yes. Yes, that will be acceptable."

Had the witches known all along Biggs was compromised by the vampire contagion? Was that why they let him into the sanctuary?

Cavendish turned to Biggs. "What do you say? It's up to you."

"I'll stay." The agent's poker face was once again firmly in place.

"Fine, but I want you in earshot." She handed him her field telephone. "Update the Cottage regularly, no matter how mundane the report, understood?"

"Yes, Ma'am."

A steady flow of intelligence from the Library would surely do wonders for her career. They'd have to figure out how to feed her only the least damaging information.

"That's settled, then." The witch beamed with satisfaction. She clapped her hands together. "Mr. Biggs can stay. Though, Ms. Cavendish, don't think this changes anything. Your kind are not welcome in Cheyne Heath. Mr. Torvalds, you would do well to hire more help. I'm sure poor Mr. Foster would welcome it."

She ushered Cavendish out.

The moment the door closed behind them, Biggs staggered and dropped the field telephone. Callum rushed over to catch him.

"I don't feel well," said Biggs. "I don't feel well at all."

Rafe led them down to a sub-basement Callum had only visited a handful of times, where the librarian kept all his analytical instruments. The floor was divided into a series of bays down each wall, each bay set off from the ones around it by half walls of wainscoting below and pebbled glass above. In each bay was a different device, some complex machines built out of cranks and clockwork, some made up of glass bottles filled with colored liquids suspended on metal frames, some nothing more than an oversize feather, a cotton sheet, or a cluster of lightbulbs, each on their own stand. He took them to a bay in the back where he asked Biggs to lie on a leather examination couch, a dentist's chair that could have been built by Dr. Frankenstein, and proceeded to strap straps to his body linked to the base of the chair by wires. Jessica watched, spectacles perched on her buzzed scalp, from a stool to one side.

His whole body shaking with cold, Biggs drew Callum near. "I have to tell you something."

"It's going to be fine. Rafe's taking care of it."

Standing behind the chair out of Biggs's line of sight, Rafe shot Callum a worried glance.

"Listen to me!" said Biggs between spasms of cold. "This is what she wanted. Cavendish. She told me to look for excuses to get me in among you. She's the one who sent me here after Trentham Abbey. To spy on you."

Though it wasn't a surprise to Callum, it was good to have his suspicions confirmed. "It's okay. We knew she'd try something."

"I don't deserve your help."

"Nonsense. I meant what I said. You're welcome here. We'll take care of you."

"Please lie back and try to relax, Agent Biggs," said Rafe.

Callum joined him at the console attached to the back of the chair as the librarian threw switches and turned dials. The chair began to vibrate quietly.

"This device will determine if there is any Chaos-borne interference in your body's natural functioning," said Rafe. "When I activate it in a moment, if it detects anything, we should see something register here."

Five backlit gauges lined the top of the control panel. Rafe flicked a switch and all five immediately maxed out, the pointers swinging all the way to the right. The machinery under the chair began to whine, and Rafe turned off the power. He exchanged a dark look with Callum and walked around the chair to face Biggs. "I'm afraid Callum was correct. There's no doubt you've been infected by this new vampire contagion."

"Something's happening." Jessica slid off the stool, and Biggs's eyes rolled back in his head. He began to convulse, the couch rattling beneath him as his arms and legs flailed around.

"Help me hold him down." Callum leaned over the agent, held his arms, and pressed his weight into the agent's torso to immobilize him as Jessica grabbed his ankles to still his legs.

Rafe opened a cabinet to reveal a wall of instruments but stood paralyzed before them.

"Do something!" shouted Callum.

Rafe seized a small blue velvet sack and rushed to Biggs's side. "Can you expose his chest?"

Callum clambered up on the couch so he could kneel on Biggs's pelvis and press his torso down with one hand as he ripped open Biggs's shirt with the other. Rafe removed from the sack what looked like a large rubber stamp the size of a man's palm with symbols embossed on the flat surface. He hesitated, the stamp held above Biggs's exposed chest. "This will hurt him—"

"Just do it!"

Rafe pressed the stamp hard into Biggs's skin, and the agent's entire body contracted, his mouth open in a silent scream. The librarian removed the stamp and the agent collapsed, unconscious, his body still. Smoldering on his chest was a charred brand of the symbols on the stamp.

"The sigils will arrest the progression of the contagion," Rafe stepped back and tossed the stamp onto a nearby tray, "but it won't last forever. It might not even last the night."

"Do you think you can get it out of him?" said Callum.

"It's not a foreign organism like a virus or a bacterium. The blood or saliva, or whatever entered his body from the vampires at Trentham, have catalyzed a change within him. He's as Chaos-kissed as any of us."

And that meant there was no cure.

Rafe looked at the equipment around him.

"Hopefully I can find something in the Library that will help him."

30

TO BE ON THE safe side, Callum and Rafe wheeled Biggs into one of the isolation cells at the far end of the sub-basement.

"You must get some rest," said Rafe. "Both of you. I'll take first watch. See you in the morning."

Callum and Jessica returned to the surface in silence, their feet dragging as they trudged up to the residence.

"You okay on your own?" she asked as they reached the landing of the common room and her and Rafe's bedrooms.

He hugged her. "I was going to ask *you* that."

"See you in the morning, then."

"Yep."

She shuffled down the corridor, arm held out so her fingertips could graze the wall.

In the attic, he ran himself a steaming hot bath. He could leave the dirty water in the tub overnight and use one of Rafe's devices to denature any threat it might cause to others in the morning. He stripped off his clothes and examined himself in the mirror. Dried blood was smeared all across his face and neck, his hands and chest. Downstairs, the grandfather clock chimed one, and the thought of Rory sprang into his head. Without thinking, he found Rory's number on the side table where the phone sat and dialed.

"You've reached Rory Mackay." The answering machine. Something so humdrum, but a lifeline to the real world outside the Library. "Please leave me a message after the beep."

"It's Callum." He had no plan for what he might say, so he let his exhausted mind tumble words out of his mouth. "I'm sorry for calling so late—"

The phone clicked.

"Callum! I'm sorry. I promise I wasn't screening."

"Did I wake you?"

"No, no. I was winding down with a video. Takes me ages to get to sleep after a shift."

"I'm so sorry for not coming to see you."

"S'okay. You said you might not be able to. I'm glad you called." With his Scottish accent, his "you" came out like an old-fashioned "ye," and Callum would have given anything to sink into his arms. "You had a busy night?"

"Yeah. It was kind of a shitshow. You remember that guy we were with the night you and I met?"

"Big chappy? Held himself like a soldier?"

"That's the one. He's a work colleague. His name's Biggs. He got … "

What could he tell Rory? He got bitten by a vampire and was about to turn into one himself?

"He got sick."

"Oh, I'm sorry. Is it bad?"

"Yeah. There might not be a cure."

"That's rough."

"Listen, it looks like my nights are going to be full for a while. I'm not going to have time to get together."

"That's okay. How about tomorrow for lunch? You could come over to my place."

Callum looked at his gruesome reflection, standing there naked and covered in blood. There was no way he could get into something intimate with anyone, no matter how much he liked Rory.

"Yeah, that sounds great. Can I bring anything?"

"No, it's fine. I'll make me Ma's haggis recipe."

"Um, okay."

"I'm kidding. I'm a vegetarian. No, just bring your handsome self. See you at one?"

"I'll be there."

It wouldn't be pleasant, but it was better to tell Rory in person he couldn't see him anymore. It didn't feel right to disappear like he usually did.

Callum awoke after five hours of sleep troubled by dreams of Rory and he being stalked through Trentham Abbey by a vampire with violet eyes. At least his body was clean after delaying sleep as long as he could to bathe before collapsing into bed. Now all he had to do was get the gear to denature the water from the equipment cases in the downstairs closet. He pulled on clothes and caught himself thinking he should spruce up his wardrobe to look good for Rory. He chided himself for being so vain and needy. What he wished he could have with Rory would never work.

In the common room, he found Rafe sitting at the table reading his way through a stack of books, taking notes on a pad so thumbed-through, the pages wouldn't lie flat. He looked dreadful, his hair oily and unkept, with great dark circles under his eyes.

"Didn't you get any sleep?" Callum shuffled over to the coffee maker to pour himself a cup.

Rafe looked up, startled.

"Oh, yes. Plenty of sleep." He returned to his work, reading and scribbling, scribbling and reading.

"How long?"

"Hmm?" Rafe didn't look up.

"How long did you sleep?"

"Oh, twenty, thirty minutes."

Coffee mug in hand, Callum sat next to him. "You have to stop. You're not going to do anyone any good without sleep."

He held Rafe's wrist so he couldn't write.

"I think I'm making progress." Rafe squinted at Callum, his face pleading, as if Callum might send him to bed without his supper. "Biggs seems to have stabilized. The sigils are working. If I can find the right combination, I might be able to devise tattoos like yours that will keep the contagion in check. Although, we'll have to find someone who can do them. Do you think the alchemist who did yours is still taking commissions?"

"He was older in nineteen-sixty-two than you are now. No, I don't think he's still taking commissions."

Rafe looked up from his work, his expression so distressed, Callum wished he hadn't said anything.

"But I'm sure I can find someone else to do it. Come on, let's get you to bed."

He took Rafe by the elbow to remove him forcibly from his books.

"But—"

"The books will be here when you wake up in a few hours, I promise you. Sleep's the best thing you can do for Biggs right now."

As he made sure Rafe changed out of his stale and ruffled clothing into his pajamas and got into bed, he wondered if this must be what having children would be like.

"There's a volume in the restricted collection I think might be … " Rafe trailed off as his head sank into the pillow and sleep overcame him.

He found Jessica pacing up and down aimlessly outside Biggs's cell, the door open.

"My turn," he said. "How's he doing?"

She joined him at the door.

"Rafe says he's okay," she whispered. "He's awake, but all he does is lie there."

"Yeah, I know how he feels."

They hugged, and Callum kissed her on the head.

"Check in on the old man, would you?" he whispered after her as she headed off. "I just got him into bed."

She nodded and shuffled away into the dark.

"Are you hungry?" Callum perched on an unforgiving wooden chair by the bed. Biggs lay in a fetal position turned toward the wall.

The glass of water on the side table was still full, the boiled egg and toast on the plate next to it untouched.

Callum sat in silence, Biggs's side rising and falling as he breathed, for what seemed like an hour.

"I don't feel anything," the agent mumbled to the wall. "Shouldn't I feel freaked out, or angry or something?"

"That's probably the sigils on your chest suppressing the Influence inside you."

Callum almost said 'magic,' but the word seemed trivial, fantastical, and he began to understand why the sorcerers called it Influence.

Biggs rolled onto his back.

"Is that what it's going to be like from now on? Either I'm sedated, or I'm a vampire?"

"Probably not." Callum did his best to sound hopeful. "Rafe thinks he can find something he can tattoo on your body that will keep you human. The Library has a long history of helping people."

Biggs looked at the tattoos on the back of Callum's arm.

"Like you?"

"Yep."

"When it happened to you, was it like this? Like me?"

Callum shook his head. "I don't remember how it happened. I lose my memory every fifty years." It felt strange to be so open with someone he had been at odds with for so long. "All those books upstairs in my room? Those are my journals, letters to myself telling me who I am, what I've done."

Biggs sat up and leaned his back against the wall. "There's hundreds of them. How old are you?"

"Don't know."

"When you lose your memory, what happens?"

Callum slumped back in the uncomfortable chair. He was all in now. "I wake up feeling like crap—"

"You wake up? It happens while you're in bed?"

"No, not last time. I was in Leicester Square. It felt like I was waking up from a bad night's sleep."

"And you lost all your memory?"

"Not all of it. I knew where I was. I knew how the world worked, but I didn't know who and what I was. And these were gone." He rubbed his hand up and down the tattoos on his arm. "Which is bad for everyone around me. Things start to malfunction. Not only equipment. People, too. And things appear, things they send your lot out to kill. But I didn't know that would happen. I was lucky this time. The Librarian back then kept me on a short leash."

"That was good of him."

"No, he was an arsehole. We hated each other."

Biggs laughed, a bark tainted with bitterness and regret, but at least it was an emotion.

"He got me back here and found someone to rework the tattoos, and I was fine."

"You got your memories back?"

Callum wondered what it would be like to have full memory of all his life. Could a brain even retain that much?

"No, but one of those books has everything important I need to know. It's like a how-to pamphlet." He put on his best BBC announcer voice. "'You've lost your memory and nearly killed people in the process. Here's how to put your life back together.'"

Biggs smiled again. Not a laugh, but Callum would take the victory.

"You got one of those for me?"

"Not written down, but Rafe, Jessica and I have all been through something similar. We can help you find your feet again."

Biggs's expression turned dark. He slumped six inches further down the wall, his body tense, his gaze locked onto nothing.

"So I can worry about turning into a vampire for the rest of my life?"

Callum sighed, leaned forward, and put what he hoped was a comforting hand on Biggs's ankle.

"I'm not going to lie to you, mate. It's not going to be easy. But the three of us have all learned how to make the best of it. We can help you do the same."

Biggs crossed his arms, hugged himself tight, and buried his chin in his chest. As Callum prepared to settle in for a long day, Biggs surprised him.

"What time is it?"

Callum looked around the room. No clock. He stuck his head out the door and found one on the wall.

"Almost noon."

"The Cottage will be expecting a report. Where's the field telephone?"

"Upstairs, I think. You okay on your own for a bit?"

"Yeah, but lock me in."

"That's not necess—"

"Lock me in!" Biggs growled.

Callum returned ten minutes later with the field telephone and Rafe, carrying an armful of books and looking much refreshed, in tow. They watched, impressed, as Biggs called in his report. He handled himself with more control than Callum thought he could have were their situations reversed, weaving a convincing story of dull, mundane goings-on.

"They have spare living quarters here. I'll have better access if I'm *in situ*. Nah, don't worry about it. I'll go back to my flat this afternoon and pick up my things."

"I can go to your flat for you," said Callum when Biggs had hung up. "Are you all set on your own? I have an errand to run."

I need to tell a hot guy I'm into I can't see him anymore.

31

Callum stopped for one last look in the mirror and shook his head, irritated at his own vanity. The idea was to break up with the guy, not seduce him. He felt a selfish heel for leading the man on when he had no place in his life for even a dalliance, let alone a relationship. They slept together once, and he was already planning out a life for the two of them. What a fool.

A knock on the door behind him startled him out of his reverie.

"Callum? May I come in?"

Edgar Newman stood smiling in the doorway in one of his many near-identical tweed three-piece suits, his white teeth and hair catching the noontime glow pouring in through the skylight.

"Edgar? What are you doing up here? Is something wrong?"

"I'm afraid there is, my darling."

A feeling of disjointedness, of being out of sync with reality came over Callum at the odd familiarity.

Edgar stepped into the room and closed the door behind him.

"It's my own fault," said the old scholar. "I should have known. You're so fiercely determined. You always have been. And so curious and inventive. I love you for it, but it's created a problem I can no longer ignore. If I don't do something about it, Sathanas will step in, and I can't put you in that kind of danger."

"What are you talking about, Edgar?"

He approached Callum and caressed his cheek.

Callum flinched at the unwelcome touch and knocked his hand aside. "You shouldn't be up here. The residence is private. Did Rafe invite you up?"

"I can't tell you how much it hurts me, my darling, to see you under these circumstances."

A blue shimmer like the reflection of water in morning sunlight shone across Edgar, and the dapper, white-haired man vanished, replaced by a tall and broad figure with chestnut brown hair that fell to his shoulders dressed in a deep blue frock coat with a loose white shirt tied at the neck, and slender blue trousers that tapered down to black leather boots. His face was perfect, every line, every feature beautifully proportioned. His skin was deep golden yellow, and his eyes were violet flecked with gold. The fragrance of grass and wildflowers and summer heat flooded over Callum and made him want to swoon, to fall into this creature's arms.

"Who are you?" he whispered.

"I am your lover, Callum. I am Emrys of the Sultry Glade, though you will not remember my name. You will not remember walking with me hand in hand through the summer fields of Annwn, nor lying with me under the stars. I promise you, my beloved, we will have our day again in twenty years when I shall pull the veil from your eyes and bring you into the light. We will be together, I promise you."

Part of Callum felt the twinge of threat, felt the distress of being held against his will, but whatever instinct he had to protect himself was drowned out by the man's beauty. This Emrys of the Sultry Glade reached caressed Callum's cheek once more, and Callum's entire body lit up with pleasure, every nerve ending alive as blood flowed to his extremities.

"Or perhaps, if my plan goes well, we will be together sooner. But that won't be possible if you continue on this path. Much as I detest it, I must humor Sathanas. I need his knowledge of the twilight realms if ever we are to make the crossing, and I am to have my revenge. I cannot allow you to interfere further."

He took Callum's hand in his and pushed up his sleeve to reveal the tattoos. Callum gasped as the beautiful man ran his fingertips over the exposed ink. His tattoos shivered across the entire span of his body.

"All I need is time, and this should buy it for us. I regret the pain it will surely cause you, but it cannot be helped."

Emrys of the Sultry Glade pulled Callum close and kissed him, parting his lips with his tongue, and Callum felt his breath leave him as if he might pass out.

Emrys pulled away from the kiss and Callum felt his edges soften as he lost himself in those violet and golden eyes.

"You will understand how important this is when next we meet, I assure you. You will see I could have acted no other way."

Callum stopped for one last look in the mirror and shook his head, irritated at his own vanity. The idea was to break up with the guy, not seduce him. He touched his fingers to his lips, remembering the pressure of Rory's mouth against his, the warmth of his tongue snaking into him. He wanted Rory so badly, wanted him by his side to bask in his presence, but he couldn't imagine a way to make it work.

A wave of anger filled him up. His fists clenched and all his muscles tensed with fury. The warded walls of his attic, which usually brought him comfort, felt like a prison cell, the thousand volumes of journals a weight that threatened to crush him.

Fuck the wild magic, he thought, that had robbed him of a normal, mortal existence. Fuck the curse that stopped him from falling in love and growing old and dying in his lover's arms. Why couldn't he enjoy the affections of a kind man who put Callum's wellbeing before his own? After everything Callum had done to help others?

He inhaled deeply and pushed the air out in a ferocious huff, blowing out all the worry, all the fear that kept him meek and withdrawn, that made him retreat to his cell and lock himself away.

His irrational fury had driven him across the neighborhood to Rory's door with every intention of taking what he felt he deserved, but the sound of the Scot's distorted lilt through the intercom blew all his selfish verve away. He slunk up the stairs, confused. Was it so wrong for him to want to be happy and to do something about it? He had a responsibility to make the most of his curse, to think of it as a gift that let him help so many people. His happiness meant nothing as long as others could be tortured by Chaos like him.

By the time he reached Rory's flat, he had no idea what to do.

"Hey, hot stuff." Rory grabbed him by the collar of his jacket, pulled him inside, and kissed him full on the lips.

Not wanting to be a jerk and pull away, Callum let the kiss linger, taking in the feeling one last time. He'd made up his mind.

"What happened?" Rory brushed his fingertips lightly over the bandage plastered over Callum's neck.

"Oh, nothing. Me being clumsy. What's that amazing smell?" Something delicious was cooking in the kitchen, and he used it as an excuse to break away.

"Baked farro, lentils, and feta cheese in a tomato sauce. It's nearly ready. Can I get you a drink?"

"A glass of water, please."

Rory winked and grinned. "Make yourself at home."

He disappeared into the kitchen. A small one-bedroom with a tiny kitchen that was little more than a closet off the living room, his flat was welcoming and comfortable: a plush sofa with a hand-knit blanket draped over the back; a sturdy coffee table with a large book of paintings by Turner and a ruffled copy of the Sunday paper; a television on a wheeled cart pushed to one side; a small bookshelf filled with well-worn paperbacks. There was even a stack of board games on one shelf. No magic, no artifacts imbued with Chaotic power, no stacks of journals of lives he couldn't remember. It was all so cozy and normal, and Callum wanted it with every part of him.

He took a seat at the small dining table, and they talked as Rory brought in a jug of water, glasses, and, finally, a pan of delicious food. They talked about the news, which Callum never read, television, which he never watched, and films, which he went to every free moment he had. Their conversation only paused when it was time to tuck in, and Callum became momentarily overwhelmed by the meal. He had eaten precious little in the last twenty-four hours and didn't realize how ravenous he was. He could wait a moment longer before breaking it off.

"How's your colleague doing?" said Rory eventually, bringing Callum back to earth.

Callum thought a moment before speaking, figuring out how to be truthful without giving anything away.

"He's stabilized. They think they might be able to help him after all."

"That's good. I'm glad to hear it. It seemed like you were all getting on well at the pub. He seems like a good guy."

Callum smiled, thinking of all the times out in the field he had wanted to kick Biggs in the backside for being an obstinate bastard. "He has his moments."

He almost reached for Rory's hand but stopped himself. This would be the time to break up with him, or he could let the moment pass into whatever was about to happen between them. Maybe he was making it harder than it needed to be. It wouldn't be the first time. Maybe there was a way to make this work.

Rory took his hand and kissed his palm. Callum let his body think for him.

"That was … " Rory sank back into the tangle of sheets and blankets, pulling Callum's arm across him. "Something else."

After the terror and the blood loss of the previous night, Rory's meal should have put Callum in a coma, but their lovemaking had been urgent and intense.

"Was that okay?" Callum worried he had ruined it letting himself be overtaken by his emotions.

"Yes!" Rory stroked Callum's cheek gently with the back of his hand. "Afternoon dates are my new favorite thing!"

Callum settled his head on Rory's chest. Taller and broader than Callum, he felt like a safe place to rest, even if only for a little while.

"What happened to your tattoos?" Rory stroked his arm.

Callum closed his eyes, ready to drift off. "Hmm?"

"They've gone. They vanished."

Callum awoke with a start and pushed himself up. His arms were bare. He jumped out of bed and went to the mirror on the cupboard door to look at his back. No tattoos. His pale skin was completely unmarked.

"No no no no!"

He grabbed his jeans from the floor and pulled them on, not bothering with his underwear. He could feel the wild magic building already, a nauseating heat burning deep within him, spreading up his spine.

"I'm sorry, I have to go!"

He pulled on his shirt and grabbed his shoes. The Library's Rover was shielded, protecting its passengers from the effects of Chaos, but it should work the other way around as well. If he could make it there in time, he could get back to the Library without causing too much damage.

"What's wrong?" Rory was out of the bed and halfway toward him before Callum realized.

"Stay back! I don't want to hurt you!"

Any genetic aberration in Rory's body, any hereditary cancer, could potentially erupt, full-blown, under the effects of Callum's wild magic and kill him.

"How are you going to—" Rory's eyes widened with fear. "Oh, no," he whispered.

A loud, concussive crack came from his body, and he doubled over, crying out.

"I have to get to the basement," he panted, breathing deeply to recover from the spasm.

Another crack rang out, and the Scot collapsed to his knees, threw his head back, and roared with pain. Before Callum's eyes, Rory's teeth began to lengthen and sharpen. His sprawling beard spread over the rest of his face. His eyes changed, his irises growing to fill his sockets, and his entire face began to lengthen.

"What's happening!?" Callum stood paralyzed, unable to comprehend the transformation afflicting Rory. The smell of cold, damp nights filled the room, a fragrance that would have been fresh and sweet were it not for the bitter, coppery taste of Chaos spreading in the back of his throat.

"Get out!" Rory's voice deepened into a low-pitched growl as his thick, dark hair spread down his naked back. "I could hurt you. Or worse!"

"If it's a curse, you can't hurt me." Torn between fleeing and helping, Callum stooped over him.

"The basement!" Rory's voice was barely more than a dog's howl. The transformation accelerated, Rory's body cracking and reforming itself until the man was gone in the blink of an eye.

A fierce, snarling wolf crouched where he had fallen.

"Fuck," said Callum.

The wolf, three times the size of any wild canine Callum had ever seen at London Zoo, readied to leap at him.

Callum leapt first, and their two bodies slammed into each other. He wrapped his arms around the wolf and pinned it to the ground, steering clear of the ferocious jaws that snapped at him. He slipped an arm around the wolf's shoulder and head in a half nelson wrestling hold, pressing its head down into its chest. The wolf struggling against him every step of the way, Callum stumbled to his feet and hauled the beast out of the bedroom.

The house was a small, modern building—one of the few new buildings in the run-down neighborhood of Cheyne Heath—with thick walls and sturdy faux-industrial doors. He lugged the snarling, writhing beast down past the front door to the one other flat in the building without anyone coming out to see what the commotion was, and found the stairs to the basement in the back. Heat searing up through his spine into his brain, he managed to get the two of them safely downstairs. A storage room stood on each side of the building with heavy security doors facing each other across a short passage between them.

One was open, the door ajar. Callum shouldered his way through and, with all his might, hurled the wolf into the room. The wolf growled and twisted to get back on its feet, but Callum slammed the door shut just as the wolf threw itself at it.

The door held, the wolf's body creating little more than a muffled thud. A heavy chain and padlock hung from the door. Callum slipped the chain through the handle and clicked the lock shut. He peered through the door's small, wire-reinforced window. The wolf paced in circles around the empty cell, snarling and howling, but no sound came through the door.

Rory had been prepared.

Heat bloomed in Callum's head, his temples afire with pain so intense he staggered and collapsed to the floor as the bulb in the overhead light grew brighter and brighter until it exploded and plunged the basement into darkness.

32

IT TOOK HIM A moment to recover from the surge of Chaos. The muffled howl of the wolf—was it still Rory?—seeped through the storage room door as he rolled over onto his hands and knees and used the wall to steady himself. His shoes, socks, and underwear were all upstairs, but at least he had the keys to the Rover in his pocket. The car was parked a few doors down. If he ran, he could get to it in under a minute, minimizing the amount of damage he might cause on the way. He walked the five paces to the stairs. The surges of wild magic in his body were coming in slow pulses, with the same ebb and flow as waves crashing on a beach. Each surge made him wobble on his feet, but he thought he could make it.

The house was dark as he made his way up to the ground floor, the electrics taken out by the Chaos. He opened the front door and stuck his head out to get a bead on the car, keys in hand. The street, a small residential back street in a quiet part of Cheyne Heath, was empty. He put his head down and ran the dozen yards to the car, setting off car and house alarms as he passed, but he made it into the Rover without causing anyone damage.

"Please work." He turned the key, hoping the car's shielding would protect its mechanisms. To his relief, the engine growled into life.

He found a parking space in front of the Library and dashed inside, not bothering to pull the bolt and lock the door behind him. He made it to the first floor of the residence without seeing anyone, only to run headfirst into Jessica on the landing, bowling her over.

"Callum!" She untangled herself from him. "What's … Oh!"

Another surge of Chaos raged up his spine and radiated out of him. Jessica's eyes shone like golden stars through the sapphire lenses of her spectacles. She collapsed back and shook, her body wracked with some kind of seizure. He hovered over her, unsure if he should try to help, or if running away would give her the best chance of recovering from the mess he had brought down on her.

"RAFE!" He cried out at the top of his lungs. "RAFE!"

A salt-and-pepper mop of tousled hair stuck itself out of the common room door.

"Dear boy, what is it?" He saw Callum and Jessica entangled on the floor and ran toward them, dropping his cane.

Callum sprang up and retreated to the stairwell. "Stay back! Don't come any closer!"

Rafe stopped a few feet from Jessica as another wave rushed up Callum's spine. He backed up the stairs to hide behind the wall.

"Something happened to my tattoos." He showed Rafe the pale, unmarked back of his arm. Rafe's eyes widened as a golden shimmer rippled across his body.

"Bugger!" Rafe's skin became coated in a layer of dust. He raised his arms and they disintegrated into sand that poured from the sleeves of his shirt and spilled over Jessica on the floor. "I'm afraid I'm not going to be use—"

His entire body disintegrated.

Callum wailed, turned, and ran up the remaining stairs. He reached the attic breathless, slammed the door shut, and threw himself on the bed, sobbing.

He had no way of knowing how long it took him to pull himself together, but the violent surges of wild magic stabilized into a steady flow that made Callum giddy, like he was high. He began to pace the attic floor, his mind racing as he tried to think of what to do. He tried calling the emergency line of the Cottage for help, but the phone line buzzed and whined loudly when he held the handset to his ear, the sound of children cackling echoing in the background.

Neither Jessica nor Rafe had been downstairs with Biggs, so perhaps they felt he had stabilized enough that he no longer needed supervising. Perhaps he would make his way up from the Hidden Galleries eventually, would see Jessica and call for help.

He roared with frustration, not daring to leave the protection of the attic for fear of making everything worse.

Exhausted by the pacing, he was curled up in a corner when a knock came at the door.

"Callum?"

It was Jessica. Still giddy from the ebb and flow of wild magic surging within him, he clambered across the floor.

"Sweetie, are you okay?" He pressed his cheek against the door.

"I'm … I'm fine. Johnny's here. He helped me snap out of it."

"What happened to you?"

"I had a vision. I got lost … " The bewilderment and confusion in her voice hit Callum like a hammer. He had done that to her. He pressed his hand into the door as if he might reach through it and comfort her. "I need to put Rafe back together."

"There's a box on the dresser in his bedroom. It has everything you need—"

"I know, I know. He gave me the lecture."

"Callum, ducky." Johnny's melodious voice seeped through the door into Callum's brain and calmed the churning anxiety in his body the tiniest fraction. "I don't quite understand what's going on, but she's a strong girl, and she's coping well. Put her aside in your mind so we can focus on you. What do you need? It's dangerous for you to come out, I take it."

"I have tattoos that keep the magic inside me in check, but they disappeared. I don't know why. I need to find someone to redo them, someone who won't be affected. There was an alchemist in the sixties who did it for me, but I doubt he's still alive."

"The sixties?" Johnny's surprise was evident in his voice. "I didn't realize you were so long-lived. You must give me the number of your plastic surgeon."

Callum laughed despite himself.

"Don't worry," said the sorcerer. "I know the perfect person to work on you. She's extremely gifted. You'll love her. Hang tight. The cavalry is only a heartbeat away."

"Wait, there's something else."

"I'm at your service, sweetie darling. You're not my first princess trapped in a tower."

"Do you know about Rory?"

How do you out someone for being a werewolf?

"Do I know about Rory, ducky? You'll have to be more specific."

"When it's unchecked, the magic inside me sometimes triggers things in people, things they prefer to keep hidden. I was with Rory when the tattoos vanished."

"Ah. I see. Yes, our Rory is a bit of a Diamond Dog, isn't he. A moonwalker, a Hound of the Wild Hunt."

Relief flooded through Callum. He wanted to cry. "He changed. I managed to lock him up in a storage room in his basement before he did any damage. Can you check on him for me?"

"Consider it done. Keep your chin up, love. Help is on the way."

He found the volume of his journals that contained the detailed instructions on how to recreate the tattoos, and sat with his back pressed against the door as if somehow being as close as possible to the outside world might set him free all the sooner.

"Dear boy," came Rafe's voice eventually through the door. "I'm all back together. Jessica did an exemplary job."

"Johnny's getting help. He says he has someone to do the tattoos."

"Well, that's excellent," said Rafe. "Jessica and I shall remain here with you until they return."

"How is Biggs?" There was so much shielding between the Hidden Galleries and the rest of the building, it was unlikely the agent would have been affected, but Callum still dreaded the thought.

"He's doing quite well, under the circumstances," said Rafe. "You have nothing to worry about. Get some rest until help arrives."

"Where's Jessica?"

"I'm here," came her voice from beyond the door. "I'm fine, too. You don't have to worry about me."

"What was your vision?" said Callum. "When you collapsed."

"It was you." Her voice was weak, shaken. "In the countryside. You were bound to an altar in the middle of a ring of stones, like Stonehenge, but smaller, all carved with symbols. A tall man with violet eyes had a hand on your head. He held a large gem in his other hand above you. You were screaming, Callum. You were in so much pain. I tried to help you, but I couldn't—Oh, thank god."

"Hello dears," came a new voice, a woman. "Millicent Hargreaves, at your service. Johnny tells me someone needs some Crafted inking. Would someone put on the kettle? We'll have a cup of tea, and you can tell me all about it."

33

"VERY WELL," SAID Millicent. "Your friends have retreated to safer pastures. I'm coming in."

"Wait!" Callum pressed his hands into the door as if the witch might suddenly barrel through. "Are you absolutely certain you can protect yourself? The alchemist who helped me last time had an entire suit of copper mesh."

"I've been a hard-working woman since I was thirteen, Mr. Foster. I can assure you I know how to protect myself. Now, open the door."

He unlocked the door and opened it a crack before darting to the other side of the attic, getting as far away as he could. The door swung open and there stood a slender woman of medium height in her early thirties. Her hair was an artful mess of tightly wound tufts and short, thin braids. She wore a knee-length dress of bright pink cotton with royal blue puffy mohair knitted sleeves, and her round, makeup-less face was adorned with five pale jewels glued above each eyebrow. She carried with her a large leather case, like an old-fashioned doctor's bag.

The fingers of her free hand touched a bee-shaped brooch pinned to her dress, probably her talisman, the source of a witch's power. She smelled to Callum, as did all witches, of nothing, a void in his senses that always unnerved him.

She grimaced. "Ugh, I see what you mean. Nasty. How on earth did you get yourself into this mess?"

"No idea." He shrugged. "Can't remember."

She smirked at his weak attempt at levity. "How unfortunate. Well, fear not. We'll have you back out and about in no time."

She strode over to the bed, put down her doctor's bag, and opened it up to peer inside and remove a leather box and a stack of white hand towels which she placed on the bed.

"So, what is it you want done? A heart with barbed wire around it? A rose with your mother's name? I'm particularly fond of mermaids." She smiled with such humor and confidence that, for a moment, Callum felt that things might turn out all right.

"Here." He handed her the volume with the tattoo design schematics. She took it and flicked through the pages to look at the instructions.

"Ingenious." She looked up at him and touched her bee brooch. "Yes, I get the general idea."

She shut the book and tossed it onto the side table.

"Don't you need to examine it more?" The alchemist had stopped every five minutes to check the diagrams.

She shook her head.

"It's pretty simple, but very old-fashioned. There's improvements I can make. All right." She put her hands on her hips. "Get your kit off, and we'll start."

He hesitated, suddenly awkward at the prospect of stripping naked before her.

"Lady, preserve us." She waved dismissively and returned to her case to take out more equipment. "I've seen it all before, and I'm not the least bit interested. Lie face down on the bed, please."

The process was as arduous as he remembered, but Millicent worked quickly and efficiently, starting at his neck and making her way down the length of his body. With every jab of her needles, with every line and swirl etched across his skin, he began to feel better, the wild magic calming itself, turning from a stormy sea to a bubbling hot spring. By the time she got to his heels, the late afternoon sun blazed through the window, lighting up the wall in a golden glow, and his head was clear.

"All right." She wiped off her needles and put her equipment away. "There you go. I adapted the sigils so the tattoos can interface more smoothly with the Influence inside you. And I reinforced the binding. It'll be much harder to burn off. It might give you a chance to get somewhere safe before it's all gone."

He started to get up, but she touched his head lightly to stop him. "Stay put until sunset and the evening star hangs in the firmament. You don't want anything touching the ink until the sigils have cured in."

"I don't know how to thank you," he said, his face half muffled by the pillow. Artifact dealers always wanted hard cash, but witches and alchemists usually operated on a barter system, and having the Library of the Damned owe you one was nothing to sneeze at.

"One good turn deserves another. I'll send your friends in. You can move around, but no sitting or leaning against anything until sunset, understood?"

"Got it. Thank you."

"How is he?" Rafe stood with Jessica at the door as she left. They must have been waiting there for hours.

"Right as a river," said the witch. "You can go in."

"If it's not an imposition, could I ask for your advice on another matter?"

"I'm here to help. May I use your kitchen to clean up?"

"Two flights down. The loo is at the end of the hall."

"The kitchen will do for now." She disappeared downstairs.

"It's good to see you in one piece, old man. I'm so sorry." Rafe sat on the bed, Jessica next to him, and Callum did his best to dispel the discomfort he felt to be lying face down and stark naked in front of them. "What happened?"

"I don't know. I was with Rory, and the tattoos suddenly faded."

"You were *with* Rory?" said Jessica. "Must have been some hot sex."

He swatted her knee in a playful rebuke, careful not to touch anything with the back of his arm. "There's nothing like it in the journals. It's never happened before."

"Except for when you lose your memory," said Rafe.

Callum buried his face in the pillow trying to make sense of it.

"Why now?" He turned his head to the side to be heard. "With all this vampire stuff happening? According to the journals I've lost my memory every fifty years like clockwork for centuries. Why did the tattoos burn out twenty years early? And why didn't I lose my memory?"

"All good questions, dear boy. And we'll discover the answers together."

There was a tentative knock on the open attic door.

"Is it okay if I come in?" said Rory. "Your friend let me up."

"Guys," said Callum. "Could we have a moment?"

"Of course." Rafe patted Callum awkwardly on the back of his head, one of the few safe places to touch him until the tattoos were set. "I'll see if Ms. Hargreaves can help us with our downstairs guest. Come on Jessica, dear. Let's leave these two young ones in peace."

Jessica snorted a laugh.

"Watch it, girl," said Callum, feeling good at being able to joke with someone despite everything that had happened.

He crawled backwards to slide off the bed without turning and smudging the ink and pulled the top sheet with him to cover himself. Even though he and Rory had seen each other naked, this conversation would be hard enough without being completely exposed, the fresh tattoos throbbing with heat on his back.

"Are you okay?" they both said at the same time and laughed.

"We should talk about what happened," said Rory.

"Yeah." Callum nodded, but they both stood there awkwardly, neither of them able to start.

"This was all because of my curse," Callum blurted out, desperate to fill the silence. "It usually happens every fifty years. The wild magic inside me burns out of control, and I lose my memory."

Rory frowned, confused. "But you know who I am? Who you are?"

"It was different this time. The tattoos got burned away, but I didn't blank out. I've no idea why."

"Wait, *every* fifty years? But you're, what, thirty at most?"

"I'm older than I look. Those books?" he gestured with his free hand to the laden shelves. "They're my journals. They go back seven hundred years, but I think I'm older than that."

Rory opened his mouth to speak, but no words came out. He sank to the armchair and rubbed his face, trying to knead the reality of what Callum had said into his consciousness.

"You're immortal," he said.

Callum exhaled deeply. And shrugged. "Maybe? Immortal's a big word. I'm hard to kill. And, so far, it seems I can't be cursed a second time. That's why I wasn't afraid to help you when you changed."

Rory frowned. "You're hard to kill? That means people have tried to kill you in the past."

Callum nodded. "I wasn't entirely truthful with you. Working for the Library isn't only dealing with books. I help people like me and you. People who have been Chaos-kissed."

Rory frowned again and stood. "I'm not Chaos-kissed. I'm not cursed."

It was Callum's turn to frown. "You turned into a wolf. I had to lock you up in the basement."

"Aye, I did, but it's nae a curse. It's my birthright. It's something I'm proud of. I'm a Hound of the Wild Hunt."

"I'm sorry, but you were worried you were going to kill me."

"We only ever don our hound-body at the full moon. I was raised to know how to protect others from the hound. Normally, you would have been perfectly safe from me. I didn't expect to transform at two o'clock on a Thursday afternoon, three days waning gibbous, and especially not here."

"Why not here?"

"The witch's sanctuary. It's the only place where the hound can remain asleep. When I left Colmuir, I had to conceal my hound-body, or my people would find me and take me back. Someone told me if I could find a witch, they could make me one of these."

He stood and held out the carved bead on the leather cord about his neck. "It only works in Cheyne Heath, in the witch's sanctuary."

"Why do you have a cell in your basement, then?"

"It's the way I was raised. My people might be homophobic, insular bigots, but they know how to keep themselves safe."

Rory took Callum's free hand.

"Careful of the ink," said Callum.

Rory dropped it. "I'm so sorry."

Callum checked the back of his hand. "No harm done."

"Callum, the change was different this time. When I transform, I usually lose all sense of myself, and the hound takes over. This time, it was me in my hound-body. I was acting wild because I freaked out, but after you left, I calmed down. I was fully myself. That's never happened before. I've never even heard of it in the loresongs."

"You're not a werewolf?"

Rory chuckled. "No, I'm not a werewolf. Me mam used to tell us if we misbehaved, the werewolves would come in the night and take us. If I wound someone, they don't become like me. I'm not cursed."

Outside, the last warm glow of daylight above the rooftops died, and the ink on Callum's back cooled all at once. He should be happy. The unchecked Chaos within him had done no permanent harm, and Rory wasn't someone else he needed to save. His change had an explanation, a strange one that would take some time to get used to, but he wasn't in a position to hold it against the handsome Scot. And yet, something within him wouldn't let him be at ease, as if it were only a matter of time before another unknown disaster befell him and the people he cared for.

"A Hound of the Wild Hunt? What does that mean?"

Rory grinned. "It's a stupid legend about where we came from. When the faeries still walked the land, we were their stewards. We would take on our hound-bodies at the equinox and solstice and run beside our faery lords when they rode out to put the fear into the hearts of the people. Now we sit around making babies, pining for the old ways, and waiting till our faery overlords return. It's a nightmare. It's why I left. They were going to force me to have babies with a kinswoman from Ireland."

Callum went to the window to make sure the sun had fully set. The evening star glittered above him. He shivered from the chill in the room and not as a sign from his tattoos that something was amiss. He wrapped the sheet around his shoulders for warmth.

"Callum, I like you. I like you a lot. I know this is new, and my situation is complicated, but I think we could be good together."

"*Your* situation is complicated?" Callum turned away from the window to face him and pulled the sheet tighter. "In twenty years, you'll be pushing fifty and I'll still look like this. If we still know each other, this," he reached an arm out from under the sheet to show Rory the tattoos running up it, "will happen again, properly this time. If we're still together, I'll forget you completely."

"Twenty years is a long time."

Rory took a step toward him, but Callum moved away and picked up one of the journals on the table by the armchair.

"It's not, though. Not for me."

Rory came up behind him and slipped an arm lightly around his waist.

"My whole life," said Rory, "I was forced to keep my needs in check, to hide who I was and to put my kin first. I came here to get away from that, to follow my desires. I want you, Callum. I'm willing to take the risk that you'll forget me in twenty years, if you're willing to be with someone whose relatives assume their hound-bodies and run wild under the full moon."

He leaned in and kissed Callum on the bare, unmarked skin of his neck.

A week ago, Callum would have said no, would have sent Rory packing. Even this morning, he had fully intended to break it off, but something had changed within him. Standing in his attic cell with the people he loved and had hurt downstairs, he felt trapped by his curse, held hostage and abused by it, forced by it to live a life he didn't want. And here was a man who he did want who was offering himself to him.

He turned into Rory's embrace and let the sheet slip from his shoulders.

<h1 style="text-align:center">34</h1>

THEY KISSED, PRESSING THEIR bodies into each other, Callum growing aroused against the rough denim of Rory's jeans, but their embrace wasn't about sex. They had seen each other for who they truly were. Their secrets were out in the open, and they were choosing each other with open eyes.

"Callum!" Rafe burst in. "Wonderful news. We might have a solution for Agent Biggs. Oh!"

At the sight of Callum and Rory's embrace, his face flushed, and he ducked back behind the door.

"Apologies, dear boy. That was indescribably rude of me. Carry on, carry on! We're all down in the kitchen if you want to join us."

He pulled the door shut behind him.

Callum sighed.

"I can go if you're needed." Rory nuzzled Callum's ear.

"I should head down and see what's going on. It's a tiny corner of Bedlam here at the moment." He went to the cupboard and took out clean underwear and clothes. "Come with me. Maybe you can provide a fresh perspective."

He did his best to fill Rory in as he dressed, half expecting the man to excuse himself never to be seen again, but Rory took it all in his stride. Perhaps when your entire family turns into wolves at the full moon, your mind is more open than most. Even talk of vampires didn't faze him.

The common room was packed with more bodies than Callum had ever seen in there. A group of witches Callum had met once or twice before, friends of one of Rafe's exes, had taken over the kitchen. A huge copper pot sat bubbling away on the stove, tended to by a diminutive, rotund bundle of witchy cheer wielding a hairbrush in one hand and a wooden spoon in the other. At the table a gray-haired Indian witch dressed in a vibrant teal and gold sari sat knitting strands of copper wire, straw, fabric, and yarn into a tight band at a furious pace, gossiping with a Chinese witch dressed in a canvas shirt and denim skirt with close-cropped hair. Rafe sat on the couch chatting with his ex, Agnieszka, a stern Polish witch Callum had never got on with, even though his friend had doted on her. Tucked away in a dark corner, Millicent and Jessica sat on a plush bench leaning toward each other with the unmistakable body language of attraction. It looked like Callum wasn't the only one getting lucky tonight.

"Rory, darling!" The final visitor to the common room, a witch with flowing jet-black hair, dark eye-makeup, and an elegant black satin blouse, threw her arms in the air at the sight of the tall Scot and rushed over to embrace him. "How marvelous to see you!"

"Aren't you a sight for sore eyes." Rory hugged her back. "How're the boys?"

"Timothy is his usual sweet self, and Edmund gets worse and worse. I don't know what I'm going to do with him." She rolled his wooden bead in her fingers. "Johnny tells me this failed. I'm so sorry. I don't know how it could have happened."

"There were unforeseen and exceptional circumstances. Gosha, this is my friend, Callum."

"Your friend? How lovely!" Her eyes sparkled as she offered Callum her hand. "Gosha Armitage. Delighted to meet you. My mother," she nodded toward Agnieszka, "has told me all about you."

As Callum shook her hand, she slipped her free hand into the pocket of her jeans, and Callum felt a tingle across his tattoos.

"Hm." Gosha raised an approving eyebrow. "Millie did an excellent job, as usual. She's got you locked down tight."

"Ladies!" trilled the witch at the stove. "Your presence is requested!"

"Come see me next week." Gosha patted Rory's chest and peeled away from them. "I'll have another stab at the charm. And bring Callum. Elsie, what have you got?"

The other witches converged at the stove, Rafe's ex, Agnieszka, and Millicent Hargreaves leaving their romantic entanglements to join in. The grandfather clock outside chimed eight.

"Oh, crap." Rory looked at his watch. "I'm going to be late for my shift. I have to go. I'm sorry."

"No worries." Callum squeezed his hand. "Want to come back here after?"

"It'll be after midnight."

Callum cocked a thumb at the witches gathered over the pot on the stove. "I'm sure this will take a while. I'll keep an ear open for the doorbell."

Rory pulled him into a short, hard, passionate kiss that took Callum's breath away.

"I'll be back." Rory grinned and disappeared into the hall.

"Did I hear right." said Jessica. She and Rafe joined him to watch the witches work. "He's a wolf in sheep's clothing?"

"A hound, apparently. Of the wild hunt."

"Look at you, walking on the wild side." She elbowed him affectionately in the ribs, and he wrapped an arm around her, squeezing her close.

"The two of you look like you're having a good night," he said. "Will we be seeing more of Agnieszka and Millicent?"

They both made dismissive noises that Callum found entirely unconvincing.

The other witches stepped out of the way so Millicent could join the diminutive round witch at the stove. With one hand touching her bumble bee brooch to access her power, she leaned over the pot and wafted the fumes toward her.

"Very good, Elsie. That will do nicely."

The witch, Elsie, beamed from ear to ear.

"Shreya." Millicent turned back to the Indian witch. "Do you have the cuff?" Shreya handed her the completed three-inch band of knitting. "Thank you."

Elsie passed Millicent a ladle. She placed the cuff into its bowl and dipped it slowly into the liquid, letting it soak it up into its fibers, and stirred the pot. All six witches began to mutter to themselves under their breath, and tingling waves spread across Callum's tattoos from his heels to his head.

"This is fascinating," whispered Jessica, pushing her spectacles up on her head. "I can see them all vividly all of a sudden."

The tingling grew in intensity across Callum's back, strengthening to sharp pricks until it abruptly stopped, and the witches grew silent. Millicent drew the ladle out, the cuff in its bowl. The knitting had turned from yarn and wire into a tight mesh of copper and gold. She placed it in her palm and presented it to the others, who all hemmed and nodded approvingly.

"I think this might work." The gems over her brows caught the light and glimmered as she widened her eyes with delight.

The crowd was more than the rickety lift could manage, so Callum manned the control panel, ferrying the witches down to see Biggs in small groups.

"You and Rory look good together," said the witch Gosha, in the last group to go down along with her mother. "He's a good man.

Strong. Reliable. Always there when you need him. He's helped me out many times."

"You make him sound like a house dog," said Agnieszka. "He's a wild animal. And you let him live in our home! He could have savaged us in our beds!"

"And yet," said Gosha, not bothering to turn and address her mother directly, "he did nothing of the sort. In fact, he stopped your goose from being cooked how many times? Three, was it?"

Agnieszka harrumphed, scowled, and forcefully crossed her arms. Callum hadn't seen her in a year or so, but she was as cranky as ever.

"I understand you know my mother quite well," said Gosha, turning a tart gleam in her eye on Agnieszka. "Imagine my surprise to learn today for the first time my own mother has been having a torrid affair."

"I don't know about torrid." Callum stopped the elevator at the right floor, steadying himself as it lurched. "Rafe's more the quiet type."

"He is a kind and generous man," snapped Agnieszka. "And enough of a gentleman to keep a hard-working woman's business to himself!"

Callum opened the gate and Agnieszka stormed out, her daughter at her heels.

"How could you not tell me you had a boyfriend … "

Callum left them to bicker as they walked ahead of him to join the rest of the group at the other end of the sub-basement, the witches craning their necks to see into the work bays around them, taking in as much as they could. It was a good thing Rafe had no one to answer to aside from the mysterious current Master of the Dagger of Buckingham Palace, who let Rafe get on with it. According to Callum's journals, the Library wasn't always given this much rope. The Hidden Galleries were hidden for a reason.

The witches and Jessica had fanned out around the door to Biggs's cell. Rafe stood in the open doorway. The room was dark. Rafe reached in and flicked the light switch on and off, but nothing happened.

"Um, Callum?" He stepped away from the door. "Would you be so kind?"

Wishing he had thought to retrieve his knives before coming down—before the previous night, when had he ever needed them in the safety of the Library?—he ducked into the nearest bay and found a scalpel on a worktable before pushing through the crowd.

"Excuse me, ladies."

The witches, more excited than perturbed at the prospect of a vampire in the next room, parted for him.

"He's very dashing, isn't he?" whispered the portly witch, Elsie, loud enough for everyone to hear. "If I were a younger woman … "

"If you were a younger man, maybe," said the Chinese witch, and Elsie tittered, her laughter a musical pealing of bells that echoed through the dark gallery.

The air in the cell stank of garlic and sulfur, but Callum didn't know if the intensity was something to do with Millicent's tattoos. Not sure what good it would do if Biggs had fully turned, he held the scalpel down by his side.

"Hey, mate," he said from the doorway. "We've got you more help."

He edged his way deeper inside, his eyes adjusting to the dim light from beyond. Biggs had buried himself under the covers and turned to face the wall. Callum could hear him muttering to himself.

"What's that, mate?"

He crept toward the bed and perched on the table beside it.

"The temple burned," whispered Biggs. "The shrine to his majesty was reduced to rubble and ash. Wave after wave of the traitor's minions swarmed over the battlements. The dukes of Hell turned on their master and tried to kill him, but he was still too powerful. Even the dagger forged from a dragon's heart extracted from the molten cauldron at the center of Hell wasn't enough to kill him, so they exiled him. They cast him out of Hell to walk among us."

Biggs rolled over onto his back, and his eyes glimmered blue in the faint light from outside. Callum lurched back, but he wasn't fast enough.

Biggs lashed out and snatched his wrist, holding him fast with a hand like cold iron.

"He seethes with anger. I can feel it. If he finds out I'm here, he'll come for me, Callum. Don't let him take me!"

He released Callum's wrist and curled up into a ball, the twin glimmers of predator's eyes extinguished.

Callum sat on the edge of the bed.

"It's okay, mate." He put a hand on Bigg's back, ready to lurch away if Biggs should attack, but the agent sobbed into the mattress. "We've got you help. I don't know if it will bring you all the way back, but I promise I'll find a way if it doesn't."

He sat like that in the dark, gently stroking the agent's back until his sobs faded away.

"I'm going to turn the light on, okay?" he said eventually and reached for the lamp on the bedside table.

The dim bulb shone like a beacon in the dark illuminating Biggs's face. His skin was pale, almost white, even in the warm glow of the lamp. Dark circles lined his eyes.

"We're ready for you," Callum called back to the door.

Millicent edged in, her jewels reflecting the lamplight, as the others crowded around the doorway to see. She took a chair from the wall and sat next to the bed.

"Don't worry, Agent Biggs." She placed a small, quilted handbag made in the shape of an earth globe on the bedside table. "You're under my care, now."

From the handbag, she took out a blue silk handkerchief embroidered with symbols in gold and copper thread, a large, faceted crystal button, and the cuff the witches had been working on, laying them out on the small table. "Lie on your back, please."

Biggs didn't move, so Callum rose to ease him into position. "Come on, mate, let's get you tucked in."

Millicent tensed at the sight of Biggs's reflective eyes and deathly pallor, but otherwise suppressed her reaction, her expression a mask of serene calm. Callum got him onto his back.

"He's so angry, Callum," Biggs whispered. "Don't let him get me."

"I won't. I promise. You lie back and do what Millicent tells you, okay?"

Biggs nodded and pressed his head into the pillow, closing his eyes.

"The recipe will take a few minutes to complete," said Millicent. "I need you to remain perfectly still for the duration, understand?"

Eyes closed, Biggs nodded again.

"If he starts to move around," she leaned in to Callum to whisper, "you'll need to restrain him."

She reached across the bed to place the crystal button in Biggs's right hand, and then the handkerchief on his head, the point of one corner placed at the center of his forehead between his eyebrows.

"May I have your left hand?" she said as she sat, and Biggs reached his arm out.

She slipped the cuff around his wrist, past his military-issue watch, and replaced his hand by his side.

"This may tingle a little."

Touching her bee brooch talisman with one hand, she held the cuff on his wrist and whispered under her breath. Warm waves began to flow across Callum's tattoos, an unfamiliar sensation in the presence of a witch casting spells. Millicent must have made more changes than she had told him about. He would have to ask her for a rundown of what she'd done, if only so the next person in twenty years could reproduce it.

The odor of sulfur spiked, dwarfing any lingering garlic smell in the room, and Biggs began to moan.

"Ladies." Millicent touched two fingertips to Biggs's temple. "Ladies, I think I might need your—"

The bed began to rattle, the legs scraping the floor, and Biggs's moan turned into a wail.

The bed lifted six inches off the floor and slammed down, making Millicent and Callum jump back. It rose and slammed itself down again, and bright cracks of burning red spread across the walls and ceiling.

"Ladies!" cried Millicent. "Your help, please!"

The Chinese witch grabbed Callum by the sleeve and pulled him out of the room so she and the others could squeeze in. They crowded around the bed, each of them taking out the mundane objects that were their talismans: a hairbrush, a rolling pin, a thimble, and a tube of lipstick.

The bed floated up in the air and stayed there, Biggs himself lifting off it, his body rigid.

"I WILL BURN THEM ALL!" He cried at the top of his lungs. "I WILL TEAR DOWN THE GATES OF HELL, AND MY ARMY WILL SWARM THE FIELDS OF GEHENNA! THE LAKE OF FIRE WILL BE QUENCHED BY THE BLOOD OF MY ENEMIES! MY ARMY WILL RIP OUT THEIR THROATS WITH TEETH LIKE KNIVES! THEY WILL FEAST ON THE BLOOD OF MY ENEMIES AND GROW STRONGER UNTO THE THIRTEENTH POWER UNTIL NONE MAY STOP THEM!"

The witches pulled the bed away from the wall so they could encircle it and joined hands, each of them speaking in tongues louder and louder to match Biggs's raving. The heat at Callum's back grew to the burning of hot coals as the stench of sulfur crescendoed, threatening to overwhelm him.

"I!" shouted Millicent, the jewels on her brow glowing red with the light of the growing cracks in the walls. "COMMAND! YOU! TO STOP!"

And all of a sudden, Biggs held his tongue, the bed collapsed to the floor, the glowing cracks vanished, and Callum's back grew cold. The stench of sulfur and garlic was gone.

Jessica swooned into Rafe's arms and he and Callum carried her to a nearby work bay where he laid her out on a gurney. Rafe found a bottle of smelling salts and waved it under her nose. She jolted back to her senses and pushed it away.

"Strewth! I was a little woozy, that's all!"

"What happened?" said Callum. "Did you see anything?"

She pushed herself up off the gurney.

"Charred rocks and jagged peaks. A whole desolate landscape."

The witches filed out of the cell, animated and chatting as if they had just come from a play at the theater. Millicent emerged last and joined Callum and the others in the work bay, her expression bright and enthused.

"I think that went quite well. Haven't had to deal with a possession like that in a few years. It gets the blood going, doesn't it? Better than the helter skelter on Brighton Pier."

"Possession?" said Callum.

"Something like it, anyway. Couldn't quite get it all out, but the recipe beat it back a good amount. Your friend should be okay for the time being, but he can't go on like that forever. The cuff will stop it from taking him, but the vampire contagion will eat away at him from the inside."

"Can't you get it out of him?"

"Not without an unadulterated sample of the contagion. Hair of the dog sort of thing. If you can get your hands on that, I should be able to rout it out of him."

"Where do we find an unadulterated sample?"

"The blood of a vampire, obviously. One from the same source. I won't need much. Only a milliliter or two."

35

THE IDEA OF SOMEHOW securing a sample of vampire blood was too much for Callum to process. His body and mind were exhausted after the turbulence of the day, so he opted for checking in on Biggs.

The agent was sitting up in the bed when Callum entered, Rafe at his back. Biggs's hair and clothes were ruffled, but his complexion was ruddy, and all traces of the dark circles under his eyes were gone. He looked like he'd returned from a quiet weekend away.

"How are you feeling?" Callum asked as he perched on the edge of the bed.

"Good. Yeah, great." Biggs beamed from ear to ear. He reached his arms out in front of him, squeezing his fists and bending his elbows to feel his joints and muscles. "Amazing."

He inspected the cuff.

"This thing makes me feel like a million quid. What time is it? I'm tired of being cooped up in here. Let's go out for a drink. That pub of yours was fun. Let's go th—"

His eyes rolled into the back of his head, and he slumped against the pillows.

"Biggs!"

"Let me get in there." Millicent pushed Callum out of the way before he could do anything to help.

She clasped her bee brooch talisman with one hand and laid the other on Bigg's brow. Biggs began to snore, the quiet rustle of someone sleeping deeply.

"He's fine," she whispered. "He needs rest. Let's leave him alone."

She ushered them back out into the open gallery. The other witches were milling around, chatting animatedly and admiring the gallery like a tour group in a stately home.

"I wish Eleanor were here," said the portly witch. "She knows where all the good stuff is. Like all that angel pornography. Do you remember that? Wings everywhere! I've never seen the like. And so tasteful."

"Elsie Dearing," declared Agnieszka. "There will be no prurient lollygagging! This is an educational institution. Such behavior is unseemly in a woman of your position!"

Elsie tittered into her hand. "Oh, you're no fun."

"That's absolutely correct." Agnieszka waggled an accusatory finger at her. "I am a hard-working woman who has no time for lurid distractions. Rafael." She turned to Rafe. "You should talk to my daughter about your devil problem. She has plenty of experience with creatures no decent witch should tolerate, and she spends half her time staring into the void. It will be good for her to be useful for a change. As for the rest of us? Ladies, our job here is done. Let's be off."

She spread her arms as if to scoop up the other three witches and carry them out. Elsie, the Chinese witch, and the Indian witch all groaned with disappointment.

"I want to see the weapons again!" said the Chinese witch. "All those swords and daggers."

"Make an appointment like everyone else." Agnieszka turned to Rafe and gave him the slightest, most condescending nod of the head. "Rafael, you may call on me when it suits you, but not between the hours of nine o'clock and two."

Gosha turned to Rafe and Callum, away from her mother, and rolled her eyes as the ladies shuffled off to the elevator.

"I'd be happy to help in any way I can. Let's have a cup of tea, and you can tell me all about it."

They left Jessica behind with Millicent to keep an eye on Biggs and made their way up to the workroom floor and the grimoire in its protective armature.

"These braziers are fascinating." Gosha approached the one tucked out of the way in the corner of the room. "How do they control Influence like that?"

"It's a technique devised by our founder." Rafe joined her to admire the brass container cast in the shape of a stylized flowering thistle. "John Dee, the sorcerer laureate to Elizabeth the First. A trade secret, I'm afraid, but without it, the concentration of Chaotic Influence within these galleries would run quite out of control." He took from his pocket a pair of embossed white suede gloves and offered them to her. "Put these on and I can show you the grimoire."

"Is it safe to take it out of the frame?" Hands gloved, she sat at the armature.

"Best not."

Callum took a seat out of the way and looked up at the clock. Ten. Only two hours till midnight and Rory's return. He shook himself to bring his mind back to the present. He needed a day off. Or maybe a year.

The witch, Gosha, took her talisman in the shape of a tube of lipstick, slid it into her palm inside her glove, and began to inspect the grimoire perfectly, page by page, Rafe hovering over her ready to answer her questions. Callum rested his chin in his hand and watched the second hand sweep around and around, falling into a dreamy reverie of radiant, handsome, violet-eyed men, a succession of gallant lovers stretched back through the ages.

After half an hour, the witch sat back and removed her gloves, slipping the lipstick into a pocket.

"Interesting." Her gaze grew distant as she processed what she had seen.

Callum snapped out of his daydreams and pushed away the deep unease that had crept over him.

"It might work," she said, "but not how the author intended. It's a clever ritual. Whoever came up with it had an extremely good understanding of Influence and the Without, but it relies too much on brute force. It lacks the subtlety to pierce the veil."

"I'm terribly sorry," said Rafe, wrinkles of confusion creasing his brow. "The Without? That's not a term I'm familiar with."

She started to speak but stopped, perhaps to collect her thoughts, or perhaps to decide if she was prepared to say whatever was coming next. Callum recognized the dilemma well.

"There's the Within and the Without," she said, finally. "The Within is us, the material world. The Without is whatever is beyond."

"What … What's beyond?" There were many things Rafe dealt with, Callum knew, that defied logic, but were all rooted in the real world, all rooted in the senses, in the land, and in people. Though Rafe's concept of reality was more sophisticated than that of your average man on the street, his knowledge of reality stemmed from the books and artifacts housed in the Library. And none of them contained this information.

"Many places, many things," said Gosha. "There are several different Heavens. There's the land of the Fae. There's the realm of dreams and nightmares, and a realm of art. And there is Hell."

"Hell is an actual place?" Rafe whispered. "It exists?"

"The way you and I exist? No, but the demons and devils of Hell walk their own ground, live their own lives, fight their own wars."

"Have you … Have you been there?"

Callum cringed. Given the assertion the Church had made for centuries that witches consorted with the Devil, Rafe's question might be taken as hugely offensive, but Gosha simply grimaced and shook herself as if to dispel the thought.

"Lady, preserve us, no. I have watched it from the outside, though. It's not pleasant."

"And the souls of the damned go there after death?"

"That's the huge mistake everyone always makes. We don't have souls the way religions teach. There's no afterlife beyond the mark the person has made on the world and on those who knew them. Ghosts and such are imprints of the person on the Influence around us, copied fragments of strongly held emotions and beliefs."

"Then how are there heavens? How is there a Hell?"

"Because we believe in them. Because we want them to exist. What lies beyond the Within is shaped by the human psyche. The Without is a reflection of what makes us who we are, for better and worse. The sorcerer who wrote the grimoire didn't understand that. Hell is not a realm with a wall you can knock a hole in to reach through and pull someone across from the other side."

"But the ritual does work at some level," said Callum. "I've seen it with my own eyes. It summoned a demon."

As he described the creature that had emerged from the circle and almost killed him, he remembered how something had made it leave Biggs alone. Could it have been the vampire contagion dormant in his body?

Gosha looked pale and shaken by the time he had finished.

"I need to check," she said.

Her eyes unfocused and her body became deathly still.

"What happened?" said Rafe. "Is she alive?"

Callum rounded the table to crouch before her and check her pulse with two fingers on her neck. "It's like when Jessica goes deep into one of her visions. Her heart's still bea—"

She came to, her face suddenly stricken with panic. "Something broke through. There's a rent in the veil. I've seen it happen before. Creatures from the Without can sometimes break through if motivated enough."

"So, it was a demon?" said Callum. "And the master of this new kind of vampire might be a demon as well?"

She nodded and rose. "It's entirely possible. I have to go. I can close the rent, but everything I need is in my kitchen. Be careful with that book. If there are other creatures from Hell walking around the Within, it wouldn't take much to draw them to it, and it might pull through something truly nasty. I'll send word through Millicent when I've finished the job."

36

CALLUM ACCOMPANIED GOSHA UP through the Hidden Galleries and to the front door, dragging his feet with a heavy head as exhaustion threatened to get the best of him.

"I could say I don't mean to meddle," said Gosha at the door, "but I'm a witch, and it's what we do. Rory's a wonderful man. Kind-hearted, intelligent, loyal. He's the only one my eldest will listen to." She squeezed his shoulder. "It's early days for the two of you, I know, but you could do much, much worse than letting him into your life. Give him a chance."

He leaned against the door jamb and took in the cool night air as she crossed the street, got into a battered black Mini Cooper, and drove away.

He half-wished he hadn't invited Rory to come back, he needed sleep so badly. On his way through the lobby to head upstairs and rest for the half hour before Rory was due back, exhaustion overwhelmed him. The idea of walking all the way up to his attic was too much. He slumped into one of the uncomfortable wooden chairs dotted around the room and buried his head in his hands, thoughts of vampires and demons from Hell running through his mind. What he wouldn't give to forget about it all, if only for a day. He knew he had no choice but to push forward and through to the end. If only the Library had the resources of the Cottage. They could send a squad of agents to deal with the problem and await the results in safety. But even that wouldn't be enough for him. Letting others risk their lives, when he was the one with the best odds to walk away from the fight alive, would be cowardice. They needed the Cottage's resources to rout out the vampires, but how to get them involved without giving away Biggs's secret?

Callum's tired mind wandered again and thoughts of a violet-eyed man who would somehow make this a little better, a little more tolerable, crept into his imagination. Did Jessica's vision mean there was someone out there he was destined to be with?

The doorbell rang, making Callum jump and feel strangely guilty.

"Hey, lover." Rory stood on the doorstep, tall and fresh-faced despite the late hour.

Callum grimaced at the word 'lover.'

Rory laughed. "I regretted it the moment the words came out of my mouth. You okay?"

Callum smiled, hoping to cover up any ambivalence he might be giving off.

"Yeah, long night. But better now you're here."

He tugged Rory inside, pushed the door shut, wrapped his arms around his shoulders and kissed him. They stood like that for what seemed to Callum like a blissful forever, the turbulence of the day wiped away by the sensation of Rory's lips and tongue, and the pressure of Rory's body against his. Callum only pushed away when he felt his limbs grow heavy and sleep threatened to overwhelm him. Not a good look to fall asleep in a lover's arms mid-kiss. "Sorry. I'm practically hanging off you."

"I can whisk you off your feet and carry you upstairs if you like?"

Callum smirked and ran his fingers through the thick, dark thatch of Rory's hair. "I bet you could. Want to see the Library? Rafe usually keeps it locked up tight after hours, but he's downstairs working. Come on. I'll give you the tour."

He threaded his fingers through Rory's and drew him with him through the double doors.

Rory's jaw dropped at the sight of the stacks and galleries.

"Wow. These are all books about magic?"

They strolled arm-in-arm through the stacks.

"Most of them. If not about magic, then about the strange stuff associated with it. I wonder if your people are in here somewhere. I should ask Rafe."

Rory reached out to take a book off a nearby shelf but pulled his hand back. "Is it safe to touch them?"

"Go ahead. The dangerous stuff is all downstairs."

Rory took out the book, a clothbound volume, and thumbed through page after page of medieval woodcarvings of people being tortured by hideous creatures.

"Yikes." He put the book back. "Were Gosha and the ladies able to help?"

"They were amazing." Callum pressed Rory against the bookshelf and kissed him. "You missed an exorcism. Shaking bed, floating bodies. The only thing missing was a torrent of green bile."

Rory whistled quietly.

"It looks like they were able to help my colleague a little. Now I have to get a sample of blood from another one of the vampires. Millicent says she can use it to cure him completely." He watched Rory closely to see how he reacted.

"Is it like this for you every day?"

"Not every day, but yeah." Callum looked up to hold his gaze. "I don't blame you if it's all too much and you want to skip out. There's always a lot going on."

He took in how it felt to be in Rory's arms, absorbing every detail for fear that it would soon be taken away from him.

Rory pulled Callum to him and pressed his head against his chest.

"Vampires are definitely a new one on me," said the Scot. Callum was close enough to hear his voice rumble through his ribs. "But I've seen a thing or two. Colmuir's full of weird goings-on, but the clan keeps it all locked down with an iron fist. They think they're caretakers of the land for their faerie masters. And I've helped Gosha out with a lot of the crazy shit that goes on around here."

He pushed Callum far enough away that he could look him in the eyes. "What I'm saying is, I'm used to hero types who run toward the problem when everyone's running the other way."

They kissed again, for ten minutes, an hour, the rest of the night? Who could tell?

"What's it like?" asked Rory when they came up for air. "When it happens, and you lose your memory?"

Callum thought for a moment, searching for the right words. He'd never had to describe it to someone else, as far as he could remember.

"It's disorienting. Frightening. I don't forget everything, only who I am and everything that's happened to me up to that moment. After that it gets worse, because the Chaos stirs up and gets dangerous. I know enough to run. The librarian back then—he was an ornery, untrusting fucker—was already on the lookout for it happening. He got to me before I could do much damage. But after I've got my tattoos back and everyone around me is safe, there's a quiet, a simplicity to not knowing anything, which is weird, because how would I know that? I keep to myself a lot. I have a journal that's all advice to myself about the loss to get me through the first year. Apparently, it's always the same."

"It must feel terrible not to remember."

"It's not great, but maybe that's a blessing? I've read through all my journals at least twice. I can't imagine what it would feel like to carry all that around with me all the time."

Rory pulled him closer again and nuzzled his ear. "I'd love to see them. Will you show me?"

Callum chuckled. "You just want to get me into bed."

"That is completely accurate." Rory grinned, took him by the hand, and led him upstairs.

37

CALLUM AND RORY CAME down from the attic to another full common room. The Library hadn't seen this much activity since the last fundraising gala a decade ago. Around the table sat Rafe with his usual stack of books, Jessica and Millicent sitting close enough to touch as they each nursed a mug of coffee, and Biggs dressed in one of Callum's shirts and a pair of his jeans. The agent radiated health and vitality as he wolfed down a full English breakfast and guzzled down a pint glass filled with milk. The others stared at him, mesmerized by the gusto with which he was tucking in. Even Rafe was unable to tear himself away and return to his books.

"Callum, mate," mumbled Biggs around a mouthful of banger and chips. "This breakfast's amazing. Grab yourself a plate. Whoa!" He registered Rory coming in behind Callum. "You're the fit bartender. Nice one. Glen Biggs."

He gave Callum a wink worthy of a Benny Hill sketch as he put down his fork and wiped his hand on his t-shirt before offering it to Rory.

"Pleased to meet you, Glen." Rory shook it, and Biggs nearly wrenched his arm from its socket with an over-enthusiastic pump.

"Nah, nah." Biggs returned to his feast. "Glen was my dad. Call me Biggs."

Rory followed Callum to the kitchen and shot him a quizzical smile, to which Callum could only shrug, bemused.

Callum grabbed himself a slice of toast and a mug of coffee and sat down next to Millicent. "Geoffrey was like this before he turned," he whispered from behind his mug. "Are you sure your spell worked?"

Millicent, dressed in black leggings, a white silver minidress, and a fluffy, cloud-like fake fur jacket, touched her bee brooch.

"It's all as it should be," she whispered back. "The contagion is dormant within him, but it's adding its Influence to his own. Keep an eye on him after dark, though. It might start to get frisky."

His plate empty, Biggs put down his knife and fork, pushed his chair back from the table, and belched loudly.

"Beg pardon." He got up to refill his coffee.

Rory sat himself down next to Callum with a bowl of Corn Flakes. He spread his legs so their knees touched, and it was all Callum could do to stop himself from running his hand up the tall Scot's thigh.

The hypnotic spell cast by Biggs's breakfast broken, Rafe closed the unread book before him and centered it on the table before him, his usual preparation to speak.

"The way I see it," he interlocked his fingers and rested them on the book, claiming the attention of everyone around the table, "our first priority is securing an unadulterated sample of vampire contagion for Agent Biggs. If there is a nest out there, we must find it and get to it before the Cottage burns it out. Secondly, we must find out more about this demon that is the source of the contagion. How is it turning people? What is its purpose? I think I can use the grimoire to summon it the way it seems Lucinda Cooke did, but then what? How do we contain it? Can we send it back to Hell, or must we find a way to destroy it?"

"Demon," whispered Rory.

Unsure of how much would be too much for Rory to handle, Callum had glossed over this part of the Library's current affairs, but in for a penny, in for a pound.

"Yeah." He squeezed Rory's wrist, as if he could keep him from bolting. "There's still time to back out."

Looking less sure of himself, Rory took Callum's hand in his own, raised it to his lips, and kissed it gently. The soft warmth against the back of his hand made Callum want to throw him down on the table and take him there on the spot.

"Do you have a map of the British Isles?" said Millicent. "I can cast a finding for you."

"That would be most helpful, Ms. Hargreaves." Rafe gathered up his stack of books. "I have a whole setup in the Hidden Galleries that you can use. And while you're at it, I'll call Edgar Newman to come and help me further delve into what the grimoire has to offer."

"Looks like I won't need this." Millicent placed the bag of flour she had borrowed for her finding spell carefully on the desk of the catalog room so as not to spill, and approached the map and pendulum set up with the cautious optimism of an antiques dealer appraising a potential find. "This will make it a lot easier. Jessica, will you help me?"

She reached out, clasped Jessica's hand, and positioned her next to the map table. Standing behind her, hands on her shoulders, she murmured into Jessica's ear.

"Keep your eyes open and tell me what you see."

They've definitely been at it, thought Callum, happy for Jessica having found someone after a year of increasing isolation as her frustration with her curse deepened.

"Cor, this place is amazing!" Biggs started opening the card catalog drawers and peering inside, his exuberance unnerving Callum.

Millicent took the desk chair and wheeled it to a place next to Jessica by the map table. "Agent Biggs, if you please."

"Yes, Ma'am." He sat in the chair bolt upright as if about to be reprimanded by a superior officer.

She patted him on the chest, gently pushing him back in the seat. "Do relax, Agent Biggs. It will go much more smoothly if you don't put up a fight."

He blanched, and Millicent chuckled.

"Only joking. You won't feel a thing. Now, let's see."

The door opened and Rafe slipped in to stand next to Callum and Rory behind the desk, well out of the way of the proceedings.

"Have I missed anything?" he whispered.

Callum shook his head. "She's just getting started. Is Edgar coming?"

"Strangest thing. He said he has to go away for a while. Apparently, he has a sister in Anglesea who has taken ill. He has to go and take care of her."

Millicent laid one hand on the pendulum framework and touched her brooch.

"Mr. Torvalds," she said, "your device is quite impressive. Is it your design?"

"Do call me Rafe. No, the Library acquired it from a Catalan alchemist at the end of the nineteenth century. Unfortunately, it requires constant tuning to make it work properly in the British Isles. It can be a bit of a beast, I'm afraid."

"It's perfect. Needs a little tweak here and a little push there … " She closed her eyes to concentrate. "That's it."

She took from the pocket of her giant puffball of a jacket a pink marble egg and handed it to Biggs.

"Hold this please, Agent Biggs, and do your best to clear your mind. Jessica, take a good look at the map as it is now. I want you to tell me when anything changes."

"This is exciting," whispered Rory and squeezed Callum's hand.

Millicent pulled the pendulum to one side of the map, closed her eyes, and muttered something under her breath. Callum felt the no-smell of witchcraft. The stirring of magic in the room caressed his tattoos, like Rory's fingers delicately tracing their lines. The witch had tinkered deeply with them. They had never been so sensitive before. Millicent released the pendulum.

The heavy weight swung in an erratic ark over the map, sometimes changing direction, sometimes tracing figure-eights or even more complex patterns.

"I see a great forest over Bermondsey," said Jessica, her spectacle pushed to the top of her head. "A dam breaking in Kent. The water swallows up three villages. White horses galloping across Northumberland. An old woman lying naked under the moon on the Yorkshire moors."

"No." Millicent scowled at the map. "That's not right. That shouldn't be happening."

She walked behind Biggs, placed her hands on his shoulders and closed her eyes.

"The connection is clear. I can feel the contagion calling out to its other hosts, but there's something—"

With a creak and a thunk, the pendulum's chain snapped, and the weighted bob fell to the map, the pointer embedding in it somewhere near Cardiff. Everyone except Millicent jumped.

She walked over to the map and peered at the bob.

"You found it!" Rafe bustled over to her side, but she shook her head.

"No, it's a misdirect. Jessica, anything?"

"A flock of white doves flying over Canterbury Cathedral."

Millicent picked up the bob and ran a fingertip over the hole it had created.

"Something's playing with us, putting on a show to get us to go to the wrong place. I'm afraid all I managed to do is mark your map."

She handed the brass bob to Rafe.

"I have another idea, but it's a long shot. It pains me to say it, but Craft might not be the best tool for the job. A creature of the Without has no concrete material substance. Whatever form they take is cobbled together from ambient Influence, which would make them hard to trace at the best of times. If the creature knows someone is looking for them, they'll likely have the resources to protect themselves from being found. I've heard of such things happening."

She cupped her palm and held it in front of Biggs. "Spit please."

"Beg pardon?" said the agent, unsure of what she was asking him.

"Into my hand. Spit. I need your saliva."

He rolled his tongue around in his mouth and summoned up a small trickle of saliva that he dribbled into her palm. She took a white linen handkerchief from her pocket, wiped the spittle from it and muttered to herself.

The handkerchief ignited in a burst of white flame. She dropped it, and it disintegrated into ash before it hit the floor. She grimaced.

"So, that didn't work. Anyone else have an idea?"

38

"FOLLOW ME, EVERYONE." Rafe, in his best tour guide mode, guided everyone back into the elevator to the laboratory level. "This way, please. No time to dilly-dally."

He stopped them in a work bay halfway down the gallery, this one arranged like a New-Age spa treatment room. The dividers were covered in tapestries depicting lotus flowers and serene vistas. Instead of a medical-grade overhead light, there were Japanese-style floor lamps and brass candelabras. Instead of a gurney or treatment chair, there was a massage table with comfy pillows and bolsters, and an expensive-looking cashmere throw rug. Rafe proceeded to turn on the floor lamps, turning them down low, and light the candles.

"Do make yourself comfortable, Agent Biggs," he said when satisfied with the ambiance.

"What exactly is your plan, old man?" said Callum as Biggs sat on the massage table and puffed up the pillow.

"Mesmerism, dear boy. That's right," Rafe patted the table, addressing Biggs. "Lie down. There's a good chap."

He took from a Chinese apothecary cabinet at the back of the bay a stone bowl filled with dried sage leaves, which he proceeded to light and waft the smoke around the reclined Biggs.

"Franz Mesmer's work may have been debunked by the medical establishment, but from the perspective of sorcery he was spot on. His theoretical *Lebensmagnetismus* describes the psychospiritual force of Influence almost exactly. You said earlier, Ms. Hargreaves, that the vampire contagion exists as a reservoir of Influence within Agent Briggs."

Millicent frowned. "I don't think I used those exact words, but okay."

"I believe we can communicate with the vampire contagion indirectly through Agent Biggs's subconscious mind, and through it, discover the location and the intentions of its source."

"Sounds plausible." Millicent nodded her approval.

From the cabinet, Rafe took five small, black crystalline rocks and placed them along the center of Biggs's torso. Next came a tuning fork, which he struck and placed on each of the rocks. Between the sage, the lighting, and the pleasant ringing of the tuning fork, Callum felt himself getting sleepy. Of course, that could also be because he and Rory didn't spend the entire night in bed actually sleeping.

"These will attune themselves to your inner reserves of Influence and will allow you to descend into a deep mesmeric trance."

He dangled above Biggs a small quartz crystal pendant attached to a silver chain.

"Let your body relax, Agent Biggs," said Rafe, "and follow the crystal with your eyes." He swung it slowly above Biggs. "Take five deep breaths. Five … Four … Three … Two … One … "

Biggs eyes closed, and his breathing settled into the shallow rhythm of someone fast asleep.

Rafe took another of the crystalline rocks, placed it on Biggs's forehead, struck the tuning fork one last time, and applied it to the rock.

"There we are. That should do the trick. Step back from the table, please, everyone. We don't want our proximity to interfere with the process. Now, Agent Biggs. How do you feel?"

"Relaxed." Biggs voice was little more than a soft whisper, the voice of a dreamer coming from far away. "Peaceful."

"Splendid, splendid." Rafe moved to the cabinet and paced back and forth as he always did when he was thinking. "And where are you? What does the world around you look like?"

"I'm lying on the table in the basement of the Library."

"Are you alone, Agent Biggs? Who is with you?"

"You are. And Callum and his fella. And Jessica and the witch. And the other."

Everyone, even Millicent, looked around nervously to see if there was someone else with them. Callum wished he'd brought his knives down with him. Did he need to carry them always now? The Library used to be such a sanctuary.

"And who is this other?" asked Rafe.

Biggs paused before responding.

"It doesn't have a name. It's just the other."

"Well, that's a step in the right direction," Rafe whispered to the others. "I was worried we'd have more floating and bed-rattling. Can you describe the other," he addressed Biggs again.

"It's tall, pale. Its skin shines like the moon and its eyes glitter like the stars."

"Sounds like a vampire to me," whispered Rory.

"Does the other have anything to say, Agent Biggs?"

Another pause.

"No. It's dancing. It wants me to join it."

"Tell him not to," whispered Millicent, "or he'll undo the recipe that's keeping him whole."

Rafe nodded vigorously in agreement. "Don't dance with it, Agent Biggs. It is imperative that you do not dance with it. Do you understand me?"

"Yes, don't dance with it. I understand."

"Ask it to show you where it came from."

Another pause.

"It wants to take me there. I don't want to go. I don't trust it."

He sounded to Callum so frail and lost, nothing like his usual bull in a china shop.

"You're right not to trust it, Agent Biggs," said Rafe, "but it's important we find out where it's come from. If there's any sign of danger, I promise I'll get you out safely. Will you go there for us?"

He reached into the cabinet, took out a large noisemaker made of two strips of wood bolted to a smaller block at one end and carved with symbols of *mathematica infernalis* and held it at the ready near Biggs's head.

"Yes," said Biggs. "Yes, I'll go. It's taking me by the hand. We're out on the street. The moon is full."

"The moon?" whispered Rafe. "It's ten in the morning."

"The visions of astral projection often obey their own logic," whispered Millicent. "If this other is a representation of the vampire contagion, it'll shy away from sunlight, even in an imaginary setting."

"We're in the countryside," said Biggs. "It's taking me to a house, a big, sprawling old house. Like on the telly."

"A country estate?" said Rafe. "Can you describe it in more detail?"

"There's so much stuff in here. Vases and statues and paintings all over the place."

"Is it a museum? What kind of objects? What period?"

"Old, it's all old. Like, super-old."

Rafe scowled in frustration, but it was too much to ask Biggs to identify old works of art. Football players, maybe.

"There's a man in here. It's taking me to see him. He's sitting on a throne. Oh, god. The throne is made of people. And they're still alive. I don't like it. Get me out of here. I want to go home."

"One moment longer, Agent Biggs. Can you describe the man?"

"Tall, slim, blond hair. Handsome. He's surprised to see me. Oh, god. His eyes! His eyes!"

Biggs began to shriek at the top of his lungs, a desperate keen that cut into Callum's brain. Rafe stood over him, ritual noisemaker in hand, frozen with horror.

"Rafe!" Callum shouted to be heard over the din. "Get him out of there. Now!"

Rafe snapped into action and whacked the wooden clacker against the heel of his hand over and over again. The clacker boomed unnaturally, each strike the rumble of distant thunder. After thirteen strikes, Biggs fell silent, and Rafe stopped. The agent opened his eyes and yawned deeply.

"Cor." He sat up, bright and refreshed as if he hadn't been screaming at the top of his lungs five seconds ago. "I'm parched. I could murder a cup of tea."

39

"I HAVE AN IDEA," said Jessica, "but you're not going to like it."

Rafe hooked his cane into the crook of one elbow, rubbed his eyes, and sighed. "What is it? What are you going to do with my precious collection?"

"Nothing bad." She grinned. "I promise you. Come on. What we need is on level four."

"Level … That's where the most dangerous artifacts are housed!"

She shrugged. "I said you wouldn't like it."

Rafe growled with frustration. "Very well. If needs must."

Jessica led them back to the elevator to the sub-basement she had taken Callum to after he lost time.

"Dammit!" she cried as she stepped out of the elevator.

She ducked and threw her arms up to protect her face, but nothing came at her. Callum pushed through the others to get to her side.

"What's happening? What can I do?"

He drew her into a hug to use his body to protect her but, other than the faint taste of coppery Chaos, he could sense nothing out of order.

"The artifacts are all worked up." She pressed her face into his chest. "It's like flocks of birds hurling themselves at me in waves. Can you get me to the middle of the floor? The rest of you gather up the braziers and bring them to me. They should dampen this madness."

Callum shuffled her down the aisle, shielding her like a bodyguard protecting a movie star from the paparazzi. Behind them Rafe instructed the others how to carry the braziers without disrupting them. It took them only a few minutes to create a square of safety. Callum unfurled himself from around Jessica, and she opened her eyes a crack.

"Thank heavens." She pushed her spectacles up onto her shaved head and blinked several times.

"This is fascinating." Millicent leaned in to inspect a brazier. "Excellent workmanship."

"Callum, move one of the desks over here, and bring the chairs." Jessica launched into a long list of instructions, including retrieving half-a-dozen artifacts, the announcement of each one met with indistinct grumbles from Rafe.

"May I look at your spectacles," said Millicent as the others set off to retrieve their assigned items.

Jessica bowed her head so the witch could take them off herself in a gentle and intimate gesture.

"My friend, Gosha, had a problem a bit like yours." Millicent examined the spectacles. "Visions that got out of control. She came up with an ingenious solution. I bet I can adapt it to help you out."

Millicent returned the spectacles to Jessica's head and let her hand linger against her cheek. Callum shot Rory a wink and led him deeper into the gallery so the girls could have some time alone.

"Here, Biggs," said Jessica. She pulled out a chair for him.

The table and chairs had been set within the square of braziers, and five artifacts had been laid out over a green felt pad Rafe had placed on the table. Biggs took his seat and sat there quietly, peering with interest at the artifacts. Millicent's treatment for the vampire contagion had turned him from his usual stern and grumpy to affable and easygoing. Callum hoped it would stick.

In the center of the table stood the crystal ball Jessica had used to find out more about Callum's loss of time. Spread out around it, he, Rory, and Rafe had deposited a brass crown, a cigar box, a Ouija board, a large square of thin metal, and a long brass rod with a ball screwed to the end.

"Fascinating." Millicent hovered over the table inspecting the objects with the interest of a hungry person at the head of the line for a buffet table. "Each has strong etheric properties. Obviously man-made, but they don't bear the mark of High Influence."

"Madame Morozova, who created them," Rafe brightened at the prospect of giving a lecture, "was an untrained occultist in the mid-eighteen-hundreds, a competitor of Madame Blavatsky. She was completely self-taught, never initiated into the sorcerous arts, and yet she had an innate understanding of Influence and created several fascinating artifacts of power purely by harnessing wild magic."

Millicent winced at his use of the word "magic."

"Lean forward for me," Jessica asked Biggs.

He did as he was told, and she slid the metal plate behind him.

"Madame Morozova," she rearranged the other objects to her satisfaction, "created this to photograph people's auras. We're going to use it to keep the goblin inside you in check. We don't want it giving us away. This," she took the Ouija board and placed it near Biggs, "we'll use to talk to it. And this," she opened the cigar box and took out a well-used deck of mass-produced tarot cards, "we'll use to understand it."

Millicent's eyes lit up at the sight of the cards. "Ooh. May I?"

Jessica handed them over, and the witch proceeded to cut and riffle them with the skilled dexterity of a croupier or a close-up magician. The cards danced under her control, cascading from one hand to another. She riffled and cut the deck one-handed.

"Nice."

She placed the deck on the table, tapped it three times, drew the top card, and laughed at the sight of it before sliding it into the middle of the deck.

"Ah, bless. Nothing like a well-loved deck," she mused to herself and realized everyone was staring at her.

She shrugged. "What? Witches and oracles. You wouldn't understand."

"This," Jessica reclaimed the attention of the group, "will show us what's going on. Rafe, your tuning fork, please."

Any objections Rafe might have had at his precious artifacts being commandeered by another had been replaced by admiration at her confidence and ingenuity. Many a night by the fire, while Jessica had sulked in her room, had Rafe bemoaned her lack of interest in training to be a librarian. After tonight, any objections she might claim when he once again grilled her about it would certainly fall flat.

Jessica struck the tuning fork on one of the braziers and both began to vibrate with clear, harmonized tones. She went around to the remaining braziers and did the same. The entire gallery began to hum, along with Callum's tattoos, and all his muscles softened as his nervous system ramped down several notches. He hadn't felt this calm in a decade. Jessica went around her arsenal of artifacts, touching the tuning fork to each. The air crackled and the pungent fizz of ozone filled Callum's nostrils as the coppery taste of Chaos that was ever-present when he was down in the Hidden Galleries strengthened.

"There," she said when she was finished. "We're ready to go. Millicent, would you be our interpreter?"

"My pleasure." Millicent took the seat across from Biggs, the large crystal ball between them, and shuffled and cut the deck, placing it by her left hand when she was finished.

"Ready when you are." She crossed her hands on the table in front of her and sat back in the chair.

Jessica picked up the golden crown and placed it on Biggs's head.

"Cripes, that's heavy." He adjusted it to sit better. "Oh."

His eyes widened.

"Oh!"

Purple mist began to swirl within the crystal ball, and Jessica took her seat at the Ouija board.

"And we're off." She began to spell out words on the board, sliding the planchette across the polished wooden surface with both hands.

"You who are the other," she said, narrating the words as she spelled them. "You who lurk within this man, speak to us, I command you!"

Ripples like the reflections off moonlit water shimmered through the mist within the crystal ball.

Millicent dealt three cards from the deck. "It's sulking. It doesn't like the way my recipe is holding it in check. Give it a poke."

Jessica picked up the brass rod and gave the metal sheet behind Biggs a good rap. It clanged with the impact, and electricity arced across its surface.

"Bloody hell!" cried Biggs and shot up out of the chair.

"Sit. Back. Down." Jessica thrust the rod at him for emphasis. "And don't move. It's only a little shock. Surely a big man like you can take it."

He scowled and sat.

Millicent drew another card. "That woke it up."

"You who are the other," said Jessica as she spelled out her words. "Reveal yourself to us."

The mists within the crystal globe parted to reveal a hideous, angular face with pale skin and far too many teeth. Its eyes were vertical slits that opened to reveal blue-burning coals. The smell of sulfur hit Callum's nostrils strongly enough to make him cough and splutter.

"You okay," whispered Rory.

"Yeah, yeah. I'm fine," Callum whispered back. "I'm allergic to evil."

Rory's eyes widened with amazement, and Callum squeezed his hand.

"Not really," he said, and thought twice. "Well, sort of. I'll tell you later."

Millicent drew a string of cards. "It's hungry. It doesn't like how I've restricted it."

Jessica looked up at Rafe and Callum. "We need to know where its master is, right?"

"Find out how many bloodsuckers he has," said Biggs. "And get as much intel as you can about the terrain. The Cottage strike team will need it."

Jessica scowled, thinking what to spell out next. "We'll need to flatter it. Disembodied spirits can be extremely narcissistic."

"How, my dear," said Rafe, "Do you know so much about disembodied spirits?"

"It's not my first time using this stuff."

Rafe's eyes narrowed. "When this matter is resolved, we are going to have a serious talk about your future with the Library."

"Hush, please. I need to think."

In the silence, the heat coming off the braziers in the low gallery baked into Callum's skin and a single bead of sweat formed at the nape of his neck. As it trickled down his spine, the ink of his tattoos contracted with a deep chill, all the way down his back from head to tail. What was this? A form of premonition new to Millicent's design?

He shivered.

Millicent drew a pair of cards from her deck. "It wants to know why you're holding it prisoner."

"You who are the other," Jessica's hands danced across the surface of the Ouija board as she spelled out the words, "are too powerful."

The apparition's head within the orb snapped around to face her, as if it had heard her speak. It drew back its lips to reveal rows of sharp teeth. A dark, pointed tongue danced across them.

"Your power terrifies us. If we set you free, what will you do to us?" She looked to Millicent as the witch drew more cards.

"Ugh." The witch grimaced at what she saw. "It says it'll sink its teeth into our necks and drain us of life. Delightful."

Next to Callum, Rory shivered. He wrapped his arms around him from behind and leaned his chin on Callum's shoulder. Callum's inked back lit up at the contact, every curlicue and angle of the tattoos bright with electric charge as the wild magic within him was suddenly stirred up. It only lasted a moment.

"You who are the other," Jessica spelled and spoke, "we are too scared to free you, but perhaps we can take you to your master."

"It likes that idea." Millicent drew a succession of cards. "Huh. It wants to deliver us to its master to add to his army in the great war. Great war?" She looked up at the others. "Does that mean anything to you?"

Rafe shook his head. "Ask it for more information, my dear," he said to Jessica.

"You who are the other, what is this war?"

"The master will tear down the gates of hell," said Millicent. "His army will surge across the plains of Gehenna. The bodies of the damned will dam the river Styx. The citadels of the mighty will fall before his wrath. He will rain his revenge down upon the usurpers who ripped him from his throne." She grinned. "That's a movie I'd watch! Love a good battle."

"You who are the other, we want to join your cause. Where can we find your master?"

"It wants us to free it," said Millicent, "so it can feast on our blood and pass onto us its master's gift."

"No. You who are the other, show us your master."

Millicent drew more cards and frowned.

"It's going around in circles. All it can talk about is blood. Well, that's insulting! It says our blood is thin and weak, and only the rich blood of the damned will slake its thirst."

Jessica lashed out with the rod and struck the metal plate at Biggs's back. Electricity arced across it and around Biggs's body, but he gritted his teeth, grunted, and stayed put.

"You who are the other, show us your master!"

Within the orb, the apparition's eyes burned brighter. It threw its head back in a silent roar.

Millicent drew cards. "Nope. Now it says it's going to suck the marrow from our dying bones."

Jessica struck the metal plate twice in quick succession. Biggs yelped and gripped the chair, his knuckles turning white, but he didn't move. Callum wasn't sure he could have done the same. Being technically immortal didn't mean he didn't feel pain.

"Show us your master!"

The gruesome head disappeared in purple mist to be replaced by a view of the Library from the street. The perspective shifted, lifting high above the earth, the streets flying by below.

"It's heading toward the river," said Callum, recognizing the terrain.

The apparition followed the river, speeding past the Isle of Dogs and Greenwich, past Woolwich and Dagenham, and began to slow before the river turned north toward the Thames Estuary. It began to drop and sped toward a large, decrepit-looking warehouse on the riverbank.

Callum leaned in to see if he recognized where they were.

"That's not the country house Biggs described in his trance."

"Scrying isn't an exact science," said Millicent. "Perhaps the demon moved since then."

"Stop it!" Rafe flapped his hands urgently as the image of the warehouse in the orb grew. "The demon already knows about Biggs. If it discovers we're looking for it, we could lose our advantage."

"Stop," spelled Jessica, but the warehouse grew larger within the orb.

She struck the metal plate, and the image dissipated into purple mist.

"Cripes!" said Biggs, struggling not to move.

The warehouse appeared again, drawing ever closer.

"No!" Jessica jabbed at the word on the Ouija board with the planchette and rapped a staccato rhythm on the metal plate.

Biggs gritted his teeth, scrunched his face up and moaned in time with her beat. In the orb, the warehouse was replaced with the gruesome head. It screamed and spat, blue fire seeping from its eyes. Biggs's head lolled to one side, and he slumped in the chair, unconscious.

"Enough!" Millicent dropped the tarot cards and rushed to Biggs's side.

Jessica stopped hammering and pulled the crown from his head as Millicent inspected the cuff around his wrist. The gruesome head vanished, and the orb turned clear.

"He's okay," said the witch, a hand on Biggs's forehead. "The contagion is back in its cage."

"I know where that was," said Rory. "Purfleet."

40

CALLUM CAREENED DOWN THE stairs to the lobby, the leather scabbards containing his knives clipped to his belt and strapped to his thighs.

"Come on!" cried Biggs with one foot out the door. "The more daylight we lose, the harder this gets!"

Millicent thrust a small leather pouch into Callum's hands as he headed for the door.

"Use these to gather the sample. I only need one, but there's extras just in case."

"What about the field telephone?"

Jessica hefted the enormous black brick of a communication device, appearing that much larger by her diminutive height.

"Leave it," said Biggs. "Those things break down all the time. I can use it as an excuse for not calling in."

Callum took the time to steal one short, passionate kiss from Rory before leaving.

It was almost a straight shot down the A3 from Cheyne Heath to Esher. They made it to the Cottage by two in the afternoon, with less than five hours till sunset. Only forty-five miles away, Purfleet would be no more than a twenty-minute flight in the Cottage's choppers, thought Callum as he turned onto the Cottage's nondescript drive. Would four hours be enough to rout out the vampire nest?

"They'll carpet-bomb the place," said Biggs, clearly thinking along the same lines, "if we don't play this right."

"The demon's the unknown factor." In the back seat of the Rover sat a thick sheaf of papers hastily photocopied on the enormous machine Rafe had bought with a large portion of the Library's annual budget. "But we've enough evidence to make them believe us."

Cottage security was its usual implacable wall, only made worse by Callum carrying his knives. Biggs kicked up a stink this time, demanding to see Esme Cavendish, but his stock had plummeted substantially in the past forty-eight hours, and it took twenty minutes of insistent cajoling and thrusting Rafe's papers into the hands of a clerk from Biggs's unit for them to be let through. They both nervously eyed every clock they passed as they were led through the rabbit warren of nondescript corridors. It was after three o'clock before their escort admitted them to Frayn Unit's incident room.

Only three hours to sundown.

Callum thought of Rory, of his strong arms and broad chest, of his beard and rakish smile and gray eyes. Who knew how long before he could lose himself in his embrace once more?

He put the thought out of his head.

The incident room was alive with activity. Three-quarters of the desks were full with oracles working at their divinations, and other more mundane operatives having intense and hushed conversations on phones. Those who weren't at their desks stood with Esme Cavendish, her hair tied into a severe braid that dangled down her back like a Valkyrie's sheathed broadsword, examining Rafe's papers.

She stormed through the huddle of agents and bore down on them. Callum resisted every instinct to drop back into a defensive stance.

"Why did you waste time by bringing me all this in person?" She waved the photocopies in her hand at Biggs. "I left you the field telephone for a reason!"

"The device malfunctioned, Ma'am." The bright, energized man Biggs had become since the witches' recipe was gone, replaced by his usual fiercely dour wall of military gruff. "And it was important you see the documentation to understand the extent of the threat."

"Demons from Hell!" She massaged the bridge of her nose between finger and thumb. "We have no precedent for this at all. There's nothing in the record to suggest the scope—"

An overpowering fragrance of lavender filled the room as Euphemia Graham entered dressed in a navy wool skirt suit styled like a nineteen-forties governess tailored tight to her angular frame like armor. Everyone immediately fell silent and stood.

"What's the commotion?" Her clipped, icy tone cut through the sudden quiet.

"A new imminent threat, Your Grace." Cavendish bobbed in a curtsy as she spoke.

"Show me." Graham snaked out a skeletal arm to take Cavendish's papers.

She looked Biggs and Callum up and down with a cold, calculating eye before turning her attention to the photocopies.

"Mr. Foster," she scanned the top sheet, a page from the grimoire, "you are quite transformed since the last time I saw you." Her upper lip curled into a sneer as she read. "Summoning rituals. This stinks of witchcraft."

She looked up at Cavendish.

"Is the intelligence credible?"

Cavendish turned back to her gaggle of operatives and snapped her fingers. One of them, a small, mousy young woman, bustled forward and curtsied.

"Well?"

Graham looked down her nose at the girl as she handed the copies of the grimoire back to Cavendish.

"W-we have a ninety-percent rating of certainty with a five percent margin of error," stammered the girl.

Graham sighed.

"Let me be clear." Without projecting, her voice suddenly boomed throughout the incident room, and the smell of lavender intensified. "We are not saying with any certainty at all that Hell and the Devil exist, and one of his minions is threatening the security of the realm. Do you all understand?"

Everyone in the room except Callum bowed or curtsied and murmured their assent.

"Find me a plausible explanation that will not alarm the Sphere of Faith." Her voice returned to its normal volume. "The last thing I want is bloody Bishop Worsley breathing down my neck. Hideous, spiteful man! And why am I only hearing about this now, when I have an entire building of oracles at my disposal? Am I to believe that Rafe Torvalds and his company of cursed sideshow freaks have a better intelligence-gathering apparatus?"

Graham's eyes narrowed and turned toward Callum, but he knew better than to respond. Even if she weren't a sorceress of great power, she could have him thrown in jail for the remainder of what might be a very, very long life.

Cavendish began to respond, but Graham cut her off.

"Don't answer that." She sighed. "Get rid of it. Napalm the whole town if you have to. I want the threat eliminated and all evidence of it erased. Have Rumors and Whispers come up with a cover story for whatever course of action you decide on."

She turned to leave.

Biggs looked at Callum with desperation in his eyes. If they blew the nest up, he was screwed.

"You can't," said Callum.

Graham stopped and spun on her heel to face him, her expression a mask of disdain. Had she suddenly grown three inches taller?

"I can't?" Her voice was cold and brittle as ice. "I can't what? Protect the subjects of the realm from a threat to their existence?"

Callum could have counted his interactions with Euphemia Graham on one hand, but they had been enough for him to truly despise her.

"The demon—"

"Not a demon, Mr. Foster. Devils and demons are the fantastical fictions of drugged prophets, and the bugbears of weak minds."

"The entity, then. Whatever created this new vampire contagion is not of this Earth. My source assures me it has no physical form. Destroying the vampire nest with brute force might get rid of the vampires, but there's no guarantee the attack will have any effect on the entity, and we'll have destroyed any evidence that might lead us to it."

Graham approached Callum, her black stilettoed heels clicking on the floor as she walked, and stopped uncomfortably close. She glared at him, and the smell of lavender crested once more as the whorls and curlicues of his tattoos shivered with cold, lighting up in a sequential pattern. She was probing him in some way; he didn't need to understand how Millicent had altered the inking to know that.

"Not of this Earth?" Her voice dropped to a dangerous purr. "Listen to yourself. Your source was a witch, I've no doubt, and I bet I know which one. You'd do better to steer clear of her and her sisters-in-Craft. You can never trust a witch. They only ever care for themselves."

Based on the past twenty-four hours, Callum could easily debate the point, but he had no desire to get in the middle of this feud between Euphemia Graham and the witches of Cheyne Heath. He glanced up at the clock.

"We have two and a half hours left until sundown. That should be ample time for us to do a sweep of the building and extinguish anything we find."

"Us, Mr. Foster? I assure you; I have the situation quite in hand. We don't need knife-wielding Chaos-kissed guttersnipes such as yourself getting in the way." She turned to Cavendish. "Who do we have on standby?"

Cavendish, an operative skilled in politics as well as tradecraft to have risen to supervisor in Euphemia Graham's ranks, remained as impassive as a marble statue, not even a wrinkle of tension evident on her face.

"Frayn and Ayckbourn, Your Grace."

"Two of my finest, Mr. Foster. Why don't you go back to your den of thieves and harlots and—"

"You need me. Curses, contagions, covert attempts to use High Influence against me," he smiled his best guileless, disarming smile even as he revealed he knew she was doing her damnedest to pry with her sorcery as he spoke, "none of that will work against me. I'm not your enemy, Your Grace. We're facing something unnatural and peculiar, both things I have ample experience with. I only want to help."

She stood there, frozen in place, her breath so shallow, she might have been a mummified corpse on display in a museum.

"Very well." She turned to Cavendish. "Keep him in line. I don't want to have to tell the Palace I've compromised an asset of their precious Library of the Damned."

She sneered at Callum as she turned on her heel and stalked away.

"So ridiculous." She strode out of the incident room.

Callum could feel the relief sloughing off Biggs in waves.

41

THE HELICOPTER LURCHED INTO the air, and Callum did his best to not white-knuckle the edge of the seat. Something about the possibility of every bone in his body shattering and his organs being reduced to mash and not dying made the slightest chance of a fall from a great height terrifying. He tried a deep breath to steady his nerves, but Esme Cavendish had insisted he and Biggs wear tight mesh armor that covered their upper bodies from neck to wrists, the Cottage's latest artifice to counteract vampire bites. No matter how much he tried to convince her he didn't need it, she refused to budge, and now he couldn't even take in enough air to blow out a birthday candle.

The thought of a cake covered in so many candles it became a ball of flame popped into his mind, but it didn't do much to calm him.

In the seat next to him, Biggs stared out the window at the receding lawn of the Cottage heliport, a scowl on his face. He had expected to be given back his command of Frayn Unit for the operation, but apparently things moved fast in Euphemia Graham's organization. The entire unit had been replaced, and Biggs was out of rank.

"We'll land beyond the tree line surrounding the target and make our way there on foot," crackled the voice of Agent Stevens, Frayn's new commander, through the earpiece Callum had been given, a rubber plug that molded itself to his ear when he put it in. It had no connection to any communications equipment, nor even a power source, but it smelled strongly of lavender. "You are here in a strictly advisory capacity and will remain behind your assigned group under agent Biggs's protection."

Callum nodded. Once they hit the ground, he and Biggs had their own agenda to follow. The specimen bottles Millicent had given him were safely concealed in his jacket pocket.

As they headed east, the low afternoon sun shining at their backs, Callum felt a prickle across his tattoos and the noise of the engine and rotors vanished in an odd silence that pressed against his temples and eardrums. They began their descent to Purfleet just as he was getting used to being in the air.

"What are you doing?" said Biggs as Callum shrugged off his jacket and began to pull off the ridiculous mesh armor. He and Biggs had hung back as the two units made their way forward through the trees.

"It's useless." Callum tossed the mesh into a bush. "It'll get in the way. You might as well take yours off."

"Some of us aren't cursed immortals."

"True, but some of us have already been infected by the vampire contagion."

Biggs frowned, grumbled, and took his off as well.

Callum drew one of his knives. It glowed with a soft, eerie radiance in the late afternoon gloom.

"See that." He held the blade up to Biggs. "Don't know what that means, but it's definitely not good."

"I say we outflank the teams. Head down to the river, approach from the docks, find a way in that way."

Callum nodded and peered through the trees at the uniformed agents heading away from them. "They're going too slowly."

Biggs glanced up at the tree canopy and pointed at a flock of birds circling and pinwheeling above them. "See that? Look carefully."

Callum stared, doing his best not to blink. After a moment the birds dissolved into a formless mist before solidifying again.

"That's probably another chopper," said Biggs, "waiting for a signal to drop ordinance on the building."

"Wankers! She promised she wouldn't."

"We'd better run."

Callum dropped from the window into the gloom of the warehouse, gulping down great breaths as he tried to recover from keeping up with Biggs. Callum worked hard to keep fit, but Biggs had outpaced him easily, tearing off ahead. The agent crouched next to him showing no signs of fatigue.

"There's a door down that way," Biggs pointed off into the gloom, "and windows. Probably offices. Come on."

"Hold up," gasped Callum. "I think I ruptured a lung keeping up with you. I need a second."

—*Field ops in place,* came a voice through Callum's earpiece.

"Now we know they're taking this seriously." Biggs adjusted the tiny bundle of alchemical technology in his ear. "Cavendish doesn't leave HQ for much of anything."

They were in a low, broad open area, maybe a factory floor when this building had still been functional. Grimy windows let in hardly any light at all, but Bigg's eyes caught it and glimmered.

Callum unsheathed one of his knives. The eerie radiance emanating from the blade cast a faint glow.

"Open your mouth."

"What?" said Biggs. "Bugger off."

"Open it!"

Callum held the blade up to Biggs's face to inspect his teeth and breathed a sigh of relief when no nasty pointed fangs stuck out at him.

"Happy?" whispered Biggs, pushing the blade away.

"How are you feeling?"

The agent scowled. "I'm fine. Great, as a matter of fact. It feels good to be doing something. Can we wrap up the therapy session and get on with it?"

—Frayn one in position.

The other teams, four in total, checked in.

—Biggs, status check, over.

Biggs touched the earpiece to respond. "Holding back by the tree line."

—Stay put until you hear my signal. Copy?

"Copy."

He dropped his hand and raised a querying eyebrow to Callum.

Callum flipped his knife around to reverse his grip so he could hold it close to his body and obscure the glow. "Lead the way."

Biggs pulled from the holster tucked under his armpit an alchemically doctored service revolver, the black metal etched with elaborate symbols, and edged forward. It looked more like a museum piece than something that could take down a vampire.

They clung to the wall as they made their way around the empty factory floor. Green paint flaked off the battered metal door, rendering it a shadowy portal in the gloom. Callum placed a hand on the knob and pressed one ear to the door. He heard nothing, and the only smell reaching his nostrils was stale urine.

He turned the knob and opened the door carefully, expecting a chorus of creaks and scrapes to announce their presence, but it gave way quietly.

Beyond was a windowless corridor, lined with utilitarian office doors, each with a grimy, mesh-reinforced window that let through the barest glow of wan light from the fading sun outside.

At the end of the corridor, two figures stood huddled around one of the doors, peering inside.

They turned almost immediately, their irises shimmering bright in the half-gloom, and Callum smelled garlic and sulfur.

"How did you two get out?" said one of them, a man.

The male vampire and his female companion didn't wait for a response. They shimmered into movement, covering half the twenty yards between them and Callum in a fraction of a heartbeat, but Biggs aimed his gun and fired twice in the same infinitesimal instant.

His strange, alchemical gun was doctored to be silent, sound converted to concussive force that felt like someone slamming cinder blocks into Callum's head, and terminal to the undead. The two vampires roared into clouds of flame lighting the corridor in a fiery burst that burned out before Callum's heart finished its beat.

He staggered back against the wall, his ears ringing.

"How did you move that fast?" he gasped.

Biggs, seemingly unfazed by what he'd done, aimed his weapon up and out of the way. "Dunno."

The blade of Callum's knife had picked up the outflowing energy of the agent's weapon and the twin fireballs, and radiated a ruddy golden glow, the burning sky of a late summer sunset. He shoved Biggs against the wall with one hand, held the blade up to his face with the other, and searched the agent's eyes for the slightest hint of predatory shine, but the whites of his eyes glistened with moisture.

"What!?" whispered Biggs. Thicker set and taller than Callum, he could have easily knocked him away.

"Just checking." Callum released him and sheathed his knife. "You're feeling okay?"

"Yeah, yeah I'm fine."

"If you start feeling funny, you tell me, right?"

"I'm fine! I can feel the bloody thing inside me, but whatever the witch did to me has it tied up in knots."

Callum relaxed, but only a fraction. "Next time, give me a chance to bleed one of them."

"Fuck. I didn't think."

"What were they looking at?"

—Alpha team entering from the north, came a voice through Callum's earpiece.

—Beta team reaching western entrance.

"We need to get a move on before they take out the nest." Callum edged down the corridor toward the door the two vampires had been peering into. He still couldn't get over seeing them straight-backed and coherent, and not the stooped feral monsters he was used to.

"What's taking so long," came a voice from two dots of glimmering blue at the dark end of the corridor. "It's start—"

The glow of the vampire's eyes streaked toward them as Biggs flung open his telescopic baton with a crack and struck the air two feet in front of him. The vampire, slowed enough by Biggs's blow to be visible, stumbled to one side, hitting the wall hard with preternatural momentum. Without hesitation, Biggs rushed it, not moving as fast as the vampire, but certainly faster than a normal person should be able to, and struck it hard with the baton over and over again, keeping the vampire off-balance, giving Callum enough time to slip out the small specimen bottle Millicent had given him and pop it open.

Callum and Biggs descended on the vampire, pulling it to the ground and kneeling on it with all their weight to hold it down as it struggled, its arms pinned, but, as Biggs whaled on it with the baton and Callum attempted to slice open the vampire's canvas trousers to draw blood from its thigh, the vampire found enough purchase to throw them off. Callum and Biggs tumbled across the floor.

Biggs was up a heartbeat before Callum, throwing himself at the vampire again, tackling it as it tried to rise, not moving so fast now. He slammed it into the wall.

The vampire roared with anger and tried to lash out with a backhanded fist, but Biggs, his combat training melding with whatever unnatural reserves of speed and strength the contagion within him had granted him, blocked the blow.

The vampire's entire body blurred in the dim light as it tried to attack Biggs, but the agent twisted its arm behind its back and brought it down with his full weight, wrapping his arms and legs around it like octopus tentacles. The vampire struggled, knocking them around like a sneaker in a washing machine, but Biggs held fast.

"Get on with it!" he growled. "I can't hold on much longer."

Callum leapt on them, pressing his knees into the vampire's neck and abdomen and leaning in with his full weight. He fished out Millicent's vial, unscrewed it with his teeth, and attempted to grab the vampire's wrist, but the blasted creature wouldn't cooperate. It twisted its arm out of Callum's fingers.

"Hold his arm still!"

Biggs did his best to pull it back at an angle that would have dislocated its shoulder had it been human, stretching out the muscles to the breaking point until the whole arm was effectively paralyzed. Callum leaned over and, with the tip of his knife, cut lengthwise into the vampire's forearm, digging deep into the flesh and severing its artery. The flesh immediately tried to knit itself back together, but the alchemical silver blade made muscle, sinew, and blood vessels sear into a carbonized mass that refused to heal. The vampire roared.

Instead of blood, what seeped out of its arm was the same inky fluid that had spewed out of the demon in Lucinda Cooke's office. Thick and viscous, Callum struggled to get it into the vial, nearly losing it when the vampire made one last concerted effort to shake them off, but he filled the small glass bottle and screwed the cap back on with his teeth.

He reached out and leaned on the vampire's face, pressing its head back as it gnashed its teeth. Its chest exposed, he plunged his blade into its heart.

"Clear!" he shouted. Biggs released it. They scrambled back as the vampire ignited, burning bright and hot for an instant, leaving behind it only ash and the knife, its blade glowing like a lingering ember.

"You got it?" gasped Biggs. Callum held up the vial, and the glass glittered in the glow of the blade. "Let's get the fuck out of here."

"Wait." Callum slipped the vial in his trouser pocket, pushed himself to his feet and snatched up the knife. "I want to see what they were looking at."

He edged toward the office door the vampires had been looking through and stood back from the afternoon light coming through the grimy window embedded in it in case there was something on the other side he would rather not see him. Through the window he saw the telltale shapes of huddled people.

"Cover me." He placed one hand on the doorknob as Biggs stepped into position, weapon up.

Callum turned the knob slowly, unlatching the door, and, leaning back in case something came out at him, he opened it the tiniest crack. Inside, six people—men and women, Black, White, and Asian— clustered together against the far wall. When they saw him, they whimpered and shrank away, pressing themselves against the far wall.

The memory of a mound of bloodless canine corpses flashed across Callum's mind. These poor people were intended as food.

"Bugger!"

42

A DOZEN PEOPLE WHIMPERED and cringed away from him when Callum opened the door and pressed themselves into the outer wall of the empty office.

"It's okay!" he sheathed his knife and spread his hands to show he wasn't a danger to them. "We're here to get you out. We're going to get you to safety."

They didn't believe him.

Biggs pulled him back. "How the fuck are we going to do that? If the backup teams see a dozen unknowns running through the woods, they'll cut them down."

The last remnants of Callum's fantasy of sinking into the safety of Rory's strong arms evaporated. He pointed to his earpiece. "How do I get this thing to work?"

"Touching it with two fingers will make it live."

"Cavendish." He pressed the disk into his ear. "We're in the building. They're holding civilians prisoner. We have to get them out. Cavendish?"

There was no response.

"Cavendish? It's not working."

Biggs pressed his earpiece. "Agent Biggs to Control, over?" More nothing. He took the disk out of his ear and turned it around in his fingers. "They're muted."

He removed his weapon from its holster. The victims whimpered as he pried a strip of alloy off its hilt.

"Clarke was a genius with this stuff. She showed me a thing or two."

He folded the strip of alloy back and forth until it snapped, then used the corner of one of the pieces to fiddle with the surface of the disc. Satisfied with his efforts, he held the strip against the disc. The alloy glowed dimly and fused itself to it. The smell of lavender filled Callum's nostrils.

"Give me yours." Biggs traded his for Callum's. Callum put his back in and tried again.

"Cavendish, we're in the building. I repeat, we're in the building. They're holding civilians prisoner, probably for food." More whimpering. "We've got a dozen innocents here. We have to get them out."

The disk crackled to life in Callum's ear.

—*What the bloody hell are you doing?* Cavendish's clipped icy tones dripped with frustration. *You're not supposed to be in there! The M. O. D. will skin us up if anything happens to you.*

"Ministry of Defense?" whispered Biggs, confused. "Why the fuck do they care?"

Callum shook his head. "Not the Ministry, the Master of the Dagger. The bigwig at the Palace who oversees all this."

—*Commander Stevens get them out of there immediately!* barked Cavendish.

Callum pressed the disk in his ear again. "We have a dozen innocents here. We're going to bring them out through the windows facing the river. Do not shoot."

—*No,* said Cavendish. *It's too great a risk. What if they're infected like Lucinda and Geoffrey Cook? Commander Stevens, send someone to escort Foster and Biggs out, and evacuate your team. Shoot anyone else on sight, infected or not. We're going to firebomb the place.*

Unaware that their lives were still about to end, but by fire and not tooth and claw, the prisoners began to stir, thinking they might have a way out.

"Wait!" said Callum. "We might have a cure."

—*What do you mean?*

"The Library found a consultant who's confident they can make a cure. There's no need to k … " He stopped himself, realizing the prisoners could hear. "There's no need to take extreme measures."

—*When the bloody hell were you going to tell me this?!*

"I'm telling you now. We haven't tested it yet, but we're confident it will work."

"We are?" whispered Biggs. "The witch bird didn't seem all that optimistic."

"Shush," said Callum, his fingers off the disc.

—*Fine,* said Cavendish. *But we'll keep them for observation. We'll keep them, this time, Foster. I'm sick of your amateur dramatics.*

"There's another thing," said Callum, dreading her reaction. He doubted the small vial of blood he'd harvested would be sufficient to heal a dozen people if they needed it. He turned away from the prisoners and stepped out of the room. "The main ingredient of the cure is vampire blood. We need one of them."

The earpiece crackled loudly and fell silent.

"If there's a chance we can save them … " he said.

—*Yes, yes. Very well. Stevens, we need a vampire specimen taken … alive? Undead? Undamaged? Just get me one of the bastards. Once you have it, clear out. Do you copy, over?*

—*Understood, Ma'am.*

"We can get the prisoners out," said Callum.

—Very well, but do it quickly. The second you're clear, I'm raining down fire on this shitshow!

"Understood." Callum released the disk and turned to Biggs. "I'll herd, you cover."

"Got it."

The prisoners now only too happy to follow Callum's orders, they got them out through the windows they had entered by without a problem, Biggs guarding them from the cover of a cement pillar, his gun drawn. He stood so still as Callum gave each prisoner a boost to reach the open window he might have been made of the same stuff as the pillar. It made Callum's skin crawl.

"Biggs," he called the agent over with a harsh whisper as he hoisted up the final prisoner. The rest waited on the outside, ready to be escorted to safety. "You go."

Biggs broke his uncanny stillness with a shake of his head. "No, you."

Callum sighed. *Are we back to this version of Biggs now?* "If there are other vampires out there, you're the best person to protect those people."

Biggs scowled, and Callum took out the vial of vampire blood. "And you need to get this to the witch. We don't know how much longer you have before the contagion wins."

"I'm not abandoning a member of my unit."

Part of the anxious grip around Callum's heart that had held fast since the helicopter ride softened. To Biggs, Callum and Jessica had always been hangers-on, an intrusion into the smooth running of his command. He'd never referred to Callum as part of the team. "Mate, I'll be fine. Your wellbeing and their safety are what's important. I can take care of myself. Have been since long before you were born."

The agent's brow furrowed. "Fuck, I hate this shit."

"I know, but we need more vampire blood in case that lot are infected, and I don't trust your colleagues to do the job."

"Yeah." Biggs holstered his firearm and slid across the open warehouse to the window. "I don't either."

He reached for the window ledge to pull himself up and stopped. "Don't get yourself killed." Callum opened his mouth to remind him he couldn't die, but Biggs cut him off before he could speak. "Or whatever happens to you. Don't forget Cavendish's about to nuke the whole building. Have you ever been burned to ash before?"

He had a point. "I'll be careful. I promise."

"Once she gives the order, you'll have about sixty seconds to find cover."

"Sixty seconds. Got it." He slapped the agent on the shoulder. "Get out of here."

Biggs hoisted himself up effortlessly and vaulted out the window, the soft thud of his landing accompanied by the murmurs of the prisoners as he led them away.

Callum turned and headed back to the offices.

He returned to the corridor and followed it deeper into the building, checking offices along the way in case there were more imprisoned victims. He felt light, the weight of responsibility lifted a fraction by the knowledge that Biggs had made it out with what he needed to rid himself of the contagion, leaving Callum free to search for the demon and take out a few more vampires along the way.

He heard voices coming from the end of the corridor, past a pair of double doors. The blade he had out still carried some of the glare of the burning vampires from earlier, so he slid it back in its scabbard and pressed one ear to the doors, but all he could hear was a muffled conversation. He pushed the door open as quietly as he could, giving himself a gap as slender as the blades of his knives to see beyond.

The chamber on the other side was large and open, two or three stories high with iron catwalks around the walls. At one end, two men stood huddled together, one taller, with broad shoulders and chestnut brown hair that fell to his deep blue frock coat, the other dressed in a white suit with close-cropped blond hair and a pair of dark sunglasses despite the gloom in the rapidly fading evening light that came through the grimy windows.

"There," said the man dressed in white. His voice was deep and rough, the charismatic raggedness of a lifetime's consumption of cigarettes and whiskey. "You almost have it. Hold the spark steady. Don't reach for it. Let it come to you like a lover under your spell of seduction. That's it."

The two men shifted slightly, and Callum could see between them. The taller one held a mote of light, a glow of deep orange and red, the fiery residue of a summer sunset or the dying embers of a bonfire. The rotting-egg stench of sulfur wafted over Callum with such strength he would have gagged were it not for the sweet underlying smell of warm, humid air, fragrant with summer flowers.

"I get it," said the taller man, his handsome chiseled features turned fiendish by his summoned light. He smirked and his eyes widened with excitement. "I see it perfectly. So elegant. I'm in awe."

The man in white patted the taller man on the back.

"Oh, nonsense, my friend. You would have discovered it eventually. You were very close before we crossed paths. I only wish I could help you further. My experience of the realms without is limited to my own, something I shall rectify as soon as I sit once again upon my throne. We made a bargain, and I stand by my agreements, despite the reputation the weak minds of this realm have lumped upon me." He sneered.

"You mustn't be too harsh on them." The other's voice was soft and melodic. The sound of it caught Callum's breath and made the world grow distant. "They live stunted lives bounded by their mortality, too short to understand anything beyond their immediate urges. They're not like us. They don't have our perspective."

He closed his hands like a book and the mote of light faded.

"I wish I had more time to spend here with you." The man in white grinned wistfully. "My people look upon this realm and its denizens with such disdain. We laugh at the way they fear us, but you have given me a whole new perspective. If your mortals could cross over to my realm, what delights of agony and perfection we could show them. Perhaps once my new army has brought death to my people, once they understand what it means to be extinguished completely, perhaps then they will finally appreciate my rule." He spread his arms as if to encompass the entire chamber, took a deep breath, and sighed.

"Banishing me here was truly the best thing my usurpers could have done for me. Your people were wrong to judge you lacking. Leaving your brilliance to languish here was such a mistake. How much they have lost. I hope you find their realm and inflict upon them the vengeance you so justly deserve. Now you know the secret of crossing you can create an army of your own." He raised his hands and shrugged impishly, a bizarre, camp gesture at odds with the brittle rasp of his voice.

"I have an army, dear Sathanas." In the growing darkness, the taller man shimmered with the same starlight glow of Callum's blades under a clear night sky. He was breathtaking, his beauty awakening in Callum a longing that felt both new and familiar, yet another confusing remnant of his lost centuries. "As fierce as the one I created for you, awaiting my call. Now, with this … "

The tall and beautiful man wriggled his fingers, and a burning glow rippled across them, illuminating the evil grin that spread across his face.

" … All that's left is to find my people."

The man in white, Sathanas, clapped the taller man on the shoulders. "And with the knowledge I've given you of the realms without, you are certain to. Whatever help I can give you once I've reclaimed my throne will be yours."

He wrapped his arms around the taller man and kissed him. The kiss was long and passionate, and Callum felt a stab of cold jealousy sear through his gut forcing him out of the glamor the tall and handsome man had trapped him in and back to cold reality.

A vampire appeared out of nowhere, a smear of darkness suddenly turned solid. It was a young man, early twenties, dressed in tweed trousers and a brown sweater with leather patches at the elbows. He bowed to the man in white.

"The sun has set, my lord."

The man in white turned to his beautiful companion. "Will you stay and watch? You could even come with me. I would love nothing more than to show you the delights of Hell."

The beautiful man cupped the other's cheek. "When we've both achieved our goals."

The man in white sighed. "Emrys, my darling. Your love of mortals is commendable, but your favorite is little more than a pet. He can't give you the love someone like us needs to be fulfilled."

"I know, but I need him. Without him I will never achieve my revenge."

They kissed each other lightly on the lips and separated as more dark smears around them resolved into the pale forms of vampires between them and Callum.

"Until we meet again," said the man in white, and his beautiful companion slipped away into the gloom.

More and more vampires filled the large, open chamber. Callum touched his earpiece. "Cavendish, there's more of them. Lots of them. I count thirty or forty."

—*Goddammit!* Cavendish's voice crackled in his ear. *Where are you? I have a dozen whimpering civilians here. Taking care of them is supposed to be your job.*

"I'm still in the building. There's a central chamber where they're all gathering. The demon's here as well."

—*All units withdraw immediately! Stevens, have you captured a specimen?*

—*Negative, command.*

—Fucking hell! You're all useless. We'll send the civilians to a quarantine center and shoot them if they turn. Get out of there, the lot of you. I can't drop the bloody bombs until you're clear.

—Understood. Frayn Unit withdrawing.

—You, too, Foster. No fooling around this time. The bombs are dropping whether you're in or you're out. I don't care what the Master of the Dagger says.

The earpiece crackled again and fell silent.

The rising stench of garlic and sulfur threatened to overpower Callum as more vampires shimmered into the chamber, the thrum of excitement palpable in the air.

"My ferocious army," said the man in white, the demon, Sathanas. His unnaturally loud voice filled the chamber. "My dire warriors! The moment has come. See the land you will reclaim with your viciousness."

He turned toward the wall behind him and raised his arms. A rent appeared in the air, a jagged severing of the stuff of nature, revealing a hellscape beyond. Black, ragged spires thrust up into a burning sky, between them flowing rivers of lava and flame. The rent grew and grew until it filled the space. The vampires edged forward in their excitement.

"Wait, my army!" The demon pulled off his sunglasses revealing eyes that were little more than slits in his head containing dark, smoldering coals. The stench of sulfur spiked in intensity and the throng before him stopped. "Patience. You must gain strength if you are to face the Lords of Hell."

He clapped his hands and the crowd parted, the vampires all turning toward doors opening on the other side of the chamber. Into the great open space stumbled a crowd of wailing and whimpering people, fleeing from the darkness beyond. The leading edge stopped at the sight of the wall of pale, fanged creatures. A handful of vampires behind them pushed the prisoners forward.

"Feast, my warriors," said the demon.

Callum pressed the earpiece so hard it threatened to pierce his eardrum.

"Cavendish, abort! Abort! There's more civilians here. They're about to be killed."

The earpiece crackled deafeningly in his ear. He yanked it out and tossed it away. He unsheathed his knives, kicked the door open, and roared at the top of his lungs as he burst into the fray.

43

HIS BLADES GLOWING RED with the absorbed light of the flaming hell-portal, he launched himself at the nearest vampire, a young man in a gray hooded sweatshirt with dark skin turned glistening black by the vampire contagion. Turning to see what the commotion was, it unwittingly exposed its neck to Callum. His blade sliced cleanly through, severing its head from its body, both exploding into flame and leaving no more than a sprinkling of ash behind.

That got the horde's attention. Fifty pairs of glimmering eyes and deadly fangs glistening in the hell-light turned toward him.

Callum cursed himself under his breath for acting on impulse without the thinnest sliver of a plan. At least the vampires had forgotten about their victims. He only had to stay functional long enough that Cavendish and Frayn Unit could get them out. Assuming Cavendish didn't firebomb the place regardless.

Sufficiently wary of him for killing one of their own, they fanned out around him. Should he flee back the way they came in and draw them away from the civilians? That would only lead them away from Cavendish's strike zone if she cut him loose.

Fuck it, he thought as a strange calm washed over him. In all the years he could remember, he'd never been so close to death.

As the vampires approached, he drew his blades across the back of his forearms one at a time to smear them with blood. Perhaps that would give him the edge he needed. If he were reduced to a spatter of biological material by the bombing or the vampires, would he still be conscious? Knowing his luck …

The first vampire to break the line, a middle-aged woman in a smart business suit, blurred toward him, moving faster than he could track, but he knew he was her target. He stabbed at her, slicing through her sleeve and breaking skin, a strike insufficient to ignite her but enough to get a few cells of his blood into it. It felt the effects immediately, its eyes widening in shock, and stumbled back into a pair of its comrades. It burst into flame, igniting the others and taking them with it.

Callum was only partially aware of the explosion. Three vampires came for him from behind. One grabbed him by the neck with arms like steel bars, while the second seized his arm, locking it straight and pulling it back. A sickening wrench tore through his shoulder, but he managed not to drop the knife. The third vampire fumbled the hold on his other arm, and, though it was strong, it left him enough range of motion to bend his elbow and knick its skin with the tip of his blade. The vampire released him immediately, freeing his arm. He swung up and across his body and stabbed the vampire at his neck in the eye. It released him, screaming, as the first vampire went up in flames. Callum swung again, sweeping his free blade under his other arm and stabbed the third vampire in the heart. It went up as Callum's blood did its work on the second, leaving him standing free between two pillars of flame that burned themselves out in an instant.

The rest of the horde caught on quick. A vampiric blur skimmed across the dusty cement floor and knocked his legs out from underneath him. He fell hard on his back, flailing his arms as he went down in a vain attempt at taking out the vampire that had struck him, but three others jumped on him before he could recover and roll himself up. One kneeled on his right arm, incapacitating it, while the other leaned its weight across him in a violent embrace, as the third stood on his wrist, immobilizing him.

The vampire leaning across him tore his t-shirt to get at his neck as Callum flailed his head around. If it severed an artery, he would be useless in seconds. It tried to seize his head and press it down but, despite its strength, Callum was able to evade its hold and it sunk its teeth into his chest, tearing the skin over his collarbone.

The second his blood seeped into the vampire's mouth it pushed itself off him, rolling away and wiping desperately at its tongue as if it could cleanse its mouth of the blood, but the Chaos in it took hold quickly and up it went, close enough to the other two that they flinched away from the flames lest they ignite as well.

Callum curled up into a fetal position and rolled over onto his front, pressing one hand against the cut both to help it seal and to smear the blood seeping out of it around.

A pair of hands seized him by the shoulders and threw him across the floor. His hands slick with blood, he gripped his blades fiercely to not lose them as he crashed against the wall, a broken rag doll.

The vampires understood the knives were a threat—how could they not? The blades lit up the chamber around him like twin storm lanterns—but the blood he had shed was too much for them. He could see the hunger in their eyes as they crowded around him.

He pressed himself to his feet, sliding his back up the wall, and held the blades out, pointing at the horde.

"Who's next, arseholes?"

It was only bravado. Sixty seconds into the encounter and he was battered, bruised, and struggling to hold his head up. He hoped the civilians somewhere beyond in the dark had the sense to flee.

Four vampires launched themselves at him, two little more than kids in jeans and trainers, the others in fancy suits, in a blurred wall of movement, and Callum tensed, but three powerful concussive waves battered into Callum from the catwalk above, and the three vampires to his left ignited. The fourth, one of the kids, held its arms up to protect its head, exposing its chest. Callum thrust forward in his best fencing lunge and stabbed it in the heart, the blade sinking in to the hilt. The vampire ignited around it.

The remaining thirty or forty vampires scattered, blurring into the darkness. Across the chamber, a handful of civilians had remained, cowering in a corner, too terrified to save themselves.

"RUN!" shouted Callum at the top of his lungs, hoping to shock them into action, but they were beyond cajoling.

A figure dropped in front of him from the catwalk. Callum held up his knives and crouched, ready to fight.

Biggs's pale face grinned back at him in the ruddy glow of hell-light.

"I guess I don't have anything better to do than be your babysitter." He grinned, the comfort of seeing a familiar face lessened by the way the glow caught his features.

Biggs swept out his gun arm and fired off two shots, and two blurs staggered from the darkness and ignited in columns of flame.

"ENOUGH!" shouted the white-suited demon in another unnaturally loud cry that filled the chamber. The stench of sulfur crested, and Biggs staggered, his free hand pressing against his temple.

"Fuck, that hurts," said the agent.

"What's he doing?" said Callum.

"THESE ARE NO MORE THAN TRIFLES! HOW WILL YOU FACE THE ARMIES OF HELL IF YOU CANNOT EVEN BRING THEM DOWN! Must I do everything myself?" Though his volume dropped to a normal level, the brittle rasp of his voice still carried across the room.

"He's stoking up the thing inside me," said Biggs. "It's fighting to get free."

"Can you resist it?"

Biggs scowled. "Yeah, yeah. I can handle it."

From the darkness the thirty-odd remaining vampires blurred into the light thrown by the hell-portal and stood arrayed across the chamber. Biggs didn't hesitate. He raised his gun and shot three times, the concussive blast buffeting Callum's ears, half-deafening him. Three vampires disintegrated in bursts of flame. Biggs tried to shoot again, but the gun clicked, out of bullets. As he released the magazine and reached for another, three vampires blurred toward him, grabbing him before he could finish. He struggled valiantly, but even with the blessing of strength and speed the contagion had given him, they disarmed him and wrestled him to the ground.

Another five blurred in around Callum, surrounding him with his back to the wall. They were all moving differently: more organized, less impulsive. Callum glanced at the watching demon behind the wall of snarling undead. The air was thick with the stench of sulfur. The demon had the vampires beguiled, turning them into an extension of its will.

Three of the five vampires bearing down on Callum blurred toward him. Instinctively, he crossed his blades in front of his chest and swiped out. One blade nicked the vampire to his left. It went up in flames, singeing Callum's side and cheek. The other two didn't even flinch, the demon's control forcing them to act against their own self-preservation. The second vampire was too close to the roman candle that its comrade had become and caught fire itself. As its flesh ignited, Callum ducked, shielded his head with his arms, and rolled through the flames. He emerged on the other side in a crouch and launched himself, both knives held ahead of him, into the nearest vampire. The blades buried themselves in its chest and it exploded.

The remaining two vampires who had approached him, plus three more from the waiting horde, tackled him faster than he could see and brought him down in a tangle of limbs as strong as steel bars. His assailants pulled his arms back and knocked his knives from his grasp. The one at his back gripped Callum's head and began to twist. He tensed his neck as much as he could, but the vampire's strength was unsurmountable. Callum's vertebrae creaked as the connective tissue was stretched to its maximum. The vampire could have snapped his neck in an instant, but the demon controlling it wanted Callum to suffer.

His head began to swim, but the wrench and tear of muscle and bone never came. The vampire exploded, singeing off half Callum's hair and burning his scalp.

A handful of vampires lit up in a random scatter that radiated outward from Callum and Biggs. The remaining vampires headed for cover as the silent concussion of spell-doctored gunfire reverberated through the chamber until the open space was empty, save for Biggs and Callum. Cries of shock and angry roars rang out from the catwalks above as vampires blurred up the walls to take out the Cottage's forces.

Biggs scrabbled around, found his gun, and fired at the demon, three concussive blasts that left Callum's ears ringing. The competing stenches of sulfur and lavender threatened to turn his stomach and leave him retching on the floor.

The enchanted bullets struck the demon, tearing into its white suit, three shots to the chest, but the creature didn't even flinch with the impact. The burning coals in ragged slits that were his eyes intensified as it grinned maliciously.

"Fool!" it rasped as it spread its arms as if to prove its point. "I'm not of your realm. Your weapons can't harm me."

Callum didn't take his word for it. He'd killed many a monster with his knives. Alchemical silver was a versatile material. He ran at the demon, legs pounding against the unyielding concrete floor. He might not have one of these new vampire's speed and strength, but he hurtled across the open space and flung himself at the demon, striking it with his full weight and knocking it down. He leapt upon it as it tumbled and pinned it to the floor. Biggs coming up behind aimed his gun at the demon's head with locked arms.

"So, you're Emrys's little pet," said the demon as casually as if they had met in a coffee bar, "his fair dove, his Chaos-kissed love. You reek of his magic."

Callum ignored its blather and stabbed both blades down into the demon's chest. Its flesh gave way like lard, no resistance of sinew, no crunch of bone to get in the way.

The demon chuckled. "Goblin blades, how quaint."

Biggs emptied the clip of his gun into the demon's head. The bullets crumpled against its scalp and the pressure of the shots slammed into Callum's ears.

"Enough of this folly," said the demon. "I am too close to achieving my goal to let you ruin it for me, no matter your fae prince's desires."

With no more than an easy swat, the creature knocked Callum off him and sent him skidding into Biggs, who dropped his gun. It rolled onto its side and pressed itself up into a crouch. The stench of sulfur crested, making Callum's eyes water. It began to change. Its body grew, the dapper white suit replaced by gray, leathery skin. A giant pair of wings unfurled from its back, and a barbed tail sprung from its hindquarters. When it stood, it had grown to twice the size of a man, and its leathery wings spread out across the chamber. The thin membrane that spread between the gnarled bones glowed in the hell-light from the tear in reality behind it. It beat its wings and rose from the floor, a woodcut print of the devil from a medieval bible brought to life. Callum had seen many strange things in the life he could remember, but a deep-seated fear gripped his innards with icy cold.

"We have to go." Biggs pulled Callum to his feet as the demon soared up to the ceiling of the chamber.

"What about the civilians?" As Callum retrieved his knives, he glanced across the empty floor.

"Frayn Unit got them out. Come on." He seized Callum's shirt and dragged him back the way they had come. "Cavendish gave the order. The bombs are coming."

44

CALLUM AND BIGGS BURST through the doors to the corridor they first came in by and ran through darkness with only the stored hell-light of one of Callum's blades to light the way. Callum's heart beat in his chest with the power of a barrage of cannons as they raced to get out before the Cottage's bombs hit. The thought of burning to ash without death taking him fueled his legs and overrode the fatigue of his muscles, but halfway down the corridor, a spell hit him from out of nowhere and knocked the wind out of him.

The buzzing chatter of distant crickets filled his ears and the fragrance of damp grass in summer washed over him as he tumbled into a heap of bones and leaden limbs. A delicate blue shimmer brought light to the dark corridor and the demon's handsome companion stood between him and the way out. Behind him, Biggs ran on, oblivious that Callum was no longer at his side.

The glow caught the white of the handsome man's shirt and turned it the blue-gray hue of a bright full moon.

"Callum!" said the man. "What do you think you're doing?"

He approached and stood over Callum, looking down on him like a disapproving schoolteacher.

Callum pressed himself up sharply, jumping to his feet, and unsheathed his second blade. The blood-red glow faded and turned a gentle blue as the alchemical silver caught the light of whatever spell this creature had cast to stop Callum. He bent his knees, softening his joints as he readied himself to fight, wondering how both this creature and the demon knew him.

"You were helping the demon. Who are you?"

The handsome creature scowled at him and waved at the knives. His hand blurred, leaving firefly trails behind it. "Put those things away. They're useless against me. I made them for you."

The spell made Callum's head spin and the tattoos on his back prickle. He shook his head to bully some clarity back into it. "These were made for me by a Venetian artificer. What are you? Another demon?"

A sneer of disgust spread across the creature's face. "No, I made them for you. You insisted on getting involved with the Library and its affairs, and I needed you to be able to protect yourself. You're far too important to me. What made you think it was a mere mortal who created them? Your journals? Half of what you've written in them is fiction. Why must you cling to the details of mortality? I made you undying to free you from those chains."

Callum frowned. He wanted so badly to learn the truth of who he was and how he came to be, but he wasn't about to believe the first stranger who claimed to know his secrets. He wasn't that much of a fool, no matter how much wild magic burned inside him.

"You made me? You're the one who cursed me?"

The creature recoiled as if he had been slapped, appalled by what Callum had said. "Curse you? I did no such thing. You begged me to make you more like me."

"A demon?"

The creature raised a threatening finger between them. "Watch yourself, mortal! I'm no filthy beast from the pits of Hell. I am Emrys of the Sultry Glade. I am your mentor and lover. You will show me respect, even if you have no memory of me!"

The creature's eyes glowed, two pinpricks of cool violet light, and his edges blurred, losing definition as he merged with the spell-light that surrounded them. His skin and clothing sparkled with flecks of gold. Overwhelmed by the beauty, Callum's eyes filled with tears that spilled down his cheeks.

"I'm tired of this," said Emrys of the Sultry Glade. "You must behave yourself. You're making me look bad. I can't leave you wandering about unchecked, not when you make yourself as much of a nuisance as you have these past few days. You've changed, Callum. What's got into you? You were always such a willing companion. You've not vexed me this much in three thousand years."

"Three thousand? What are you talking about?"

The creature's expression softened, and he reached out to caress Callum's cheek, but Callum flinched away, took a step back and raised his knives in a defensive gesture.

"I can see it's time you returned to me," said Emrys, "even though it's ahead of schedule. You will leave your life and attend me directly. Now that I have the means to reach the lords of the Fae, I will need the wild magic I bestowed upon you to help me locate them. This will hurt, but it is necessary I return your memories to you."

The creature raised a hand and the glow around him intensified, as did the scent of summer nights that threatened to make Callum swoon. Callum's tattoos crackled with electricity and grew hotter, the heat scorching his flesh. The creature scowled and dropped his hand. The heat, the glow, and the fragrance all dimmed.

"What have you done?" The creature looked up as if hearing something in the distance, and Callum smelled a faint trace of lavender. "Oh, Callum. You'll have to get yourself out of this on your own. If you fail, rest assured I will find your remains and return you to life. It will be painful, but I cannot risk losing you."

The glow vanished, taking the creature with it, and Callum breathed deeply, gasping for air as if he had been holding his breath for the past minutes.

Minutes! The bombs were coming.

He turned and ran, his heart ready to burst as he sped for the windows. The smell of Lavender grew stronger and stronger as the Cottage's enchanted bombs approached. He vaulted out the window and fell to the grass outside without pausing to catch his breath and sped for the tree line.

The ground shook and a great wave of force knocked him off his feet. Winded, he rolled onto his back to catch his breath, expecting to see the warehouse reduced to debris and flames, but it remained standing, untouched and lit up by a shifting aurora.

"Impressive, isn't it." Biggs stood over him. "I've seen them use that kind of device before. It looks fine, but underneath all that it's completely flattened." He crossed his arms and looked down at him. "What the hell happened to you? You were right beside me, and then you vanished."

45

"HE MADE YOU?" said Biggs as they trudged through the woods to the rendezvous point. "What does that mean?"

Biggs wasn't Callum's preferred confidant in matters of his curse but, limbs heavy with exhaustion, brain foggy and confused, he desperately needed to make sense of what the demon and the handsome man had said.

"He claimed I asked him to do it, to curse me. He said I was three thousand years old."

Biggs snorted, thinking Callum was joking, but the agent saw the expression on his face. "I'm sorry mate. Three thousand? Is that possible?"

The night air was cool, the damp from the river a freshening mask against Callum's skin that helped him think.

"I suppose so? I have records going back eight hundred years. Why not another thousand or two?"

Biggs shook his head. "I don't know how you handle it."

Callum had never thought about how strange it was to be him. It was all he knew. "Maybe it's because I can only remember things for fifty years. Less mental clutter."

"Wait," whispered Biggs as he put out an arm to hold Callum back and took out his gun with his other. Ahead, in the near pitch black under the tree canopy, stood a group of figures. Biggs edged forward, gun held down in both hands with arms locked. Callum readied to draw his blades, holding off for fear they might absorb what little ambient light there was and give them away.

Biggs relaxed as he approached the figures, holstered his gun, and waved Callum closer. The dozen prisoners they had freed stood huddled together in a cluster, facing out to scan the woods around them in all directions.

"Thank god you're here," whispered one of them, a woman in her sixties dressed in a quilted cotton coat.

"Why are you hanging around?" said Biggs. "I told you the rendezvous point was five hundred yards that way."

The woman gestured for him to keep his voice down. "There's something in the woods. Can't you feel it?"

Biggs drew his gun again and turned to Callum. "Is there?"

Callum sniffed the air: no sulfur, no garlic. Only the lavender emanating from Biggs's gun. He shook his head.

"All right," said Biggs. "Follow me. Callum, in the back."

If there were vampires, the light from Callum's blade would be the least of their problems, so he slid them out of their scabbards. They gave off only the faintest glow, but in the darkness, they might as well have been lanterns.

Five yards on, Biggs whipped up a hand to signal them to stop. Figures moved through the woods toward them from their right, lighting their way with flashlights. Before Callum knew it, they were surrounded, the unmistakable sound of military-grade firearms being trained upon them rustling and clicking in the dark.

"It's Biggs," said a voice from behind the glare.

The lights and weapons dropped toward the ground as muttered swearing whispered through the trees and Commander Stevens approached, his white face catching the glow from his flashlight. "You've got civilians?"

"Twelve," said Biggs. "You?"

"Fifteen went on ahead. Got four more back there."

"Thanks for the backup."

Stevens eyed Biggs with an expression that telegraphed his mistrust. "You looked like you could handle yourself okay."

Biggs shook his head. "Nah. My luck ran out. You hadn't arrived, I'd be a puddle of blood on the floor."

He peered into the gloom behind Stevens. "Where's the rest?"

"We lost four."

"Fuck, mate."

"Yeah. Let's get the fuck out of here."

While Biggs and Stevens commiserated in their emotionally repressed security services shorthand as they led the group to the rendezvous point, Callum's eyes darted around, catching on any glimmer of movement in the now dimly lit woods. The civilian was right. Callum could feel something watching them. He smelled nothing other than the musty loam of woodland earth and sorcerous lavender, nor did he feel any tingling in his tattoos, but something had his nerves on edge and his every sense straining as the canopy began to thin around them the closer they got to the road.

The smell of sulfur hit him a second too late. Wings flapped and a dark mass swooped down out of the night sky and snatched away the two civilians in front of him. Someone ahead turned at the sound of wings, saw the two bodies go up, and screamed. Gunfire erupted from Frayn Unit in a soundless cacophony of pressure waves from their doctored ammunition, and the remaining civilians dropped to the ground, trying to press themselves into the earth as the gunmen swept the sky.

Without warning, two of Commander Stevens's underlings were ripped into the air, screaming.

"We need light!" shouted Stevens.

One of the agents pulled a flare gun out of his belt and fired it into the sky. Not a conventional flare, a fist-sized globe of golden light soared above them, revealing the angular, stooped shape of the winged demon standing in the trees not ten feet away from them. The agents fired, but the demon spread its wings, undeterred, and hurtled toward them, snatching up two of them and taking them with it high into the night sky, beyond the reach of the dimming flare.

Biggs raised his weapon to join the remaining three agents' gunfire, but Callum put a hand on his arm to stop him.

"There's no point," he shouted to be heard through the jarring barrage of pressure waves. "We need to save these people."

"GET UP, YOU LOT!" shouted Biggs. "Before it comes back. RUN!" Happy to be thrown a lifeline of hope, no matter how tenuous, the civilians fled in a chaotic spread as the younger, fitter ones surged ahead. "Get to the road!"

Commander Stevens and his two remaining agents came up the rear, weapons pointed toward the sky.

"Your bullets won't work!" shouted Callum as he did his best to pull an older couple along with him.

The agents dropped their guns and pulled out sidearms. Behind them, unseen by anyone but Callum, a dark shadow whipped across the grass, the demon's wings spread like a giant manta ray.

"IT'S COMING!" shouted Callum, pointing desperately at the creature, but it snatched up the two underlings before they could turn. They emptied their guns into it, but it didn't make a difference. They were gone in seconds.

"It's picking us off," said Callum with what little breath he had to spare as he ran, Stevens catching up with him.

"Can those fancy fucking knives of yours kill it?" growled the commander. Callum shook his head, saving his breath. "Fucking useless. We need to get to the van."

The demon fell like a boulder from the sky, spreading its wings at the last second to break its fall and sweeping away two of the civilians.

Their group had numbered twenty when they had come together in the woods, now they were down to eight.

They made it to the road before they saw the creature again. All eight of them, even Biggs and Stevens, highly trained ex-military, were huffing and puffing, their strides slowing with fatigue as it touched down between them and the command van. The agents within came out firing, but, unaffected, the demon spread its wings and grinned, revealing rows of sharp, deadly teeth. It ran at them, catching the wind, and lifted off as it sped toward them, graceful and terrifying all at once. The second it moved, Callum pushed toward it through the huddle of exhausted and desperate people.

Bullets and knives might not work against it, but it could be tackled. Free of the huddle, he ran at it with every last ounce of strength he had, dipped his shoulder at the last minute and crashed into the center of the demon's mass before it could grab him with its clawed hands. They tumbled sideways, the demon landing on its back with Callum atop it, but it wrapped its wings around itself and used its momentum to roll to its feet. It lashed out at Callum with one arm, a horned elbow stabbing at his head, but he ducked and spun, grabbing the edge of the creature's wing. He clambered across its back and wrapped an arm around its neck as it thrashed to dislodge him, but Callum held fast, squeezing the demon's neck in the crook of his elbows as hard as he could in a choke hold, hoping it shared human physiology, but Callum didn't even tire it. It beat its wings and the road dropped away from them.

"Time to die, faerie pet," shouted the demon over the rush of air as it flapped its wings. "Your master will be unhappy with me, I've no doubt, but we'll work through it."

The demon dropped and spun in faster and faster circles until Callum became light-headed. The orange glow of light pollution in the overcast sky began to dim.

He blacked out.

46

HE AWOKE TO DARKNESS and comfort, with no memory of who or where he was, the restful oblivion of a deep sleep.

It didn't last long.

The world slammed into him one sense at a time: a searing pain across the back of his body; a throbbing in his head and gut; voices coming at him from a great distance, growing louder and louder; a rumble beneath him, his body sliding around on a hard surface thrown this way and that. Full consciousness returned in an agonizing bloom from the depths of his mind.

"SOMEBODY GET ME A FUCKING ESCAPE ROUTE!" A woman's voice. Young. Icy, rounded vowels and clipped consonants heated up by anger and fear.

The surface beneath him lurched, and he was thrown into a hard metal wall.

Callum opened his eyes to bedlam.

What little space there was in the command van around the workstations along one wall was taken up by Biggs, Stevens, two civilians, and another agent holding on for dear life. Esme Cavendish sat in the driver's seat driving like a maniac, slamming the wheel from side to side as she peered up through the windshield at something above them.

"I CAN'T SEE THE BLOODY THING! DILLON, GET ME A FIX ON IT!"

Dillon, a young Cottage agent manning one of the three workstations, gripped the desk with one hand to steady himself as he fiddled with switches on a plastic box, a large pair of headphones on his ears.

"I'm not reading anything," he squeaked.

Something large and dark swept by them, and Cavendish swerved sharply to the right to avoid it, slamming Callum against the side of the van. A stabbing pain like shards of glass digging into him lanced across his back and limbs and he groaned.

"Well, it's fucking reading us!" shouted Cavendish.

"You're alive?" Biggs pressed one hand on the roof to stabilize himself. He leaned down to help. "Can you stand?"

"Yeah, I think so." Holding him to help him up to his feet, Callum got a whiff of him. Lavender, sulfur, and garlic mixed together with the smell of his stale sweat. His face was pale and damp. "You look like shit."

"Says the guy who fell out of the sky on his head. Cavendish wanted to leave you there, but I insisted we bring you with us. I didn't think you'd wake up. Looked like you'd shattered your spine."

Callum rolled his head to feel out his neck and immediately regretted it. Shards of glass stabbed into his back and limbs, the pain subsiding to a low burning across his skin. His bones should take the same time to heal as anyone else's. What were these new tattoos Millicent had inked on him?

"It's trying to get to me," whispered Biggs. "That's why it's not hitting us. I can feel the thing inside me thrashing against whatever the witch did to hold it in check. It hurts like fuck."

"Is it going to break through?"

Biggs shrugged. "Fuck if I know," he whispered. "Have your knives ready in case I go feral."

"How would I know the difference?"

"Fuck off," said Biggs at the gibe, but Callum could tell from his eyes he was grateful for it.

"I'm not going to kill you."

"Yes, you will!" Biggs hissed fiercely at Callum. "You should have killed me at Trentham like I asked you. You owe me that. I don't want to end up like one of those things. Swear you'll do it!"

"I swear," he said, nodding sharply to put a conviction into his pledge he didn't feel. Pain rippled across his tattoos from the movement.

A loud thud came from the roof, and the metal buckled.

"It's on top of us!" shouted Dillon.

"Yes, I can tell!" Cavendish shouted back. "Hold on!"

She yanked the steering wheel first to one side, then the other, over and over, making the van careen across the road as she tried to shake the creature off. The added weight made the van tip precariously with every lurch, but the creature held fast. Biggs groaned and clutched his head, and Callum put a hand on his knife hilt in case the agent lost control, though he was unsure if he could follow through.

The creature's claws burst through the roof, and, with a great creak, it tore a section off. Red glowing eyes peered down at them from the darkness and the two remaining civilians wailed with terror.

The wailing didn't last long. It reached down, snatched the two civilians up and yanked them into the sky.

"How long before it comes back?" shouted Cavendish.

"Ninety seconds minimum," shouted Stevens.

Ninety seconds could be an eternity or a blink of an eye.

It was the latter. The entire back half of the van ripped away, leaving only the floor. Biggs lurched forward, pushing Callum down and making his back scream with pain as the demon grabbed Stevens and Dillon and yanked them away.

"It's not going to take me," whispered Biggs. "It knows it's only a matter of time before it has me."

Behind them, part of the van screeched and sparked as it dragged on the ground. Cavendish spun the steering wheel hard to the right, sending them barreling into a ditch.

"Out! Out!" She kicked out the driver's side door and ran for the dense patch of woodland on the side of the road. Callum and Biggs jumped from the back of the van in pursuit, jagged pain piercing into Callum's back as his feet hit the dirt and with every strike of his feet on the ground.

They caught up with Cavendish in the densest part of the copse of trees.

"Why the fuck don't weapons work against it?" she gasped, doubled over leaning against a tree.

"It's not of this realm," said Callum, his head throbbing. "It has no physical form." He caught a whiff of sulfur in the breeze. "It's coming."

"Stay perfectly still." Cavendish pushed off the tree. "I mean it. Don't even twitch. Hold your breath if you can."

She removed from her pocket a palm-sized disk halfway between a pocket watch and a yoyo and teased from it a thread with a coppery gleam. She stepped away from the tree and spun the contraption around her head, sweeping it through the night air in a slow and steady arc. The fragrance of lavender kicked up strong and thick in Callum's nostrils, blocking out all trace of the sulfurous stench, and the air around them shimmered with the haze of a summer mirage.

The beating of enormous wings sounded above them, passing them by, heading away from the road.

"We can move under this slowly," Cavendish whispered, looking up at the sky, "but my arm will get tired, and then we're fucked. There's a safe house in Battersea. I can contact HQ from there."

Cutting through the nighttime silence came the sound of a train passing and slowing.

"Train station's nearby," said Biggs.

The half hour it took them to walk to the station was a slow, torturous trudge through a field of phantom lavender, Callum growing steadily nauseated by the smell the further they went. Cavendish's device hid them from the sight of normal people as well as the demon, but the radius of the yoyo-like contraption meant they had to navigate carefully to avoid people, trees, buildings, and cars. After ten minutes, Cavendish began to droop, the arc of the device growing smaller and lower.

"Can I take over," asked Callum.

Cavendish shook her head, her face fixed into a scowl of contraction. "It has to be me."

"Maybe I can help."

Between them, they figured out an awkward arrangement. Callum, holding her wrist, helped her keep her arm up and spinning the yoyo as they walked. It made their progress even slower, Callum's tattoos screaming in fury at his exertion, but the demon swept over them five times without noticing.

The station was empty when they arrived. Apparently, no one was heading to London at eleven o'clock on a Tuesday night. Unable to hold her arm up anymore, Cavendish let the yoyo spin down and they huddled together on the platform under shelter, pressing themselves back against the wall to make themselves as invisible as possible to the sky. Cavendish cradled her sore arm and did her best to massage life back into it. Callum's arm felt fine. It was his tattoos that were complaining. Waves of stabbing pain flowed across his limbs and back. What had Millicent done to him?

"Who has cash?" said Cavendish as a train braked into the station, an expectant hand held out.

Callum and Biggs fished out their wallets. They only had three pounds fifty between them.

"Absolutely useless!" hissed Cavendish.

"If I'd known we'd be taking the train, I would have gone to the cash machine," Callum snapped back, exhaustion getting the better of him. "I didn't think I'd need cash at a vampire hunt!"

The train stopped and they hopped on, walking straight into the conductor.

"Tickets, please," said the young woman.

Cavendish took from her pocket a plate of brass with rounded edges about the size of a credit card engraved with complex symbols and held it up so the conductor could look at it. The smell of lavender filled the small enclosure between the two cars.

"Oh!" the conductor exclaimed quietly, mesmerized by the plate, her eyes alight. "That's beautiful."

"We have tickets," said Cavendish.

The conductor nodded, blinked, and moved on.

Cavendish slid the plate back in her pocket. "We're not supposed to use these on the general public. If Ms. Graham finds out … "

"If Graham finds out and we're still alive," said Callum, "I doubt she'll give a damn about a little gentle suggestion used on a train conductor."

Cavendish grimaced. "You'd be surprised."

A blond-haired man in a white suit wearing heavy dark glasses stepped into the next car at the other end. The demon had found them. Callum pulled Cavendish and Biggs into the well in front of the train door out of view. "It's the creature. The man in white."

As Cavendish leaned cautiously forward to peek, Callum shot a worried glance at Biggs.

"It's my fault," the agent mouthed silently.

"Fuck," Callum mouthed back.

"He's got his own way of dealing with the conductor," said Cavendish. "How did he find us?"

"It must be me," said Callum. "He can probably sense the curse."

Cavendish grunted and glared at him with withering disdain. "Always a liability, Foster, and never an asset." She peered around the corner again. "He's taken a seat, and he's chatting to the other passengers."

"If he can track me, he doesn't exactly need to do anything while we're on the train." Callum glanced at Biggs. The agent's face was practically white.

Callum peered out as the demon looked in their direction. It smiled, took off its glasses, and winked at him with its ragged eye slits and burning coal eyes.

In a wave that fanned out from the demon through the quarter-filled car, the passengers stood and filed into the aisle toward them.

"We've got to move." Callum shoved Cavendish into the next car, but the wave of people falling under the demon's influence caught up with them, hands reaching up to hold them in place, bodies stepping into the aisle to block their way.

As Callum and Biggs tried to push their way through, twisting arms and prying hands from them, Cavendish drew out her brass card and held it up above her head.

"Our sovereign lady, the Queen," she proclaimed loudly to the carriage, "chargeth and commandeth all persons—"

The smell of Lavender crested, mixed with the unmistakable scent of old, varnished wood that reminded Callum of the Library's forest of bookshelves, but a passenger reached up and grabbed her arm, knocking the card out of her hand, and the smell subsided. Cavendish dropped to her hands and knees to find it, and a scrum of bodies wedged itself into the narrow aisle.

"Help me!" she shouted, a cry of anger and frustration.

Biggs, powered by the contagion with strength he shouldn't have, picked up passenger after passenger and threw them to the side, sacks of laundry to be caught by the next row of enthralled late-night commuters, while Callum dropped to scour the floor at Cavendish's side. He spotted the chip of brass under a nearby seat.

"Here." He grunted as a passenger clambered over the seats to drop on his back and grab at his arm. His tattoos screamed at the impact. He gritted his teeth, clenching hard against the pain, and kicked the passenger off him, leaving him free to grab the chip and pass it to Cavendish.

She snatched it from him and stood, raising her arm again.

"Keep them off me," she gasped, catching her breath.

Callum and Biggs clustered near her, one on each side of her in the aisle, wrestling the passengers back.

"Our Sovereign Lady the Queen," her voice boomed through the carriage and the mixture of lavender and old wood returned, "chargeth and commandeth all persons, being assembled, and peaceably depart to their habitations, or to their lawful businesses, upon the pains contained in the Act made in the first year of King George the First for preventing tumults and assemblies. God save the Queen."

The passengers all stopped what they were doing and returned quietly to their seats.

"What was that?" said Callum, arms up and legs braced in case they began to swarm again.

"The Riot Act of seventeen-fourteen," said Cavendish, visibly unnerved by the sudden peace. "It's a borrowed enchantment. I'm not supposed to use it. There'll be hell to pay if we get out of this."

The demon appeared in the doorway at the end of the carriage, his horrific eyes covered by his dark glasses. He clapped his hands as if to awaken a sleeping child.

"Come, come everyone. Back to work," he said.

The smell of sulfur grew potent, and the passengers rose, turning on them once again. Cavendish raised her artifact, snapping it up above her like a soccer referee signaling a caution, and launched into her recitation once more. The combined stench of lavender, wood, and sulfur was almost strong enough to make Callum vomit. But he swallowed it down. He'd need days in the olfactory equivalent of a dark room after this.

The demon began to lose the battle. It scowled as the passengers returned to their seats, sitting quietly.

"Figure out a way to get us out of here." Callum reached for his blades out of habit as he approached the demon, even though they were useless against it. Fists and feet would have to do.

The demon sneered at him. "I don't understand how Emrys has put up with you for three thousand years. Your sexual prowess must be extraordinary."

"You'll find out in a second, because I'm about to fuck you up." Callum cringed inwardly as the words left his lips. He was dreadful at snappy comebacks. He should learn to keep his mouth shut.

The air shimmered around the demon. Its skin turned gray, and horns began to grow from its scalp beneath its rapidly thinning hair.

"Uh-uh." Callum launched himself at the creature, barreling down the aisle, his tattoos tearing at his flesh.

He tackled the demon, knocked it on its back, kneeled on it, and pressed his forearm into its throat. The transformation to its horrific winged form reversed itself.

"You can't kill me," it grunted.

"Looks like we're evenly matched, then."

Callum drew his arm back and punched the demon in the head with as much strength as he could muster, hitting him again and again. A human face would have been reduced to a bloody pulp, but the demon's head remained unblemished.

With a great roar of frustration, it freed one arm and seized Callum by the throat, its fingers clenching with strength enough to crush Callum's windpipe given enough time, but Callum yanked at its wrist and broke the hold. He twisted its arm around, but it felt wrong. Expecting sinew, muscle, and bone, instead it felt like twisting a thick bar of rubber. Holding the arm away, he spiked his free elbow down into the demon's temple.

Something shifted beneath the creature, and it pistoned up off the floor, throwing Callum back into Biggs. Its hideous wings unfurled behind it, cramped by the confined space.

"Get him into the loo," whispered Cavendish around Biggs's shoulder. "I can seal him in."

"You stay," said Callum as Biggs hoisted him back on his feet.

"Fuck that," said the agent, and pushed Callum toward the demon.

Callum twisted and used the momentum to slam his shoulder into the demon's chest. It stumbled back. Its wings cushioned its fall, tangling around it in the process. A feral growl rippled from its throat as the wings retracted into its body, its suit gleaming in the bright light of the train car.

Biggs pushed past Callum and swung a fist at the demon's head. It flinched and tried to avoid it, but the agent's fist connected and knocked its head violently to one side. It clutched its face, and, as it turned back, Callum could see a red welt spreading across its cheek. Somehow Biggs was able to hurt it.

"Keep going!" he shouted, and Biggs swung at him again with the precision of a trained boxer.

A look of fear spread across the demon's face, quickly obscured by its shifting form. Its entire body turned leather and gray, its hands becoming claws as horns sprouted from its bald head. No wings this time to get in its way.

It swiped at Biggs with its claws, but he stepped back with a dancer's grace and pressed forward again, pounding at the demon with fists like hammers, driving it back past the passengers to the end of the car and the toilets.

The extra foot or two of space was all it needed to regain the advantage. It pressed its back against the door to the next car and kicked out at Biggs, sending him flying across the floor and knocking Callum down like a bowling pin. The stench of sulfur intensified, and Biggs wailed, clutching his head and curling into a ball at Callum's feet. The demon stalked toward them.

Cavendish slid next to Callum holding her artificed brass plate up before her as if presenting her identification and began to mutter a song to herself. As the smell of lavender increased, the lights began to flicker on and off. With every moment of darkness, Callum felt his brain turn over in his skull. His tattoos seared heat into his body. In the darkness, the train car became transformed into an old Victorian-style car, the country outside lit up by a brilliant moon, all returning to normal every time the lights flickered back on.

The demon clutched its head, disoriented. Callum knew how it felt. With every shift from present-train-car to past, his tattoos screamed at him, pain arcing along his back and limbs. He inhaled deeply, the breath steadying his nerves as the horror approached him, red eyes glowing in the darkness of the Victorian car.

Callum may not have been as strong as the demon, but he was fast, and he knew his way around a body. In any normal fight, he did his best not to cause injury. Now he didn't have that worry. When the demon lunged for him, he stepped back beyond its reach, grabbed one arm and twisted as it lurched forward, pulling the arm behind it and making it stumble. In the cramped aisle of the train, he didn't have the room to throw it. Instead, he pulled it sideways so its barbed head bashed into the back of a seat. Gripping the demon's arm tight, he stepped back, away from Cavendish and Biggs toward the toilets at the end of the car.

"You want me, wanker?" He sneered and taunted the demon, gesturing for it to come at him as he edged closer to the end of the car.

Its long talons sliced into the seat upholstery as it steadied itself, ripping out chunks of fabric and foam. It ran for him, claws out, ready to swipe at him and rip him in two, but Callum was ready. The aisle down the car was a channel that directed it into a single path. He lunged sideways between the seats leading one leg out in front of it at the last possible moment. It collided with his hip in a sickening crunch, and his tattoos screamed at him.

The demon tumbled hard into the floor, rolling to a stop. It pulled its limbs underneath it, ready to launch itself at Callum, but Callum ran leapt toward it: one hop, two hops, building momentum as he swung his leg, and kicked the demon as hard as he could in the head. The blow knocked it onto its back.

Pain lanced up Callum's leg into his hip and lower back. His tattoos seared into his flesh, but he ignored the pain. He grabbed the seats in front of him and vaulted over the demon before it could roll off its back in the confined space. He slid his arms under its shoulders from behind and held it in a wrestling grip, every muscle fiber in his body straining as it thrashed about to get free. If they hadn't been in such a confined space, The demon would have easily thrown him, but the seats helped contain it as Callum dragged it toward the end of the car.

Past the seats, where the car widened, the demon's thrashing battered Callum against the sides of the train, and the searing pain of his tattoos doubled. He clenched his teeth against the pain, clamping down with every fatigued muscle in his body as he corralled the monster toward the sliding door to the toilets with no idea how to get it in there.

A crazed roar came from deep within the flickering car, and Biggs, his face bright red with exertion, slammed into them, rushing them and bundling all three of them into the door to the toilet. In a scrabble of arms and legs, between the two of them they pried the door open without losing the demon, pushed it inside and slid the door shut. It slammed against the door over and over again, the metal buckling under the assault, and Biggs and Callum grabbed the handle, pulling with all their might to keep it closed.

The disorienting flickering stopped, and Cavendish darted in beside them. She pressed her brass chip against the door and muttered a few words. There was a flash of purple-white light and the battering stopped. The train pulled into the next station and a passenger, lost in her own world, oblivious to what had happened, got off.

"That'll keep it in check until it reaches Fenchurch Street. Come on." Cavendish hopped off after the passenger and beckoned Callum and Biggs to follow. "That bloody thing cost a fortune. I don't relish having to explain to my superiors how I lost it."

They followed her to the nearest phone booth where she picked up the handset and spoke into the transmitter. "April is the cruelest month, breeding lilacs out of the dead land, mixing memory and desire, stirring dull roots with spring rain. This is Cavendish. I need a team. Strange incursion on the nine twenty-eight to Fenchurch Street. High-level incidence. Extreme caution advised."

Waves of thick lavender spewed out of the confined booth, wafting over Callum. His entire body wretched, and he turned away from the booth and vomited, his tattoos throbbing dully like a headache that had spread to his entire body.

Biggs placed a hand on his back, the agent barely able to stand up himself. "You okay, mate?"

Callum slumped to a crouch with his back against the phone booth and rested his head on his knees.

"No idea."

47

A COTTAGE HELICOPTER CAME to pick them up within half an hour. This time Callum was too battered and weary to pay it much mind. It dropped them off at a private heliport near Canary Wharf where an unmarked car whisked them away to Fenchurch Street Station.

The car drove up to quiet chaos of the non-magical kind. After midnight, the streets were empty but for fleets of police cars, black vans, and ambulances in a perimeter around the station. The car screeched to a halt at the police cordon, and Cavendish, one hand on the door before the car came to a full stop, was out and enmeshed in the investigation in seconds.

"Helicopters caught up with the train at Dagenham," a young woman who could have been Cavendish's clone read from her notepad as Callum and Biggs eased themselves out of the car, "and followed at a safe distance as units converged here. Air surveillance indicated no unusual activity en route. The police evacuated and isolated the area.

The train is empty on the tracks. Stoppard and Pinter Units are in position awaiting your orders."

A uniformed inspector approached them and bowed his head a fraction of a degree. "Ms. Cavendish."

"Chief Inspector Webster." She scowled at him.

"We're ready for you." As he gestured for them to follow, a whiff of lacquered wood rolled off him.

"Hang back," Callum whispered to Biggs. "Too many sorcerers. We don't know what they might pick up."

Biggs nodded and stayed by the car as Callum followed Cavendish across the cordon. Webster eyed Callum coolly, scanning him up and down—Callum's tattoos, throbbing like a healing wound, shivered— and promptly ignored him.

He led them past the barriers to the stairs above the platform where the train from Purfleet stood, four teams of armed responders in ranks around the train car.

"My people are quite capable of handling this," said Cavendish.

"With no concrete evidence to suggest that is in fact, the case, I assigned two of my teams to support you." He raised an eyebrow as he delivered his rebuke, Callum happy to see a Cottage official brought down a peg after all the hassle they gave the Library.

A Cottage agent ran up the steps, stopping two beneath Cavendish.

"We're ready, Ma'am. Countermeasures according to your specifications."

"Execute at will," she said.

Only Callum noticed her clench one hand into a fist.

The chief inspector mumbled into a walkie-talkie as the agent scurried down to his team. The smell of old wood and lavender wafted up from the platform as the twenty-odd agents and police officers readied themselves, some raising their weapons, others wielding strange objects that looked like medical implements from the nineteenth century.

When they moved, the two Cottage teams acted like a single, multi-limbed organism as they poured into the train from multiple doors.

Three long minutes passed, Callum barely breathing, his heart pounding in his chest, before the commander emerged.

"It's gone, Ma'am," he called up.

"What!?!" Cavendish sped down the steps, Callum and the chief inspector at her heels.

The unit commander stopped her at the train door.

"One moment." He touched his earpiece. "Secure for the Guv'ner. This way, Ma'am."

Agents with weapons up inside the car made way for them to pass through as they climbed aboard. A faint smell of sulfur hung in the air, and Callum's tattoos shivered.

"Wait." He put a hand on Cavendish's shoulder.

She shrugged him off with an irritated glare, but she took the hint and hung back to let Callum go first. The toilet door was open, Cavendish's brass plate embedded in it. The compact space within was empty, but something nibbled at the edges of Callum's perception. He slid out one of his knives and held it up to catch the emanations in the air, and the agents all shifted, a dozen index fingers curling around triggers, ready to fire if something nasty poked its head out, even though they knew it wouldn't do any good.

He held the knife out in front of him and waved it slowly through the air. It glowed with a dim crimson sheen no brighter than a child's bedroom night light.

"There's a localized spell. Pretty weak." He waved the blade over the brass plate, but he smelled no lavender, and the blade didn't change color. "It's not your artifact. Do you have anything that can negate it?"

One of the agents lowered her weapon and fished in a pocket with her free hand to retrieve a brass cylinder with three dials on it.

"You know how to use it?" she asked as she passed it to him.

He took the device and nodded. They had several of them in the Library's inventory, not as powerful as the ruined Scepter of Labrax, but would do in a pinch. He twisted the three dials until the cylinder thrummed under his fingers and pressed the button to activate it. Static rippled out away from it.

The release of the illusion came like a gentle sigh, a lifting of weight off Callum's shoulders. The open, unmarked door to the toilet turned into twisted metal as the illusion masking it fell. The interior was a mangled, ripped up disaster.

Callum turned to Cavendish. "It must have walked right past your people. It could be anywhere now."

The debriefing was long and torturous in its repetitive tedium. Callum was taken into one of a line of unmarked vans to be questioned first by a bland agent of the Cottage, yet another Cavendish clone who reeked of lavender, and an equally bland uniformed member of the Metropolitan Police Force who reeked as strongly of dusty old wood. Callum knew the fuzz had sorcerers in their ranks, another of those many certainties of which he didn't know the source. In the thirty years he could remember, he'd never come across a sorcerer-cop in person.

The Cottage agent went first, reading off a long list of questions about the incident which Callum did his best to answer. When she was finished, the police officer asked his own list of questions, most of them identical to the other agent's. Lavender and old wood swirled around him as the two sorcerers analyzed his responses. What they were looking for, Callum couldn't tell, but he answered as carefully as he could so as not to give Biggs away. It was exhausting.

When he finally stepped out into daylight and the morning chill, his head pounded in time with the throb of his tattoos.

Already free of his own interrogation, Biggs came over, wearing a baseball cap pulled down over his eyes, and handed Callum a cup of strong and sweet milky tea. "We're free to go." He dangled a set of car keys in front of him. "I got us a ride."

"No slip-ups, I take it?" Callum sipped his tea as he followed Biggs past the cordon.

"I think we're clear."

"And you have the sample of blood?"

Biggs patted his shirt pocket as he looked up at the pale morning light and shielded his eyes. His skin was bright pink, as if he had fallen asleep in the tropical sun. "Why is the sun so bloody strong this morning?"

Callum's tattoos burned like hot iron pressing into his flesh when he tried to sit back in the passenger seat. He pulled the seatbelt out, giving him enough strap to lean forward against so at least his back wasn't touching anything. The backs of his thighs were agony, but he could endure until they got back to the Library.

They drove in silence as Callum's weary mind tried to make sense of what had happened. Within him a void opened up now that every assumption he had based his life upon, even his sense of self, seemed a lie. Could he trust what the creature had told him? What had he called himself? Emrys of the Sultry Glade.

Callum let the name and that handsome face hang in his mind, dangled above his inner chasm of forgetfulness hoping for some inkling of recognition to clamber up out of the dark, but nothing came.

Every cell in Callum's body thrummed with the anticipation of being home and quiet and safe as Biggs followed him up the steps to the Library. All he wanted was peace and quiet, a cup of tea, a soak in the tub, and days of sleep. It felt like nothing less would give him the strength he needed to sort out the mystery the stranger and the demon had laid out before him. The demon had called Callum Emrys's pet. What could that mean?

The feeble spirit strengthening within him with every mile closer they got to Cheyne Heath and home crashed when he opened the door to find a crowd of bodies standing there. It didn't matter that among them were friends and people he would trust with his life. All he wanted was the quiet of his attic.

Rafe, Jessica, and Millicent stared up, mesmerized, at Johnny balancing precariously at the top of a ladder dressed in skin-tight blue jeans covered in sparkling glitter, a white tank top, and a construction helmet. Rory stood at the foot of the ladder holding it steady.

"Please be careful!" said Rafe, a look of horror on his face as he gnawed at his thumb.

"It's absolutely fine, darling," said Johnny as he screwed something into the ceiling. "This is the last one, I promise. Did anyone ever tell you; you look like an older Hugh Grant?"

Jessica looked up at Rafe through her spectacles. "He's right, you know. Put twenty years on him and you'd be twins."

"Oh, stop it!" He swatted at her. "You're trying to distract me."

"Yes, we are," she said, eyebrow raised. "You're being ridiculous. He clearly knows what he's doing."

"Rory, ducky." Johnny slipped his screwdriver into his comically large toolbelt. "Give me the thingamajig."

Rory passed him up what looked like a velvet pouch small enough to fit in his palm. A memory of being held by those hands flashed through Callum's mind, and he cringed. With all this new information, he didn't have room for the Scot in his thoughts.

Johnny sprinkled the contents of the pouch into his hand and blew it up at the cut glass pendant he had screwed into the ceiling. The smell of sandalwood wafted down at Callum.

"There." Johnny thrust his hands on his hips and turned to stare down at them. "All done. Glamors and illusions will no longer work within these walls."

He let go of the ladder to wave his arms in a theatrical bow, but the ladder rocked, and he slipped and tumbled into Rory's arms.

"My gallant hero!" His construction worker costume transformed into a cloud of tulle and shiny lamé in a facsimile of a fairy-tale princess's gown.

"You did that on purpose," said Rory as he let Johnny slide down to the floor.

"Can you blame me?" Johnny winked and squeezed Rory's ample bicep. His dress changed into a pair of black leggings and a black crepe Victorian undertaker's coat with a shocking pink pocket square. "Mr. Foster!"

The attention of everyone in the room turned to Callum and Biggs standing in the doorway in a commotion of welcome. Jessica ran at him and wrapped her arms around him. Pain lanced across his tattoos from the back of his hands and feet.

"Ow, ow, ow!" He eased her away from him with a gentle push.

"Are you okay? What happened?" She looked up at him, arms spread wide with desire to hug him again.

"Let's see. In order," Callum counted off on his fingers. "Vampires, hostages held to be feasted on, more vampires, the demon, a portal to Hell, more hostages, vampires again, carpet-bombs, the demon again, a fall from a great height, a desperate escape, and a few hours of interrogation. It was, as they say, a massive cock-up. Oh, and I think I met the man—the creature—who cursed me."

This caused another commotion and a round of questions he ignored as he shuffled over to a hard-backed chair pushed up against one wall and eased himself onto it, taking care only to sit at the edge so as little of his body touched it as possible. Millicent pushed her way through, knelt before him and caressed his face lightly with her fingertips.

"Good thing I made those alterations," she said. From the folds of her oversized black judo outfit, she took out a small magnifying glass about the size of a ten pence coin on a slender six-inch brass handle and peered through it at him. "All things considered, I think it held up quite well."

"What alterations?" said Callum.

"It seemed a waste for you to have all that Chaos within you and not put it to good use. The tattoos are acting as a conduit for it, harnessing it to your will. Either your curse or your own sense of self-preservation took advantage of the upgrades to prevent catastrophic damage, though I wouldn't rely on them. There's only so much the tattoos can do for you. And there will often be a cost, as you've discovered. When you have time, I'll show you the ropes. Now." She looked up at Biggs. "You did secure the sample, did you not?"

Biggs took the vial from his short pocket and handed it to her. She held it up between finger and thumb to inspect it.

"That'll do." She stood and peered at Biggs through her magnifying glass. "And not a moment too soon." She turned to Rafe. "To the kitchen."

"Oh, we have all sorts of equipment downstairs you can use," said Rafe, clearly excited to show her.

"Your kitchen will do." Millicent was clearly not impressed with what he had to offer.

"Darlings!" Johnny bowed extravagantly, his appearance transformed into a colorful Regency dandy. "My job here is done. As exciting as this all sounds, I have my own path to walk. Toodle-oo."

He twirled, and his outfit returned to his black jeans and undertaker's coat as he left.

48

THERE WAS NOTHING SO formidable as a witch in a kitchen, thought Callum as he, Rafe, and Jessica stood back to let Millicent get on with it. She planted her big leather doctor's bag on the table and proceeded to take out and neatly arrange rows of bottles and jars filled with powders, colored liquids, and odds and ends like buttons, yarn, and sewing needles.

She pulled out a chair and pointed at it.

"Sit and take your shirt off," she said to Biggs, who complied meekly. The red sunburn went as far down as his collar, the remainder of his skin so pale it was almost gray. "Rory, would you assist?"

Under her instructions and watchful eye, Rory combined ingredients into a bowl while she took Biggs's pulse first from his wrist, and then from his neck, and then inspected his eyes and shined a flashlight in his ears with a doctor's proficiency. When Rory was finished and she was satisfied with whatever vitals she was taking from

Biggs, she heated Rory's mixture over the stove in one of Rafe's pots and pans.

While she worked, Callum, Jessica, and Rafe retreated to a corner so he could fill them in on the events of the night before.

"A portal to Hell," said Rafe when Callum finished. His gaze grew distant, no doubt staring off into the library's stacks, and his voice grew dreamy. "Labrax mentions such things in one of his volumes. He was convinced they were possible. He had an entire cosmology of other realms, but he never succeeded in creating one. I wonder if—"

"Rafe." Jessica squeezed his arm. "Stay with us."

The librarian blinked and looked sheepish. "Apologies. My biggest question is why open a portal to Hell? Is the demon trying to bring others of his kind through?"

Callum shook his head. "Other way round. It made this new kind of vampire to be soldiers in its army to conquer Hell."

Rafe exhaled loudly and shivered. "An army of vampires. A terrifying thought. But how did it create them?"

"The other one," said Callum, "the man who said he made me. He helped him somehow. And taught him how to create a portal in return."

Jessica removed her spectacles and cleaned them with the hem of her white cotton button-down shirt, something she often did when she was processing. "So, this tall, handsome stranger said he made you three thousand years ago?"

"He said I asked him to make me. The demon called me the man's pet. I think we were lovers. And I don't think he's human. People don't give off that kind of fragrance, not even sorcerers."

"What did he smell like?" Jessica laced her fingers through his and gently squeezed.

Callum's breath grew shallow at the thought. Yearning washed over him, gripping his limbs, his heart. Separation from something he desired more than anything, something that could never be. He turned to find a chair so he could sit and bury his head in his hands to block out the world, but his tattoos throbbed in protest at the movement, and he thought better of it.

"He smelled like summer." Callum swallowed to clear the knot that had tightened in his throat.

Rory, Millicent no longer in need of his help—she was hand-sewing lengths of colored ribbon around Biggs's limbs and torso—came over to join them. Callum knew he should be happy to see him, but the feelings that emerged were too powerful, too confusing.

"Hey," said Rory.

"Hey." Callum smiled weakly. "I'm sorry. We're dealing with Library stuff. It's a bit complicated. Can you give us a second?"

A moment of hurt flashed across Rory's face. "Oh, sure. No problem."

He recovered quickly, smiled, winked, and went back to Millicent and Biggs. Two days ago, Callum's heart would have raced with excitement at that wink, now it fluttered anxiously. Jessica and Rafe exchanged a worried look.

"I don't think I can handle Rory right now," Callum whispered, dropping his gaze so as not to look at the handsome and kind Scot. "My head's spinning with all this."

A memory flashed across Callum's mind: " ... *no matter your fae prince's desires ... "* the demon had said.

"Do you know anything about faeries?" he asked Rafe. "The demon said this Emrys is one of them."

"One of the Fae?" Rafe ran his fingers through his hair as he considered. "There's plenty of lore about them. I have an entire stack of volumes in the collection, but it's mostly folk tales. There's nothing about their true nature or if they even ever existed. I've never come across any trace of them."

Callum looked over at Rory, now seated across from the table watching Millicent work on Biggs. The agent was rapidly transforming into a living maypole with all the ribbons she had wrapped around his bone-white muscled arms and torso. Rory glanced over at Callum, caught his gaze, and smiled, though the curl of his lips was a weak remnant of his usual charming, confident grin. Callum smiled back, but it was nothing more than a shape masking the confusion he felt.

He sighed. "I think Rory might know something about them. They're connected to his people."

"The Hounds of the Wild Hunt." Rafe cocked his head to one side and stared at the window. No doubt he was planning a path of research through the Library and its archive. "I must see if there are references anywhere in the catalog."

He blinked, shook his head, and breathed in a sharp, invigorating breath. "To the collection, I think." He placed a hand on Callum's shoulder, careful not to touch his tattoos. "We'll find answers for you, my boy. I promise."

He smiled, soft crinkles forming around his eyes, and slipped out of the common room.

"I'm ready." Millicent put down her needle and thread and stepped back to inspect her work. "Gather round everyone."

Biggs beckoned to Callum with two fingers. "A word, mate." He kept beckoning Callum forward until they were almost cheek to cheek. "If this goes pear-shaped," he whispered, "promise me you'll do me in. And not like at Trentham. Promise me you'll put me down. I don't want to kill anyone like that."

"I promise," Callum whispered back.

"Given what happened last time we dealt with Agent Biggs's condition," said Millicent, "perhaps don't get too close." She looked around the room. "And maybe hold onto the furniture."

Callum and the others all stepped back as she took out the vial of vampire blood and poured it onto a white handkerchief.

"When I'm finished," she said, "this will be harmless, but until then, be careful. It's quite dangerous."

She placed the empty vial in her doctor's bag and held the bloody handkerchief up by two corners. The smell of rotten eggs wafted at Callum. Muttering to herself, she flapped the handkerchief as if trying to get dust out of it, and the smell vanished, replaced by the absence of odor that happened whenever a witch performed magic. She held the handkerchief above Biggs's head and draped it over him, wincing as if it might explode.

Everyone tensed.

Nothing happened.

"Well," said Millicent, bright and cheerful as if she had put the finishing touches on a cake. "Good job all round, I say." She beamed at the others.

"What, that's it?" Biggs furrowed his brow, confused.

"Pretty much."

As one, the handkerchief and all the ribbons fell from Biggs's body. Everyone jumped.

Millicent took out her long-stemmed, tiny magnifying glass and peered at him through it. "Hmm." She frowned.

"What?" Biggs crossed his arms as if to cover his modesty. "Did it work or not?"

"Hm. Ah." She took out a crystal pendant on a long silk cord and dangled it above his head. It began to sweep around him in an irregular circle, sometimes approaching, sometimes moving further away. After three rotations, she caught it and returned it to her bag. "I have good news, and I have bad news. Yes, the spell did the job. It will hold the contagion in check without decaying. The bad news is, the contagion has already seeped into you quite a bit, so you might experience some … changes. You should probably avoid daylight, garlic, rock salt, and silver of any kind. You must never kill or cause anything larger than a housecat to be killed with your own hands. And steer clear of blood or dead animal flesh. I recommend becoming vegan to be on the safe side."

"Vegan!" The look of disgust on Biggs's face would have been comical under any other circumstances.

Millicent squatted before him. "You must be extremely careful going forward, Agent Biggs. Even the suggestion of death could inflame the contagion to the point of burning out the spell entirely. If that happened, you are so steeped in it at this point, you would change into one of those creatures on the spot."

"I thought you could cure me." Biggs looked stricken, a small child being given the worst news of his life.

She placed a hand on his knee. "I had hoped for a better outcome, but that was never going to be possible." She looked up at Callum. "Now you, Mr. Foster. I want to see how my handiwork has held up."

49

EVEN WITHOUT THE DOOR closed, the dampening effect of the wards and sigils embedded into the walls of his attic room had a calming effect on Callum's nerves.

"Take your shirt off, please." Millicent placed her doctor's bag on the bed and clicked it open.

"Do you know anything about faeries?" Callum slipped off his sweat-and-blood-stained t-shirt and tossed it into a corner.

"Other than in storybooks, I'm afraid not." She held up a small doctor's hammer for testing reflexes, placed it against Callum's breastbone, and inspected it through her small magnifying glass. The hammer thrummed gently, the vibration seeping into his chest and settling his heartbeat.

"Gracious Lady!" Her face hardened with shock. "What did you say you did to yourself?"

"The demon dropped me from a hundred feet in the air onto a country road."

"In that case," her expression brightened, "the tattoos were remarkably effective, though I wouldn't do that again anytime soon, if I were you. Turn around."

He turned away from her and felt the calming thrum of the hammer trace across his back.

"Hm," she said. "And it looks like someone tried to tamper with them. The demon?"

"No, the faerie." Even with the constant strangeness of life in the Library, the words felt bizarre to say.

She slid the head of the hammer down the back of his jeans to press it against his sacrum. "It looks like your faerie tried to rip the tattoos off you by force. That might have worked with your old ones, but these are not merely physical ink. I took the trouble to imprint them on your subtle anatomy as well. They'll require deep esoteric manipulation to extract."

She removed the hammer and walked around to face him.

"I have good n—" she began but saw the expression of dread on Callum's face. "The tattoos will take a lot of beating and hold the kind of injuries you sustained in the fall, but they only take the injury into themselves. They don't heal you."

She paced up and down, stroking her face with the back of her hand as she moved across the room, her expression a scowl of concentration.

"If anything else happens to you now, you'll feel it. Suffer too much injury and the tattoos could fail entirely and your Chaos will be released. You might not be able to die, but it could mean years of agonized incapacitation. And, of course, I can't help you with a spell. The wild magic inside you would rip it apart. But."

She stopped and turned around, one finger held high, a glimmer of excitement in her eye.

"I could make an addition to the tattoos, add a sigil that would allow a witch's spell to work on them, and you indirectly."

"Wouldn't that make me vulnerable if I meet the faerie again?"

She shook her head and stalked over to the bed to retrieve her tattoo needles from the doctor's bag. "Only a witch's Craft would work. And they'd have to know the sigil was there. And examine it to understand how it works. Only you and I would know of its existence. If I can't be reached, you'll always have the option of finding another hard-working woman to help you. What do you say? It'll take me all of five minutes."

Grinning, she held up a needle and a pot of ink.

Callum didn't need to ponder the offer. Anything to feel better. "Let's do it."

"Take down your pants and lie face down on the bed."

He hadn't been naked in front of others this much since the seventies.

True to her word, she finished the alteration in a matter of minutes.

"There you go." She muttered something that sounded vaguely French. A wave of cool ease spread across his back, his arms, and legs. "That will help move along the healing process, but your injuries were severe. It will still take some time, possibly weeks, and you need to be careful until then."

He slipped off the bed and pulled up his trousers. "I can't thank you enough."

"As I've said before, I'm sure the opportunity to demonstrate your gratitude will crop up before long." She packed her tools away and clicked her bag shut. "It usually does around here. I'll be back in a day or two to check on you."

Rory came up the stairs as she left. "Hi," he said from the doorway. "How are you feeling?"

This was going to be a conversation Callum would have done anything to avoid. He didn't want to end this thing with Rory. It had been sweet, and arousing, and comforting, all things Callum yearned for. But suddenly it was too much. The sight of Rory suffocated him.

He needed to end it, but the Scot might have information that would help him. How could Callum ask for his help and reject him in the same conversation?

His muddling took too long, and the gap between them soured. "Hi," he said, finally. "Better." He grabbed a clean t-shirt from the dresser and slipped it on. The tattoos were sore, but it was the ache of a good workout, not near-fatal injuries partly healed.

Rory stepped across the threshold into the attic, his expression expectant, hopeful, his hands thrust into the pockets of his jeans in an attempt to look casual. Twenty-four hours ago, Callum would have had those jeans off him in a heartbeat. Instead, he tidied the rumpled bed covers.

He turned back and started to speak, but Rory spoke at the same time, their words crashing into each other.

"Did I do something wrong?" said Rory.

What had Callum been about to say? Probably something weak and idiotic.

"No, no. Not at all."

An excuse popped into his head, a fully formed list of reasons to open a chasm between them: reasons why his work was too important, reasons his immortality would make their relationship impossible, reasons why his memory loss made him only half a person and not fit for companionship. But knowing his curse might not have been inflicted upon him against his will, that he had asked for it, that the person who had done this to him might have been his lover, that he might be *three thousand* years old … He had always thought of himself as a defended tower, immune to attack from the outside world, perpetually enduring. Now he felt as vulnerable as three huts on an open plain.

He no longer knew what or who he was, and the emptiness, the sudden loss of solid earth beneath his feet, made him want to slam the attic door and seal it up forever, to go from an eternal presence to a permanent absence. But he was spent and weary, and even that was too much for him.

"Come sit with me." He sank to the edge of the bed and patted the place next to him.

He told Rory everything he knew about himself, which wasn't much, and everything he had learned, which was precious little more, and filled it out with everything he felt, unburdening himself on the kind and gentle Scot. As he talked, it struck him how this was the perfect way to get rid of Rory, to show him what a broken mess he was, but Rory sat there unflinching, taking it all in, his broad, open expression soft and compassionate, even taking Callum's hands into his own.

Callum finished. For a long minute, Rory said nothing, and Callum held his breath.

"You think this Emrys was a faerie?" said Rory, and Callum exhaled.

"Yes, but what does that even mean?"

Rory stared off into the distance, lost in reverie. He picked up Callum's hand and kissed his palm. "I never thought they could be real." He blinked and returned to the room. He ran his thumb softly across the back of Callum's hand, careful not to touch the tattoos. "Which is ridiculous, given my entire village changes shape every full moon."

"What do your people say about them?"

"They were strange and powerful creatures who ruled the land thousands of years ago. I always thought of them as gods, but my mother said they were of nature like us, because they came from us."

"Came from us? What does that mean?"

"They're born of wild magic, and wild magic comes from us, all of us. They're not benevolent, though. They're wild like magic, to be feared. The stories tell of how we were created to be their soldiers, to keep the people in line. The Wild Hunt existed to scare the crap out of the locals. From their fear came wild magic, and the Fae would feed on it. But something happened, and the Fae abandoned us and left the land. Those who stick to the old ways are convinced they'll return one day, so they do everything in their power to keep us as we always were."

"That's why you left?"

"My boyfriend and I were going to be forced to take wives the elders had picked out and make babies. Brodie and I were going to run away together, but they got to him, convinced him to stay. He told the elders about our plans so they'd stop me. I ran for eighteen days to get away from them."

Rory's eyes glistened with tears, and bitter anger tinged his voice.

"I'm so sorry." Callum slid across the bed and slipped an arm around him to comfort him.

"It's fine." Rory wiped his eyes. "I should have seen I wanted it more than he did. He always cared more about his reputation in the clan than he did about me." He leaned his head against Callum's chest. "But that's all ancient hist … " He stopped himself and chuckled. "Not so ancient, I guess. You've got me beat by a few thousand years."

He lifted his head and pulled Callum into a kiss, but Callum pushed away.

"Rory, I don't think this is a good idea."

The Scot ran his fingers through Callum's hair and smiled. "So, we both have shitty ex-boyfriends. I'm not going to let that get in the way of us."

Callum closed his eyes. It would make his life so much simpler to break it off, but he was so tired, and Rory was so kind. Callum crumpled against him, ready to fall asleep even there. "I need to rest."

Rory slid up on the bed, drawing Callum with him. He fluffed up the pillows and lay back against them, opening his arms. "Come on." He patted his chest.

Callum sank into his embrace and was out before his head came to rest.

50

CONSCIOUSNESS CRASHED INTO HIM like a falling stack of library books.

"Callum! Wake up!" Jessica stood over him, shaking him awake.

"I'm up, I'm up!" He pushed away from Rory's embrace, rubbed his face, and glanced at the window. Sunlight had crept around the chimneys outside to cast golden geometric shapes across the hardwood floor. "What time is it?"

"About noon. You have to get dressed. The Palace has sent a car for you and Rafe. They're waiting downstairs." She hovered between the bed and the door, a bundle of anxious jitters.

"Shit!" Callum clambered out of bed. Any remaining fogginess snapped out of him harder than if he'd chugged back a shot of espresso or been slapped in the face. The Library's only oversight was the Master of the Dagger, who gave it broad license to direct its own affairs, but when the Master demanded an audience, the Library always jumped.

Callum tumbled out of bed, stripping off his trousers and socks, and even his underwear. He'd never felt more exposed than the previous two times he had been called before the Master of the Dagger in his current memory. He wanted to feel as well as look his best. It took him five minutes to don his one good suit, which he only wore when the Palace called.

"What's the Palace?" Rory stretched out his long limbs.

"The big boss," said Jessica, gaze fixed intently on Callum as if her focus could make him get dressed faster, but all it did was make him fumble and get his fingers caught in his shirt sleeves.

"What, like the Prime Minister?" He joined her by the door.

"Higher than that."

Rory's eyes grew to the size of twin full moons. "Buckingham Palace?"

"Yeah," said Jessica. "Well, no. St. James's Palace, but yeah." She turned back to Callum. "Come on! They've been waiting down there for twenty minutes."

Callum finished with his necktie and tied his shoelaces. "How do I look?"

"Fine, fine," said Jessica. "Rafe's in the common room."

As Callum headed for the door, Rory stopped him to adjust his tie, pat down his collar, and run his fingers through his hair. Rory winked and raised a flirtatious eyebrow. "Handsome."

How had they left it before Callum passed out? They clearly hadn't broken it off. He had no idea how he felt about that and didn't have the time to think it through.

"Mr. Torvald and Mr. Foster, such a pleasure to meet you. My predecessor had only good things to say about you both." The Master of the Dagger shook their hands, his warm, inviting smile only slightly undermined by a tangle of extremely British teeth and the mismatched colors of his eyes. "I must apologize for our first meeting being a summons of such magnitude. Have a seat, both of you."

In his forties, the Master of the Dagger was tall, slender, and fashionably dressed for a member of the Star Chamber of the Palace of St. James in a black crepe three-piece suit and bone-white dress shirt. His predecessor had been a voluptuous woman who always favored clothing fifteen years out-of-fashion, and the three scowling sorcerers—Euphemia Graham, head of the Cottage, among them—sitting on the other side of the enormous dining table could have been plucked from a film set in the nineteen-thirties.

To Callum's surprise, the Master of the Dagger pulled out a chair on the same side as Callum and Rafe and sat with his back to the sorcerers, the table between them making their role in this meeting clear. Euphemia Graham, imposing in her black Chanel suit, curled her lip, tensing her eyes at the slight, but the other two sorcerers seemed oblivious. The second sorcerer, dressed in the magenta robes of an Anglican bishop, smiled amiably, waves of pungent frankincense, the mark of his sorcerous cabal, wafting off him, while the third, a stern elderly gentleman in a stuffy pinstripe suit, looked thoroughly bored, the proceedings beneath him. An undertone of old wood surrounded him, marking him as the head of the cabal of sorcerous police officers.

The Master of the Dagger caught Callum's glance in their direction. "Mrs. Graham, Bishop Worsley, and Lord Griffiths are merely here as advisors to the Star Chamber." He opened a leather folio and took out a pen to make notes on the legal pad within. "Let's get started, shall we? I'd like to hear your account of the past few days."

His smile was warm and genuine, his accent cheerfully working-class, unusual in anyone from the aristocratic shadowy council that oversaw the supernatural goings-on of the British Isles.

Rafe launched into a comprehensive account of the missing persons investigation that had uncovered vampires and demons, omitting any reference to Biggs's and Callum's unique personal situations, and Callum took up the tale when his was the more immediate perspective. Euphemia Graham would sniff out any falsehood immediately, so they both spoke with care, avoiding outright lies to direct questions that might give away the Library's negligence in allowing artifacts to be stolen, or its recklessness in harboring an individual under the effects of the vampire contagion, or the near catastrophe of Callum's tattoos failing. When it came to Callum's curse, it was impossible to know exactly how much the Master of the Dagger or the sorcerers knew, but he kept the details to a minimum and flat out lied when the questions became too intimate. Callum didn't care if Graham knew he was lying. These facts were his own to keep. She had no right to them.

When they were finished, Callum, Rafe, and the sorcerers watched and waited as the Master of the Dagger finished his notes, stabbing and scraping at the legal pad in an unruly scrawl. He finally stopped and looked back over the pages.

"A demon," he said without looking up. "Your thoughts, Bishop Worsley?"

The bishop, his skin pale and lined, taught and dry against his bones, adjusted his robes and the silver cross that hung around his neck. "Though the Sphere of Faith acknowledges the Devil, as a principle, to be a real and present danger to the souls of the subjects of the realm," he plucked imaginary fluff from his collar and tossed it behind him like salt to ward off misfortune, "demonology is an extensively documented, categorized, and regulated art that mines the darker aspects of the mortal soul. It doesn't manufacture fantastical creatures from imagined nether realms."

"And yet," the Master of the Dagger paged back through his notes, "Mr. Foster witnessed a portal to Hell itself, and was dropped from a great height by this demon."

"Self-proclaimed demon," the bishop shifted deeper into his seat, crossed his legs and laid his hands on his lap, staring at the back of the Master's head, "and who's to say what Mr. Foster actually saw? Thanks to the intervention of Mrs. Graham's stormtroopers, we will never know."

"The regulations surrounding vampire contagion are extremely clear." Graham, too, stared at the back of the Master's head. He refused to turn and face them as they spoke. "Any outbreak must be burned out immediately and all traces expunged. The safety of the nation depends on it."

"Interesting how you invoke regulations whenever it suits you." The bishop addressed the air above the center of the table. "Yet again, your jack-booted shock troops stamp out any hint of the unusual, any morsel of revelation. I thought your role was to uncover secrets and explain mysteries, not to hoard them for yourself."

Graham turned away from the bishop, letting one long, skeletal arm drape down the side of her chair. "I am bound by duty to the realm, as are we all. It's rich that you, of all people, accuse me of hoarding knowledge."

The Master rapped the end of his pen against the table sharply, silencing them both.

"Please tell us," he smiled, unaffected by the squabble behind him, "Mr. Torvalds, that you have a plan to resolve this."

"Most certainly, Lord Master." Rafe took out a series of photocopies from a manila folder and handed them to the official. "The grimoire that Mr. Foster recovered—"

"The one Ms. Cooke used to summon the demon?" The Master pored over the pictures.

The bishop cleared his throat. "To use the word 'summon' assumes the authenticity of what are, as yet, unverified phenomena."

The Master sighed. "What terminology should we use?"

"'Invoke' would imply the act of faith upon which such a ritual depends."

The Master made a note on his pad. "Invoke, then. This was the volume Lucinda Cooke used to invoke the presence. Is that acceptable to you, Bishop?"

The bishop smiled, his eyes creasing with satisfaction as he glanced slyly toward Graham, who stared ahead without acknowledging.

"Perfectly, Master of the Dagger. The language we use in these matters affects our understanding. Imperfect language will surely lead us to incorrect conclusions, which we cannot risk when the souls of the realm are in jeopardy." The bishop glanced toward the third sorcerer, but Lord Griffiths remained impassive, as if contemplating more important questions. Or pondering what he would have for tea.

"Yes, quite." The Master spread the photocopies out in front of him, drawing the attention of Graham and the bishop behind him. "Do go on, Mr. Torvalds. These are pages from the tome?"

"Yes, Master." Rafe edged forward in his seat. "It details the ritual she used."

"Oh!" The Master wrinkled his nose in disgust at a line of script on one of the pages. "It requires sacrifices?"

"I have devised modifications that will allow us to perform the ritual without them. I propose to summon the demon and capture it."

The Master raised an eyebrow. "You can do that?"

"Oh yes, quite reliably. We will then be able to study it at our leisure. By my colleague's account, it cannot be killed by normal means, but I am confident I will be able to devise a way to trap it permanently. The Library's resources—"

"This entire mess," Graham pushed away from the back of her chair to sit bolt upright, her hands resting on the Chanel purse on her lap, "is a direct result of the Library's incompetence, and yet another clear example that such a ramshackle organization manned exclusively by those with their only qualification that they are victims of Chaos is a dangerous folly. A new, even more perilous variant of the vampire contagion has emerged, and we have a small window of opportunity to learn the mechanism behind it before it ravages the entire realm. My organization is the only one equipped to handle it properly. I demand the entire affair be given to me, along with all the Library's resources."

The Master of the Dagger closed his eyes and took a deep breath, all attention on him to see how he'd react.

He opened his eyes and spoke without turning to face Graham. "The charters are all quite clear on each of your roles." He spoke as if reciting words he had long grown bored of repeating. "They have stood without alteration for four hundred years, protecting the subjects of the realm quite adequately in all that time. The Star Chamber sees no reason in the current situation to alter that."

"If I may, Master of the Dagger?" The bishop leaned forward and rested his arms on the table, his hands clasped as for prayer. "Mrs. Graham does make a valid point that her organization could be a valuable resource in this matter, as could mine. Given the level of threat, would it not be better for us to put aside our differences and work together? The Library of the Damned has done excellent work uncovering what's happening." He leaned further forward to peer at Rafe's photocopies. "As have Mrs. Graham's agents in containing the threat. It would be a great disservice to the Library not to offer the help of the Cottage's corps of oracles and alchemists and my forensic demonologists."

Graham narrowed her eyes at the bishop, but he returned her suspicious gaze with an amiable smile and open hands.

"What do you propose?" The Master of the Dagger finally adjusted his chair, edging it sideways to make it easier to face the sorcerers.

"I have the perfect place to perform the invocation, a small church in Richmond. It rests on an intersection of three ley lines and is already amply warded against infernal influence. I propose the Librarian perform the invocation there with a hand-picked team of my and Mrs. Graham's best people to assist."

The Master of the Dagger nodded his approval, eyebrows hiked in surprise. "That seems acceptable. Mrs. Graham, Bishop Worsley, Lord Griffiths, you will each send a team of four to the Library tomorrow morning at nine o'clock. That shouldn't be too overwhelming a number. I will make the appropriate appeal to the witches to permit your access. Mr. Torvalds, the teams will assist you in your preparations, including transportation of any materials you need for the invocation to the Bishop's selected location. Do I need to send over a proctor to supervise, or will you all behave yourselves?"

Graham tilted her head toward the bishop in a subtle nod of respect. "I serve at the pleasure of the Crown."

"It *will* be a pleasure," said the bishop, beaming from ear to ear.

Lord Griffith merely grunted.

"Excellent." The Master of the Dagger looked pleased with himself as he shuffled Rafe's photocopies together into his folio along with his notes from the meeting. "I await with eager anticipation your reports on the fruits of this new spirit of cooperation between loyal servants of the realm."

Callum caught the expression of abject horror that raced across Rafe's face before he could corral it.

They were so screwed.

51

AFTER AN HOUR IN the car unable to say anything in front of the driver, Callum and Rafe exploded into the foyer of the Library and paced up and down, a pair of restless caged lions.

"This is a disaster!" Rafe pulled at his salt-and-pepper locks, turning his hair into an unruly mess. "Twelve of the blighters! They'll get into everything! And I haven't even come up with a way to imprison the demon yet!"

"It's fine," said Callum, not believing it. "It'll be fine. We have till nine o'clock tomorrow morning to figure it all out."

Jessica came galloping downstairs, Biggs—looking more substantial and human than before—and Rory at her heels.

"How did it go?" She slipped on her spectacles, changed her mind, and pushed them back up on her head, changed her mind again, and slid them over her eyes and glanced back and forth between Callum and Rafe. "How did it go?"

"It was a catastrophe!" proclaimed Rafe as he slumped into a chair pushed up against the wall and sank his head into his hands.

"We've got twelve sorcerers coming in tomorrow morning to help with Rafe's summoning ritual," said Callum.

Jessica's face fell. "Oh, fuck."

"I don't understand," said Rory. "Isn't more help a good thing?"

Rafe looked up from his desperate collapse. "They've been trying to get their hands on the collection for generations. They'll strip us of every last page and screw if we give them the chance."

Jessica took his hand and drew him to his feet. "We won't give them the chance. We have till tomorrow morning to figure out how to minimize the damage." She looked at the clock. Eight at night. "Thirteen hours. Plenty of time. I'm certain there are a few things in the Morozova collection we can use to keep the bastards in check. It might be as simple as setting up a workshop here in the foyer and stopping them from entering further. Perhaps we could find a way to lock down the Hidden Galleries entirely or hide the basement from them."

Rafe's eyes lit up at the possibilities. "Yes, yes! Morozova's work is serpentine enough, it might work. And I have a few treasures from Labrax you don't know about."

"Labrax? Really?" She looped an arm around his and led him into the Library, her surprise entirely unconvincing.

Rafe stopped at the door and turned back to Callum. "Speaking of Labrax. Dear boy, do you have the scepter?"

Callum's heart sank, all hope of getting away with destroying the artifact dashed. He retrieved it from the closet and winced as he presented it to Rafe.

"What," the librarian's eyes widened in horror, "have you done to my precious scepter!"

Jessica ignored his blustering and pulled him through the doors. "Yes, yes. He's a dreadful hooligan with no respect for your priceless artifacts. You can berate him later."

She turned back and scowled at Callum as the doors swung shut behind her.

"What can I do?" said Biggs.

"Go with them," said Callum. "Any insight you can give them about the Cottage will be a great help." He put a hand on the agent's shoulder. "How do you feel?"

Biggs took a second to think about it. "Good. A bit wobbly in the knees, but good." His eyes drifted and his gaze unfocused. He shuddered and brought himself back, a haunted look in his eye at whatever had crossed his mind. "I'm hungry," he whispered. "It's not right. Remember the promise you made. Don't let me turn."

"I remember," said Callum, determined not to let it come to that.

Biggs pulled himself up, slapped Callum on the arm, and followed Jessica and Rafe into the library. "Good man."

Pain lanced across Callum's tattoos and was gone. "Working late tonight, I'm afraid," he said to Rory. "This time I am going to have to kick you out."

"Yeah, yeah. Can we talk for a second, though?" Worry creased his usually jovial and carefree expression.

"Of course." Callum drew him to the chairs Rafe had vacated and took Rory's hand in his as they sat. "What's up?"

"Earlier today, after you told me about your fae lord, I realized something. I've been pushing too hard for us. I've never met anyone like you, and I've only been thinking of myself. I think we'd be great together, but I didn't listen properly. What you've been through, what you're going through, is unfathomably big. I finally understood what you were asking me. If you want to take it slow, or even break up, I'll understand … "

He trailed off as he watched for Callum's reaction.

A knot in Callum's chest that he hadn't realized was there released and relief flooded through him. For a moment his throat was so thick with the feeling of it he couldn't speak.

"Thank you," he croaked. "I appreciate that."

"I want to be here for you, even if it's only as a friend."

Callum leaned in for an awkward hug, his knees crashing against Rory's. "Going slower would be great," he said when they parted.

"Yeah?" A hint of that smile ghosted across Rory's face. "Good. That's good. Come on. Be a gentleman and walk me out."

Callum led him to the door and the front step beyond. The night was cool and clear, a sliver of dark sliced off the moon.

He slipped an arm around Rory's waist and squeezed. "Does the moon affect you at all while you're here in the witches' sanctuary?"

Rory rolled the large, carved bead around his neck in his fingertips. "With this on? Not at all."

They stood in silence, looking up at the night sky.

"Off I go," said Rory, eventually. "My shift starts at nine. Will you call me when all this is done?"

"I will. I promise."

Rory ran his fingertips over the brass plaque by the door and grinned. "Library of the Damned? Honestly, such a drama queen." He winked and stepped onto the pavement.

The stench of garlic and sulfur hit Callum first. Six figures blurred into solidity out of the darkness, but Callum already had a fistful of Rory's denim jacket in his grip.

"RORY!" He yanked the big man back with every ounce of strength he had and shoved him through the front door. He was halfway inside himself when one of the vampires seized his arm, pulled him close with machine-like strength and sank its teeth into his neck.

52

THE TEETH WERE SO sharp, Callum barely felt them. He struggled, squirming violently. Though his thrashing dislodged the vampire, and its teeth only tore at his skin, the wound was still deep enough to bleed. The vampire lapped at his neck with a rough tongue, and ignited in a blazing flash, leaving Callum free with skin singed and t-shirt burning.

Should have read the memo. The thought sprang into Callum's mind unbidden as Rory grabbed him, yanked him inside, and slammed and locked the door.

The Scot pulled off his denim jacket and used it to help Callum smother the flames and embers, the thin cotton of his shirt reduced to charred tatters.

A wave of intense pain pulsed through Callum's tattoos, making him stagger, and he felt the low throb of the wound in his neck fade. He checked himself in the mirror. The wound was gone.

I'm going to be in the witch's debt for decades, he thought as he wiped his bloody hand clean on the shirt.

He went to the front door and leaned into it with both hands, bracing his legs as if it would make a difference if the vampires tried to break the door down.

"Look in the closet," he said to Rory, hovering behind him. "Find anything that looks like silver!"

The big coat closet in the back was full of knickknacks. There had to be something in there.

"Found these." Rory held up a pair of chunky silver candlesticks.

Beyond the front door, all Callum could hear was scratching and whispers. A faint smell of garlic wafted at him, and a chill shivered across his tattoos. Rory came up behind him and placed a hand on his.

"It's okay," he said. "We can let them in."

"What?"

Rory reached for the deadbolt, and Callum brushed his hand aside, but the large Scot thrust his shoulder into Callum to push him out of the way.

"Rory, stop!"

Callum grabbed him by the waist and heaved with all his might to pull the tall slab of muscle away from the door. He spun, knocking Rory off-balance, and threw him on the floor. The Scot looked up at him with a glassy expression, as if listening to music in a far-off room. The vampires had beguiled him. He tried to get up, but Callum kneeled on him to pin him to the floor.

Rory blinked and, for a moment, Callum hoped he'd broken free, but the Scot reached up and levered Callum to one side with surprising strength, pushing him off. Callum grabbed him by the belt and leaned back with all his weight to pull him to the ground. He wrapped one leg around him and tried to twist the Scot's treetrunk arm behind his back, but Rory swiveled, pulled it free and, with one big hand, pushed Callum down.

Rory turned for the door, but Callum tackled him low, trying to knock the Scot off-balance, but Rory brushed him aside, knocking him to the ground. Callum tried to get to his feet to stop him, but Rory was too close to the door. He wrapped his arms up under Rory's shoulders in an attempt to put him in a headlock, but Rory was tall enough that Callum couldn't get leverage.

Rory unlocked the deadbolt, and would have opened the door but for Biggs, who darted out of nowhere, yanked him back, and threw him across the foyer to crash into the doors to the collection.

"Sorry, mate," he said as he bore down on Rory, but halfway there, he clutched his head and fell to his knees groaning.

Callum ran to his side, but the agent pushed him away. "It's okay. I can handle it. Check on your boyfriend."

"What the hell happened?" said Rory, free of the beguilement, as Callum helped him up.

"The vampires had their hooks in you."

"Thank the moon they released me. There was no way anyone was going to stop me opening the door."

Callum nodded over at Biggs struggling to get up like a drunk after several shots beyond his limit. "I think they're more interested in him."

They tried to help Biggs up, but he shrugged them off and hauled himself to his feet on a side table.

Rory walked over to the front door and laid a hand on it. Callum twitched, thinking he might have been beguiled to do it, ready to dart over and stop him.

"Why haven't they broken through?" said the Scot.

Biggs took a deep breath and shivered. "They can't. The bastards have to be invited in."

A memory of Lucinda Cooke at the door flashed through Callum's mind. She had only entered once Rafe and Jessica had asked her in. "How do you know this?"

The agent went to the door and pressed his ear against it. "I can feel their frustration." He frowned. "Did you get a look at them? I thought the bombardment last night got them all."

Callum thought of bodies being yanked into the dark sky by sharp talons. "We assumed the demon killed the rest of your team and the other survivors. It must have turned them instead."

"Then we're in serious shit." Biggs scrunched his eyes shut and massaged his temples. "If they can't get in, they'll find a way to get us out."

As if on cue, the lights went out. Callum's eyes quickly adjusted to the dim, warm glow cast by the two braziers by the doors to the collection. "Is it worth calling for help?"

Biggs shook his head. "If they cut the lights, they cut the phone lines, too."

"What about your field telephone?"

"It's upstairs. But it's a piece of shit. I wouldn't rely on it getting through."

Callum thought for a moment, Biggs and Rory staring at him expectantly, their faces pale in the gloom. Between them, Rafe and Jessica might find an esoteric solution. He turned to Rory and squeezed his arm. "The door to the emergency stairs to the Hidden Galleries is to the right of the lift. Would you go down and tell them what's going on? Tell them we need a solution to call for help."

"And make sure they stay down there," said Biggs. "It's deep enough to protect them from being hypnotized by the vampires. They're on the sixth level."

"Why didn't the witches challenge them when they entered the sanctuary zone?" said Biggs as he and Callum headed up through the dark staircase. There were no braziers upstairs. Finding their way around was going to be fun.

"Change of allegiance?" said Callum, his breath labored as they climbed. He needed a vacation. Or at least a decent night's sleep. "They're not with the Cottage anymore. The witches seem mostly concerned with keeping sorcerers and their underlings out."

"I hate magic." Biggs's irises glimmered in the darkness, not with the full reflective glow of a vampire's predatory eyes, but with enough sheen to make Callum itch for the security of having his knives strapped to his legs.

"Yeah. It's not my favorite, either."

After a tense half hour of going through the Library's upper floors, making sure all the windows were sealed, and moving furniture to block them, Callum and Biggs made their way down into the Hidden Galleries with the field telephone. Callum lit the way down the stairwell with one of his knives held aloft, the blade giving off an eerie purple light absorbed from the wild magic around them. Callum's fresh white t-shirt glowed in the light, illuminating their faces as they descended. Biggs eyed the blade nervously.

They found Rory awaiting them in the stairwell on the fifth level. His eyes widened at the sight of the glowing blade and the muddy streak of phosphorescence trailing it. "They're in the card catalog." He ushered them through.

In the drawer-lined office, Rafe and Jessica had pulled apart the apparatus designed to track outbreaks of Chaos across the country. On the table beneath the brass armature and the map of the British Isles on the wall sat an artifact made of lacquered wood, wires, and valves that looked like a cross between a vintage radio and a musical instrument from a fifties science fiction film. Rafe and Jessica had attached it to the armature with a tangle of copper wires, the pendulum tracing slow circles above them casting eerie moving shadows in the light of the single brazier in the corner.

"Magnificent!" Rafe waved them over to the apparatus and patted the table. "Put it right here."

The field telephone placed to his satisfaction, he attached a wire to the phone's casing with a crocodile clip and placed the handset on the wooden device. "This little marvel is hand-cranked. I'm certain it will do the trick."

He cranked the handle a few times, thumbed a brass ball toggle switch on the side of the device, and the valves and bulbs attached to it crackled and lit up bringing welcome light to the room. He turned a knob and static hissed out of the device's speaker. The pendulum stopped at an unnatural angle, its tip pointing toward the handset. He stood back and admired his work.

"Now, which of us has the least wild magic in them?" He looked at them expectantly. "Agent Biggs, why don't you give it a try."

Biggs approached the table. "What do I do?"

In the harsh, angular light of the glowing bulbs, Rafe's expression of excited enthusiasm took on an air of derangement. "The artifact is a psychospiritual amplifier, you see. It draws on the stuff of magic and ramps—"

"Rafe." Callum did his best to interrupt his train of thought as gently as he could. "What does he need to do?"

"Oh! Yes, of course. Pick up the handset, visualize who you wish to talk to, and speak." Rafe stepped back and ushered the rest of them to the other side of the desk. "Too much Chaos will throw everything off."

Biggs picked up the handset and held it away from him like a dead and rotting fish. "Visualize?"

Rafe bounced up and down on his toes as if itching to explain in more depth. "Picture whoever you want to talk to. Imagine yourself doing it. Oh! Who should he be calling?" Rafe turned to Callum for an answer.

"Esme Cavendish," said Callum and Biggs at the same time.

"Capital!" said Rafe. "Imagine Ms. Cavendish at her desk in her office, or anywhere you've seen her a lot."

"The incident room," said Biggs.

"The incident room! Excellent. Picture her there. Picture yourself talking to her. You can do it!"

Looking entirely unconvinced, Biggs held the handset to his ear and mouth.

"Close your eyes," said Rafe, "and picture it."

Biggs did as he was bidden and spoke. "Cavendish, it's Biggs. Merida, Argyll, Aberystwyth, Tooting. Condition black, over?"

The speaker in the device erupted into a grating screech, the hiss and cry of a thousand terrifying creatures. The sound grew louder and louder, bouncing off the walls of the office, threatening to deafen them. Rafe raced to the machine and threw a switch. The device fell silent, but Callum's ears rang as if he were standing inside a church tower at high mass.

"Forgive me." Rafe took the handset from the agent. "I thought the spell keeping your contagion in check would shield you, but I was obviously mistaken. What do we do now? The rest of us are infused with far too much Chaos."

"Rory isn't Chaos-kissed," said Callum. "Would you be willing to try it?"

"Of course! Anything to help." The Scot took Biggs's place at the device. "Who should I try and call? I've never met this Cavendish person."

"Your witch friend," said Callum. "What was her name? Gosha?"

Rory's face lit up with relief at the thought. "Yeah, I can do that."

Rafe cranked the handle, flicked the switch, and passed the handset to him. "Whenever you're ready."

Rory closed his eyes and took a deep breath before putting the handset to his ear. "Gosha? Gosha, it's Rory. I'm in the Library. We're surrounded by vampires. I need your help." He exchanged a glance with Rafe.

"Keep going," said the librarian.

"Gosha, can you hear me? I need your help." The speaker crackled and a low hiss seeped out of it. "I can hear whispers."

Rafe joined him at the device. An electronic hum thrummed out through the speakers, growing louder the closer he got. He turned a few dials, flicked a few switches, and withdrew to the desk with the others. The hum abated, leaving only the hiss. "Try again."

"Gosha, it's Rory. We're stuck in the Library. There's vampires outside—"

"Blood," came a voice from the speaker, a throaty, harsh rasp, "and power. Hungry, so hungry. The master compels me. I will rip out their throats and fill myself with their blood, and I will revel in their death."

Another voice joined it, repeating a similar litany, and a third and a fourth, until the room was filled with grim and violent chatter.

"Turn it off," said Callum, unable to take the haunted expressions growing on the others' faces.

Rafe rushed over to the device, flicked the switch to deactivate it, and the room fell silent. "Excuse me, dear fellow."

He took the handset from Rory and placed it to one side on the table. He took out a screwdriver from his pocket, unscrewed a panel in the side of the device's cabinet, and fiddled around, disconnecting and reconnecting wires. Finally, he stepped back and turned to the others.

"It's no good," he said, stricken. "There's too much Chaos down here."

"Even with the braziers?" said Jessica. "What if we brought a few more in? Or tried it down in the vault. The insulation down there is absolute."

Rafe shook his head. "The Library's vast reservoir of Chaos would all still be there beyond the line of protection. Our signal can't get through. I'm afraid we're on our own."

Callum never suffered from claustrophobia, but the walls suddenly felt far too close and the air unbearably hot and oppressive. He paced back and forth to get some movement in his body before his skin began to crawl and he ran upstairs to open the doors. The vampire beguilement didn't work on him, but he might end up letting them in just to get out of there.

A faint glimpse of an idea emerged from the fog in the back of his fatigued mind. He stopped and turned to face the others, all of them staring at him anxiously. "That vast reservoir of Chaos might be exactly what we need. If we extinguish all the braziers and let it run free, either the witches or the Cottage's oracles will pick it up. Someone will be sure to investigate."

Biggs nodded. "Cavendish's got three seers on this place at all times waiting for you to fuck up."

Rafe scowled. "We'll be obscured from their view by the witches' sanctuary!"

"They can't see you directly," said Biggs, "But Cavendish got approval to rig up some kind of early warning system. Something about ley lines and astrological concordances. It takes up a whole floor."

"Outrageous!" Rafe's face turned the shade of a light rosé wine. "I shall have words with the MOD about this!" He remembered their predicament and distress washed over his face like the return of an evening tide. "If we get out of this."

"We'll get out of this," said Callum, faking confidence he didn't feel. Odds were, he would get out of it in some shape, even if it took him a few decades to heal enough to be human again, but he couldn't rely on that with the others in jeopardy. Rory especially. Rafe, Jessica, and Biggs had no choice but to be there. Rory was only stuck with them because of him. The possibility of signaling the Cottage wasn't enough. They needed something else. "What about the summoning? Could we do it ourselves? If we trap the demon, we could force him to call the vampires off."

Rafe brightened at the idea. "We do have everything we need here, and between the grimoire and references I found in Labrax I'm reasonably certain I can devise a way to contain the demon permanently."

Callum started to feel better about their prospects. "Good. I'll work my way through the Library and extinguish all the braziers while you set up the summoning."

"I can help," said Rory.

"No!" chimed in Callum, Rafe, and Jessica at the same time, startling the tall, strapping Scot.

"All that wild magic bouncing around won't be good for you," said Callum. "You could end up like one of us."

Rafe went to the desk and piled his books and papers into a stack. "We'll set up down in the vault. You'll be perfectly safe there."

"I'll come with you," said Biggs.

"No," said Callum. "It's too risky."

Biggs grinned. "Wasn't asking, mate."

53

“ARE YOU SURE YOU want to take the risk,” said Callum as they made their way up the stairs to the surface.

“My job’s to protect you,” said Biggs, unfazed by the eight flights. “If I can’t do my job, what’s the point?”

Callum knew the feeling. He needed a hobby. Maybe something easy like martial arts or fencing. No. Too much like work. Knitting? Needlepoint? Flower arranging?

The main floor of the Library, which housed the books that were only theoretically deadly, glowed warmly, the avenue and the pathways lit invitingly by lines of braziers.

“How do we turn these things off?” said Biggs in the respectful hush of someone taught at a young age to fear the wrath of a vexed librarian. “Blow them out?”

“I’ll show you.” Callum led them to the main doors to the collection and through to the lobby where two braziers stood sentry.

"We need to extinguish them sequentially all the way down to the vault to stay protected."

"I thought you couldn't be cursed twice."

"The historical record would suggest so, but by the time we get to the vault, there'll be more wild magic flowing freely in here than I'd care to mess with. Things can get unpredictable." He ran a hand over his tattoos. "Artifices like this and the spell Millicent cast on you to keep the contagion in check might break down."

"Mm. Understood."

Callum squatted at the base of the nearest brazier and removed the front panel. Behind it was a blue gemstone about the size of a fist mounted on a pewter stand resting in a brass bowl covered in symbols of the *mathematica infernalis*.

"Turn the bowl ninety degrees clockwise so the star is pointing at you." He reached into the base to show Biggs how to do it, and the brazier dimmed to black as he turned the bowl. A shiver raced across his tattoos. "Do the other one."

As Biggs removed the plate on the base and turned the bowl, Callum stepped back into the library and the protection of the braziers within.

"Leave the cover." He said, beckoned the agent inside. "One less thing to do when we turn them back on. You take that side. Work from the wall to the center aisle and back to the stairs."

There were seventy-two braziers on the main floor, more as a barrier of protection against what lay beneath than any effect the books housed in the stacks might have. The more they extinguished, the more Callum's tattoos shivered, though he couldn't tell if it was because of wild magic, or his anticipation of it. He'd seen far too many horrors when Chaos was whipped up into a frenzy. Probably just as well he lost his memory every fifty years.

They worked efficiently, Callum a little faster at doing his side than Biggs thanks to years of experience. He stood at the elevator waiting for the agent to finish, listening to the silence, all the hairs on his body standing on end, the bitter taste of copper building in the back of his throat.

Glass tinkled to his left. A deafening bang and blinding flash erupted behind one of the bookshelves, the tall and heavy wooden frame shielding Callum and Biggs from the blast. The bookshelf toppled over, and torn pages fluttered through the air, a flock of confused paper birds settling to feed.

Wood splintered explosively near Callum's head, and Biggs, appearing out of nowhere, tackled Callum, knocking him to the carpet as the wood-paneled wall behind him popped and splintered. Biggs dragged him behind a low bookshelf, shielded from the shattered window above.

"We've got to put out the fire!" Callum tried to rise, but Biggs grabbed him by the belt and yanked him down as a bullet whisked past his head. A book behind him splintered and ripped.

"Keep your head down!" Biggs crouched near the edge of the bookshelf and peered out. "They can't be serious. They'd have sent a proper incendiary device through, or worse. I think they're just keeping the pressure on."

The flicker of flames danced on the bookshelves around the flash bomb, and the smell of burning paper filled the air.

"They're doing a bloody good job!" Callum could see one of the library's many fire extinguishers nearby, but he'd have to break cover to get it. "Can you distract them?"

"Don't you have a sprinkler system?" Biggs looked up at the high ceilings.

"The building was built in the seventeenth century. Of course we don't have a fucking sprinkler system." Callum crouched, ready to run for it.

Biggs grabbed a handful of books from the nearest shelf. Callum shook his head. Rafe was going to go spare when he saw the mess.

"On three," said Biggs. He counted down and began throwing books in the air, each one torn up by bullets before it fell.

Callum put his head down and ran, grabbed the fire extinguisher, and made his way around to the fire as Biggs poked his head out and flicked V-signs at the sniper, ducking back to safety before he could be hit. Callum reached the blaze without a second to spare. One entire bookcase was burning. He emptied the fire extinguisher and doused the flames, destroying hundreds of priceless volumes.

With the fire out, darkness reclaimed the library.

"I think we're okay." Biggs edged toward the stairwell. "The flash bomb was to give them something to see us by."

They made it to the stairs, leaving burning the five braziers Biggs hadn't managed to extinguish before the attack. Five wouldn't do much once all the others were out.

By the time they had put out all the braziers on the first sub-basement, the taste of copper was so strong in Callum's mouth it burned like hot peppers. The cabinets began shifting in the dark, the entire floor creaking and swaying like a wooden ship in rough waters. Floor by floor, the weirdness increased. Strange lights flickered in the dark, and doors and arches that shouldn't be there led off into mystery. The seventh sub-basement had already transformed before they even got there. Vegetation was everywhere, vines hanging down from the ceiling, strange and disturbing flowers blossoming on every surface giving off sickly radiance. On the tenth sub-basement, where Rafe had tried to help Biggs, a flock of ravens cawed and fluttered through the work bays. By the time they got to the lowest floor and the vault, Callum's shoulders were up by his ears, his neck a solid column of barbed cables.

The vault was a room where all the dangerous items were kept at the back of the lowest sub-basement. Sealed off from the rest of the floor by an iron cage over the entrance with two gates, the stone walls and arched ceilings were carved with a dense grid of *mathematica infernalis* that isolated the vault completely from the world around it. Inside, metal industrial shelves lined the walls wrapped with treated copper wire crafted to make them inert and impervious to the books and artifacts they housed. When the gates were closed, no magic, wild or otherwise, could come in or out.

The overwhelming coppery bitterness in Callum's mouth faded the second the inner gate clanged shut.

Rafe and Jessica had, with Rory's help, rearranged the shelves, pushing them all up against the walls. Jessica and Rory were still struggling with a final shelving unit, doing their best to drag it without scraping up the floor or toppling it. Rafe knelt in the cleared-out center of the room referring to the grimoire and two other books as he painted geometric shapes and strange symbols on the stone, the layout a hundred times more elaborate than the summoning circle Callum and Biggs had found at Lucinda Cooke's house. Classic Rafe. He never did anything half-hearted.

"How did it go?" Rafe looked up at the rattle of the gates. "Everything okay up there?"

"Yep." Callum exchanged a glance with Biggs, who had gone to help the others move the shelving unit. Telling Rafe about the fire would only distract him. Let him live in the bliss of research and problem-solving he was in for a few hours longer. Assuming they got out of there alive. Rafe would be easiest to save. Take his cane away from him, or even push him outside the vault with all the braziers down, and he'd turn to dust. The others were a different story. Perhaps he could hide them in the many new corridors and rooms that had appeared on their way down, though it would mean exposing Rory to more Chaos than any normal person should ever have to experience.

"I've cross-referenced the grimoire." Rafe put the finishing touches on an intricate white curlicue of *mathematica infernalis* with a paintbrush, "with Labrax and I've come up with modifications that will ensure the demon remains contained within the summoning circle. And Jessica was able to locate two artifacts in the collection that will act as sacrifices."

He waved his brush at a cheerful round porcelain teapot and a rusty garden trowel that sat awaiting their moment on a folding table pushed up against one of the metal shelving units.

"And what about once we have it?" said Callum. "Do you have a way to compel it to call off its vampires? Do we have a way to kill it?"

"Regrettably, no." Rafe scowled as he leaned in to get a better look at his work. "There is no way of killing it. The grimoire and Labrax are both quite clear. The demon is not of this realm and thus cannot be killed by anything from here. We would require something that came from Hell itself to kill it."

"And we've not got anything like that?" Callum walked over to the nearest shelf half-hoping he would find a red barbed trident lying there. All he found was a crumpled-up Kleenex and a Monopoly set with the board and all the pieces laid out as if for a half-played game.

"No, dear boy." Rafe put his brush to one side, scrunched his eyes up and raised his arms to stretch out his shoulders.

Callum sighed. "Perhaps we can ask it to tear its own throat out."

Rafe patted the pocket of his blazer. "Fear not. I have something I'm confident will put the screw to it."

"I've an idea." Jessica emerged from behind a shelving unit in the corner wiping her hands on her fashionably ripped jeans, Rory and Biggs in tow. "There's a bottle from the Richard Francis Burton collection. It was said to once contain a being of immense power. Perhaps we could use it to trap the demon. I know where it is. I could get it."

"A genie's bottle?" said Callum, surprised he could still be surprised in this place. "Do genies exist now as well as faeries?"

"No, no, no!" Rafe waved his hands urgently at her as if she were about to lay hands that very moment on the bottle. "Those artifacts are highly volatile. The bottle could explode. Or worse."

"Will the circle hold the demon indefinitely?" Callum walked the circumference toward Rory.

"Perhaps?" said a sheepish Rafe.

"Do you have another solution?

"Not yet, no."

"We should at least consider it, don't you think?"

Rafe sighed. "Yes, I suppose so. For once I would like a solution to our problems that doesn't involve a threat to the fabric of reality."

The thought of all the strange changes outside in the galleries flashed across Callum's mind and he exchanged another wary glance with Biggs.

Jessica darted toward the gates. "I'll get it."

Callum and Rafe chimed in with a joint "No!" One foot outside and the unfettered Chaos would overwhelm her with visions, not that Rafe would have known. The librarian shot him a confused look. Callum was usually on Jessica's side.

Jessica scowled and mouthed "traitor" at Callum.

Rafe beckoned to her. "Help me with the sacrifices, please. Once we get them set up, I'll be ready to begin."

Callum made his way to Rory around the remainder of the circle. "How are you doing?" he asked.

"Turning the braziers off released a ton of wild magic into the library?" Rory's broad forehead wrinkled with thought.

Callum nodded and lowered his voice so Rafe couldn't hear. "Things are getting mighty peculiar out there."

"Like what happened to you at my flat when your tattoos vanished?"

"Something like that. Why?"

Rory looked over at the gates, lost in thought. "No reason. Just thinking."

"Excellent!" Rafe stepped back from the circle. He and Jessica had placed the teapot and the trowel each in their own smaller circle butting up against the big, empty one filling three quarters of the room. "We're ready. Stand back, everyone."

The others did as bidden, edging back against the shelves as Rafe picked up the grimoire and took from it a sheet of yellow legal paper covered in his dense scrawl and cleared his throat. He proceeded to read from the paper a long sequence of gibberish, short concussive syllables that bore no resemblance to any language Callum had ever heard.

After about five minutes of this, Rafe stopped and swallowed. "Gracious, what I wouldn't give for a glass of water!"

"Is that it?" said Jessica. Rafe nodded. "Not very impressive."

"Perhaps I should give it another go." He flipped his crib sheet over and turned it upside down. "Ah, I see what I did."

He launched into another five-minute barrage of blabber, but, by the end, nothing had happened.

"That should have worked." He looked plaintively at Callum. "I swear it should have—"

The three overhead lights flickered and waves of sulfur overwhelmed Callum's nostrils. The shelves began to rattle and shake, skittering on the stone floor. Two of the lights exploded in a shower of glass, and the remaining one dimmed almost to darkness.

In the circle stood the demon, its skin gray and leathery, its wings wrapped around it. Its horned head and burning coal eyes peered out from behind them. It tried to spread its wings, but the circle contained him like a glass cylinder. It roared, a deafening, metallic chorus of voices crying out in pain. It slashed at its containment with its talons, and the air glowed like bright, golden neon around them, but the containment held.

It threw its head back and roared again, even louder, and the room spun around Callum. Jessica and Rafe beside him doubled over and retched at the intensity.

The one remaining overhead light flickered, and the gargoyle disappeared, replaced by the blond man in his white suit and dark glasses.

"Oh my," it said in its whiskey-and-cigarette-soaked voice. "And here I was about to sit down to a nice glass of sherry and an episode of Prime Suspect."

54

CALLUM DIDN'T BUY THE flippant remark. The demon's tension was clear in its body, its hands half-clenched into fists, the expression behind its dark glasses fierce. The smell of sulfur rose and fell in waves. It was testing the circle, searching for cracks with which to pry itself free. It spotted Biggs and the stench of rotten eggs made Callum gag.

"Progeny," said the demon, "assist me."

Biggs, leaning against the shelves, staggered and caught himself on the nearest post. "Fuck you, wanker!" He hoisted himself back to his feet.

The stench intensified further, and Jessica moved to help him, but Callum held her back, one hand on the hilt of his blade in case the witch's spell failed.

Biggs smirked, an angry leer, but he stood his ground, and the demon gave up. The stench of eggs receded to a low funk that ebbed and flowed, merging with the bitter copper of Chaos in the back of Callum's throat.

"The faerie's pet," said the demon, laying eyes on Callum. "I cannot comprehend what your master sees in you. A doxy like you should be compliant, respectful."

Callum knew it was supposed to be a taunt, felt some stirring of emotion deep within him, but the handsome faerie was a stranger to him, and the jibe sloughed off him.

"Call off your vampires." Callum approached the circle.

The demon scowled, confused. "Vam-pyre? What a peculiar word. What does it mean?"

"The men and women you infected with your contagion. Call them off."

"Oh." The demon raised an eyebrow, at once irritated and amused. "You mean my progeny? My glorious host? My savage army that I shall lead across the divide to slaughter my usurpers and subjugate the feckless and revolting denizens of Hell?"

He looked Callum up and down, his contempt clear.

"Make me."

"Rafe?" said Callum.

The librarian, wiping his mouth with the back of one hand, took from his pocket a tube of toothpaste, the old-fashioned kind made of soft metal with a key attached to the end to help squeeze out the paste. He crouched and laid it in a small circle connected to the larger summoning diagram.

"I'm offended, little man," said the demon. "I keep my teeth perfectly clean." He opened his mouth to reveal pearly white teeth and a pair of sharp fangs. He ran his tongue across them and smacked his lips. "All the better to rip your head off with."

Rafe turned the key half a rotation and a dollop of white toothpaste bulged out of the tip. The intricate network of circles and symbols flashed and sparked. The demon grunted, its entire body seizing. When the spasm released, it sagged to its knees.

"How unexpected," it croaked, looking up at Callum with murder in its eyes.

"Call off your thugs," said Callum.

"Such a pretty pet." The demon got up, wincing as it moved. "Pretty lips, pretty neck, pretty wrists. So many places whence to draw blood. Does your faerie lord bleed you when you fuck? No? You should let me show you how exquisite the feeling can be."

Rafe twisted the key again. The bulge of paste at the tube's tip grew bigger, the circle flashed, and the demon moaned as its body spasmed.

"Jessica," said Rafe. "Get the bottle."

"Be careful." Callum caught her before she opened the inner gate. "Its rough out there." He spoke softly, hoping Rafe and the others wouldn't hear, but the librarian glanced up to listen. "Like when my tattoos failed."

"It's okay. I'll be fine." said Jessica, though her expression wasn't convincing. "Millicent showed me some tricks to control the visions."

"A bottle?" The demon watched her intently as she unwound the chain that held the inner gate and stepped through. "A good vintage, I hope. Or perhaps the blood of a virgin. It's quite a delicacy in the plains of Tartarus. Hard to come by, of course. Where are we exactly?"

The demon looked around the vault and wrinkled its nose.

"Is this your Library of the Damned? I don't think much of it. Mine is so large it straddles the Acheron. Where are your tomes of bone and flesh? Where are your scrolls of agony and despair?"

The smell of sulfur rose again, cresting sharply. Callum looked over at Biggs, but he seemed fine. If the demon wasn't trying to get to him, what was it doing?

"You won't be able to get through," said Callum, reasoning the creature was trying to contact his army. "We're completely sealed off in here. No magic in or out."

"So I see." The demon looked around, annoyed.

"The bottle my friend is fetching," said Callum, "will hold you quite nicely. We'll put you on a shelf where you'll remain forever. And it won't be pleasant. Rafe?"

Rafe wrang out a little more toothpaste. The glob from the tube dripped into the stone floor. The circle sparked, and the demon convulsed. Callum had no idea if Rafe could follow up on his threats, or even stuff the bloody creature into this Aladdin's bottle Jessica had found. All they had to do was last long enough for the Cottage's oracles to pick up all the undamped Chaos coursing through the library.

The demon collapsed, sprawling on the confined stone circle. Panting, he stared up at Callum, an evil smile spreading across his face. "Perhaps I shall make you *my* pet. If this is an indication of your lovemaking, we will do well together."

His eyes flicked down to the symbols on the floor, and the noxious stench of sulfur crested again.

"I recognize this script." He pushed himself up on his hands to better peer at the markings along the circle. "This is fae-wrought." He sat back and chuckled—deep-throated and gleeful, as if he hadn't been writhing in agony on the stone floor—and looked around the vault. "This entire building is built of fae-tempered essence."

The demon stood and ran its fingers through its thick blond curls. "Your master and I did more than share our bodies when we fucked, little pet. We exchanged knowledge and power. He showed me many things, including the Bright Art of his people."

The stone beneath Callum's feet began to vibrate, a deep thrum that shook his bones and made his teeth rattle in his gums. The symbols of *mathematica infernalis* in the summoning circle began to glow, their radiance spreading to all the protective symbols carved into the vault until the entire room was bathed in soft radiance.

"Rafe!" said Callum as he drew his knives, for all the good they would do against the demon. "Squeeze the tube!"

The librarian reached for the toothpaste, turned the key, and more white goop dripped out onto the stone floor. The demon's body locked up, but the spasm didn't wipe the smile from his face.

"I can't keep this up for long," wailed Rafe. "Once the tube is empty … "

On the other side of the circle, Biggs locked his elbows and aimed his gun at the demon's head.

"Minions … " The demon barked the word out, each spasm of his body choking them off. "Please … Enter … And … Finish … This."

Darkness fell, the glowing symbols and the one remaining light in the vault extinguished. Two red-burning coals hovered in the darkness where the demon stood.

Biggs fired at it. The room shook with the silent blast of his rounds.

The demon, once again a towering fright of talons and teeth, lashed out at Biggs and knocked him across the vault with a wing.

"Everybody out! Now!" Callum sheathed his knives and launched himself at the creature, barreling into it with all his weight to knock it off its feet. Weapons might not affect it, but he could slow it down long enough for everyone to get out.

The demon levered itself up with its wings, but Callum slipped around it, tangling its limbs with his own in a violent reflection of a lover's embrace, and held fast. The demon roared and flailed, knocking them about, crashing against the walls and shelves. Callum's tattoos throbbed with pain as the witch's magic tried to keep him in one piece, pain strong enough to leave him curled up and crippled on the floor, but he clenched his jaw and held on for dear life.

"Callum!" Rafe cried out from within the cage between the two gates. The others were already outside.

Callum released the demon mid-thrash. The creature threw him across the floor in the direction of the exit. Callum rolled and was up on his feet and through the first gate in seconds. Rafe slammed the gate shut behind him and bound the chain with a padlock the size of a dinner plate to seal it. He pulled out the key and stumbled back as the demon loped over to the iron bars. It rattled the cage with one hand and reached through the bars with the other, but the lock and chain held, and Callum and Rafe dodged away and out the second gate into the gallery. The demon rattled the gate and roared as Rafe sealed the outer gate with another giant padlock, but the demon couldn't get through.

Rafe dropped the key to the padlock and raised his empty hands, his eyes wide with shock. "My cane."

His skin turned dusty, and his hair wisped away as his body began to decompose.

"It's okay, old man." Callum wrapped his arms around his friend and carried him into a corner, leaving a trail of sand and dust behind them. "You'll be safe here. I'll come and find you. It might take a while, but I'll put you back together."

"You're a good frie—" Rafe's entire body turned to dust and ran through his clothes like the sands of an hourglass. His clothing, suddenly empty, collapsed on the pile of dust around his shoes where he had stood a second before.

Biggs looked up at the ceiling. "The vampires are in the building."

Behind him Rory doubled over and moaned. Callum ran to his side.

"It's happening." Rory pushed Callum away. "Don't freak out this time, yeah?"

Rory shrugged off his jacket and pulled off his shirt, his pale, muscular torso catching the dim phosphorescent glow in the gallery.

"What the fuck's he doing?" said Biggs as Rory kicked off his shoes and shrugged out of his trousers and underpants, leaving him naked before them.

The transformation happened quickly, much quicker than before. Rory keeled over, roaring in pain, and fell to his hands and knees. By the time he hit the floor, a giant wolf stood in his place, its eyes shimmering in the gloom, its jaws open in a snarl.

55

"CRIKEY!" Biggs pulled out his gun and aimed it at the wolf … the hound … at Rory, but Callum pushed the agent's arm down before he could fire.

"No! It's okay … " Callum stared into angry, feral eyes and doubted himself. "I think? Rory? Is that you in there?"

The hound growled, a low rumble more tiger than wolf or dog. It bared its teeth.

Callum edged sideways to put himself between the hound and Biggs and held out an open hand. The hound tensed, crouching imperceptibly, readying itself to attack.

"Rory, it's me. It's Callum. You know me."

The hound wrinkled its snout, and the tension melted from its body. It whined with curiosity and edged forward to sniff Callum's hand.

"Rory?" said Callum.

The hound—Rory—barked and pushed forward to lean against him, but it—he—was as tall as Callum's hip, and almost knocked him over. Callum resisted the temptation to crouch down and scratch the hound's neck.

"Okay, then," he said as Rory looked up at him and Biggs.

"Fuck," said the agent. He turned his head sharply, his eyes unfocussed, as if listening to distant music. "They've found the stairwell. They're in the first level."

"You should stay down here," said Callum. "All we have to do is survive until the Cottage comes."

Biggs shook his head. "No."

"But the contagio—"

"I said no. There could be dozens of them. You won't stand a chance."

"They can't bite me. Well, they can, but … "

"What about when the strike teams get here? You saw what that thing," he shrugged at the raging creature behind them, "can do on its own. Imagine what it can do with help?" He nodded toward the ceiling. "Didn't he turn all those people to make an army? We have a chance to at least whittle down their numbers."

"But you'll—"

"You gave me your word you'd take me out."

Callum frowned.

Biggs sighed. "I've worked with you for how long? I know you're not a killer. You're a soft git who thinks he can save everyone. Sometimes you can't. Sometimes you have to take lives so others will be safe."

It wasn't only the chance that the vampires might overpower the strike teams, that Jessica and Rory might get killed, and Biggs might turn. If the demon and its minions seized the library, they'd have control over all the artifacts within it. What havoc might they cause? How many innocents living their lives in blissful ignorance of magic, wild or tamed, might suffer?

Callum breathed deep and rubbed his eyes as if the pressure might clear his thoughts.

"All right," he said, finally.

Rory barked, ran toward the stairwell, and stopped halfway there. He turned back and barked again.

"He's got the right idea." Biggs lifted his weapon, barrel pointed to the ceiling. "We've got about two minutes before they reach us. We need to find cover. I've got three more clips. You got anything other than your knives?"

Callum unsheathed them. The blades glowed a dark and evil purple, becoming balls of luminescence as he spun them. "Just these."

Biggs sighed. "Yeah, we're fucked."

They caught up with the hound and wove their way through the shelves and cabinets to the elevator and stairs. Biggs hung back, crouched and half-hidden by a large shelving unit containing jars of things Callum would prefer not to know about preserved in a purple fluid alchemically treated to neutralize wild magic.

The hound at his hip, Callum edged into the blind spot of the stairwell door and put a hand on its pelt … *His* pelt. Even with the hound's enormous size, it was impossible to think of it as Rory.

"Stay," said Callum.

The hound looked up at him with an unmistakably human expression in its eyes Callum could only interpret as "watch it."

A concussive thud reverberated through the ceiling.

"Flash grenade," said Biggs. "Making a big entrance. They must be going down floor by floor. Sounds like they're upstairs. Get ready!"

Callum backed up putting a large, old-fashioned iron safe between him and the door.

"Rory!" He beckoned the hound to join him. The enormous bundle of fur, more wolf than dog, padded away from the door to his side.

One breath. Two. Five. Ten more. Callum's heart pounded in his chest. When the blast hit, it was almost a relief.

Though he was shielded by the safe from the flash and the concussion, the bang tore through the low gallery, deafening him. Smoke filled his lungs, and he struggled not to collapse in a fit of coughing. As he stepped out from behind the safe, three soundless shots from Biggs's gun buffeted against him, clearing some of the smoke. Three columns of flame exploded and were gone. Callum slipped into the blind spot by the door, wary of getting too close to the elevator cage in case someone thought to drop down through the shaft.

Gunfire rang out, conventional gunfire. Short staccato bursts exploded out of the barrel of a semi-automatic weapon poking through the gap in the door. Bullets sprayed through the gallery, splintering wood and shattering glass. Wet, bloated specimens flopped onto the floor, and Callum caught the ghastly, sodden movement of things that should have been dead.

The security door was ripped from its hinges in a deafening groan that cut into Callum's teeth, and the remaining smoke swirled as vampires flowed through. Biggs let loose, and blast after blast lit up the gallery, filling it with stifling heat. Callum counted ten vampires down. How many people had the demon turned?

Biggs's wall of enchanted bullets stopped, and the shelving unit he was hiding behind crashed down on him as a blurred vampire smashed into it. Two others converged on the agent, and the hound roared and leapt at them, a wake of smoky tendrils flowing behind it. It landed on the back of one of the vampires, a woman in her sixties dressed in a tweed overcoat with a silk scarf wrapped around her head. It buried its jaws into the back of her neck. The vampire tried to shake it off, flailing her arms violently, but the hound held on, sinking its teeth deeper and deeper. It wrenched back and severed the vampire's head from its body, both of which burst into flame.

Okay! Don't have to worry about him, then.

The vampires moved with their dizzying speed, but the smoke gave them away. A wave surged toward him, and Callum stabbed at the vampire's chest with both blades, burying them in its chest to the hilt. The creature, a young man who could have been no older than eighteen, didn't explode straight away, so he must have missed the heart. He stabbed deeper and scooped the blades inward. Flames erupted from the boy's eyes and mouth, consuming him from within.

Callum lost count of how many vampires flowed through the door—another five? ten?—but most of them weren't interested in him and the others. As a second and third vampire came for him out of the misty smoke, he could see the remainder flow past Biggs and the hound to the end of the gallery and the caged door where the demon thrashed and roared trying to escape.

Callum panicked. He hadn't thought to take the key to the gate from Rafe before he turned to dust. He had to make sure they didn't find it. He turned to run back to the vault, but something wrenched his arm back and spun him around. Taloned fingernails slashed at his cheek, drawing blood.

Callum wiped the back of a blade against it, smearing blood across his face and knife. "That was foolish."

The vampire, a balding man in a business suit, eyes crazed at the scent of blood, pulled him close in an iron grip, but Callum shut his eyes and stabbed up through the vampire's jaw. Heat seared his face, the blaze flashing through his eyelids as the vampire combusted.

He opened his eyes to find three vampires, a woman in a cocktail dress, a man in a battered flasher's raincoat, and a nurse in scrubs, surrounding him.

He held up his blades as they approached, ready to do his best, even if it meant bleeding on them and hoping some got in their eyes or mouth, but before he or the vampire could move, the nurse's head cleaved in two and she combusted.

The other two flinched away from the blast. A long, thin spike of wood thrust through the vampire in the cocktail dress's chest, and she went up. A knitted lace shawl—half spider's web, half fisherman's net—fell across the remaining vampire, the threads cutting through it like a cheese slicer, and it went up in flames.

Behind it stood Jessica, her sapphire spectacles glittering in the light of the fires spreading across the gallery. "Leave it to the lesbian to clear up the gay boy's mess!" She looked down at the remains of the lace shawl. "Bugger. Didn't think that would be single use. Rafe will kill me."

Dressed in white gloves and a white robe all inscribed with *mathematica infernalis* to protect her from the artifacts in her hands, she slid the long wooden spike into her belt and picked up a five-foot peacock feather from the smear of ash where the vampire she had struck it with had exploded.

"Is that a knitting needle?" said Callum.

"And a feather, some marbles," she pulled a handful of blue and green glass orbs from the robe's pocket and held them out for him to see, "a silver cocaine spoon, and some poker chips. All early experiments of Madame Morozova, before she perfected her technique. All extremely dangerous."

She slipped them back into her pocket and grinned, a mad monk laden with precious relics of her arcane religion.

Behind Callum came a canine whimper. The hound and Biggs struggled with two remaining vampires, Biggs's former coworkers dressed in military fatigues and much better fighters than the poor souls the demon's last batch of minions had yanked off the streets. Biggs had his gun in one hand held aloft, his arm pinned to the cabinet behind him by his assailant as they struggled for control. The hound and his attacker were all savage teeth and claws in a tumble across the floor.

"What the fuck is that?" said Jessica.

"My new boyfriend." Callum crouched to launch himself at Rory, but before he could move, Jessica lobbed one of her marbles at the vampire with all her might. The green orb shimmered as it flew through the air. It struck the back of the vampire's shoulder, and the fabric began to smolder and disintegrate, glowing embers drifting away in the heat.

The marble wasn't enough to make the vampire ignite, but it slowed it enough to give the hound, Rory, the opening he needed to roll the attacker on its back and sink his jaws into its neck. With a sickening crunch, the hound bit hard and yanked, severing the vampire's head from its body, and jumped away as it burned to ash leaving a body-shaped smear on the floor.

Callum launched himself at Biggs. The agent saw him coming and shifted to turn the vampire's back toward him. With one smooth sweep of his arms, Callum encircled the vampire's head, crossed his blades, and pulled. The blades sliced through flesh and sinew, severing the vampire's spine. Its head lolled to one side, its body ash before it hit the floor.

The hound, Biggs, and Callum stood panting, gulping air with exhaustion and shock. Biggs doubled over, groaning. He tumbled forward and rolled himself into a ball.

"It's starting," he barked between moans. "I'm losing control."

Rory growled, his hackles rising as he lowered his head and exposed his teeth, ready to leap at Biggs.

Callum stepped between him and the agent. It was Callum's responsibility to see this through. With one foot, he rolled Biggs onto his back and dropped to the floor, one knee pressed into the agent's chest with all his weight. He dropped one of the knives so he could grip the other two-handed, and raised his fists, ready to stab down at the agent's heart. In the gloom of their secluded corner, Biggs's eyes shimmered in the blade's glow. Not the full reflective glow of a predator, but enough to make Callum's tattoos shiver. A faint whiff of garlic and sulfur wafted up at him.

"I'm sorry, mate." He thrust down, but Biggs raised his hands and grabbed Callum's wrists to stop him, already too strong for Callum to break the hold.

"Wait," said Biggs. "Not yet. I can help. I can kill it."

Callum glanced nervously at Rory, and the hound edged around Jessica for a clean shot at Bigg's head. "How?"

"If I turn, I can kill it," said Biggs. "It said as much in the vault. It created an army to kill the demons who stole its throne. I'll hold out as long as I can to get close. It won't take much to put me over the edge."

Callum frowned. "It's a terrible plan."

Biggs gestured with a nod to his weapon on the floor behind him. "Take my gun. Do you know how to use it?"

Callum had spent enough time in a shooting range to acquit himself with a firearm. He wasn't the best shot, but five rounds would be enough. "I do."

"Use it on me when the job's done, yeah? And give me one of your knives to help me get close to it."

"Jessica, bring me the gun, please."

She scurried over to it, picked it up by the grip with a finger and thumb, and held it out for him. He took it, and only when he had sheathed his knife and had it pointed at Biggs's head did he shift his weight off the agent.

"Give him the knife."

Jessica kicked it over to Biggs as the big man clambered to his feet.

"KILL THEM!" came a roar from the direction of the vault.

The vampires had found the key.

56

BIGGS WAS ONLY HALFWAY off the floor, Callum's knife in his hand, when the smoke blurred with ghostly figures dragging pale tendrils behind them. One grabbed Jessica from behind. Without thinking, Callum shot it in the head before it could hurt her, wasting one of the five rounds he had to take Biggs out. The vampire, one of Biggs's former compatriots, went up in flames, and Jessica fell hard to the floor on her backside. The hound leapt at seemingly nothing but collided with another ex-agent, sinking its teeth into the vampire's shoulder. The two fell to the floor in a rolling tangle of vicious teeth and claws. The hound's growls reverberated through the gallery. To Callum's surprise, the thought that it was Rory beneath all that fur turned him on.

Jessica, bless her ferocious heart, lobbed a marble at the hound's foe from where she lay, and hit it on the back of the head. Its hair went up in flames, the rest of it igniting in quick succession. The hound yelped and jumped away, only to be grappled by another former

Cottage agent. While they struggled, a fourth vampire descended on Jessica, but she already had her knitting needle out. The vampire impaled itself on the wooden spike as it fell on her and went up in a flash.

"Bloody hell!" cried Jessica, curling into a ball and covering her head to protect herself from the flames.

Another ghostly vampire surged over its comrade struggling with the hound to get Jessica while she was down. Callum used up another round taking it out. She yelped as the figure burned above her and scrabbled away to hide behind a storage cabinet on the far side of the gallery's central aisle.

Biggs, now on his feet, shouldered Callum out of the way as another vampire surged at them, knocking Callum down. Adept and deadly with a knife, Biggs slashed and jabbed at the man who he must surely have been on missions with only weeks before. He was getting stronger, faster, a sure sign that Millicent's spell was fading. In the struggle, the vampire turned, moving between Callum and Biggs. Callum Shot it in the head.

Biggs stepped through the flashfire. "What are you doing! Those are supposed to be for me! You've only got two left."

"They're not going to be much use if you don't survive. I have other ways to kill you."

Biggs convulsed and groaned, his face scrunching up into a mask of pain. He fell to his knees hard and clutched his head. "I can't … hold on … for much longer."

With a flash of golden flame at its back, the hound darted round the corner into their alcove. It took one look at Biggs and growled, teeth bared and hackles rising. Callum spun to face the central aisle, bracing himself for another wave of vampires, but nothing came.

"DAMN YOU TO THE PIT OF ABBADON!" roared the demon. "MUST I DO EVERYTHING MYSELF!"

Callum turned to Biggs. "Get your shit together, mate. We'll hold him off as long as we can. Rory?"

The hound reared up on its hindlegs and spun to stand at Callum's side. Callum slid the gun into his belt, praying he wouldn't accidentally shoot his own cock off, and retrieved his second blade from the floor where Biggs had dropped it. He sank into his joints, ready to run. "Now!"

With Rory at his heels, he rounded the corner to find the demon hurtling toward them, its wings tucked back behind it to keep them free of the shelves and cabinets that lined the narrow aisle. The ground shook with each pounding stamp of its cloven hooves. The hound leapt at it, aiming at its legs, and buried its jaws in its thigh. The demon roared with pain and grabbed at the hound, sinking its taloned fingers into its fur, but Callum was on it before it could draw blood. He tackled it, wrapping his arms around its waist and knocking it off-balance. The hound released its leg and jumped at its head, bounding up Callum's back, its claws scraping his flesh.

The hound toppled the demon onto its back and snapped at it, trying to sink its jaws into the demon's throat. The demon barely held it away. Callum dropped onto the monster's abdomen, adding his weight to the hound's to hold it down.

"BIGGS!" he cried.

Callum smelled the agent before he saw him, a powerful odor of garlic adding to the acrid stench of sulfur emanating from the demon's body. Biggs yanked Callum away, his arm a piston that hurled Callum rolling across the floor. Callum caught and righted himself as Biggs tossed the hound aside, sending it crashing into a nearby cabinet, and took its place at the demon's neck.

"My child," said the creature. "You have finally surrendered to me."

Callum smelled the surge of sulfur as the demon tried to exert its hold over Biggs, but the newly born vampire's teeth were already in its throat.

The monster screamed a wail of desperate terror. It flailed at Biggs, thrashing and rolling, trying to dislodge him.

"Rory!" Callum barreled forward so he and the hound could hold the demon fast as Biggs drained it.

Blood spewed everywhere. Biggs was only able to drink a fraction of what spurted from the demon's body as its cries grew louder and more desperate, soaking Biggs and Callum and matting the hound's pelt.

The demon weakened. Its cries softened into wretched sobs until it finally grew quiet and still. Its body grew dry, its skin tearing like aged parchment.

Biggs released the demon's neck. His face was deathly white, his eyes glimmering dangerously in the gloom, his fangs shining in his bloody mouth. Bloody tears streamed from his eyes, and he looked around the gallery as if seeing it for the first time.

"It's so beautiful," he whispered. "It's all so beautiful."

He collapsed off the demon's body onto his back and stared up at the ceiling. The hound turned on it, growling, its every muscle taught, its body an arrow of threat aimed at his neck.

Callum rose, wiped his hands on his jeans, and pulled the gun from his belt, locking his arms as he aimed it at Biggs and edged closer. He loomed over the agent and aimed the gun at his head.

"Please," Biggs whimpered.

Callum steeled himself to shoot this man who had, over the past few days, become his friend. As the hound approached, ready to strike, he exhaled and tensed his finger around the trigger.

"Please," Biggs whimpered again. "Don't kill me."

He sobbed and rolled onto his side, curling himself up into a ball, one arm protecting his head, the other held up to hold Callum at bay.

"Please don't kill me. I don't want to die. Do whatever you want. Keep me locked up here in the basement forever, I don't care. I want to live, even like this."

His entire body rigid, Callum could barely breathe. Vampires were vicious creatures, the vampire contagion a scourge that could take over the entire country if people like him didn't remain vigilant. And this new breed of vampire the demon had sired was even worse. Not merely feral predators, they were intelligent and lethal, an entirely greater level of threat.

"Callum." Jessica came up beside him and placed a white-gloved hand on his arm. "Do you have to kill him?"

"He's a threat to all of us." Callum couldn't believe the words coming out of his mouth. A week ago, he would never even have contemplated killing a friend. "There's no cure."

"But do we know that for sure?" She looked up at him through her sapphire spectacles. "No one's ever had a reason to try and find one. You, me, and Rafe have all found ways to help ourselves in the Library. This is just another curse."

"But what if the contagion gets out? What if new nests start popping up with this new breed of vampire?"

"We can make sure it doesn't. The vault will hold him. No magic gets in or out."

Callum shook his head. "We can't trust it. The demon was able to get through and invite its minions in."

"Then we'll find a way of fixing it. We have the entire Library at our disposal, and all the witches of Cheyne Heath if we need them."

The hound growled and sank into its paws, ready to attack.

The vault, the demon, and Callum were connected through the fae lord, Emrys. Helping Biggs might mean helping himself in the process. It was only a thought flashing through Callum's mind, but the selfishness of it filled him with disgust. Biggs wanted to live. That should be enough.

"Rory, back off," he said. The hound looked up at him. "But stay alert. Biggs, on your feet."

"Thank you," said the agent as he rose. "I know I don't deserve it."

Callum waved at the vault gates all the way at the other end of the gallery with the barrel of the gun. "Get in the vault."

Biggs vanished in a blur, streaks of misty tendrils trailing after him. The gates clanged shut, and Biggs stood in the vault, laughing and looking at his hands like he was tripping on magic mushrooms.

"Quick," said Callum, running after him. "Get the key."

57

CALLUM AND JESSICA PEERED through the locked gates at Biggs lying on the stone floor across the summoning circle, staring at his hand with childlike wonder as he waved it slowly above him.

"This explains so much," said Jessica.

"What do you mean?" Callum looked over at the pile of shoes, clothes, and dust that was Rafe's current state of being. They had to get him back together, but with the braziers still out, that would be impossible.

"At Trentham Abbey I saw them all wandering around the grounds like a bunch of undergrads on mushrooms. They must have all been tripping like him."

"Fuck." A chill ran down Callum's spine. "We were lucky. If they'd had their wits about them, we would have been completely screwed."

Crashing after the stress of the night, he yawned. He shook himself and gulped down air trying to wake himself up. The hound ... No, Rory. How was he ever going to get used to that? Rory lay curled up next to him with his snout resting on his crossed paws, his tail twitching.

"We have to get these two back to normal." Callum glanced up at the clock on the wall, seven in the morning, and looked around the gallery. Autumn leaves wafted across the stone floor, and a flock of sparrows chirped and chattered atop the shelves and cabinets. "And this place, too. The Cottage is sure to be here any moment. I can't believe they're not already."

"They're probably still negotiating with the witches to be let into the sanctuary."

"Speaking of." Callum suddenly realized how focused and capable she was acting. "How come you're not zonked out in a corner yourself?"

She grinned and slipped off her robe. Underneath, she wore a sleeveless black muscle shirt and black jeans. Her bare arms were wrapped in leather straps and Rosary beads. The smell of frankincense, clean and pungent, wafted up at him, cresting over the coppery taste he was certain he was never going to be rid of.

"Religious magic?" An image of Bishop Worsley in the magenta robes he wore to the audience with the Master of the Dagger popped into his head. If any of the high-level sorcerers got wind of what had almost happened down here, they'd all be out of a job, and who knew for what purpose the contents of the Hidden Galleries would be used?

"Something like that." She ran a hand over the straps. "This paraphernalia has enough juice to cut my visions down to a manageable level."

"That's great." He was genuinely happy for her, but he didn't have the time to feel it. "I'll get the braziers back up and running. You take care of Rafe. And Rory will need clothes."

Callum worked his way up from the vault to the ground floor, brazier by brazier, each sub-basement stranger than the last. The more braziers he lit, the more the strangeness abated, like the remnants of dreams that faded upon awakening, but even when he ignited the final brazier by the doors to the book collection, the Library hadn't quite returned to normal. The enormous apple tree that had grown out of a wooden bookshelf in the center of the collection remained tall and strong, squirrels and sparrows darting about among the thick boughs that towered up toward the ceiling.

The high window was still shattered, the shelves in the middle of the floor splintered by gunfire and sodden with extinguisher fluid. Perhaps he could get Jessica to leave Rafe disintegrated for a couple of days while he cleaned up the mess.

A commotion coming from the foyer disrupted Callum's mounting despair at the damaged collection. A high-pitched, musical voice cut through the doors.

"No! You cannot go in. I must insist you wait here respectfully until Mr. Torvalds comes for us."

Callum pushed through into the foyer, taking care to draw the doors closed behind him, and found himself behind a line of three witches—Millicent, dressed in a silk kimono with slicked-back hair, Rory's friend, Gosha, in black denim and a motorcycle jacket, and Elsie, the chipper diminutive witch who'd helped with Millicent's first spell for Biggs—protecting the Library from a line of scowling figures. Euphemia Graham, Esme Cavendish, and five of their plain-clothes agents looked ready to storm the building. The Master of the Dagger, slender and dapper in another immaculately tailored suit, smiled, seemingly unfazed by the whole situation.

"This." Euphemia Graham pointed at Rory's friend, Gosha, with an arrogant flick of the wrist, "is the troublemaker I've informed you about. Her presence is a deliberate provocation."

"My presence," said Gosha, elbows clasped and arms across her chest, an implacable barrier in black, "is necessary to make sure you don't get up to your usual tricks."

"Ladies, please." The Master of the Dagger spread his long slender arms as if to hug them all to his breast. "This is not the time for old contretemps."

"Ah!" twittered Elsie, spying Callum behind her. "Our dear Mr. Foster has arrived. I yield the floor to him."

"Everything ok?" muttered Millicent out of the corner of her mouth. "We were ready to send in a squad."

An image of witches dressed in combat gear wielding rolling pins and brooms flashed across Callum's tired mind. He did his best not to giggle.

"I've had better nights," he whispered back, "but it all worked out in the end. Ladies," he put on his best party-host face, "gentlemen. How may I help you?"

Euphemia Graham pointed up at the clock above the library doors. The gold trim in the cuff of her black Chanel suit glimmered in the morning light shining through the windows. "It is eleven o'clock, a full two hours past the assigned start time for the summoning ritual. We demand an explanation!"

She glared at Callum, and the scent of lavender kicked up in the room.

The Master of the Dagger coughed sharply, and Graham dropped her hand, bristling as if she'd been verbally rebuked.

"What Mrs. Graham meant to say," the Master of the Dagger smiled broadly, "is that we became concerned when you failed to appear for the ritual. We are here to make sure everything is all right. We would have been here sooner, but negotiations with the esteemed sisters-in-Craft took time, as they rightly should. The Library is usually so reliable. *Is* everything all right?"

Callum could see how this Master of the Dagger had got the job. His predecessor, an impatient and irate woman, was a nightmare to work with.

"Yeah, sorry about that," he said. "We had a bit of a rager last night."

"This is outrageous!" Graham drew herself up and clutched her Chanel purse to her body, a slender spike of couture-clad aggression. "The security of the nation is at stake! I demand to see your superior!" She turned to the Master of the Dagger. "This is yet another example of the Library's reckless incompetence."

The Master of the Dagger smiled at her, this time with considerably less charm. "We'll see, shall we? Mr. Foster, is Mr. Torvalds available to offer some explanation?"

"He's getting himself together," said Callum. "As I said, it was a long night. Perhaps you could come back later?"

As if the witches would allow it. Two intrusions into their sanctuary in the space of a week was more than they'd allowed in the five years since establishing it.

"Argh!" Purse raised to swat anyone out of her way, Graham surged toward the library doors. "Take us to Torvalds this instan—"

The doors swung open to reveal Rafe, fully himself, covered by a fine layer of dust that made him look like he'd just been taken out of storage. It would take a few hours for all of him to reabsorb.

"Mrs. Graham, Lord Master." He beamed at the visitors with enthusiasm that bordered on the deranged. "How may I help you?"

Graham turned her back on Torvalds and spread her arms dramatically as if she had solved an impossible proof. "You see, Lord Master? This is why I insist, at the bare minimum, that the Library have official oversight by someone qualified to assess the value and the danger of their efforts. They are, and always have been, inefficient, incompetent, and unreliable."

"Yes, Mrs. Graham," said the Master of the Dagger with the barest hint of a sigh. "This morning's negligence would seem to require explanation. Mr. Torvalds?"

"Lord Master," Rafe tilted his head in a subservient bow, "I fear we rather had our hands full with the case last night, but I'm happy to report the problem solved. Jessica? Would you?"

He stood to one side holding the door so Jessica and Rory could drag in the desiccated corpse of the demon and place it down in the middle of the foyer. Rory, barefoot and dressed in Jessica's white robe which only went down to his knees and elbows, quickly stepped behind Callum and Gosha. The witch raised a quizzical eyebrow. He grinned and tapped his wooden bead, once more tied around his neck.

"Are you naked under there?" whispered Callum.

Rory waggled his eyebrows. "You can find out for yourself later."

"What on earth!" exclaimed Graham as she and the others crowded over the corpse. "You had the gall to perform the summoning on your own after you were expressly ordered not to! Lord Master, what more must happen to convince you?"

"Hm." The Master of the Dagger stooped to inspect the corpse. "I'm impressed. You did this all yourself?"

"Thank you, Lord Master," said Rafe. "I won't say it was easy, but we saw an opportunity and seized it with gusto. I'm quite happy with the way it turned out. Of course, we couldn't have done it without the help of Agent Biggs. Which does make me want to revisit the question of allocating funds for more staff."

The Master of the Dagger smiled, genuinely this time. "Glad to hear it, Mr. Torvalds! I've always thought you could expand your scope given the resources. I'll accept your proposal at your earliest convenience."

"Where is Agent Biggs?" said Graham, the fragrance of lavender spiking once more.

"I told him he could have a bit of a lie down after the events of the evening," said Rafe. "In fact, I would like to request Agent Biggs be relieved of his duties at the Cottage and be assigned to the Library on a permanent basis. He's been so helpful."

"Impossible," said Graham. "He's one of my best operatives."

Rafe and Graham watched the Master of the Dagger as he pondered. "My understanding is, Mrs. Graham," said the Master finally, "that you are already about to embark on a new recruitment drive thanks to recent events. I'm sure you can find suitable replacements for all your lost personnel. My office will be happy to assist you. And what about this?"

He gestured to the demonic remains.

"You're most welcome to it," said Rafe, to Callum's surprise. He wasn't usually so generous. What went into the Library rarely came out again.

Graham was clearly surprised as well. She and Cavendish shared a meaningful glance, and Cavendish waved the agents forward to pick up the corpse.

Callum leaned toward Rafe from behind and whispered. "Are you sure?"

"Oh, yes." Rafe patted his breast pocket and whispered back. "I cut off its thumb. It'll be enough to study."

"How generous of you," said the Master of the Dagger. "And so, I can mark the matter resolved? We can all go back to our days confident that no nasty surprises will come at us out of the dark?"

"In this case," said Rafe, "yes."

"Then we'll leave you to it. I will expect a full report by the end of the week."

"Certainly, Lord Master."

Graham's face tensed in a mask of fury. "You're just going to leave it at that? Not even a slap on the wrist?" She bore down on the Master of the Dagger poking her purse at his chest, though careful not to actually touch him. "This favoritism is a clear violation of your regulative authority! The Librarian expressly disregarded your direct instructions, and you're letting him get away with it! I demand there be consequences, or I will take this all the way up the ladder to the very top!"

All emotion dropped from the Lord Master's face, an effect much more daunting than Graham's bluster. "Be careful, Mrs. Graham. You'll discover it less a ladder than a greasy pole. The Star Chamber doesn't take kindly to demands from below. Remember that you serve at the pleasure of the Crown." He turned to Rafe. "Mr. Torvalds, I value your autonomy, but Mrs. Graham does have a point. Incidents such as this are far too dangerous to be handled by the Library alone.

You should have brought this to my attention at the first inkling of its magnitude."

"Yes, Lord Master," said Rafe, contrite.

"Going forward, I will require weekly reports from you. Nothing formal, but I want to be kept in the loop."

"That's it?" Graham spluttered. "I demand—"

The Master of the Dagger raised a finger and an eyebrow without bothering to look at her. The crisp fizz of lightning and summer rain filled Callum's nostrils, and Graham fell silent. "You demand, Mrs. Graham?"

Her mask of fury turned soured to one of worry, the shift of expressions dancing across her face. She opened her mouth to respond, but closed it again without saying a word.

The Lord Master glanced down at the demon's corpse. "Take your spoils and go." He beamed at the witches. "I'm sure these kind ladies have enough to get on with without having to babysit you."

Eyes downcast, Graham ushered Cavendish and her agents to shuffle away with their prize and swept out imperiously behind them, followed by Elsie and Gosha fast on her heels. Millicent stayed behind.

The Master of the Dagger paused at the front door. "Weekly reports, Mr. Torvalds."

Rafe frowned.

"I am on your side, Mr. Torvalds." A twinkle glimmered in the Lord Master's eye. "How about tea on Thursdays? We could meet at the Palace. Or Fortnum and Mason! They do an excellent afternoon tea. I'll have my secretary call you. Good day."

The door closed behind him. A weight of tension left the room and everyone exhaled.

Millicent held up Jessica's arms and ran her hands over the straps and beads to inspect them. "Did it work?"

Jessica nodded. "Beautifully. It took a bit of getting used to, but yeah."

Millicent's inspection turned into an embrace. "I've already thought of improvements."

"You were amazing," said Rory, looking partly ridiculous and partly insanely hot in his too-small robe.

Callum threw his arms around his neck and kissed him.

Behind them, Rafe opened the doors to the collection. Birds chirped in the boughs of the apple tree.

"Will someone please explain what's happened to my precious library!" he cried.

WANT MORE ?

The journey doesn't have to end here! Craving another taste of the CHAOS-KISSED world? I've got you covered with these exclusive extras:

A HOUND OF THE WILD HUNT

Follow Rory in this FREE short story as he escapes the clutches of the sinister cult that raised him hidden deep within the Scottish Highlands.

SPELLS & DRUGS AND ROCK 'N' ROLL

This FREE novelette throws Gosha and Johnny into a wild night on the town that explodes into unexpected danger. Can they handle the chaos when the spells start flying and the music turns deadly?

Join my mailing list and be the first to know about new releases, exclusive content, and more!

wvfitzsimon.com/free-book-hound/

ACKNOWLEDGMENTS

The longer I work as a writer, the more amazing people I meet who are willing to selflessly help getting a book ready for publication. My great thanks to Sandy Blaine, Lisa Simon, Lynn Witwer, James Wright, Richard Cartwright, Judith Mortimore, the Casco Bay Writer's Project, and the SFFH group. Thanks also to Curtis Wallin for his kind guidance on the cover.

And most thanks of all to Kris.

ABOUT W. V. FITZ-SIMON

W. V. FITZ-SIMON is author of fantasy novels filled with adventure, eccentric characters, and intricate magic systems. His bestselling "Waking the Witch" and award-nominated "The Third Secret" feature a queer sensibility and blend humor, excitement, and wonder. He lives in Portland, Maine with his husband where he knits sweaters, plays board games, and teaches yoga.

www.wvfitzsimon.com
witold@wvfitzsimon.com
www.facebook.com/wvfitzsimon
www.instagram.com/wvfitzsimon